THE HOMECOMING

"I love that kind of simple, extravagantly expensive outfit. But most of us need a bit more shimmer to shimmer." Angie's smile was catty. "Ali could come in a barrel— even in jeans—and look stunning."

Sitting very still, Nora followed Angie's eyes. It was as if a gun had been fired off behind her back. She wanted to touch herself to see if she was hurt . . . if she was bleeding. Somehow she had managed not to see Ali. But there she was—life-size. Stunning in a black silk T-shirt and a single strand of gold and gray pearls. Deep in dialogue with cousin Harold Brett. Behaving as if she cared.

Nora's color rose and she dropped her eyes. The old foolishness had begun again. Tic tac toe . . . who would get the dough? Millie's millions. She or Ali?

Other Avon Books by
Davidyne Mayleas

NAKED CALL

THE GARDINER WOMEN

DAVIDYNE MAYLEAS

AVON BOOKS ⧉ NEW YORK

THE GARDINER WOMEN is an original publication of Avon Books. This work has never before appeared in book form. This work is a novel. Any similarity to actual persons or events is purely coincidental.

AVON BOOKS
A division of
The Hearst Corporation
1350 Avenue of the Americas
New York, New York 10019

Copyright © 1993 by Davidyne Saxon Mayleas
Published by arrangement with the author
Library of Congress Catalog Card Number: 92-97290
ISBN: 0-380-75690-0

First Avon Books Printing: May 1993

AVON TRADEMARK REG. U.S. PAT. OFF. AND IN OTHER COUNTRIES, MARCA REGISTRADA, HECHO EN U.S.A.

Printed in the U.S.A.

RA 10 9 8 7 6 5 4 3 2 1

PROLOGUE

Millie
1992

EVERY MORNING the sky was blue . . . somewhere in the country. But the blue sky over Southern California was not the same blue as the blue sky over Kansas. It wasn't a matter of smog in La Jolla. Or lack of smog. Or nearness to the ocean . . . as well as to the desert. The sky was California blue . . . not Kansas blue. The tall, slender woman standing on the narrow sidewalk outside the Scripps Memorial Hospital gazed at the sky and compared it with memories. The California sky had none of Kansas's calm. What it had was blue vigor—or variety—the vigor and variety of the people who lived beneath the California skies. From one end of Kansas to the other—from Topeka to Wichita to Goodland— wherever one set "country folk" down . . . that was where they could have been born. Not so in California. In California the blue air was full of odd accents, voices from distant lands. Transplanted people come to seize the future. Bacon and eggs for breakfast was new to them. Chiquilas were familiar. Or hot soy milk. Tapsilog. Pho.

Millie Gardiner remembered she hadn't eaten breakfast . . . another brain scan. She sighed. That was why she'd come alone . . . not mentioned her appointment with Dr. Keller to either of her granddaughters . . . or anyone else. Nora was

astute. She knew how to think. What questions to ask. Much
as Millie did. Nora would want to know the diagnosis . . .
the prognosis . . . the treatment. But this crisis, and it was a
crisis of sorts, had no clear answer. She'd seen her own careful questions evaded. She'd been given answers that were no
answers. Bull . . . her father would have said. Nora would
have done better. She'd insist. And keep insisting until—from
sheer exhaustion—he'd tell her as much truth as he had. Millie thought about that. Maybe, she decided . . . maybe I don't
want the truth. Ali, with her tanned legs sans panty hose,
would be solicitous and tactfully amusing. She'd try to charm
the doctor . . . then shrug her shoulders and suggest Millie
and she tootle up to Costa Mesa and check out the new Saint
Laurent or Odeon collections. No! She was in no mood for
Ali. Or Hiram? Hiram, her son, was in Geneva. Just as well.
She didn't want company. Not the company of any relative
or friend. At this moment all the company she could take was
the human race at large . . . energetic and impersonal. The
strangers passing by—all ages, races, male and female—were
not strange at all. They were more her natural element. She
watched them hurry in and out of the hospital doors that
automatically slid open when anyone drew near. A mother
with a baby in a walker, an old man in a neat sport shirt
seated in a wheelchair pushed by a young man in tennis
whites, three Mexican women in sundresses, two giggling
teenage girls in short shorts and T-shirts—one a black-haired
Asian, the other a California blonde—a workman looking
puzzled. In and out of the hospital doors they went.

Now and then a woman glanced at her enviously. Standing
quietly, wearing a white silk shirtdress cinched at the waist
by a black patent leather belt, the breeze whipping around
her legs, she looked carefree and expensive. With her white
hair pulled back in a tight chignon, the years only intensified
her remarkable cheekbones, her deep-set and almost china-
blue eyes. There were faint lines radiating from the corners
of her eyes and deeper lines alongside her wide mouth. But
her chin and neck were firm . . . no sagging skin. It was a
face that had lasted . . . beautiful when young and patrician
in age. The essential structure was there. Rich . . . , the envious women thought as they eyed her. She was. But what
could money buy for her? She felt as if she'd been up all
night drinking brandy and black coffee.

Each year—for the last six years—she'd made a five-million-dollar donation to Scripps Basic Research. Hoping, perhaps it might add a few years to her time on earth. Praying she would never have to ask for a return on her investment. But when the warnings came, she'd asked . . . and there was no return . . . nothing. Months back she'd had a CAT scan. After that magnetic resonance imaging. Then an even newer invention, a PET scan—positron emissions topography. Lately she had the grim feeling the world was overstocked with miraculous medical technology but short of great doctors . . . the kind who could examine a patient, take some tests . . . and then, drawing on a backlog of years appraising human animals, say—and with authority—this is what's going on. And be right. Such doctors were in short supply. After the examination, she'd paused to speak to Dr. Keller—technically a genius in neurophysiology—to discuss the reports. They talked for an hour. She remembered snatches of the conversation with a wave of chilled relief that mercifully washed her mind clear.

"Can I go on doing anything I like?" she had asked.

"Anything. The more you do, the better. Enjoy yourself."

"Do you think I'm being a bit hypochondriacal?"

"It's possible. Perhaps that's exactly what it is."

At which point there passed between them a sign—in the eyes only—that they both knew he was letting her down gently.

She smiled at him, but her smile was only courtesy. "No. That isn't it. At any rate, will I suffer much?"

"Why do you have to suffer?"

"In order to live."

"My dear Millie," said the distinguished doctor. "Isn't living exactly what I've been telling you to do? You know as well as I that medicine has only partial answers. As a science, it's in its infancy. You may live to be ninety . . . in good health."

Millie chose not to argue. He thought he had deceived her with double-talk. The truth was she had played with him. She'd never told him about the other doctors. Other opinions down the years. Symptoms . . . dormant so long, now awakened. She'd wanted a fresh, unbiased opinion. He'd given her one. No answers. Thank you for your time, Dr. Keller.

What Millie Gardiner brought away from this meeting was a conviction that for her the future was—as she'd been warned

many years ago—more finite than not. She must live from
day to day. It would be a matter of taking the assault of life
full in the face. Dr. Keller had said she might live to be
ninety. Yet why speak of living unless it was possible she
could die tomorrow? Unconsciously she started to sing to
herself in a clear, soft voice. . . .

"Then beat the drum slowly and play the fife lowly,
These words he did say as I passed boldly by. . . .
So, sit down beside me and hear my sad story,
For I'm a poor cowboy and I know I must die. . . ."

It was a meager memento from the early morning of her
life, when once life had seemed both harsh and golden at the
same time and the horizon stretched away to infinity. Until
the rain stopped falling and the wind and the dust came. . . .

A young woman in baggy white pants, pulling a small boy
by the hand, passed her . . . then turned back and smiled.

"I have a record of Woody Guthrie singing that. It's The
Cowboy's Lament. My father loved it. But you got the words
wrong. I know them by heart. The first stanza starts . . ."
Her voice was pure and musical.

"As I walked out in the streets of Laredo
As I walked out in Laredo one day,
I spied a poor cowboy all wrapped in white linen . . ."

She stopped and hummed the last line. "That's how it
goes."

Millie smiled back. "Thank you."

"It's sad. My father loved it. He loved everything western.
I used to sing it for him."

Millie tilted her head. "You don't anymore?"

Grim laugh. "No. He died. So I married a cowboy . . . in
memory of him. Only he was a midnight cowboy. My father
once said, 'You need a man to go to hell with.' I found one.
Now the bastard won't pay child support. Is that a Calvin
Klein you're wearing?" Millie nodded. "I got two Calvin
Kleins in my closet. Found them in a resale, discount boutique in Hillcrest."

Millie smiled.

"I know what's good. When I graduated from UCLA, my dear departed father gave me a Rolex watch. Then Mike happened. And Noodles was born." She gazed down at the boy. "So Mike—my ex—sold it. Is that a Rolex you're wearing?"

"No. A Piaget."

"Not cheap either. Bet you keep your Rolex in the vault. It would make you a mark. You're rich." Without leaving time for Millie's answer, she hurried on. "I wish I had tons of money. . . . "

"Hello," Noodles said to Millie.

"Hello." She smiled at him.

"He's cute," his mother said. "But he doesn't come cheap. I love him but love costs money. Tonsils today. Teeth forever. I used to think money wasn't important. Love was the big number. Now money's all I think about. Rent. Taxes. Car insurance. Food bills. Noodles." She glanced at Millie's hair. "I hope when I'm your age I'm filthy rich and look as good as you do. This is one lousy country to be old and poor in. Maybe Sweden . . ." she shrugged and started toward the entrance to the hospital. Then she stopped, looked over her shoulder and said, "Have a nice day."

Millie smiled back and watched her go, feeling an odd kinship. The young woman had bills to pay. Food. Car insurance. Rent. She too had rent to pay. A different kind of rent. Rent for time . . . month to month . . . she'd lost her lease. Not on a house . . . on her future on earth. Dr. Keller's evasive words said little . . . yet said all there was to say. They had stripped her down . . . robbed her of her small, hard-won sense of safety. Her condition—in sharp contrast to the elegance of her clothes—teetered on bankruptcy. It gave her the sensation of déjà vu . . . of being again the young Millie Thorne, full of bravado, frightened and flat broke. Clawing and struggling to keep going . . . paying her way with the only currency she had. Now everything else fell away from her . . . nothing remained but how best to pay the rent. Like the young mother, she must get on with it and see. After all, there might be ways. First and foremost, Millie was an incurable optimist.

The white stretch Cadillac turned into the circular driveway and pulled up in front of her. The driver, dressed in a short-sleeved white shirt and light gray pants—his summer uniform—slid from behind the wheel, ran around the front of the car and opened the rear door for her.

"Sorry to keep you waiting, Mrs. Gardiner. A van broke down on the Genesee exit ramp."

"It's all right, Mario. I'm in no hurry." Millie stepped into the car and relaxed into the deeply upholstered rear seat. "Drive to the Del Mar beach, Mario. I want to see the ocean."

The driver nodded.

The long, luxuriously appointed car eased away from the curb. Except for the slight pressure Millie felt as her back sank farther into the upholstery, she would not have known that the limousine had started. She glanced wearily at the white cellular phone that Miss Kratz had had installed. More technology. She must call Nora to set up a meeting at Channel 18. No. She'd call later. The doctors had left her wrung out and spent . . . awakening sleeping memories of the past. A past she had stubbornly disowned . . . afraid if she remembered it would threaten the present. But more and more often these days, memories insisted on returning . . . as if trying to tell her something. She was too weary now to fend them off. She would let them come. She would go back to that far-off land of her childhood. . . .

She remembered when the blinding white sky of long ago was dark with clouds of dust and the earth was no longer rich. Then her clothes were ragged overalls and the car didn't move smoothly . . . when it moved at all. Another time, another place, another car . . . another self. All she had to do was close her eyes and allow that other self to come to life. And it was as if that day was now. She was a child clinging to the safety of her father's hand.

The land was flat and the soil parched. Here and there a spiral of dust—the locals called it a "devil's tail"—caught by strong wind, twisted its way high into the pale white sky. The soil, which a few years before had been rich and dark and had given birth to rows of yellow-and-green corn so tall a man couldn't see over the field, was now pale brown dust and cracked earth.

Off on the western horizon, the white sky merged into a brown cloud moving swiftly eastward. Another dust storm was coming. The sheriff, Andrew Thorne and Millie stood

close together in the shade of one of the few trees remaining
on the land. Millie clung to her father's hand . . . he was a
tall, lean, weatherbeaten man with no more flesh on him than
a scarecrow. Father and daughter were dressed alike . . .
threadbare overalls, bright colored cotton handkerchiefs tied
around their necks, cracked straw hats and worn sneakers.

The sheriff wore a faded tan uniform with a sheriff's star
pinned to the shirt, a white handkerchief around his neck and
a wide-brimmed hat stained with years of sweat. He was
heavyset with a round face and a huge stomach that hung
over his tightly buckled gun belt.

"Andy, I got no choice. I'm real unhappy that it's come
to this. You know that," the sheriff said.

Andrew Thorne gently pushed Millie behind him . . . as
if to shield her from what was about to happen . . . what had
already happened. He clawed at his thin hair with a dirty
hand. The squint lines fanning out from the corners of his
eyes, his high cheekbones and deep grooves running from
his nose to his square jaw gave his big-boned face a look of
craggy strength. But his bowed head and grim mouth told the
truth. Told of deep, anguishing losses that had eroded the
spirit of a once proud and independent man.

Millie glanced up. Make him go away, Papa, she thought.

"No, Abner," Andy Thorne said. "Not much can be done
now. I don't got to like it."

"You're in good company," the sheriff pointed out. "The
bank foreclosed on the Paine farm last week . . . the John-
sons ten days ago."

"Bloodsuckers. All I needed was another year."

The sheriff shook his head. "Wouldn't do no good. Look
at the land. Played out. Every time we get a wind, more
topsoil blows away."

"The worst drought I ever seen. No money to plant a crop
and no water to grow the crop . . . even if I got it planted."

Millie tugged on her papa's arm. When he looked down,
she said, "I could help, Papa. I'm big enough to help."

"I know you are, Millie. It wouldn't do no good."

The sheriff nodded. "The farm's finished, Andy. Don
Moore at the bank doesn't want your land, but he ain't got a
choice."

"My family's owned this farm since before the Civil
War. My great-granddaddy voted to bring Kansas into the Union.

Damn! And now I lose the place." Andy stared at the house.
It was a nice house. Nothing special about it except maybe
the big porch with the swing that Mary and he used to sit on
and watch the sunsets. Gosh, he thought, it sure looks shabby.
Needs a new coat of paint. I'll do it next spring before planting. Misery crumpled his face. There wasn't going to be any
spring planting. The cloud of dust grew closer as the first
tendrils of sand reached out for them. He used the handkerchief he'd tied around his neck to cover his mouth and nose.
When the storm hit, the place'd be a bowl of dust.

"Might as well get on with it," Abner Bledsoe said, his
voice muffled by the white cloth he'd used to cover his nose
and mouth.

"Might as well."

The sound of the hammer as the sheriff banged a nail into
the tree made Millie squirm. She watched him unfold a notice
and stick it on the nail.

Millie wanted her daddy to make the sheriff stop but she
knew he couldn't. He'd told her the sheriff was only doing
his job. She searched for her daddy's hand. Without thinking,
she hugged his waist . . . trying to get closer to him. He
reached down and lifted her onto his shoulder. Together, they
stared at the white piece of paper with the black writing.

"What's it say, Papa?" Millie asked. Her thin, childish
voice sounded birdlike in Andy's ear.

"It's a foreclosure notice, Millie. Says we don't own the
farm."

"Where you going, Andy?" the sheriff asked.

"California. Or as close to it as old Benji can get us." He
gestured toward a beat-up Ford pickup truck.

"You got any money?"

"A little. When Mary died, the insurance company paid
me five hundred dollars. We'll be okay," he said with confidence he didn't feel.

"That was tough. Mary dying of cancer and your losing
the farm at the same time."

Andy shook his head. "Cancer didn't kill Mary. The farm
did. Watching the corn rot because there weren't no buyers.
Then the land dried up and blew away."

The sheriff extended his hand. When Andy shook it, he
was grateful. Sometimes the farmers blamed him for the foreclosure notices. As if it was his doing. Andy Thorne had

more sense . . . or maybe he was so beat he didn't have any fight left in him.

"I wish you all the luck in the world, Andy," he said.

"Thanks, Abner."

The men looked at each other . . . wondering who should leave first. Then the dust storm hit. Clouds of loose dirt swirled around, hiding the sun, pelting them with a hot dry rain of dirt. Andrew Thorne shifted Millie from his shoulder and held her behind him to protect her from the dirt winds. The sheriff hurried to his car. Millie watched from behind her papa as the sheriff switched his headlights on bright and drove across the field. Finally he turned onto the dirt road toward Great Bend.

Leaning against the wind, Millie and her father made their way to the old truck. All the furniture and clothes they could carry were securely roped down in the open bed of the truck. Her papa helped her into the passenger seat and then went around the other side to sit behind the wheel. As he turned the key, he prayed that the sand hadn't clogged up anything. The money he'd spent on new spark plugs and a new battery and the days he'd spent cleaning and oiling and adjusting the engine paid off. The motor started at once. He shifted into low gear. The truck bounced across the hard dirt . . . then stopped. Millie glanced sideways at her papa and bit her lip. He was looking backward through the rear window. His thin body was racked with silent sobs and tears made muddy tracks as they streamed down his dirty cheeks. She tried not to look at him. There was nothing she could do to make it better. In minutes, he stopped sobbing and turned to her. She leaned over and kissed him.

"It's all right, Papa," she whispered.

"It isn't all right, Millie. It is what it is." He started the car again, found the blacktop road and headed west. Dodge City was their first stop on the long haul to California.

Slowly the scene dissolved and Millie opened her eyes . . . wet with tears. For all the pain of remembering, this was the first time in a long time she felt safe . . . even serene. The past was not a threat . . . it was hers . . . the life she'd been given. If anything, her memories were like old friends— trusted but neglected—who returned bearing no grudges . . . offering her the strength to face the present . . . the future.

Reminding her that long ago she'd watched her world blow away . . . saw her mama die, heard her papa weep . . . saw his helpless surrender to fate. If she could survive that, maybe—just maybe—she could survive again.

PART 1

Nora
1992

Chapter 1

CHANNEL 18 was housed on Torrey Pines Road in a building that had won numerous architectural prizes. Students came from all over the country—all over the world—to see it. Then they would compare it with the Salk Institute, a short drive up the road. It led to arguments . . . pro and con each building. Nothing was resolved. The Channel 18 building was a two-story V-shaped structure made of raw concrete and glass. The effect was one of brute strength . . . no gingerbread ornamentation softened the lines. The landscaping was in keeping with the building . . . white limestone gravel, green-and-brown desert plants that needed no watering, all grouped around a huge geometric sculpture in steel and concrete. The facility perched on the cliff overlooking the ocean like the prow of an ancient ship.

Actually the building was considerably larger than it looked. There was a basement and subbasement that housed three studios, two editing rooms and a series of screening rooms. Despite all advice to the contrary—only Nora agreed—Millie Gardiner had chosen the then-unknown architect Amos Hauser to design the building. After the project was completed and had won several awards—making Houser's reputation—Millie's advisers took credit for the choice.

A man and woman were seated in a screening room of Channel 18 reviewing the third episode of a syndicated detective series the station had bought. The bloody action barely held their attention. They waited impatiently for the second commercial break. It came.

On the king-sized TV screen, a towheaded boy—about six—entered a kitchen and sidled up to a baby seated in a high chair. A pretty black-haired Asiatic woman was feeding spoon after spoon of strawberry Jell-O to the baby.

13

"Mrs. Tang?"

"Hi, Billy. . . ." She smiled at the boy.

"Can I ask you a question?"

"Ask away, Billy."

"Are you Chinese?"

The young woman stopped feeding the baby for a moment and looked at the boy. "My parents were born in China. I was born here. I'm second-generation Chinese-American."

"Can you eat with chopsticks?"

"Yes, I can." Mrs. Tang resumed feeding the baby.

"And Mickey?" The boy nodded toward the baby. "Can he?"

Mrs. Tang laughed. "Not yet. He's too young. But someday."

"They're harder to use than a spoon. Aren't they?"

"For me they're easy. But maybe not for everyone."

"Not for me. We went to a Chinese restaurant last night. Mom and Dad used them. Sissy used them. She made fun of me because I couldn't. She said I was dumb."

"Mmm. . . . Do you want me to teach you how to use them?"

"No thank you. You can only eat Chinese food with chopsticks. I like a lot of other things."

"You can use chopsticks for almost anything. I'll show you."

Billy took a pair of chopsticks out of his pocket. "Look—Mrs. Tang. Could you feed Mickey Jell-O with these chopsticks?"

Mrs. Tang shook her head, smiling. "You're right, Billy. I couldn't. But there are lots of things—"

"Nothing good. Like ice cream."

Mrs. Tang laughed. "No. Not ice cream."

"I'll stick to a spoon. Make sure Mickey learns how to use a spoon too. Even fortune cookies are better with ice cream."

Mrs. Tang watched Billy try to pick up the Jell-O with chopsticks. When he couldn't, he grinned at her.

The commercial cut to a distinguished man with a strong, square chin and short, thick, iron-gray hair . . . the kind of man who projects honesty, morality, integrity. He removed his glasses. "Glasses are good . . . sincere," the director had said, and "Speak directly into the camera." He did. His voice was a little rough, natural . . . not the too mellow voice of an actor.

"Make sure your son or daughter learns how to eat ice cream with a spoon. Chopsticks are optional. You and your baby can decide later. But either way, give your baby a head start in life by providing for its future. Start your child's college fund at Reiner & Co." There were a few more lines extolling the high return and security of the Reiner College Fund.

The commercial over, Pat Yocum, Channel 18 program director, switched off the TV. The lights went on automatically. The room was empty except for Pat and Tim Rourke, the general manager.

"Mrs. Gordon Fong is bonkers. Paranoid. So is her Asian-American League. The commercial's cute. It's not pro spoons or anti chopsticks." Pat crossed her legs and shook her tousled auburn hair. At thirty-nine she was a mite too old for that much uncombed hair. But Candice Bergen was her model. If Candice Bergen could, so could Pat. She was almost right. "There's nothing anti-Asian about that commercial."

"Agreed." Tim Rourke studied his nails. His face—with the map of Ireland all over it—was expressionless. "However, Mrs. Gordon Fong and her league have written Channel 18 thirty-two letters. Threatening a boycott. I can see them with their lousy little hand-lettered signs—'Turn off Channel 18' . . . 'Cancel WMTG's license'—pacing in front of the station. Christ! They could picket the cable companies. You know the drill. The cables disown us. No cable, no signal. No signal, no audience. No audience, no advertisers. No dough." He grunted with distaste. "Plus she means to mention it to her dear, good friend Mrs. G."

"Who will suggest we pull the commercial." A dutiful shrug. "Which gives us no choice. Since Mrs. G. owns the station."

"A fine point of law. So what do we do?" He breathed deeply. "I am suffering from a mental brownout. Think. . . . "

Pat wrinkled her brow. "I do have a thought. That commercial was run by Reiner & Co. Who does that bring to mind?"

"The raging capitalist, Mark Stern. Nora's squeeze."

"Exactly. The husband-to-be . . . our secret weapon."
Their eyes met in a canny exchange. "He's a customer's man
at Reiner & Co. How does that grab you?"

"It grabs. He's Mrs. G.'s future grandson-in-law. Nice
thinking, Patti Cake. So if Nora puts it to her grandmother,
Mrs. G. might find the commercial amusing. No matter what
the dragon lady says." Tim's face relaxed. "I can live with
that. Pat, my girl, if only you'd take a shine to Nora. Improve
your job rating. . . ."

"She isn't my type. I'm not hers."

"I heard you and Juno blew?" All friendly concern.

"You heard wrong, friend." Complacent smile. "Where
the hell is Nora anyway? This is her can of worms."

"If we don't run that commercial, we run dead air."

"What's in inventory?"

"The usual. If need be, we'll pick one. Malpractice lawyers. Discounted tires. Cosmetic surgeons. Used-car dealers.
No money down . . . leave your virgin daughter and drive off
into the sunset. We guarantee the transmission forever . . .
or until the first traffic light. Whichever is sooner." Tim
sighed. "Damn! Where's Nora?"

"I'm not her keeper."

"Peace be with you. Here's Nora." A tall girl with short,
shiny black hair—looking feminine, not androgynous—stood
framed in the doorway. Hers was a face too irregular for
conventional beauty . . . the cheekbones too wide, the jaw
too square, the mouth too full. Yet the face was charming
. . . strong and intelligent. The mouth laughed easily. The
eyes behind the horn-rimmed glasses were expressive. Friends
and co-workers regularly advised her to wear contact lenses.
Nora said they made her eyes itch. She lost them. And keeping them sterile—washing her hands whenever she handled
them—was a pain in the butt. Plus she did have a pair of blue
contacts—her eyes were gray—for festive occasions. Which
she often forgot to wear. Even as she forgot to wear mascara
. . . eyeliner . . . lipstick. Was she avant-garde or merely
eccentric? People couldn't decide.

"Nora! We need you. Mrs. Gordon Fong and her Asian
League are breathing fire and brimstone."

"She was. She is now a happy camper." Nora strode into
the screening room . . . whippet slim and long-legged in a

short black turtleneck dress over black stockings. No bangles
. . . baubles . . . beads. Only pearls and a tote bag.

"Saint Nora and the dragon. How did you do it?" Tim
asked.

"Simple, dear co-worker. When Pat showed me those unkind letters from Mrs. Fong's league, I thought she and I
should get to know each other. After all, we're members of
the same San Diego community. We must be good neighbors." She arched a savvy eyebrow. "So I decided to give
Mrs. Fong a ring. I invited her to breakfast and a friendly
chat."

"You didn't?" Pat stared with grudging admiration.

"I did." Nora grinned.

"And she accepted?" Tim asked.

"Why not? She loves the view from Café 18. We got to
know each other over croissants and poached eggs. Then we
toured the station. I introduced her to Sonia Chin." Nora
gave a rich, ribald laugh.

"To Sonny? Oh, you sly, foxy lady." Tim's big chest
heaved. Six feet tall and thirty pounds too heavy, he was a
bear of a man with a wide, toothy grin. A formidable physical presence anywhere.

"Foxy is as foxy does. I'd warned Sonny yesterday not to
leave the station after she finished the show. Breakfast could
wait. Shopping could wait. She must meet Mrs. Fong because Mrs. Fong never sees our Sonny on the sunrise show.
Mrs. Fong doesn't rise and shine until eight. But now that
Mrs. Fong and our Sonia Chin have discovered they're blood
kin—they have cousins in common in Singapore—Mrs. Fong
feels that the chopstick commercial is not anti-Asian. Or pro
spoons. She sees the humor in it."

"Nora, will you marry me?" Tim begged.

"I'd love to. But I'm pledged," Nora cooed. "And your
wife would object, lover boy. What's more, I'm an old-
fashioned type. Lousy at trysts. I'd screw it up . . . leave
lipstick on your hankie. That sort of thing."

"You don't wear lipstick," Pat noted.

"I would if I were trysting with Tim."

A small, all-out blonde, who dressed out of Nordstroms,
appeared at the door. She announced her mission in her natural, breathy whisper. "Nora. Your grandmother called. She
wants you to call her back . . . pronto."

"Right, Sheri. I'm on my way," Nora said as the girl vanished.

"Wanna trade for Mrs. Stone?" Tim asked. "Your secretary has great buns."

"Fickle man. First trysting with me, and two minutes later, lusting after Sheri's buns. Not that you care but Sheri also has great secretarial skills. Types sixty words per minute, takes dictation, wins spelling bees, punctuates, makes good coffee, waters plants and picks up my clothes at the cleaners. Not for trade. See you later, kids," Nora said as she left the screening room.

Nora faced the windowed wall in her office—gazing absentmindedly at the sparkle and foam of the ocean—while she did a lot of listening and not much talking on the telephone.

"Yes," she said, giving the word two syllables. "Yes, I'll arrange it. . . . I'll tell Mark. . . . Uhm, I see your point." She sounded dubious. "By the way . . ." She stammered and searched for words. "Mmmm . . . well." She seemed to come unmoored between one thought and the next. Finally she gave up. "You're sure that's all? Nothing else? . . . No. I've nothing else. . . . Okay. See you tonight, Millie." She said the word affectionately, gently . . . with a low note of desperation.

Slowly she put the receiver down and stared at the ocean . . . and eternity. Cathy Johns had called only a short while earlier full of concern. She'd been to Scripps to see her GYN, and when she'd pulled out of the parking lot she'd spotted Millie Gardiner standing in front of the hospital. Although they'd never actually met, there was no mistaking Millie Gardiner. She'd seen her photo often enough in one or another San Diego newspaper or magazine. It was definitely her. What was she doing standing there alone? Was something the matter? Cathy repeated that since having her breast tumor biopsied—thank God, it was benign—she was feeling edgy. Double-checking everything. She had too much to live for to risk goof-offs. And if she was being an alarmist, sorry. Maybe Millie was visiting a friend. But if something was wrong, could she be of help to Nora? No, Nora lied. Nothing was wrong. Millie was visiting a friend. Cathy was glad. Nora thought of Cathy as a friend. Not a dear, close friend like

Ali. No! Not like Ali. Ali was . . . well . . . Ali was an ex. An ex-best friend. The Ali in Nora's mind was a memory . . . a series of happy snapshots from long ago, carefully mounted in her family album. There should be a word for such a sad, human loss.

Her conversation with Cathy and now with Millie left Nora holding her breath. What was Millie doing in front of Scripps Memorial? Visiting whom? If she was visiting someone, she'd never go alone. Not Grandmother. Then why was she there? What was happening? And why hadn't Millie mentioned to her that she'd been to Scripps? Millie was no ordinary grandmother. They were even closer . . . more like mother and daughter. Once her mother had died, Millie—as much as her father—had raised her. Especially when her father was being every lonely woman's Prince Charming. She didn't keep secrets from Millie. That Millie would keep an important secret from her hurt. Millie's not telling her about Scripps gave Nora the sharpest premonition of something menacing lurking just over the horizon. Like clouds gathering in the Pacific before coming on shore.

"Wake up, Nora. It's time to tote that barge and lift that bale," a voice said. Startled, Nora turned from the ocean. Tim and Pat were standing in the doorway.

Nora blinked, rousing herself from her trancelike concentration. "Oh! Hi there, friends and viewers. Glad to have you tune in on Channel 18. . . ."

"What's up with Mrs. G.?" Tim asked.

"Mrs. G. telephoned to tell me that since you weren't in your office when she called, she wishes me to tell you that we will have a meeting Tuesday morning at ten o'clock. Roll call includes Tim Rourke, Nora Gardiner, Pat Yocum, Sim Crumb, Luddy Poole and Donna Zabriskie. That's it. Have I forgotten anyone?"

"Damn it! What's got into her?" Tim growled. "Imagine. I was in love with her at fifteen. Now she's a television maven."

"I saw *Bad Girl* eight times," Pat blurted out.

"I saw it six. I saw *Monsoon* ten times," Tim countered.

"She only made three movies," Pat reminisced. "Why, Nora? Did Max Gardiner really sweep her off her feet?"

"Off her feet and into his limo."

"Did she love him madly?" Pat asked.

"Passionately."

"Faithless witch. I thought she was in love with Milos Banska," Tim sniped.

"She was. But she was young and he was . . . well . . . Milos Banska . . . and already married." Nora took off her glasses and sucked on one of the stems. She thought about her grandmother's effect on people. Without any intent, Millie worked upon the curiosity, the imagination of both strangers and those closest. All these years later she evoked— even from Nora—intense, passionate interest. Which was as it should be. Millie was the embodiment of what Hollywood meant by "star quality." Nora looked at Pat and Tim and smiled. "You never told me you were fans."

"Why would we?" Tim asked. "You're her granddaughter. It's not safe to tell you anything."

"It's brownnosing," Pat said.

Nora nodded. There were pros and cons to being Millie Gardiner's granddaughter. Half the time she couldn't tell if people were talking to her or to Millie through her . . . as if she were Millie's front. Damn! "Okay. Brownnose. Why this sudden nostalgia for old movies? What can I do for employee relations?"

"Look. Millie Thorne was a star. When Hollywood had real stars. Like Garbo. Irene Dunne. Carole Lombard. Clark Gable. Tyrone Power. So why not let my boyish dreams rest in peace? Why is she messing around with satellites?"

"Who said she's messing around with satellites?" Nora asked.

"The grapevine whispers. The walls have ears. So do the toilets. The word is out. She's applied to the FCC . . ."

"For a license. What's up?" Pat asked peevishly. "She used to pop in now and then. Once a month. Maybe. She used Luddy's office. Now it's every week. Twice some weeks. She's even furnished an office for herself. Your cousin, Sir Lancelot, did it. You think he could kill dragons?"

Nora didn't correct Pat on bloodline connections with Lance. "No. But Lance is a fine decorator. He did a good job. So?"

"So why? Suddenly television interests her? Why?" Tim asked.

"The big screen wasn't enough," Pat said. "Now she's

into small screens. She'll show Ted Turner how to do news
. . . become another CNN.''

Nora rubbed her forehead, puzzled. "No. Its not news.
Millie says news—like history—mostly repeats itself. In
different-colored capsules.''

Pat broke in. "Then why a satellite link? Why must we be
a superstation?''

Nora raised her eyebrows. How should she know?

"Why not stick to what she's good at?'' Pat fumed.
"Handing out money. Housing the homeless. Endowing
medical research. Saving landmarks. Like the Del Mar house
that's a hundred and two years old. She restored it and made
a museum. Good works!''

Nora smiled wryly. They did keep tabs on Millie.

"San Diego needs her. We don't. Honestly, Nora, what's
up?''

"Honestly, Pat, she hasn't told me.''

"Honestly, Nora, maybe she hasn't told you exactly what's
going on, but you must smell something. Admit it,'' Tim
said.

"I admit nothing. No little bird tells me a damn thing.''

"I don't believe it. Blood is thicker. And you two are thick
as thieves. Like sisters. To think I once masturbated watching
her in a movie.'' He cleared his throat. "The balcony was
dark. I was fifteen.''

Nora made a gesture of dismissal. "Go away, friends.
Leave! Let us earn our daily bread. I have to do a memo for
Luddy. Prepare him for Tuesday . . . and the surprises Millie
has waiting for us.''

Tim wouldn't leave. "Maybe I'm wrong. Maybe she plans
to sell the station. That's what the meeting's about.''

Nora had a funny look. "Where'd you get that foolishness?''

"My voices. They talk to me constantly.''

"Give them my regards. On your way out.''

Pat stopped at the door. "You see your grandmother tonight, don't you?''

"We never talk business on Friday night.'' Nora smiled.

"Aaah, Friday. The night of the Gardiner family dinners.''

"Homey. Cozy. Think of a Norman Rockwell painting.''

"Nora, break tradition. Go to hell with yourself. Ask your

dearly beloved grandmother to send a fax on future plans. So
the staff has weekend lead time to prepare résumés.''

Nora poured oil on a troubled Pat. ''Miss Yocum, don't
get antsy. Whatever's in Millie's mind, it's not staff cuts.''

''Then ask her to messenger me a videotape of *Bad Girl*.
It's not available at Wherehouse or Blockbuster.''

''Ask her yourself. Tuesday. Before the coffee and oat bran
muffins arrive,'' Nora said. ''Now please go.''

Left alone, Nora never knew afterward how long she sat
quietly thinking about her grandmother. Her history. Her
health. Her beauty . . . even now. Her mystery. Millie Thorne
had been a star. Millie Gardiner remained a star. But that
very quality had its drawbacks. It made for Millie's loneliness
and other unknowns . . . like standing by herself in front of
the hospital. Her visit to the hospital was important only because she didn't mention it. Not to her or—as far as she
knew—not to anyone else. For an instant Nora felt again a
sharp premonition . . . as if she were standing on the brink
of an abyss. A chill ran down her spine. If Millie—her grandmother—was alone, it was a matter of pride. She would never
admit to being ill. Comfort from anyone would ease the com-
forter . . . not her. For her, it would be an insult . . . con-
tradicting the bravado of her life. There was only one answer.
Millie—until today Nora couldn't imagine the possibility—
Millie was afraid.

Chapter 2

THE SUN had vanished into the Pacific Ocean . . . the golden haze was turning to dusky purple. The April air was soft with a hint of fog drifting in from the ocean . . . fog that would settle over the land by midnight. Driving along the snakelike lanes that wound through Rancho Santa Fe, Nora was glad the twisting turns were familiar as the palm of her hand. Occasionally she took her eyes off the road to glance at a white wooden fence where, during the day, horses roamed and munched on heavily watered grass. Property owners in Rancho Santa Fe were not inclined to worry about the desert climate or the drought. If push came to shove, they'd import tank trucks of water. Then there was the nonhorsey set . . . the flower and tree worshipers. Often their houses could barely be seen through the groves of orange and lemon trees that swept back from the road. There were no streetlights in Rancho Santa Fe . . . only reflector signs to warn of hidden driveways, crossroads and turns too sharp not to be taken cautiously. Eventually Nora arrived at the high wrought iron gate extending across the entrance to Bienvenida . . . Millie Gardiner's forty-five-plus-acre estate.

At either end of the gate stood two life-size sculptured stone horses, and at the side of the gate, in a white stucco guardhouse with a red tile roof, sat a uniformed guard, Juan Carillo. His grandfather, his father, and now Juan and his brothers had guarded Bienvenida for three generations. And Millie Gardiner for the last six years. Day and night a Carillo sat in that guardhouse . . . a rifle, a pistol, a telephone and the switch that opened the gate within easy reach. Nora stopped in front of the gate.

When Juan saw Nora, he smiled and leaned out of the window. "You are late, *señorita*."

"My karma."

"Sí, señorita." Juan pressed the switch and the gate slid noiselessly open.

Nora waved and shifted into Drive. She guided her car up the winding driveway leading to the main house. As she drove, she glanced at the landscape . . . thinking of Millie . . . of Bienvenida. Six years ago Millie had left New York City, where she'd lived for so long, having decided to return west. She was homesick, she said. So she'd moved bag and baggage back to the splendid Gardiner estate . . . to Bienvenida. She'd inherited Bienvenida from Max Gardiner, her first husband. There, as a young bride, she'd been happy . . . or so people said.

The Ranch—as the more-than-six-thousand-acre enclave of Rancho Santa Fe was called—had been established in the twenties next door to Fairbanks Ranch . . . the hideaway of Douglas Fairbanks and Mary Pickford. Sixty years later, the Ranch was San Diego's equivalent of L.A.'s Bel Air and New York's Locust Valley . . . except that houses were less ostentatious and had a good deal more land. Two acres per house was the minimum zoning. Ten-acre estates were common. Twenty acres not uncommon. There were a few thirty-acre estates. Then there was Bienvenida . . . half again the size of any estate in Rancho Santa Fe. Millie said it was home.

Nora couldn't help smiling. There's no place like home . . . if home is Bienvenida. She nosed her black T-bird under the portico where Carlos waited to park her car.

"You are late, *señorita.*" Carlos opened the car door.

"Juan told you." Nora laughed as she slid out of the car. "Lord! My grandmother has more security than the White House."

Carlos thought about that. "Maybe. . . . *Señora* Gardiner believes one must be careful. The world is not always friendly."

The words reminded Nora how few illusions Millie permitted herself. Even here—with a guard at a gate—even here there was no safety. Nora gazed at the shadowy graceful old hacienda-style house. Built in the twenties—two stories and U-shaped—it had been remodeled in the late 1940s for Max and Millie and again in '86 for Millie. It stood at the crest of the highest ridge in the Ranch, commanding a view of hills and Lake Hodges to the east and the Pacific Ocean to the west. The hacienda had gleaming white stucco walls and red tile roofs . . . Addison Mizner, the legendary architect, had stripped a few Spanish monasteries to supply the original owner with authentic eighteenth-century Spanish tiles for the roof and floors. The tile roof extended over long colonnades that ran the length of the interior walls. All the public rooms opened on an inner courtyard with a wading pool, flower gardens and classic sculpture. The art dealer who sold Max Gardiner the statues whispered they'd been smuggled out of Italy . . . from the Tivoli Gardens. Very authentic. Max laughed. He didn't care. The sculpture looked authentic . . . that was enough for him.

Nora often wished she'd known her grandfather. What was he like? Why had Millie loved him? She could have loved a hundred men. At least a hundred men loved her. Why had she chosen Max? For money? Millie Thorne was a star. If she'd stayed in movies, she would have been an even bigger star. Big stars made big money. Maybe not big *big* money by Gardiner standards, but big money. So why? Love? Somehow Nora didn't think so . . . despite her father's insisting Max was Millie's great love. So why? Nora shrugged. There were no answers. She walked to the tall, hand-carved oaken doors and stood watching as they slowly opened, powered by some kind of electronic marvel that Carlos controlled. Inside, Miguel greeted her and led her through the dimly lit reception room to the main dining room with its rough beige stucco walls and exposed brown timbers.

"You are late, *señorita,*" Miguel said.

"Sssh. Juan told me. Carlos told me. Don't you tell me."

"One hour late," Miguel noted somberly. "The main course will be served shortly. *Luciana do conchinita pibil.*"

"Barbecue heaven! All's well that ends well. Seasoned suckling pig baked in banana leaves. That's what I sniffed in the reception room."

"And roast turkey for the Wolffs, who do not eat pig on Friday night. And vegetable curry for—"

"Don't tell me. For Paul Pratt, Harold Brett and Lance Webb. They have heart bypasses to cater to." Nora laughed. "We are a very multied family . . . multinational . . . multidenominational . . . multi-life-styled. It sounds like a standard gourmet menu from grandmother. Nothing microwaved."

Miguel was shocked. *"Señora* says the microwave eats food."

"I know. My grandmother believes in simmering pots and home-baked pies. Convenience foods are bad for the digestion. We've had a few differences over frozen versus fresh vegetables." Nora stepped into the glow of the dining room, lit by a huge black-iron-and-bronze chandelier. Like much of the house, the chandelier had a Spanish provenance. The dealer assured Max Gardiner it once belonged to Queen Isabella. Suddenly Nora wished she'd gone home from the station and added a few sparkles. Changed into something more festive. There were limits to California casual.

Glancing at Millie, seated at the head of the thirty-foot-long rectangular oak table, Nora felt a surge of love. Millie . . . mysterious and real. A brooding presence . . . a moody sphinx. In keeping with the fiesta spirit, she'd turned herself out in a broomstick skirt, a striking Amuzgo Indian blouse, a necklace of old gold coins. Pure peasant . . . pure star. She couldn't dress it away, wash it away, think it away. It was the essence that transformed the migrant child from the Kansas dust bowl into a legendary movie star . . . that destined her to be the wife of Max Gardiner, the spoiled, adored son of the rich and powerful California Gardiners. By turns she could be intimidating or fragile. Fragile! The thought made Nora blink. How fragile, how precarious, was her grandmother's health? Tonight she didn't look in the least fragile. . . .

Nora caught Millie's smile, taking her in like a warm embrace. It gave Nora a small, strange dread. She knew her grandmother well . . . her fierce pride. She must walk on eggshells . . . betray no concern . . . show no special knowledge. She flashed back a smile and paused to kiss Millie on the cheek. She then continued, smiling at all the smiles seated at the table. She followed Miguel and slid into the seat reserved for her at the far end of the table. Although never stated, it was understood by all that at Millie's table there were two equal heads . . . Millie sat at one and Nora at the other. Albeit, whichever head Millie sat at was a touch more equal. Mark sat on Nora's right and Dr. Abe Lombard her left. She waited for Oscar—Millie's longtime factotum—to pour champagne. At Millie's there was always champagne . . . no matter what other wines were served. Nora felt a

glow . . . a warm, human glow. The Friday nights at Millie's
had gone on for so long. They had the feeling of past times
. . . a chain of lives stretching through time.

Barron Gardiner, Nora's father, had said that the tradition
of Millie's Friday family dinners went back more than forty
years to Nora's grandfather, Max. Dark, handsome Max, who
was courtly, charming and deadly dangerous to women. When
he died after falling from his horse during a polo match in Santa
Barbara, Millie grieved for a year. There were days, he said,
when his mother wouldn't speak to him. Sometimes he blamed
himself for her grief. And sometimes Nora thought he'd spent
his entire life studying the enigma of his mother. . . .

Eventually Millie recovered and remarried. To please her
second husband, Leo Stein, she moved from California to
the Fifth Avenue penthouse. Nora remembered dinners in
New York with Millie and Leo presiding . . . dinners that
stopped only briefly after his death. Later, when Millie moved
back to Rancho Santa Fe, the dinners continued on a reduced
scale. As time passed, many family members moved west.
They wanted to be closer to Millie . . . to the source. So the
dinners grew larger until they equalled the original Friday
nights when Max was alive. Millie held them from the Friday
after Labor Day until the Friday before Memorial Day, when
she decamped for her compound on Martha's Vineyard.

Nora glanced around at the evening's assortment of guests.
Seated along both sides of the long table were cousins, nieces,
nephews—their husbands or wives—grandnieces and grand-
nephews, in-laws and assorted kin from Millie's two marriages. Relatives all . . . come to pay their respects. All
twenty-four. Handpicked out of dozens more. Millie had so
many relations from her two marriages, Margaret Mead might
have had to invent new labels for the varieties of her kinship.

Nora's spirits rose . . . listening to the orchestralike effect
of voices and laughter ricocheting around the table. The
women, glowing and perfumed and dressed to kill . . . coo-
ing, chattering, gossiping. All friends . . . more or less. They
knew much the same people . . . wore the same kind of
clothes . . . shared the same interests. Some worked out of
necessity, some ambition; some didn't work. The men seated
at the table were a sea of suits, ties and horn-rimmed glasses
or sport jackets and expensive open shirts . . . showered and

shaved and cologned to a fare-thee-well. Cracking jokes, laughing, swapping stories . . . a formidable gathering of goodwill. Having the time of their lives.

No one stared directly at Nora, but everyone noticed her. Noticed her straight-from-work clothes. No glamour. No shine. Except her nose . . . her nose needed powder. Her hair needed combing. Nora sat up straighter. She understood she was regarded as odd. It was inscribed in family lore. Nora the eccentric heiress. If she was an heiress . . .

Abruptly Mark swiveled from Leslie Kelly on his right and hissed in her ear, "Nice of you to come. Your outfit's a knockout. Nothing else to wear? Not even a towel?"

Nora smiled at her husband-to-be. Tall, strong, agile . . . with muscular legs, a golden mop of hair and the slightly arched nose seen on ancient Roman coins. Mark looked like what she imagined an English archer might.

"No time to change, dear heart. Think of it this way, my lack of glitter stands out."

"So do the glasses. You look like a math teacher." He turned back to Leslie . . . Leslie with the alabaster-white neck, red lips, lacquered blond hair—not a wisp out of place—an inch-wide diamond choker, and a red dress with a plunging V neck.

"Sorry. I forgot to put in my contacts," she said to the back of his head.

"Nora! You look so Hollywood. So chic. After-work casual. You should have worn jeans. Marlene Stewart lives in jeans. She dresses Madonna. The Gap look. I've seen jeans at premieres. White tennis pants. Even spandex. Of course, at a blockbuster premiere or charity the dress code is more formal." Angie Pratt, third cousin, poured syrup over her words. "I guess you didn't think this was a blockbuster evening?"

"I haven't seen the movie yet. I'll tell you when it's over." Nora wanted to kick the family clotheshorse . . . scintillating in a crystal beaded chiffon, bought at some pricey boutique in La Jolla.

"I adore casual cashmere . . . like your turtleneck, Nora. So classic, so back of your hand," applauded second cousin Lolly—the clotheshorse contender—shifting her white feather boa around her shoulders.

"By the way, I hear Millie's thinking of selling Channel 18," Angie prodded Nora.

"Oh! I hope not. It belongs in the family." Lolly spoke with childish authority.

"Lolly, dearest, you really should have finished high school. You still can't add." Angie dismissed Lolly with a superior smile. "Mark can get a very nice price for the station. Maybe a few hundred million. Yes, Nora?"

"No, Angie. Maybe forty million. It's a UHF station . . . not a VHF station." There was strain in Nora's tone.

"That's peanuts! Paul, you told me TV stations are hot-ticket items. Networks are going down the drain. Everything is cable." Angie pouted at her husband.

Paul Pratt had been itching to put in his two cents. "I exaggerated a little, but—"

"Who gave you that tidbit, Paul?" Nora was exasperated. "Millie hasn't mentioned selling."

"Norton James. This joker from Channel 10. We had lunch. He said Arthur Reiner and Mark were putting together a syndicate to buy Channel 18 . . ." Paul smiled blandly at Mark.

Mark turned from Cousin Leslie. He gave Paul the kindest of smiles. "Have I mentioned anything to you about a syndicate?"

Sullen. "No."

Friendly. "But you think I should have?"

Righteous. "Well, I *am* family. . . ."

Unctuous. "And family gets preferential treatment."

"You know Millie's rule." The words hung in the air. Then he asked, "Leslie, has he mentioned it to you?"

"No, he hasn't." Leslie was peeved.

Mark looked at Paul. Paul looked at Mark. Mark's look could have killed. "Right on. And when there is a deal, Paul . . ."

"Do that. A family that prays together . . ."

"Don't say 'lays together,' " Lolly said primly.

Nora half smiled. Mark was no longer listening. He was working to make back points with Leslie. Who—as luck would have it—was rich in her own right via a handsome divorce settlement. Mark prized Millie's dinners as prime hunting ground for clients. Even if, occasionally—as luck would have it—the seating arrangement backfired. And a Paul Pratt, placed nearby, could damn near derail his pitch.

Angie broke into her reverie. "Speaking of family, Ali says Bienvenida has true historical value."

Nora examined her unmanicured, square-cut nails. A standard Friday-night ritual. Homage to Ali . . . short for Alison. Ali always came up at Friday dinners . . . one way or another.

"Old Spanish tiles are so romantic. And she loves the horses. She rides as if she was born on a saddle. She told Millie she'd like to breed a horse for the Derby . . . the Belmont . . . the Preakness."

Nora's ears tingled. Something was off-key. The Ali verb had changed from past to present tense. It sounded current.

Sugary. "You ride too, don't you, Nora?"

Alerted. "Yes. But I was born in a hospital . . . not on a saddle."

Heartfelt. "Ali thanks God that Millie can still ride . . . at her age."

"Of course Millie rides. She grew up on a farm." Nora met Angie's eyes and for a moment they looked straight at each other.

"I wish I did . . . ride, I mean. Not grow up on a farm. Riding is wonderful exercise." Angie offered another Ali goody. "Millie agreed to let Ali catalog her antiques. Ali adores Millie's pieces. The Louis XV commode that belonged to Madame du Barry. The Chinese things. Ming. Han." She frowned. "Your house is Milanese modern. Chrome and steel. You don't care for antiques?"

"I care for what we can afford. At that, we live too near the ocean. Salt air isn't the best climate for antiques." Nora didn't trust herself to say more. Her political instincts were aroused. Angie could ramble from now to doomsday. She wouldn't ask questions. She wouldn't give her the satisfaction. She scanned the guests. There was Dr. Abe. The Wolffs. Lance Webb. The Popps . . . the Pratts. Et cetera. Hiram, as usual, was notable for his absence . . . by choice or chance . . . tied up with the World Bank in Washington or Geneva. But the table was filled with guests who were eager to savor the suckling pig or the roast turkey or the curry, the grilled vegetables and salad vinaigrette. Millie always gave her guests menus.

Angie was itching to talk. "You must be so glad she's back."

Nora's heart flipped. "Hmm . . . I didn't know. . . . How nice."

"You mean she hasn't called you?" Angie forced the issue. "You two are so close. See." Zing went Angie's arrow. "There she is, to the right of Digby, who's sitting next to Millie."

Sitting very still, Nora followed Angie's eyes. It was as if a gun had been fired off behind her back. She wanted to touch herself to see if she'd been hurt . . . if she was bleeding. Somehow she had managed not to see Ali. But there she was . . . life-size. Stunning in a black silk T-shirt and a single strand of gold-and-gray pearls. Deep in dialogue with Cousin Harold Brett . . . behaving as if she cared.

"I love that kind of extravagantly simple, extravagantly expensive dress. But most of us need a bit more shimmer to shimmer." Angie's smile was catty. "Ali could come in a barrel—even in jeans—and look stunning." Another dig.

"So could Nora," Lolly Popp said loyally.

"Of course, so could Nora." Angie was diplomatic.

Nora's color rose, and she dropped her eyes. The old foolishness had begun again. Tictacktoe . . . who would get the dough? Millie's millions. She or Ali? That is, besides Hiram. . . . Who would get what? Bienvenida? Channel 18? The antiques? The horses? Millie's stock-and-bond portfolio? A stipend . . . a legacy . . . a something? Her face became grave. She knew how the chance of inheriting even a small part of Millie's estate fascinated the family. How much it was the hub of private hopes. Which of the hungry mouths at the table would be satisfied? Which not? Who were the family favorites to win? She guessed Hiram and she were the odds makers' choice . . . morning line favorites to share millions. It stood to reason . . . by right of dynastic descent. Her dead father was Millie's and Max's younger son. Hiram, her uncle, their older son. Millie and Leo Stein had no children. But Leo had sisters . . . with children galore. Like Paul Pratt, his nephew. Barron had said that Leo was a big teddy bear of a man, twenty years Millie's senior and New York City real estate rich. He admitted, grudgingly, that Leo was gentle and devoted and the two were oddly well matched . . . that their life together may well have been happy. Until Millie woke one morning to find Leo dead in bed. His death added considerably to Millie's millions, but it ended her desire to marry. If her lovers were going to die on her, they would die in their own homes . . . in their own beds. It was Nora's impression her father was relieved.

But given the givens, Millie's death would be profitable for Uncle Hiram. For her. For Ali . . . Hiram's stepdaughter. Ali was bound to be included in Millie's will . . . since her mother had the good sense to marry Hiram. And from the day Millie had introduced Ali to the family, she had gone out of her way to treat Ali as though Ali was her real granddaughter. What was good enough for Millie was good enough for the family. So no matter where Ali sat, the family believed she was running Nora a close second in the inheritors' steeplechase . . . a few even felt they were neck and neck. As a consequence, the family studiously courted Ali and Nora equally. There were times Nora thought the family's obsession with inheritance was mean spirited. Unnatural. Then she remembered history. Families had been preoccupied with inheritance since the beginning. The biblical history of brother killing brother for property began with Cain and Abel. It had no end. Survival often depended on who inherited the farm . . . the estate . . . the kingdom. Everything considered, Nora decided her clan was no greedier than others. No more conniving or self-seeking. Simply blatantly human. Hoping to inherit.

"Nora, wake up. Mindy wants to thank you for getting Eugene a job," Dr. Abe said.

"Yes, I do. Thank you, Nora," Mindy purred.

"Don't thank me. Thank Millie. She said Eugene needed a job in San Diego County. The office manager's job at the station was open. Eugene has the skills. He got the job."

"You moved to San Diego, Mindy. Well . . . It is closer to Millie . . . to your Wednesday night bridge game," Angie said pettishly.

"It is, and I love it. And I love coming to the Friday dinners . . . when we're invited. But it was an hour-and-a-half drive from El Toro to here . . . each way."

"The drive was taking its toll on Eugene," Dr. Abe said. "I told Millie."

"He was developing an ulcer," Mindy said.

"And stress syndrome," Dr. Abe added.

"Now it only takes a few minutes to drive from Carlsbad to the Farm."

Nora smiled at them. Mindy Wolff, Millie's niece via Leo, was in her early forties. Young enough to enjoy a bequest . . . if Millie were so inclined. Or even a few pieces of French furniture with ormolu dripping from the marquetry. If they sold it—which they would—it would bring a pretty penny. They were barely scraping by . . . they'd appreciate a few pretty pennies. That was a plus for them. Grandmother liked appreciation. No sending coals to Newcastle for Millie Gardiner.

"By the way, Nora." Dr. Abe turned back, sipping champagne. "You and Mark have postponed things long enough. I'm concerned."

Nora expected Abe's concern. His concern was another Friday night ritual. "Don't be, Abe."

"I must be. It's time you married. A year of mourning is sufficient. Your father would rather you were happily married than grieving for him. So would your grandmother." Dr. Abe spoke with the gracious but official tone of a messenger from the gods. "We agree you've been living together long enough . . . it'll be three years in June."

Nora wished he'd shut up and knew he wouldn't. She smiled. "We mean to give up our sinful ways, Abe. Cross my heart."

Mark had overheard Dr. Abe. His look was belligerent. "We're with you, Abe . . . all the way! Any minute now I'll make an honest woman of her."

Abe's gaze never faltered. He spoke in his best professional manner . . . a hypnotic torrent of words that made Nora drowsy. "I have . . ." He repeated it. "I have your best interests at heart."

Listening without listening, Nora thought he delivered a fine sermon. Dr. Abe was a psychiatrist with a little talent and a substantial practice. He had been the family psychiatrist and counselor for many years. Blindly self-important, he was given to tireless introspection and revelations. Against all vows of confidentiality, he was known to fill Millie's ear with the foibles, follies and frolics of his patients. "The ebb and flow of human lava," he called it. Mutual friends and family members were Abe's favorite topics. Paul Pratt's mid-life crisis and the virtues of Prozac. He suggested Millie buy shares in Smith Kline. Lance's gay flings. Lolly Popp's handwashing tic. Harold Brett's masturbation compulsion. The shames, the failings, the wins, the losses . . . Dr. Abe confided the details to Millie . . . providing her with news from the family twilight zone. But despite the secrets he unstintingly shared, Millie shared nothing with Abe. Once he complained to Nora that she never confided in him . . . no heart-to-heart talks . . . no intimate moments. She was a good listener . . . better than he was, he said. When not listening, she played the role of intelligent, social animal . . . exchanging opinions about art and music, politics, world affairs, light gossip. But nothing personal . . . no private hopes, no visions, no lost causes. If it had been anyone else, Abe would have said she was superficial and let it go at that. But he couldn't . . . she wasn't. Her reserve troubled and attracted him. He yearned to know more. When he asked, she changed the subject. Sometimes he suspected she was judging him and finding him ridiculous. He was right. That much Nora did know. But she understood his dilemma. Her grandmother had always been a game of guesses . . . a puzzle within a puzzle.

With relief, Nora heard Angie break into Abe's monologue. "Excuse me, Abe. Nora, look. Ali is waving to you."

Nora looked at Ali . . . animated . . . graceful . . . waving to her.

"Nora, it's wonderful to see you again." Ali's voice floated toward her. "I hear you're the new television genius."

Again Nora was sorry she hadn't changed clothes. "This television genius is like the White Queen . . . running to stay in place."

"How's the news desk? Is the garbage being dumped properly? And what's with medical waste on the beach?"

"Gridlock is the big sweat. We're pumping for car pools. Make friends. Meet a husband. A housemate. . . ." Nora was at a loss so she asked, "How have you been . . . you . . . yourself?"

"Splendid! I knew you'd be here. So I asked Millie to invite me. Let's have deep-dish talk later." Ali's eyes were appealing.

"Post dessert." Why not? She was curious.

Mark turned and stared at her, blue eyes flashing. His warm whisper brushed her ear. "Don't see the bitch. She's poison."

"You're crackers!" Nora whispered back, licking his ear. "And why didn't you tell me she was back?"

Mark gave Nora a tender smile and murmured, "I didn't tell you because I didn't know. We are not her travel agents, sweetheart. Reiner & Co. managed her money . . . when she had money. That's all."

"No one at the firm heard from her . . . that she was back?"

"No one. Me included. I merely deposited her checks— dividends and interest—at California National. Wired the principal to her Paris bank. The way Ali spent money makes Congress look El Cheapo. You know damn well she ran through a three-million-dollar inheritance in just five years. No more interest or dividends to deposit, no principal to transfer. So no news from dear Ali. Blackout."

"Okay. I believe you."

"If I'd known I'd have warned you. That spoiled rotten Ali Cat has a fatal attraction for you, my sweet. Why?" Mark asked.

"We share memories of youth. Central Park ice skating. We saw *Body Heat* together. Three times."

"She dumped you. Not a peep out of her for five years. Not a ring on the telephone. Not a telex. No postcards from the edge. Or from the equator. Or from either pole. Only silence . . . as in silence of a tomb. Now, hallelujah! She's back and wants to play jacks. And you run up to the attic to find the jacks. Why?"

"I told you. We grew up together," Nora explained.

"I don't trust her."

"I like to live dangerously."

Mark shrugged his shoulders. "A born victim." He turned back to charming Leslie.

Nora shook her head. Mark was on his anti-Ali march. It had started years ago . . . the weekend he met her. Over the years his opinion of Ali had worsened. Once he'd said, "She's shown a knack for inheriting . . . for being in the right place at the right death." He'd said that right after Amanda's accident.

"Mark, that's ghoulish," she'd said.

"Also grisly. Ali's the grieving beneficiary of three million dollars. Statistically high . . . considering the tender age of Amanda . . . her benefactor. Not that much older than Ali herself. You're another young relative. You stand between your friend and a queen-sized inheritance. Be careful.''

Mark meant it. It made Nora feel queer. Was she missing something?

Millie's couple—she had four in-house servants—Oscar and Rosa, served dinner. Afterward some guests had brandy . . . others had port or sherry or a liqueur. At that point, Nora and Ali excused themselves.

"Isn't Millie's cook an artist?'' Nora remarked as they retired to the library for their quick gossip.

Like every room in the hacienda, the library was a treasure trove of antiques. Ali seated herself elegantly in a George III chair while Nora plopped down on the more comfortable couch that had pillow shams made from Kasel tapestries.

"An artist.'' Ali smiled. "Luciana must cost a fortune. Millie does know how to spend money.''

Nora thought, So do you. Ali's perfume gave off the scent of genetically engineered strawberries and money.

"Incidentally, I must say Mark was a pet,'' Ali continued. "Whenever I called Reiner & Co. for money . . .'' She giggled. "I mean when I had money, I received the money *tout de suite*. I'm sure I have Mark to thank for the quick action. Nora, he looks divine.'' She gave Nora an envious smile. "You must make him happy. I wish I could have done the same for Aldo—'' She broke off and swallowed . . . then a half sob . . . a shade too theatrical. "That's history. I'll tell you about it sometime. Not now.''

Tactfully, Nora changed the subject. "How was Paris?''

"I love Paris. I met this divine man, Stanley Tseng. We flew to Fiji in his jet. It was heaven. You must go.''

"I'll tell Mark,'' Nora said. Inexplicably she had a flash of a graceful diver flying through the air into a deep blue ocean . . . the words *Great White Wall* floated into her mind. Fiji. Why?

"Yes, tell Mark. He knows Stanley. In a way, he introduced us.''

"Mark introduced this Stanley Whoever to you?'' The night was full of surprises.

"Tseng. Stanley Tseng. Yes. I don't jet off with strange Asiatics. He told Stanley to look me up in Paris. Stanley did, and . . .''

"Mark knew you were in Paris?" Nora tried to keep her voice casual.

"Why wouldn't he? That's where he sent me my checks . . . when I had checks. Don't fret, Nora. It was strictly business for Mark—I mean introducing Stanley—and fun for me. Stanley is charming. And very, very generous." She managed to grin sophisticatedly and blush at the same time. "We stayed on Taveuni Island. Not touristy at all. Primitive. They're filming a sequel to *Blue Lagoon* there. And Stanley taught me to scuba dive. I'm a beginner . . . twenty feet is my limit. But I snorkeled. Tropical fish are gorgeous. And I met Ratu Sir Penia Ganatau, the president of Fiji."

With Ali anything was possible. "Does Mark know him too?"

"I don't think so. But Stanley does. Stanley knows everyone. He can introduce Mark and you to everyone who matters when you go to Fiji."

"I'll remind Mark." Nora said it and meant it.

"Enough of Fiji. Let's have breakfast before the meeting Tuesday. And have a real heart-to-heart. About life, love and the future. We must catch up."

"What meeting?" Nora wasn't sure she could believe her ears.

"Millie's meeting. At the station. I'll be there of course."

Nora could think of nothing to say. Except, "Of course."

"You know I did her office? By telephone from Paris," Ali enthused. "I told Lance exactly what to buy and where to put it."

Life was getting stranger and stranger. "I didn't know. It's stunning. He followed your instructions very well."

"It's pure Millie. . . . I'm her gofer. I do this a and that a. And I know a bit about interior design. Last week I was at Christie's with Lance. He wanted my advice on buying. They were auctioning the Hancock estate." Ali threw out sparkles like a fountain. "He was searching for pieces for his antiques shop. He found nothing. Nothing at the auction compared with Millie's collection. He's been spoiled." Ali was reverent. "It would be nice if she gave him a chest . . . like the Italian one painted with garlands."

Nora heard between the lines. Maybe Millie would leave Lance a few priceless antiques. Offhand, she doubted it.

So did Ali. "I know Lance is the son of Leo Stein's sister.

The lunatic, dead one. But Mama left him a fortune. I don't think Millie will make it a larger fortune.''

"No. She'll give Lance something to remember her by." Nora smiled. "Jewelry. One of Leo's rings . . . a watch . . . a tiepin."

Ali giggled. "He won't think it's enough. And Millie will laugh all the way to the grave. Actually, if she gives anyone her antiques, it will be Dr. Abe . . . and perhaps a little something to me. I adore antiques." Beatific smile. "Millie and Abe go to auctions together. New York. London. She taught him all he knows about antiques. I adore Abe . . . Lance too. But Lance is no true antiquarian." She stretched her arms. "Wait till you hear what I've done . . . Tuesday."

Unease settled over Nora like a shroud as she smiled at Ali. "I look forward. Breakfast Tuesday morning. Are you here to stay? Or . . ."

"To stay. Moved back last month. I rented a charming condo in a high rise in Hillcrest. Tenth floor. A terrace overlooking Balboa Park. I'm a city girl . . . except for Bienvenida. I wanted to surprise you. So I waited for tonight to talk to you. I missed you, Nora."

Nora didn't ask, Then why didn't you write or phone for five years? "I've missed you," she said, carrying on the charade.

Ali's face lit up as Ali's face could. "So we'll catch up Tuesday. A sisterly breakfast. Let's go to that place in the Del Mar mall . . . Il Fornaio. We'll get a table on the terrace and look at the ocean."

"Fine. Tuesday. Eightish? It'll give us time to catch up. . . ."

Their *danse macabre* had begun again.

The party was winding down . . . the guests were leaving. Mark nuzzled Nora's ear. "Juice up, baby. I want to run barefoot through your hair."

"See you home, you mad, impetuous thing." Nora giggled. She watched him leave . . . pausing to kiss Millie on the cheek and thank her too profusely for another "champagne Friday." Nora wished he would tone down the trashy flattery. She was embarrassed for him. All the same, she did love him . . . very much. Chemistry? Love or lust? It didn't matter. She glanced around. There was still pleasure in the air . . . the pleasure of being inside a charmed circle. It was going on as it had always . . . Friday night at Millie's. Once she had childishly believed it would go on forever. Tonight the familiar rat-a-tat about inheritance had had a chilling effect.

Nora watched Millie say good-night to her guests. One moment she could be open as the sky above . . . another instant her Olympian grandness became unsettling. Prickly. A cactus with gorgeous flowers.

Millie came toward her. "Mark has a new client."

"Leslie Kelly," Nora said dryly.

"She mentioned she might use him as a broker."

"And you did nothing to stop her . . . did you?"

Millie smiled. "Nothing. He's smart . . . I hear."

"I wish he'd stop pitching the family." Nora's deep-rooted fright surfaced. "If he loses Leslie or Paul or Digby any real money . . ."

"They are all consenting adults. . . ." Millie faltered.

For an instant they gazed at each other with pain and compassion. The past was too real for both of them.

"Mark isn't like Barron, dear," Millie whispered, stroking her granddaughter's cheek.

Nora nodded, but she wasn't sure. Her eyes blurred as she saw her father. Losing his money—Millie's money—hand over fist . . . tap-dancing on the devil's coals. In an effort to regain her footing she said, "The air is full of rumors that you're selling 18."

Millie followed her lead. "Nora, you know better. No one's made me an offer I can't refuse." The smile returned. "But thank you for charming Edith Fong. You enchanted her."

Herself again. "Building goodwill for the station. My job."

"Introducing her to Sonia Chin was a stroke of genius."

Nora laughed. "I got lucky. They're related."

"So Edith said. A happy coincidence." She studied Nora's face. "You and Ali have picked up where you left off?"

Nora almost laughed. Millie had eyes in the back of her head. "Well . . . we've picked up . . . in a way."

"Originally, she said she'd be back by Labor Day."

Nora's head buzzed. The words sounded foreign. "Ali was in touch with you? Before she returned?"

"She telephoned. Regularly. I'm no letter writer either. I'd rather telephone. Today overseas calls sound like next door."

Nora perspired. She felt like a human sacrifice trussed up and turning on a spit. "She never wrote or called me."

"I know. She said she was going to . . . eventually. She said she didn't want her affection for you to influence her. . . ."

Nora's voice was unsteady. "Influence Ali? I don't follow."

"She couldn't decide if she should live in Italy permanently. She was afraid you might persuade her not to."

"Me persuade Ali? To do anything? That's crazy!"

"That is what she said."

Millie's words triggered a feeling of betrayal in Nora. Five years had changed nothing. Millie continued to protect Ali. For a moment Nora couldn't breathe. Then . . . "You never told me she wrote to you," she murmured.

"It wasn't my place to tell you. When Ali was ready to talk to you, she said she would."

Nora was adrift. "Did she talk to Hiram too?"

"No. She felt it was too soon. Amanda's death was too fresh. She felt she'd be an unhappy reminder."

"Then you're the only one . . . ?"

"Well, Reiner & Co. And Barron. She saw him. . . ." Millie said it matter-of-factly . . . not like a woman scoring a big point.

"Ali saw my father?" Nora had trouble getting the words out.

"Yes. Barron saw Ali when he went to Rome. And later in Paris."

"He never told me."

"We agreed he shouldn't. Ali and you were close. We felt it was her business . . . and yours. Third parties had no place." Millie's tone was deceptively casual. "When are you seeing each other?"

"What don't you know?" Nora laughed without humor.

"I know you. I know Ali."

I don't, Nora thought. "We're breaking bread Tuesday. Before the meeting."

"She'll be at the meeting. She's doing work for me."

"So she said. . . ."

Just then Angie interrupted. "It was wonderful, Millie. I'm a food junkie when it comes to roast pork."

For once Nora was glad to see Angie. The conversation

with Millie had left her unnerved. She didn't want to talk any more about Ali. "Dinner was wonderful," she said. "I'll be in touch." She kissed Millie on the cheek and all but ran for the door. Once there, she paused to glance back briefly at her grandmother. Millie looked as always . . . hardly in her late sixties. The mysterious aura of beauty still surrounded her. She could have visited Scripps for a variety of reasons besides her health, Nora thought. About Ali, she didn't know what to think. . . .

Most evenings after a Millie dinner, Nora and Mark were eager to talk. They'd plunk on the couch and trade tidbits. Secrets. News. Jokes. Dirt. They'd go on and on for hours. Not this night. Nora had nothing to say . . . although Mark poked and pried. Nothing about Ali. Nothing about Channel 18. Or about Stanley Tseng and Ali and Fiji. Or about Millie and Ali. Not a word.

Sensing her upset, Mark slid over . . . slipped his hands under the turtleneck of her dress, and gently, expertly massaged the nape of her neck. His fingers were strong and sure. Cool fingers on warm bare skin. Nora arched her back . . . relaxed. His fingers were calming . . . arousing. She felt the message in them. She tilted and turned her face to him. Their lips met . . . the massage stopped. They stumbled to the bedroom. That night they made love passionately. Nora was wild . . . sex would stop her thinking. Sex would be a narcotic. Mark was astonished. Afterward Nora fell into a deep sleep. Not so Mark. He was awake for hours thinking about tomorrow. Tomorrow! Nora would be in L.A. And maybe—just maybe—he would hit pay dirt.

Chapter 3

IT WAS three o'clock . . . Pacific Daylight Saving Time. The Pacific Stock Exchange was closed. Mark sat at his desk at Reiner & Co. and completed totalling his commissions for the day. But it wasn't the usual fun. Today's take—not bad—was nothing compared to the money he'd make if Millie gave him a piece of her business. Mark had few illusions about himself . . . he was as greedy as most men . . . maybe greedier. Ambitious. A visionary. Don't forget the vision. A smart, quick outsider who could beat insiders at their own game. The kid who took Christmas and Yom Kippur vacations . . . Nora called him a double-dipper. Maybe so. Which was why he hadn't mentioned the meeting to her. Even though he was blameless. A saint. Millie had called him . . . he hadn't called her. No way! He was a saint . . . Saint Mark.

San Diego is the seventh largest city in the United States, but what Mark liked best was its small-town atmosphere. Except for the tiny downtown high-rise office area, the city was a collection of semiurbanized communities like Hillcrest and Mission Bay . . . high-rise apartment houses and single family homes abutting each other. Reiner & Co. occupied the top two floors of a twenty-story high rise on Broadway. Adjoining it—with a connecting door on each floor—was a high-rise garage with two intertwined, corkscrewlike ramps—one for going up, one for going down—and parking spaces on every floor. To negotiate the corkscrew ramps, one had to be either a good driver or a cautious one. Mark was neither. He was something better . . . a lucky driver. In the three years he'd been driving up and down the ramps, he'd never so much as scratched a fender.

Exiting the garage, Mark picked up the northbound entrance to I-5 . . . the San Diego Freeway. Rancho Santa Fe was only minutes away. Driving gave him time to think . . . to consider his approach. How to make the best impression? Be confident yet modest. His hard-nosed sales pitch about the quick money he'd make for Millie . . . that wouldn't cut it. Better talk about protecting her capital . . . taking few risks and looking for special plays with tax advantages. Tax loopholes had sex appeal to people as rich as Millie Gardiner.

Juan greeted him at the gate to Bienvenida and announced his arrival on the intercom . . . passing him along to Carlos at the hacienda entrance and then to Miguel at the hacienda door.

Mark walked through the foyer. He wished he was rich enough to afford eighteenth-century Spanish tile floors.

"Good of you to come, sir." Oscar Michaelmass was waiting for him at the end of the foyer, his English accent stagy as ever. One would never guess he'd been born a Cockney. "Oscar is a self-made man," Millie had said proudly. "He invented himself." She'd added that Oscar went to school to learn butlering and speak English with a public school accent. Which was oiled and fluent . . . even after twenty-five years of living in the States. Today, his custom-made suit was better cut than Mark's.

"Please follow me, sir," he said. "To the small library."

Mentally Mark rubbed his hands together. The small library was Millie's business room.

"They are waiting for you," Oscar continued.

Inwardly Mark did a double take. "They are waiting . . ." Who was the "they"? The question ricocheted around his brain like machine gun bullets bouncing off steel walls. Had Millie invited other brokers to compete for her account? Knowing her . . . yes! Mark panicked. What could he promise they couldn't? Service and prompt execution? No. Every broker promised that. And given the size of her account you could bet your sweet ass she'd get silky service. Maybe . . . No. He had nothing special to offer . . . except himself.

"Mr. Stern has arrived, madam," Oscar announced.

Mark gulped. His boss, Arthur Reiner, was waiting. He sat on Millie's left . . . engrossed in talk with her. Mark felt sudden relief. Maybe Arthur had been invited to make the deal official.

Millie glanced up. "Arthur, dear, Mark is here. Now

please drop this tiresome subject. Sixty million doesn't interest me.''

"Right, Millie. I hear you.'' Arthur heaved a dramatic sigh
. . . paused. "Maybe . . . maybe I can get seventy. I can't
promise it. Seventy million's a lot for a UHF license . . .
with a local audience. San Diego's not that large a market.
Twenty-seventh in the country. If the channel was in New
York City . . . well . . . that's another story. Three or four
hundred million is possible. But San Diego? No. Maybe, if
you include the real estate—the building, the studios—
although they're not worth more than—''

"Arthur, you're not listening. Seventy million doesn't interest me. Eighty million doesn't interest me.''

"Millie, you're being greedy. It's not like you. Channel 18
isn't worth more than seventy million. It's an independent. It
competes with network affiliates . . . with cable channels. There
are TV channels for sports fans, news addicts, music lovers,
movie buffs, nature lovers, money lovers. There's even a sci-fi
channel and a live courtroom channel. Channel 18 is obsolete.
Dated. It has a limited audience and no access to unique programming.''

"Are you finished, Arthur?''

He sipped his scotch, inclining his head. "For now.''

"Forever, Arthur. You deliberately misunderstand me. I am
not cash poor . . . portfolio poor . . . or land poor. For the
third and last time, tell your buyer Channel 18 is not for sale.
Not the license . . . buildings . . . or studios. At any price.
Channel 18 is shedding its caterpillar skin. The butterfly will
emerge. You'll see the start of some very unique programming.
Good evening, Mark.'' She gestured a welcome with her jade
cigarette holder.

Mark smiled weakly. He'd walked in on Arthur's ongoing
pitch for Channel 18. Hardly the moment of fleeting perfection.
"Good evening, Millie . . . Arthur.''

"Millie, why this sudden yen to turn 18 into a butterfly?''
Arthur hung on by his teeth. "We'll get to Mark shortly. First
I must remind you that—''

"Enough, Arthur.''

"Millie, remember, it was you who first suggested to me that
you might like to sell. . . .'' Doggedly he persisted.

Exasperated. "Yes. That was before . . .''

Riveted. "Before what?''

A battle of pregnant pauses. "Before I realized I wouldn't live forever."

"What are you talking about?"

"Legacies." Millie was ice-cold courtesy. "It has occurred to me that money alone isn't a good enough legacy."

"It will do for most people."

"Not for me. Arthur, the magic of money is not the fat checkbook . . . not 'round-the-world shopping sprees where you buy till you drop. It's none of those things. It's freedom to choose how to live. Even how to die. How to be remembered. I'm rich . . . so I'm free to choose. I've made plans—beyond money—for my legacy. That's why Channel 18 is no longer for sale. No more, Arthur. Or you'll wear out your welcome." Her tone was unemphatic, clipped. She turned to Mark. "Good of you to come on such short notice. It's flattering, knowing how busy you are."

Mark tried to smile. What was Arthur up to? Was all that palaver about Channel 18 just pump priming? Was he using it to lead in to the real pitch . . . Millie's investment portfolio? Mark never knew with Arthur. Originally it had struck him that Arthur Reiner wasn't cut out for Wall Street . . . especially investment banking. Too attractive to be taken seriously . . . except by women. Too soft, too much a playboy . . . a man meant only to enjoy the privileges of inherited wealth. Mark soon discovered how wrong he'd been. More than men who seemed to have ten times his natural gifts, Arthur Reiner had prospered. In time Mark learned why. Reiner was deceptive. His courtly manners and playboy looks were his disguise. Arthur was a born barracuda.

"Would you like your usual gin martini, Mark?"

Mark said yes and sat down facing them. Glancing around, he felt intimidated. Intimidated by the two life-size portraits of Millie's husbands that took up most of the mahogany-paneled wall behind her. Intimidated by the two other walls with their floor-to-ceiling bookshelves filled with books on business, economics, and biographies of business leaders. Intimidated by the window wall that opened onto a private terrace and overlooked the rolling, wooded hills of Rancho Santa Fe. Most of all intimidated by Millie . . . formidable and elegant in a red—or was that color burgundy?—silk shirt, matching trousers and a single chain of heavy, loop-in-loop gold links. The outfit on anyone else her age would have looked wrong.

When his drink materialized, Mark raised his glass in smiling salute. Millie smiled back.

Arthur broke into the family playlet. "Reports tell me you're becoming the top producer in retail sales. Your trading volume rises every week." Laughing. "You even make money for your customers."

"Making them money is a good way to keep their accounts." Mark relaxed. Arthur was selling for both of them.

"Right. Now let's dispense with shop talk." Arthur used his clubby, man-to-man voice. "This isn't solely a business meeting."

Then what the hell is it? Mark stared.

Millie exhaled a small puff of cigarette smoke. "Mark, today everyone's sex life is cocktail conversation. You miss the thrill of my generation. When lovers had secret trysts in romantic hideaways." Her tone was ironic. "But you and Nora are another breed. You live together openly."

Mark felt a light sweat at the back of his neck. "As Nora puts it, we're consenting adults."

"I understand that. Nora's father understood." Millie's tone became brisk. "I've been patient. But my patience wears thin. Tell me, do you love each other?"

Mark flushed. "I love Nora. I think she loves me. Ask her yourself."

"If you love each other, why not get married?" Arthur asked.

"Money. Or rather, the lack of money."

"Good lord, Mark! You have two incomes," Arthur exclaimed. "Plus you've done well this year. You can live comfortably on combined incomes."

Mark hesitated, then said, "A few good years do not a net worth make. We want children. Children cost money."

"A sane attitude," Arthur intoned righteously. "But I believe you'll do even better next year. There could be a partnership in your future."

Millie inserted another cigarette in her holder.

In order not to react to the word *partnership*, Mark concentrated on the nimbleness of her fingers . . . they could have belonged to a woman of thirty.

"Is money the only reason you haven't married?" Millie asked.

"It is for me, Millie. We have a pleasant life now . . . with the pluses of marriage and no minuses . . . like responsibility."

Millie's smile was kindly. "Dr. Abe suggested money might be the reason for the delay. I have some free cash to invest in the market." She was as calm as Mark was nervous. "Suppose you handle it for me? Say ten million? The commissions should solve your money problems . . . real or imaginary."

Mark had a big-eyed, bingo expression. The break he'd prayed for had arrived . . . via the back door. "It would help. If . . . well . . ." He hoped he didn't sound as eager as he felt.

"If what?"

A drum pounded in Mark's chest. He spoke confidentially, as if confessing a shameful secret. "If I could accept your account."

"Why can't you accept it?"

"Because you're Nora's grandmother. This may sound odd, but I dislike using Nora's family for business. It's against my principles." He lowered his eyes . . . glad his suit didn't fit as well as Oscar's. He looked more sincere.

"You're acting like a child." Arthur lost patience.

"I think it's important to mention my reservations." He was definitely high-minded.

A skeptical smile crossed Millie's face. "Mark, dear boy, you already have family members as clients."

"Their accounts are small potatoes. Nothing like what you're suggesting."

"You'd refuse my account because of its size?"

"Not because of its size. Because you're Nora's grandmother. Her closest blood tie. It's a matter of principles." Nora's principles, he said to himself.

Millie gazed at him with amused detachment. "Are you afraid you can't handle a ten-million-dollar account?"

"Oh, no! I can handle it." So much for playing Lancelot, the pure of heart. He sounded like a jerk. "Look . . . since joining Reiner & Co., I've covered my twenty-five-thousand-dollar draw. Add that to the fifty percent I keep out of my commission . . . it more than doubles my income. I'm doing fine on my own. Sure, I have a few family members as clients." He still had to justify himself. "But it's like I said. They're not as important to Nora as you."

"I have a thought," Millie said. "When people marry, they receive wedding presents from friends and relatives. I'll

give you the account as a wedding present. From me to Nora
and you. I know how she feels about your taking family business.'' She smiled . . . the smile of a cynical conspirator.
''That way she can't object.''

''I guess that would convince her.''

''Fine. It's settled.'' Millie the matriarch was content.
Mark was bought and paid for. This was how she liked doing
business. ''Two months after you two marry, my lawyers will
assign you the power to open an account for me at Reiner &
Co. and trade up to ten million dollars through the account.''

Mark felt he was in free-fall. A trading account!

''Next. Where will you marry? Nora has a large family.''

''As you know, I have a small family.'' Mark tried to collect his thoughts.

''Then I'll take care of wedding plans. Nora's family is
large but her father is dead. Your family is small . . . your
mother and sister . . . We'll finally meet them.''

Mark had the grace to lower his eyes. ''I don't know,'' he
murmured. ''My mother has two homes . . . the apartment
in Queens and her stockbroker. And my sister, Shirley . . .
Shirley commutes between Jackson Heights and her teaching
job at NYU.'' He continued looking at the floor as he thought
of the stopovers his sister made at seedy hotels to knock off
a quickie with a married professor.

''But you're getting married,'' Millie protested.

''Yeah. I'll call them and send them an invitation. Maybe
they'll come.'' Mark's relationship with his mother and sister
was an old story . . . one he did not wish to discuss with
Millie.

Millie long ago had had Mark's family investigated. She
already knew most of what Mark was holding back. But since
she didn't believe in guilt by association, she elected to drop
the subject of Mark's parents.

''Given the situation, persuade Nora a small wedding is in
order . . . suggest the courthouse in Vista. The bride and
groom, maid of honor and best man.''

''And you?''

''No. If I'm at the wedding, the entire family will be offended at not being invited. So I'll have the family—including
your mother and sister—assuming they'll come—to a
postwedding dinner. When you return from your honeymoon.'' She smiled. ''That settles it.''

"A civil service is perfect, Millie. In fact, if Mark agrees, I'll volunteer to be best man," Arthur said.

"Very good, Arthur." Millie beamed.

"Yes," Mark agreed. "I'd like that."

Millie spoke again. "Incidentally, I do think you handled Nora's loss with tact and patience. But her mourning period has gone on long enough . . . as has mine." Millie looked away for a second. "I overheard Dr. Abe last Friday night at dinner. He was quite right. Three years is long enough." A short silence. Then Millie went on, her tone casual and confident . . . also deliberate. "I'm a practical woman, Mark. So let me make myself clear. You mentioned children. Well, as far as I'm concerned, the point of you and Nora marrying is great-grandchildren. Mine. I would like great-grandchildren. Two, three or four. You and Nora decide."

"Two—to replace us—Nora will say." Mark's voice was low.

"Two will be fine."

Mark stood up. It was time to go. He placed his glass on a coaster. "This has been an extraordinary evening." He took Millie's hand and brushed his lips lightly over the back. "I will let you know the wedding date as soon as I know . . . Grandmother-in-law-to-be. I have to propose first."

For a moment Mark and Millie regarded each other appraisingly. Then her eyes twinkled. "Do that. When the date is set, Arthur will send me the papers to open the account." Although she enjoyed his old-world courtesies, Millie kept score like a computer.

Mark smiled, pretending happiness. But from somewhere had come a feeling of intense, intuitive, inexplicable warning.

Driving home, Mark thought about Millie. She'd engineered a merger out of which he got a wife and a ten-million-dollar account . . . in one package. Why wasn't he ecstatic? What worried him? Why the premonition of trouble? Was it Nora's reaction? No! It was something deeper, almost organic. Almost like being told that his heart wasn't well, that he must live carefully in order to survive. His mind cleared. The metaphor applied. The survival threat was Shirley. He'd learned one thing about Shirley years ago . . . she always had

her own agenda. The trick was to figure out her agenda . . .
to stay one step ahead of her . . . and survive.

Mark turned into the driveway and pressed the automatic
garage door opener. The door swung open, and he eased the
vintage Aston Martin into the garage. Good thing Nora was
in L.A. He had time to prepare for her reaction to Millie's
proposal. Millie was one smart broad . . . the wedding present idea was a beaut. There was no way Nora would turn
down a wedding present from her grandmother. Shirley was
something else. Would she come to the wedding?

Chapter 4

THE BROADCASTERS' meeting dragged on for what seemed to Nora to be an eternity. The main panel was on residuals . . . who was to get the lion's share, the studios or the networks? Channel 18 wasn't a studio and it certainly wasn't a network . . . not even a network affiliate. And it didn't produce shows for syndication. Nora wondered why Millie had insisted she cover the meeting. At ten o'clock, the conferees reported "No progress." They didn't even agree to disagree.

Afterward Nora couldn't sleep. She lay awake pondering . . . musing . . . mulling things over . . . listening to night sounds. The gray light at dawn was a relief. She checked out of the Bel Air Hotel in L.A. at five-thirty . . . revved up for her breakfast with Ali. She was tempted to call Mark. But Mark hated to be interrupted during his morning drill . . . dressing for the office was serious business. She didn't call. Driving south on the freeway, she tried not to think about Ali. No more questions . . . no more doubts . . . wait and see. The jam at the El Toro Y was worse than usual. Only by risking a speeding ticket did she arrive at the restaurant in time. Incredibly, Ali was already there . . . seated at a table at the far end of the terrace overlooking Camino Del Mar and the ocean. Ali waved. Nora waved while weaving her way across the crowded terrace. She sat opposite Ali and smiled. Ali smiled. Five years later, almost to the day, here they were. Ali preening in a belted pink chemise . . . Nora forthright in a smoky tank dress. At least these days she was a match for Ali's slam-bang chic.

Ali leaned forward and squeezed Nora's hand. "Isn't this like old times?" Sensing Nora's reserve, she added, "Of course, times change. Things aren't what they used to be."

51

What's worse, they never were, Nora said to herself. Out loud she asked, "When did you get back?"

"Early March. I would have called but I didn't want to burden you with the whole bit of my relocating."

"Does Uncle Hiram know you're back?"

"Yes. I saw him in Geneva. He called Millie and asked her to help me get settled. Which she did. I waited for one of Millie's Friday night galas . . . to surprise you."

"You did surprise me." Nora motioned to the waiter. "Bring a large pot of coffee, Tony."

"And two giant orange juices." Ali picked up the beat. Her enthusiasm was contagious. Nora was confused. She felt hurt and wary and yet glad to see her. They ordered breakfast. Ali did most of the talking . . . sounding worldly, sophisticated . . . sprinkling her speech with upper-class English and low-class French or Italian or Jewish slang.

"Merde!" she would say. Or *"Que stronzo!"* Or "You bloody well know it!" Gasoline was "petrol." An international style.

The talk turned to personal matters. Ali remarked with splendid casualness, "Millie told you why I never called?"

Nora almost smiled. She hadn't brought it up first. "She told me."

"It's true," Ali said. "You don't realize how much you influence me. How much I want your good opinion."

Nora didn't believe her . . . but she wanted to believe her.

"And I didn't want my feeling for you affecting my decision about Aldo."

"Aldo?" The new name.

Ali went on to explain in a pleading tone that she hadn't been in touch because—much to her own surprise—she'd fallen in love. "Yes. I fell in love. With an Italian count." Aldo was his name. Aldo had a divine profile . . . exquisite manners. The sound of his voice was so seductive she hardly heard the words. Now she understood love . . . Nora's for Mark. But marrying Aldo meant living in Italy. Forever. Nora and she would be oceans apart.

"If you loved him, I'd have been for the marriage." Nora gave her a wry smile. Count on Ali to come up with an original excuse.

"I did love him, but I didn't marry him. Maybe its just as well. I couldn't afford him. Aldo is the reason I'm broke. . . ."

"You're broke?" In the game they were playing, there might be some advantage in not telling Ali that Mark had filled her in on Ali's finances.

"Flat broke. I had to make nice with Aldo's family." Ali explained what making nice meant. Aldo had brothers and sisters, aunts, uncles, grandparents on both sides of his family, of both genders, who were not only time-consuming but costly. Sadly, when the time came for posting the banns, a principessa happened to drive by in her red Lamborghini. Renata was her name and she and Aldo had played doctor when children. Renata's money came from olive oil. Her family was the largest exporter of olive oil in Italy. With investments in United States government bonds, American corporate stocks and bonds, California real estate. The United States is such a safe place to invest. Given the money and the old family ties, Aldo sadly but firmly gave Ali her walking papers. So here she was . . . broke, brokenhearted and alone.

In Nora's opinion, Ali hardly looked brokenhearted. "You ran through your entire inheritance in five years?" Asked with pretended awe. "How did you manage that? You inherited three million dollars!"

"If you think it's cheap putting modern plumbing and electricity into a seventeenth-century palazzo . . ." Ali paused. "Well, it isn't."

"You didn't!"

"I did. I thought I would be living there with Aldo. I wanted the conveniences." She smiled forlornly. "Also there were the lemon trees to be pruned . . . or whatever they do to lemon trees. And the roof leaked. And the marble floors needed new marble. And the relatives live off Aldo. I paid for a cousin's big wedding. Little nothings like that."

Her eyes begged for sympathy. Nora did her best to oblige.

It was after Nora finished her *melone con prosciutto* and Ali savored the last morsel of her *uovo strapazzate con prosciutto* that Ali got down to a cozy schoolooze . . . her plans for the future. High on the agenda was Ali's new interest in a career. Work. She must earn money. She was poor as a church mouse. Nora ordered another pot of coffee.

"Actually, I'm beside myself. I may be tossed out of my beautiful condo . . . on my ass."

"For heaven's sake, why?"

"Dennis D'Arcy . . . a medical malpractice lawyer. He

owns the condo. Originally his idea was when he retired he would move out of his six-bedroom La Jolla tile-and-stucco mausoleum—he calls it Taj Mahal West—and into the condo. His fourth wife divorced him and his children are grown. They live somewhere in Washington . . . the state, not the city. Now Dennis wants to retire to Sydney. Imagine! Sydney, Australia. So he's put the condo up for sale. The price is out of reach. I can't buy it. And I love it."

"Ask Uncle Hiram for the money."

"I asked. He said no. No loans for Ali . . . until I earn a living. At least he pays the rent on my digs."

That answered a question Nora had tactfully not asked. . . . How could a church mouse afford a posh condo? Hiram was how.

"But it will all work out. I refuse to be homeless or live in a tract house with a neat little lawn and shrubs that blot up water. I'm a city girl. I need a high rise."

"I like houses." Nora didn't mean to sound defensive.

"You probably can fix locks . . . faucets. . . . I'm all thumbs. I'm good at pressing elevator buttons. And calling the handyman. Living in Hillcrest, I'm in walking distance of the Globe Theater, the Timkin Museum, the San Diego Museum of Art. It's a short drive to the opera. San Diego isn't Paris, but it is a city. The restaurants are as interesting as those in SoHo in Manhattan."

"You do want that apartment."

"Feverishly. I must think of something . . . or someone . . ."

Nora reshuffled her feelings for Ali . . . she'd had a hard go. "Maybe I can help you get a mortgage. Or Mark can . . ."

Ali's face changed. She gazed at Nora . . . her eyes shrewd as a pawnbroker's appraising a diamond. Then she was Ali again, smiling affectionately. "Thank you, but no thank you . . . you darling. But you've given me a lovely idea."

"I have?"

"You have. I will prevail. A charming tract house is not my karma. But first things first. I must make a living before I starve in my condo."

Nora grew impatient with Ali's dramatics. "Quit it! Hiram won't let your starve."

"No. But he believes in the sanctity of work. I must get a job. So I've zeroed in on an art gallery. Millie put me in touch with her friend Ivan Bonn. A darling. He has this marvelous gallery in La Jolla. His assistant moves to Vancouver in January. Ivan said I can have her job. Actually I'm ideal. I majored in art history . . . studied modern art. I have taste. And besides Grandmother, I have friends.'' She smiled. ''Wealthy friends. And my friends have friends.''

Chewing on this nugget, Nora thought an art gallery made sense. It suited Ali to a tee.

''I'll make bubkus, but it's a living. Hiram respects that. He's afraid I'll turn into a wastrel. Imagine! Now he hopes I've learned my lesson . . . learned the value of money. I know he's right. But oh, Nora! I did have a grand and glorious time running through my millions.'' She grinned sheepishly.

''I bet you did. What will you do for money till January?''

''Grandmother Millie . . . our angel of mercy. She's hired me as creative assistant on her new project. That's why I'll be at the station meeting,'' Ali said carelessly.

''What's the new project?'' Nora sounded equally offhand.

Ali smiled. ''It's hush-hush. You'll find out at the meeting. If I tell you, I'll spoil Millie's surprise.'' Her smiled dimmed. ''Millie doesn't like her surprises spoilt.''

Nora's resentment was seasoned with jealousy. Again Millie had gone out of her way to tell her that Ali and she were very close. What was Ali doing for Millie? Why wasn't Nora in the loop?

Ali's tongue came out like a cat's and flicked over her lips. ''And you? What do you do at Channel 18?''

''I'm national sales manager. I sell air time to advertisers.''

''I saw a commercial on Channel 18 . . . for dolls that wet their diapers.'' Ali rolled her eyes.

Nora laughed politely. ''That's not my turf. That belongs to the local sales manager. I'm national. My beat is big ad agencies with national advertisers. Kellogg's. Ford. Obsession, the perfume.''

''Oooh! That sounds impressive.''

Nora said ruefully, ''When I started, the word around was *pull*. Millie's granddaughter . . . no talent but snappy bloodlines.''

''They didn't know Nora. Nora the fireball . . . the workaholic.''

''They didn't know Millie. There's Millie's charity money

and the money she spends to make more money. Channel 18 is to make money.'' Nora spoke without sarcasm. ''Anyway, I think I've convinced them . . . last name and all.''

Ali's tone was respectful. ''Nora Gardiner, the Channel 18 money-making machine.''

''Not making it like mad, but earning my keep. Me and Danny.''

''He's your boss?''

''No. Danny Darroch is the station rep. Works for Blair . . . a national station rep firm that contacts ad agencies in New York, L.A., Chicago, Tokyo. Danny gets a commission on our national advertising sales. Luddy Poole, the station manager, is my boss. So is Sim Crumb, our business manager. So is Tim Rourke, our general sales manager. They'll be at the meeting. And a few more.''

''The men all married?''

Nora glanced sidewise at Ali. Her mind was clicking away. ''Sim isn't.''

''Good-looking? Should I skateboard over?''

''He wears steel-rimmed glasses . . . belongs to Donna Zabriskie. She does promotions.''

Ali grimaced. ''Naturally. Anyway, I'm off men . . . unless they offer diamonds. When a woman tires of diamonds she is tired of life. I bet they shower you with gold pieces. You must make an enormous salary?'' Her eyes shone with calculation.

''It's better than welfare. I get a base salary plus a quarterly bonus. There are fat quarters and lean quarters . . . depending on what I bring in over budget projections.'' Nora spoke quickly, disliking Ali's look. ''You interested? You'd do well in sales.''

Ali thought this over. ''No. I'll stick to selling art. One meets more interesting people in an art gallery. Ad executives only buy time. Selling art, you never know when . . .''

The words hung in the air and Nora finished them for her. ''When a wealthy divorced man or a widower or a rich bachelor is looking for a painting. You could be star-crossed lovers.'' Nora grinned.

Ali smiled demurely. ''I am good with educated older men . . . or young men eager for culture.'' Then she burst out laughing. ''Now tell me about Mark. He's still with Reiner

& Co., still flourishing? I think of him as a tycoon in training.''

"He is still with Reiner & Co. Still flourishing. Eats at his
desk so he doesn't miss a tick on the tape.''

"Does Arthur Reiner still own Reiner & Co.?''

"He does. You sound as if you know him.''

Ali laughed . . . a full, rich laugh. "Nora, I'm hurt. Years
ago I told you I met Arthur at one of Amanda's parties. You
forgot.''

Suddenly Nora remembered. The idea of Ali knowing
Mark's boss made her prickly. Floundering, she asked, "Is
there anyone you haven't known?''

"Too many. The world is full of kings and princes and
emirs and moguls and magnates I don't know . . . more's the
pity. But I know Arthur . . . intimately. Married to Dorothea
Kellman of the Kellman millions.''

"Nothing wrong with your memory. He's still very married to Dorothea.'' Nora felt as if she were a dike holding
back the sea. "I didn't think you were an 'other woman'
type.''

"I'm not. At first I thought it daring. We arranged weekend trysts. Arthur had a Manhattan pied-à-terre. We went to
out-of-the-way restaurants . . . never opening nights . . . or
gallery openings. Or anywhere someone might see us and
put two and two together and make sex. The trysts became
stifling. I felt silly. Especially the days we met for lunch and
made love. Love in the afternoon is not my style. Too back
street . . .''

"You've given up married men?''

"Completely. They're a chore. But what's Mark doing on
the West Coast?''

"The Reiner & Co. main office is in San Diego. Mark
transferred three years ago . . . when I went to work for
Channel 18.''

"East Coast or West Coast, money makes money. Being a
stockbroker can be lucrative.'' Ali started to brighten . . .
then her face became resigned. "Hiram dislikes Wall Streeters. He'd prefer I go into the art world.''

This was news . . . Ali worrying about Hiram's prefer-
ences. Nora changed subjects. "Any new man?''

"As usual it's feast or famine. This month it's famine.''

Nora made a sympathetic noise.

"But I mustn't complain. There's this marvelous hunk of childlike muscle who paints like a wild man. A cross between Andy Warhol and Francis Bacon. Imagine! Makes art out of gas stations . . . supermarkets . . . buses. Or floats big, block words in gorgeous skies. Like 'Garden of Garbage.' Or 'Prime Crime Time.' I critique his paintings. The art world has its advantages." Ali giggled. "I'm four years older than he is."

"Ali!" Nora pretended shock. "Robbing the cradle!"

"Wicked and more wicked. Decadent too. Four times a night is average. He's hard as a rock each time." She again grinned and blushed at the same time. "I've talked so much about me. Tell me more about you and Mark. Why aren't you married? What are you waiting for?"

"My father was killed last summer in a boating accident."

"Millie told me. If I'd known I'd have been here in a flash. To comfort you. The way you did with me. With Amanda. I didn't know." Ali reached over and squeezed Nora's hand.

"No one knew where to reach you." A pang of the old hurt throbbed in Nora.

"I know. I'm childish. It never occurs to me that anything can happen to people I love . . . like Amanda." Her eyes glistened with tears. "Or you. I was waiting to get in touch when I had real news . . . like my marriage to Aldo. Which never happened." She gazed at Nora bravely. "Can you forgive me?"

"I forgive you." Nora felt like a fool. "Anyway, we've talked about eloping."

"What a splendid idea. Why not elope?"

"Mark's dragging his feet."

"Mark! I can't believe he doesn't want to marry you."

"He does. He's been saving money for two years . . . for our honeymoon. Three weeks in Europe. First-class—" Nora stopped. Mark had lost the honeymoon money on a crazy stock play . . . it wasn't any of Ali's business. "He's asked me to be patient. He was patient when Daddy died. He let me put everything on hold."

Ali was exasperated. "You've been living together three years. Millie said so."

"Thirty-four months."

"Nora, it's poor taste to live together more than two years. It bores people. You must get married." Ali paused for emphasis. "An elopement's a fine idea. A civil ceremony. Why not elope to City Hall?"

"Arthur has twice suggested the same thing to Mark. A civil ceremony at City Hall."

"Good for him," Ali approved. "Please do it. I could be your maid of honor. I'd be so honored."

"You mean it?" Nora felt embarrassed at how pleased she was.

"Yes. It would be a real welcome home. Do it."

"We just might."

They went on talking until, with a start, Nora realized it was nine-thirty. She jumped to her feet.

"The meeting's in fifteen minutes. Come . . ." She reached for the check. "You're poor as a church mouse . . . this is on me."

"As your maid-of-honor-to-be, I accept." Ali gave her a sly glance. "How funny. Me . . . a maid of anything."

They left the restaurant, hurrying to the inside garage. Nora to pick up her T-bird, Ali to her—Nora gaped—green convertible Jaguar XKE. Nora's father had pointed out an XKE on the San Diego Freeway a few weeks before he died. It looked like a bullet. He'd rhapsodized over the car . . . said it was the most beautiful machine ever designed. Nora's mind was full of questions. If Ali was broke, how had she paid for an XKE? Also, old Jaguars needed a master mechanic to keep them running. Who paid the master mechanic . . . those guys cost big bucks. Ali had mentioned a Stanley Something. Said he was very very generous. Was he XKE generous? If he was, what did Ali give him in return? Sex? Sure. But a Jaguar for a whippy week in Fiji? Nora shook her head. Ali was good, but she wasn't that good. Also, if Ali sold the car, she'd have enough cash for the down payment on the condo. Or would Stanley Something spank? Nothing made sense. But Ali was like that. Nora had known her since her "age of innocence" . . . as her father called it. She'd admired Ali . . . loved her . . . was sometimes shocked by her. But understand her . . . no! Not then, not now. If she was glad to see her again, her gladness was tinged with wariness. Ali had been out of touch for five years. Not for a minute did Nora believe some man named Aldo was the reason.

"See you at the station. The surprise comes with me," Ali called back. Then she gunned the motor and hurtled from

the garage. Nora followed . . . she was in time to watch Ali
turn north on Camino Del Mar. Why north? Channel 18 was
south. Where was Ali going? And why? Why hadn't Millie
told her about Ali? Of what use could Ali be to her? Ali knew
nothing about television. Nora gave it up. Millie had her
reasons. Nora had never known a time when Millie didn't
have her reasons. Still, she was confused by a storm of questions. About Millie. About Ali. The questions drew her back
into the history of her friendship with Ali. And her feeling
of loss when Ali vanished from her life. Five years! The years
had given Nora plenty of time to think about the two of them
. . . about the time they'd been friends and the deep impression Ali had made on her from the minute they met. About
the love she felt for Ali that was too strong and too complex
to be described merely as the sexual attraction of one young
girl for another . . . although that element was certainly present. That they'd never kissed, that they'd only pecked each
other on the cheek, didn't prove a thing . . . one way or the
other. The question was pointless. Nora didn't know and
didn't care. And although in a strange way she still loved Ali,
the question now mattered even less. Ali had cared for her
once as much as she had cared for Ali . . . once anyway.
Had she really? Nora admitted she would never know that
for sure. What did she know about Ali? Why had Ali not
called . . . or written? She'd called Millie. Even saw Nora's
father. Ali would have a reason. She always had reasons . . .
reasons to justify . . . to beguile. In a way she was a game
of true or false. So how to explain her? What could one say
of their friendship? Blurred, forgotten images of Ali drifted
through Nora's mind. Was there any clue in their shared past?
Nora remembered the first time they met. . . .

PART 2

Nora and Ali
1979–1987

Chapter 5

IT WAS one of Millie's Friday nights . . . all of her favorites had been invited to the Fifth Avenue penthouse. Millie had insisted Nora's father bring her to dinner. Nora was baffled. Why? This night was supposed to be for adults only. Nora was the exception . . . the only teenager present.

"This is Amanda Gardiner." Millie introduced the stunning woman with white, Viking-blond hair to Barron Gardiner. Nora glanced around.

"Hiram's Amanda." Barron gave Amanda a tantalizing smile. "I've underestimated my brother. Where is the old boy?"

"He sends his regrets," Millie said. "Hiram is locked in the White House basement with the president . . . in a political cesspool. Amanda, this is my younger son, Barron Gardiner."

"And you're his goodwill ambassador . . . keeping peace in the family. Meeting his kin . . ." Barron's smile grew more seductive.

"That's what political wives are for." Amanda gazed at Barron with mild surprise. "You're really Hiram's brother?"

"Do you see a family resemblance?"

"A little. Around the eyes . . . the chin . . ."

"Not true. Hiram's jaw is square. Mine is cleft. Hiram is a throwback to Max the First, our grandfather . . . the founder of the Clan Gardiner. I take after Max Two . . . our father." He took Amanda's hand, squeezed it lightly and led her to a seat beside himself on a sofa. "Hiram's the ugly duckling . . . with brains. I'm the swan. Swans don't need a high IQ. Still, I'm easy to talk to, engaging . . . often quite charming."

"Well, I am charmed," Amanda admitted.

You bet she was charmed. . . . Nora knew her father.

"I try harder. What are you drinking?"

Nora watched her father make beautiful music. Her hand-some, beloved father. He charmed everyone. Men as well as women felt the fascination of his physical presence. He was light and gay, but not in the sense of being blond . . . or homosexual. Actually he had blue-black hair and a rich, year-round tan. The quality was deeper than hair and skin. When he entered a room, the air grew brighter . . . charged with excitement. The people seemed more interesting, more in-telligent, their conversation more animated, their smiles truer. A school friend once told Nora he looked like an old-time movie star . . . Cary Grant. Or was it Errol Flynn? Nora saw little resemblance between Grant and Flynn—let alone with her father—except they were all extremely handsome men. But she knew what the girl meant. Her father had a quality . . . personal magnetism. She was proud to be his daughter.

Millie broke into Nora's reverie. "And, Nora, this is your new cousin, Alison. Or Ali . . . as she's called. Amanda's daughter." Nora blinked into focus. Out of nowhere a girl appeared standing beside Millie. Her hazel eyes smiled with amused curiosity.

"Ali, this is Nora." Millie continued to do the honors.

Ali made a great show of ingenue shyness. "Hello, Nora."

"Hello, Ali." Nora realized why she'd been invited. To meet Ali. Suddenly Ali started to laugh and Nora did too . . . laughing like children over nothing. They were so pleased with each other.

Ali studied Nora . . . Nora studied Ali. Ali—unlike Nora, who dressed in the approved Miss Barclay's Country Day School fashion . . . tweed skirt and loose cashmere sweater—wore a snug, distinctly non-Barclay blue sweater and a cling-ing navy skirt. She had an animated face and a trendy tint in her dark hair that gave it auburn glints.

At dinner, over the filet of sole, Ali explained, "I adore reddish tones. Makes a woman look sexy."

Nora thought about Ali. Even without tinted hair, her new cousin looked like nobody else. She was unique. Ali was fifteen, only a year older, but everything Nora wasn't. She had an "I've been around" authority, plus style and grace and excessively good manners. At dinner she courted her new relatives. They returned the compliment by courting her. Nora was smitten. She thought—without jealousy . . . who could be jealous of someone so superior—Ali would soon be the family favorite.

After dinner, Nora and Ali slipped away to the library to talk. As she left the living room, Nora noticed that her father and Amanda were growing *intime*. Sly glances were flying between them like pigeons in Central Park circling bread crumbs. Nora wasn't surprised. This was why his cronies had nicknamed him the Red Barron . . . a killer with women. She winced inwardly and hoped her Red Barron knew what he was doing. Not like his namesake . . . shot down in flames in World War One. Nervously she looked at Millie. Millie, elegant and formidable, her Nefertiti eyes glistening, glancing occasionally at her son and Amanda with dispassion . . . as if they were specimens in a test tube. Millie missed nothing.

She paused at the door and heard her father say, "As a young man I was a poet, a dreamer, romantic. And even now at night—when the stars draw very close—I see a king in a golden suit riding an elephant over the mountains. . . ."

"You're still a poet." Amanda smiled. Nora smiled too. Her father could go on and on like that. In a way he was lying . . . in a way he wasn't.

As she leaned toward the mirror in the powder room off the library, Ali assured her, "You're right not to wear much makeup." She narrowed her eyes, smoothing on authority with Max Factor #5. "Your charm is the freshness of your complexion. London fog skin."

"Is it? Thank you." Nora accepted the word from on high. Though three inches taller and more physically developed, she already looked up to Ali.

Ali turned from the mirror and stared at her. She studied her so long, Nora began to fidget. Finally she said, "Your figure is fine. Pull up your skirt."

Nora looked blank. "Up?"

"Up . . . up . . . up! Stop being so la-di-da modest."

Nora pulled up her skirt.

"I thought so. Your legs are splendid. Your skirt's the wrong length. Not long enough or short enough. You look like the Deb of the Year . . . 1950."

Nora mumbled, "My father likes this length."

"The pattern is interesting . . . English tweed . . . classic.

But shorten it. And that baggy sweater. Cashmere or not, expensive or not, it's instant middle age.''

"My father likes it." Nora swallowed. "He likes me to dress . . . well . . . conservatively. So does the head mistress at school."

"Miss Barclay's, Amanda said."

Nora could read Ali's thoughts. Elite, all-girl Miss Barclay's Country Day School cost an arm and a leg. Nobody blinked if a daddy's girl arrived in a chauffeured Rolls. Limos were almost standard. Nora took the bus. "My mother went to Miss Barclay's," she said in an attempt to explain something that—until Ali—had never needed explanation.

"And your father went to Choate."

"Like Uncle Hiram."

"Hiram didn't *go to* Choate. He *is* Choate. Your father isn't. He's a free spirit. I can tell." Ali giggled. "Perfectly adorable. A pussycat. Amanda says he's on Wall Street adding millions to the Gardiner millions."

"Millions and millions."

"Amanda says Wall Streeters are either investors or gamblers. Your father's a gambler. Not a tight—a . . . ummm . . . tight-bottomed investor." She giggled again. "You know what I mean. I love gamblers . . . risk takers."

"He takes risks," Nora admitted. Her smile grew harder to maintain. Barron Gardiner definitely was a gambler . . . not an investor. A floor trader. An in-and-outer. Buy at the opening . . . 9:31 A.M. Sell at the close . . . 3:59 P.M. Same day. Often he bought too fast and sold too fast.

"I adore men like him. Your mother's lucky to have hooked him . . . and held him."

"Yes . . ."

"She must be a genuine ten. Where is she, by the by?"

"My mother died when I was four."

Ali did a measured performance. "Oh, I am sorry. Please overlook my foot in my mouth. Your father's a widower?"

"Yes. For ten years."

"Mmmm. My father waited two years."

Nora was confused. "For what?"

"To marry Amanda. My real mother—her name was Jenny . . . Jenny Kjytekka—died when I was five."

There was silence a moment and the two girls exchanged a look of communion and compassion.

"Amanda's not your mother?" Nora asked.

"My stepmother," Ali said dryly. "I don't think I will ever forgive Mumsie for dying."

"You will."

"I won't. Did your father love your mother?" Ali asked, concentrating on her eyeliner.

"Yes." Nora felt her heart hurt. "He cried all night after the funeral." She'd never said such things out loud before.

"So did mine. At the funeral. How did they meet?"

"They grew up together."

"Aaaah. Childhood sweethearts?"

Usually Nora resented having her personal history pawed over by anyone. But Ali wasn't just anyone. She nodded.

Ali's face brightened. "My Lord! We've so much in common. Dear, departed mothers. Grieving fathers. Of course, you've been spared an Amanda. She was years and years younger than my father." Ali pursed her lips and brushed on red, red lip gloss as she asked, "Was yours ever unfaithful?"

"You mean my father? Unfaithful? When my mother was alive?" Nora had never considered this question. She smiled. "I've never asked him."

"Mine wasn't. Henry Kjytekka was completely housebroken. After Jenny died he lived like a monk . . . for two years." Ali smiled ruefully. "Except for Ruby. And Celia. Prostitutes. Smart working girls. He paid their way through secretarial school. Then he met Amanda . . . the flavor of the month. *C'est la vie.*"

"You sound like you don't like her."

"I also dislike minimalist art, stingy men and Indian gurus."

Nora shifted uncomfortably. "A born nonconformist. Quickly bored. Hard to fool . . ."

Ali gave her a sharp look. Then smiled. "Anyway, it's not trench warfare. She'll do. Or did. We had a rather queasy family life. Now he's gone too. Two years ago. So Amanda and I signed a truce. Although we're hardly anybody's idea of a tender, loving mother-daughter act." A little catch in her voice. "I'm sure she married him for his money."

In the absence of evidence to the contrary, Nora believed her.

Ali sighed with resignation and changed subjects . . . resuming her role of adviser. "Remember. No more sweaters

two sizes too large. They look like cashmere tents. The one
thing right you're wearing is the pearls. I love real pearls.''

"My father gave them to me. . . .'' Nora faltered.

"Ah. I have a marvelous idea. I'll take you shopping with
me. Teach you what kind of clothes to buy.''

"Daddy buys my clothes,'' Nora blurted out.

"So what? It's time you stopped him. We'll do it tomorrow . . .
Saturday. Ransack the boutiques. I was meant to save you from
yourself. And your father. He forgets that once he dated
daughters. Sometimes a daughter wasn't a lady. Didn't look
or act like one. If he was lucky, she was immodest. Immoral.
Anyway, morality is a matter of opinion.'' Ali's voice was
smooth as midwinter ice.

Nora smiled. She knew her father . . . he was always lucky.

Nora and Ali went shopping. Ali was a speed shopper with
an instinct for spending. At Yves Saint Laurent, Rive Gauche,
she didn't check prices. She pointed. "I'll take that . . . and
that.'' Three silk blouses in three colors. Four scarves. A
linen blazer. Two Hermes bags.

At Chanel Boutique . . . denim jeans and sneakers.

At Bloomies a trench coat. Perfume. Joy. Chanel No. 5.

She was also a generous sponger. Amanda hadn't yet
opened a charge at Bergdorf, so Ali borrowed Nora's to buy
a brown suede tote bag she adored and a red beaded clutch.

"I swear in blood I'll pay you back. Only three hundred
and fifty dollars. A steal.''

She adored the beige pumps . . . she adored a tunic dress.

"Nora, darling, as a born-in-the-castle member of the
privileged class, would you charge these few things for me?''

Nora was embarrassed. "It's a bit too much, Ali. I never
use my father's Bergdorf charge . . . except for Christmas
presents.''

"I understand. Bergdorf isn't your thing. But you didn't
buy a button at Chanel. Or Rive Gauche. I picked out some
perfect outfits for you. Where do you buy your clothes? I bet
you have a portfolio of department store charge cards.'' Ali's
eyes were avid.

"Those stores are very expensive. . . .''

"Nora! You are Barron Gardiner's daughter. Buy something . . . anything. A Hermes scarf. A belt. You loved that

silk twill trench coat. Perfect for you. And the houndstooth jacket.''

''My closets are jammed. My father picks things for—''

''Stop him. Men know nothing,'' Ali snapped. ''Stop scrimping. Don't you know how rich your father is?''

Nora looked at Ali, wondering what to say. What not to say. She knew how her life looked to outsiders . . . she was a Gardiner. The Gardiners were rich. She was rich. Yes? No! It was done with mirrors. She didn't have a cent to her name. And her father . . .

''I don't like to waste money,'' Nora said lamely.

''You and the Kennedys. Penny-pinchers. I bet you take your lunch to school in a lunch box.''

Nora started to laugh. Ali's belief in her father's fortune was black comedy. ''In a brown paper bag. A lunch box costs money.''

''And you don't go to Miss Barclay's. You go to public high school and carry a switchblade.''

''No. I don't go to school. I can't. I don't have any shoes.'' Nora managed a sniffle and wiped an imaginary tear from her eye.

''And you don't live in a penthouse on Park Avenue. You live in Queens.''

''In a walk-up.'' Nora wished she could see Ali's face if she told her the truth. Told her that, last year, her father couldn't pay the monthly maintenance on their co-op for six months. But the building management was so awed by the Gardiner name they said nothing.

''Poor little rich girl,'' Ali sniped. ''Your father's a tight-wad. How do you stand it?''

''I suffer in silence.'' Nora shrugged. ''Heroically.''

''Oh well, forget it. I get the party line. You're on the verge of bankruptcy. So lend me your charge. Amanda will send your father a check.''

Nora surrendered. ''Okay. The tunic, the pumps—''

''And the slingbacks,'' Ali interrupted. ''I adore them.''

By now Nora accepted that Ali's second favorite word was *adore*. Her first favorite words were ''I'll take that . . .''

''Frankly, I don't understand you or your father. You're deprived. Yes, you are,'' Ali remarked impatiently as they left Bergdorf. ''With all your money you didn't even buy bath

salts. Or panty hose.'' She saw Nora's face. ''Oh well, never
mind. . . .''

Doing her homework that evening Nora thought about her
father. About Ali's words. Her illusions. Nora had no illusions about her father and didn't feel deprived. Her father
loved her . . . when he had money, he splurged on her. She
walked down the streets of her childhood remembering so much.
Christmas toys from F.A.O. Schwarz. Big birthday parties. Riding lessons when she was seven. Skiing lessons at eight.
Ballet lessons at nine. Sometimes he made a killing in the
market. Then to celebrate he might take her on a trip. He
wanted her to see as much of life and the world as he could
possibly show her. That's why, when she was thirteen, he'd
taken her to London to sit in the House of Commons gallery.
And to Rome to meet a prince who owned a kingdom of olive
groves. And to the south of France to visit a princess who
lived in a palace without decent plumbing. But they also visited yachts and villas with lawns and swimming pools and an
assortment of Fredericos and Teresas, Khalids and Omars,
Claudes and Micheles. She met one serene highness, three
dukes, two counts, and enough lords and ladies to fill Buck-
ingham Palace. Another time they flew to Paris for a Saint
L'Aurant opening. He apologized for not being able to buy
her a bow. He took her to theater parties to meet the stars
. . . to dog races . . . to horse races . . . to the Kentucky
Derby to introduce her to trainers getting ready for the ''run
for the roses.'' Her father could do this because her father
had charm. Nora felt lucky to be his daughter. If they were
often broke, it was their private joke on the world. A one-
upmanship. She was a Gardiner—an heiress—and usually she
had to count the pennies.
Barron Gardiner had received a sizable inheritance from
his father. But something had happened—it was one of their
few off-limits subjects—and he'd lost everything. After marrying her mother, he'd gone through another fortune . . . her
mother's dowry. Until all he had left was the co-op and his
seat on the New York Stock Exchange. He lived mostly on
Millie's largesse . . . and regularly lost the sizable monthly
stipend she gave him. He gambled on and off Wall Street.
He loved horses and roulette and baccarat . . . and all-night
floating crap games. He loved women and women loved him.

"Live every day as if it's your last," was his motto. He did. Yet he didn't. Nora knew how easy it was for her father to find love . . . or sex. And how hard it was for him to find peace.

Once he said, "The day God made me he had one too many."

Still, Nora's attitude toward him never changed. She believed her father had a grand—even glorious—way of looking at life . . . an extravagant heart. But somehow, in some way, he had slipped out of the normal course of what his life should have been . . . into a maelstrom. He'd been punished for his sins by being exiled from everything that mattered . . . except women. Always except women. But if he was in exile, Nora thought he bore it beautifully . . . with humor and high good grace.

Amanda sent Barron Gardiner a check. "This will cover Ali's extravagances. It won't happen again." And he sent it back with a note. "I believe in extravagance. Anyone who dies with more than five thousand in the bank has not lived."

After mailing the note his eyes were hooded with sadness . . . his stillness frightening. As though his soul had turned to salt. But there was something inside him that wouldn't let him share the hurt . . . even with Nora. All he said was, "I wish you'd been the one to splurge on fancy duds. The tote bag. Those beige pumps. I don't buy you the right clothes. I don't know what teenage girls like. But you won't spend a dime yourself. You're afraid." Silence. A cough. "It's that I spend enough for both of us."

"I love my clothes, Daddy," Nora tried to reassure him. "You do fine."

"Do I, Nora?" His eyes pleaded for approval. "I try. I'm not sure. I really do wish you'd be more extravagant . . . now and then, anyway. A spending spree is good for the soul."

"I can't help it, Daddy. I'm a miser at heart."

"Not you, baby." He drew her into his arms, hugging her. "You're like your mother. You put up with your spendthrift father. Why do you do it?"

"Because I couldn't do without you . . . that's why." She kissed him on the cheek and for a minute they smiled at each other.

Then he stepped back. "Honey, I forgot to tell you. I'm seeing Pansy tonight for dinner. Do you need food money?"

"No. I saved some money this month from my allowance."

Her father stared in wonder. "How do you do it?"

"I've a good business head . . ."

"Good thing one of us has. Are you rich enough to lend me fifty dollars? I promised to help cover Pansy's rent this month."

They burst out laughing and hugged each other again.

A few minutes after he'd left the apartment, the telephone rang. It was Ali. Warm and confidential . . . as if she'd known Nora for years . . . not weeks. "I think Hiram and Amanda are going to Europe this summer and will rent a cottage for me in East Hampton. We must get together. Where will you be?"

So their romance began . . . Nora and Ali's unending, roller coaster friendship. It survived long separations when all they could do was phone or write each other. Because Ali lived in Washington with Amanda and Hiram. And Nora lived two hundred and forty miles away in Manhattan with her father. But the more they talked and wrote, the more Nora liked her new cousin. No one had ever given her so much attention . . . so much sympathetic understanding. Still, it did occur to her briefly that sympathetic understanding was Ali's technique for getting her way. Then she felt ashamed of her ingratitude.

After graduating from Le Lycée Français in Washington, Ali went to Bennington. Nora didn't go to Radcliffe, her mother's alma mater. In her senior year at Barclay's, she switched goals. No more freeloading on Millie, she told her father. She would pay her own way. Her father—half proud, half scared—reviewed the pros and cons . . . the list of cons was endless. But Nora prevailed. She obtained a partial scholarship—tuition only—to Ohio State. And paid her room and board by waiting on tables in a fast-food restaurant.

In time Nora's faith in waiting on tables brought rewards beyond tips. In her sophomore year she met a senior, Mark Stern . . . also at Ohio State on a partial scholarship. Mark paid for his room and board by working as a short-order cook. With so much in common, how could they help but fall in love and live happily ever after? At least that was what Nora planned to tell her father and Millie . . . when she got up nerve.

Unlike One-Man Nora, Ali whirled through college from romance to romance . . . amorous and buoyant. She used and misused men with a casual disregard of the suffering she caused. Nora came to believe that deep within her, Ali was profoundly cool . . . concerned with only a chosen few. Nora was happy she was one of the chosen.

One Christmas holiday Ali telephoned Nora. "By the way, are you on the pill?"

"No. I use a diaphragm. Of course, Daddy has no idea I'm not a virgin," she added quickly. "Even Millie thinks I am."

"I would hope so. Millie's a reformed nympho. Ah, yes. I know her glorious, notorious, Hollywood history. But Millie's days of wine and roses and lust are behind her. Now she's righteous as a nun."

Ali couldn't see Nora smile over the telephone. There were some things about the family that her friend didn't know. Like the fact that Grandmother still had lovers. Nora knew of three . . . Elliott Hansen, Scott Wade and Ira Myers . . . each a highly eligible, unattached male . . . divorced or widowed. And each ten to fifteen years younger than Millie. There were probably a dozen more men about whom Nora didn't know.

"Have your GYN give you the pill," Ali advised.

"She'll ask my father's permission. He'd have a hemorrhage."

"So would Amanda . . . if Amanda knew. So I made provision. I know a perfectly wonderful GYN in New York . . . very advanced . . . believes in liberating women. He'll give you a prescription for the pill. It will get Manny's vote."

"His name is Mark. Mark Stern." Why did Ali keep forgetting Mark's name? She'd told it to her often enough.

"Mark. Sorry about that. I promise it will get Mark's vote. And your dear father will never know." Ali laughed. "By the by, Amanda finds him fascinating. Your father. You're lucky she's committed to ladyhood. She says he's the most charming man she's met in ages."

"Why lucky? That he's charming?"

"No. That Amanda's in training for the Mother Teresa medal in morality. Even in passion she follows a ladylike agenda."

A short, deep silence followed. "Exactly what do you mean?"

"Put two and two together."

"Hiram is her husband. . . ."

"You got it. Hiram is also your father's brother. Amanda won't fish off the company dock. The company being the Gardiner Family Inc. Otherwise she'd flutter her lashes . . ."

Nora snorted. "A waste of her time. If she wasn't married to Uncle Hiram, she might make a jazzy weekend for Daddy. But my father likes variety."

Ali's voice bubbled with amusement. "Amanda would see him as a challenge."

Nora hardly winced. "They all do. He is a son of a bitch with his women."

Ali hooted. "You surprise me, Nora. You're not innocence triumphant. Still, knowing how randy Amanda can get . . ."

"It would only be a matter of time before yin met yang."

"You put it so well." A heartfelt chuckle. "And we'd be stepsisters, not stepcousins."

"You really don't like her."

All traces of amusement disappeared from Ali's voice. "I really don't like her," she said flatly. Then she laughed. "I just wish I was older. Your father is fascinating. An inspiration to all dirty old men." She paused. "Incidentally, speaking of inspirations, I'd like to meet Manny . . . Mark . . . the groom-to-be."

Nora wasn't ready for that. "So would my father. So would Millie. So would everybody in the family."

"Me first," Ali insisted. "I could put in a good word for him . . . with Millie."

"Right." But would you, Nora wondered? It had recently occurred to her that Ali often said nothing . . . unless she already knew Millie agreed.

That summer Nora put her doubts to the test. Hiram and Amanda were on the Spanish Riviera; Ali was in East Hampton. So Mark and Nora spent a weekend with her. Afterward Ali said Mark was a jewel . . . she'd give him a rave review with the family. Nora decided the weekend was a success . . . Mark didn't. At first he kept quiet, which was out of character. Then he let go with a few choice obscenities. Ali was a bitch. Ali was not to be trusted. Nora should look both ways when crossing a street with her. Nora rubbed his neck, whispered softly. Mark was marrying her . . . not Ali. Inwardly, she shrugged. Maybe Ali was a woman's woman. Unless she and the man were making out on the sheets. That thought gave her second thoughts.

When Millie decided to move back to Bienvenida, Hiram persuaded her to keep the New York duplex. Her own apartment would be more comfortable than a hotel when visiting New York. Especially if she kept two servants on staff there. So except for the master bedroom, her bedroom, the apartment was available for family use . . . for meals, for sleeping, for parties. Whatever. To make arrangements, one called Bienvenida and asked for Oscar . . . Oscar had moved west with Millie.

Because she kept the apartment, Millie regularly flew east for the big holidays—Thanksgiving and Christmas, sometimes New Year's, always Easter.

So it happened that on Easter Sunday, Nora and Ali took their traditional meander up and down Fifth Avenue and compared notes about men.

"Do you want children?" Ali asked as they stared into the windows of F.A.O. Schwarz at Easter bunnies.

"A boy and a girl to replace Mark and me," Nora fumbled. "Don't you?"

"No!" The no was definite. "Amanda is a terrible role model. Suppose I turn out like her? Why inflict me on a helpless baby? Maybe I'll have a cat or a dog or a parakeet when I'm old." She gave Nora a sweet, silly grin. "But when are you and that gorgeous hunk posting the banns? Share him with the family. Let them in on your secret. I've spread the word. There'll be no opposition . . . he's graduated, hasn't he?"

"With honors. He's on Wall Street. With the New York office of a San Diego brokerage house . . . Reiner & Co."

Ali's expression grew enigmatic. "What a coincidence! I met Arthur Reiner at one of Amanda's parties."

"Mark's boss?"

"A very attractive man. Well, if Mark's with Reiner & Co. he can afford to get married. Go public. Do it!"

"Maybe I'll break the news this summer. I graduate next year. That'll give them a year to work out the invitation list for the wedding." But Nora's smile had faded. She had a sudden, unwelcome premonition. For no reason she could give, she wished with all her heart that Ali and Arthur Reiner lived on separate planets.

That summer Nora's mind was full of Mark . . . she paid almost no attention to the family grapevine. She missed the news bulletins from the front . . . the Battle of Ali and Amanda. Neither would listen to sweet reason. When Nora did hear, she shrugged. This was not news. Ali and Amanda were not on the same wavelength. Amanda was patrician dignity in a Givenchy outfit . . . Ali was Madam X in jeans. Ali's choice of clothes, her escapades with men, her shaky grades were enough to set Amanda's teeth on edge. The two were barely polite to each other.

Until, out of clear sky, one day word flickered over the grapevine that a truce had been declared. The two were reconciled. When Ali graduated from Bennington the cease-fire was signed. Peace reigned. The family applauded. Ali had matured. Amanda had mellowed. Nora was astonished . . . even hurt. Why was she the last to know? Wasn't she Ali's best friend . . . her confidant? If Ali had reformed, how come it went unmentioned in their heart-and-soul conversations?

"Listen, momma's girl," Nora said one evening on the long-distance line, "what's this flimflam about you and the reformation? And I don't mean Martin Luther?"

"Nora, love, you never understood pragmatism."

"Are you speaking of William James? Or a way of life?"

"Both. Pragmatism. The philosophy of the practical. If it works, don't fix it. I'm a born-again pragmatist."

"Meaning practical?"

"Meaning practical. My dear, departed father, in his uncanny wisdom, left his millions to Amanda and only three teensy-weensy millions to dear little Ali romping in the playpen. To be hers when she graduated college. It was Daddy's way of making sure I graduated. Daddy was practical. Of course, his ploy worked. Why else would I put up with Bennington? To learn art history? I've forgotten more about Renaissance art than the whole department knows. Including the names of the choir-boys Michelangelo buggered when painting the Sistine Chapel.''

"Enough." Nora laughed. "What's the scoop?"

"Well, I did learn two valuable lessons at Bennington. One, if I hang my pants from the top drawer of my bureau, the creases will hang out. Two, I learned how to ski. I can handle the International at Stowe . . . white ice and all. So I graduated. But now comes the switch. . . . I can't touch my money.''

"Why not?"

"Daddy. My cynical insurance mogul father put a lock on my inheritance. Made Amanda trustee of my money until I reach thirty. Then this aging crone will come into her fortune. My one chance to get it sooner is if Amanda deems me fit to manage the money myself." Ali's sigh vibrated over the long-distance telephone lines. "Now I must convince the dear soul that I'm the essence of fitness . . . a responsible citizen. I sing in the angel choir . . . not Michelangelo's. I tried that once. The sadistic bastard loved it. I hated it. It hurt.''

"Mmmm . . . I see." Nora did. She saw wheels within wheels turning in Ali's mind. "Do charity work? Prove you have social awareness? That should convince Amanda you're responsible.''

"Don't be ridiculous. Amanda thinks charity work is for social climbers. She's already climbed." Ali started to laugh. "Look who she married. Your Uncle Hiram. Currently chairman of the president's Council of Economic Advisers and heading for bigger triumphs. No. Charity work won't play.''

"Maybe Uncle Hiram could get you a job in Washington. You know . . . assistant to the assistant press secretary. Something like that. Hold it for a year and become a pillar of Washington society. Prove you're concerned about the country. Committed to the right causes.''

"Me? Work? With all the money in my family, why in heaven's name should I work?''

"It's fashionable for rich women to work.''

"It's a mistake. Women with money have no right to take a paycheck away from a single mother. Or a penniless ex-wife . . . a widow . . . an orphan. And to work for power is nutsy. If you inherit wealth—as I have—then power accrues.

And don't tell me about the inherent pleasure of a job well done. I don't believe it.''

Nora considered her own future after graduation . . . she'd be a working stiff. She relished the idea. But why argue with Ali? "Okay. I give up. How will you persuade Amanda to give you your money?''

"I don't know. Now if I happen to fall in love and marry a man of substantial means . . .''

"Then you wouldn't need the money.''

"Of course I'll need it. A woman should always have her own money . . . mad money. But it is a thought. Amanda could help me find the right man. She'd approve of my marrying a rich man.''

"Amanda? She never struck me as a matchmaker.''

"She is. For herself. But maybe she'd stretch for her loving stepdaughter?'' Ali mused. "You know, Amanda isn't the first of the Cinderella girls, but she's one of the smartest. And she's proud of her know-how. She can spot a Prince Charming with a bankroll across a crowded room . . . a crowded stadium . . . a crowded airport . . . in Grand Central Station. Anyplace . . . anytime .. anywhere. Have I ever told you about Amanda?''

Nora thought this over. "No." In their years of intimate conversations and confessions, Ali had learned all about Nora's family but Nora had learned very little about Ali's.

"No . . . I've told you nothing.'' Ali sighed. "I've a habit of lying about my past. Or giving vague answers. Then I discovered your liberal family believes in self-made men . . . like my father. That's made me rethink my thinking. I dropped a few hints, but you never got them. So I'll give you the inside scoop on Amanda. She's as self-made as my daddy . . . another overachiever. I bet you thought she married down. That she was born on the right side of the tracks.''

Nora said she hadn't thought about the tracks one way or another.

"People who are born rich don't anymore. It's unfashionable to be snobbish about one's origins. Amanda's origins weren't very lofty. Her mother—my stepgrandmother—was definitely not another Millie. She didn't *have* a housekeeper . . . she *was* one. And sometimes little Amanda Wisniewska helped with the cleaning. They were not members of high society in Sandusky, Ohio.'' Ali waited just long enough for

Nora to digest the truth. "Neither was my real mother. She began her career as a bookkeeper for the local undertaker. That's how she met Daddy. I may not have mentioned that Daddy started out in insurance by working for the local undertaker."

Nora was more impressed than ever with Ali. Her family had come up the hard way. "Are you saying your family was poor?"

"By the standards of our world today, yes. Not by the world I grew up in. There we were a hardworking, church-going, respectable family. My mother worked a five-and-a-half-day week . . . half day on Saturday. My father worked a seven-day week . . . Saturday and Sunday. They both worked too long and too hard for us to be poor. They both worked so hard they never lived to enjoy it. But we didn't belong to the Upper Sandusky Country Club. The postmaster had more social status. In time my father did build Ohio Casualty. This is America, the land of the free and the home of the eager beaver. Remember, my father started out as an undertaker's assistant. That's what gave him the idea to get into life insurance . . . to start Ohio Casualty."

"I didn't know," Nora said.

"I know you didn't know. I didn't tell you. At first I didn't know you well enough to tell you. Nora, my pet, you have a major shortcoming. You were born into a rich family. So there's a whole world you'll never understand . . . except with your head."

"I told you about my father and me. You know we've no money."

"I know you're not rich, but Millie is. It amounts to the same thing," Ali said flatly. "Oh, sure, I know now how your father runs through money. How he's often flat-ass broke. But Millie always bails him out. That's divine! And for heaven's sake, don't be ashamed of it! Be happy! If you're not rich yourself, it's great to have a rich, loving grandmother. Of course, I'd rather be rich myself. Very rich. I love the idea. One of my least attractive traits is that I envy people. When I'm a member of the privileged class, imagine! I'll never envy anyone again."

"Have you envied me?" Nora asked in a small voice.

"Naturally. Sometimes I was jealous. But usually—"

Nora cut in, embarrassed. "Skip it. Sorry I asked."

"Don't be. It's a good question. You're hard to envy. You don't flaunt Millie's millions."

Exasperated pause. "How can I? The money isn't mine to flaunt."

"Well, if it was me, I'd flaunt it. You don't spend up a storm. I would. You forget how rich she is. I wouldn't. You act like a plumber's daughter."

Nora disliked the turn of the conversation. "But now you'll be rich yourself."

There was an odd silence. Then Ali laughed. "Not as rich as you'll be someday. But rich enough. Once Amanda understands my position. She has her settlement and I must have mine."

"But if she won't agree, you still get it when you're thirty. Meantime your allowance is gigantic. You once said it could support a family of six comfortably."

"My allowance is dependent on Amanda's goodwill. And suppose she fritters away her money . . . and mine? In fly-by-night schemes . . . idiotic investments. My allowance ends."

"She hasn't yet. Besides, Uncle Hiram wouldn't let her."

"Right. Each night I thank heaven for Hiram. But suppose she tires of darling Hiram and runs off with some bearded folksinger? Remember, I know Amanda's history. It's possible. For my own good I must take precautions. I want my money while I'm young enough to enjoy it. And I want it intact."

"There is a logic in your thinking. Protecting your money."

"By the way," Ali asked, "why don't you ask Millie for a few million in trust?"

Nora laughed politely. "I wouldn't think of it."

"Okay. See. . . . That's why I don't envy you. You don't grasp the value of money . . . of being rich."

"You grasp it well enough for both of us. Well, I hope you convince Amanda to give you your millions."

"Thanks. There's always Hiram. If I went to him in tears, I think he could persuade her to do the honorable thing."

"You'd drag Uncle Hiram into this?"

"And spoil his romantic illusions about his beautiful, aristocratic wife? Never. Well . . . almost never . . . only if she forces me." Ali paused. "If I can't persuade her to do the right thing, the honorable thing, and stop trying to run my life. Then, yes, I might have a few funny stories to tell my stepfather.''

There was no doubt in Nora's mind that Amanda didn't stand a chance against Ali.

Ali and Amanda were seen everywhere together. All over the country . . . the world. They went to Paris. To Rio. To Copenhagen. To Moscow. To Rome. They took junkets that Hiram couldn't take because he had to be on tap for meetings with the president, for conferences with foreign central bankers, to march up to Capitol Hill and lecture Congress on the error of their ways. Ali and Amanda visited Nora and her family at Martha's Vineyard. A more loving mother/daughter scene Nora couldn't imagine.

"I bet it's going well." Nora laughed as they changed into bikinis for swimming and sunning.

"What's going well?" Ali asked, her eyes wide and innocent.

"Your settlement." Nora suddenly felt she was prying into things that weren't her business.

"You mean my inheritance?"

"You did mention it," Nora said, wishing she'd said nothing.

"I've decided to outwait her. I was too impatient. As you said, eventually I will get the money. And she did increase my allowance. So, for the time being I've put everything on hold," Ali said with unusual resignation.

"I think that's smart. It will all work out."

"Maybe. After all, she's the only mother I have left. And she won't be around forever, so I should enjoy her now . . . get to know her better while she's still hale and hearty."

Since Amanda Gardiner was in her late thirties, the remark struck Nora as off-key, oddly pessimistic. But she forgot it within minutes. She didn't remember it until the following winter when the news arrived from Europe. Amanda had been killed in an avalanche on a ski slope in Davos, Switzerland. The snowpack was so deep the Red Cross would have to wait until it melted to recover the body. Probably March or April. Ali was inconsolable. With her father's permission, Nora flew to Switzerland with Hiram to comfort her cousin and her uncle at the same time.

"It's terrible," Nora said, sitting beside Ali on the bed in her suite. "But at least she had a good life."

"She was so young," Ali sobbed. "We came here to celebrate her thirty-ninth birthday. That's young."

"What a shame she wanted to celebrate by going skiing."

"I told her it was silly. You don't learn to sky at her age. Pure craziness. She was an intermediate skier at best." Ali spoke with authority.

"Why do you think she did it?"

"I don't know. Maybe she was trying to recapture her youth. Begin again. Do all the fun things she never did. I know she felt she'd missed so much. I think I was a bad influence. And I should have talked her out of it."

"Ali! Please! Accidents happen. Don't blame yourself."

Ali started to sob again. "But I do blame myself. If we'd gone to the Mediterranean . . . She was a good swimmer. I feel so guilty. We were just beginning to know each other."

"I remember you said you wanted to do that . . . to get to know her better."

Abruptly Ali stopped sobbing. "I said that? When?"

"When you visited us on Martha's Vineyard. You said she was the only mother you had left, and you wanted to enjoy her while you still had her. At the time I thought you were morbid and pessimistic. After all, she was so young. But you were right."

Ali gave Nora a long look . . . then smiled through her tears. "Not morbid and pessimistic, Nora. Realistic. I far prefer to be optimistic, and I'm a terrible sentimentalist. But life has forced me to think ahead." She paused to show her respect for the dead. "And I am a fatalist at heart."

As the Swiss predicted, Amanda's body was found in April and shipped back to the States for burial. The funeral was attended by two hundred people. Later that month the will was read. The bulk of Amanda's fortune went to Hiram in trust for Ali. But to the family's surprise—not Nora's—three million from her father's estate was left directly to Ali . . . unsupervised by anyone. Though she was barely twenty-two. It was also noted that when Hiram departed this world of pomp and circumstance and economic conferences, Ali would inherit again. Clearly, Ali was a charter member of the privileged class. Nora had to smile.

Nora and Ali had a bon voyage party before Ali flew off to Paris. They shared a pizza and a bottle of Dom Perignon at Ali's apartment while Minna, her recently hired maid, packed the suitcases.

"Manhattan has lost its charm for me." Ali sipped her champagne with her pizza. "You'll love the apartment I bought in Paris."

"I can hardly wait."

"It's on the Champs-Elysées. Imagine!"

So they talked on and on as they always did . . . laughing a lot and crying a little. Ali looked more excited and glamorous than ever before. Although it was late spring, she wore an ankle-length mink coat over her jeans.

"You could come too . . . if you wanted to." Ali pouted.

"I can't. You know that. I have to graduate. My finals are next month. And I have a career plan. . . ."

"Like Mark?"

"Like Mark . . . and like television . . ."

"You're my favorite stubborn mule."

"And you're just my favorite," Nora said. "But I'll write and write and we'll run up million-dollar telephone bills on transatlantic calls."

"Buy telephone stock." Ali laughed.

"In thousand-share blocks," Nora said, swallowing champagne.

It started well. Ali wrote . . . Nora answered. Nora called . . . Ali called back. Nora wrote . . . Ali answered. Nora wrote . . . Ali didn't answer. Nora called . . . the maid said in French-accented English that Ali was out. Nora called again . . . Ali called back . . . days later. Nora wrote . . . and wrote and wrote. Ali didn't answer. Nora called . . . and called. Ali was not in. In time, Nora stopped writing, stopped calling. After graduation, Mark and she opted to tour the French vineyards before she looked for a job. On the way to the tastings, they stopped off in Paris. Sipping wine in a café and moved by a whim, Nora called Ali. The maid said Ali was in Rome. Nora didn't ask for her number. When they returned, Nora tactfully queried Uncle

Hiram about his correspondence with Ali. Hiram said gruffly that he hadn't heard from her in months. As far as he was concerned she had dropped from the face of the earth. Nora didn't know who was more hurt . . . Hiram or herself.

PART 3

Millie
1992

Chapter 6

FIVE CHANNEL 18 executives slumped around the conference room table . . . their studied attempts to appear relaxed added to the tension. Six chairs were vacant. When the door opened everyone jolted to attention. It wasn't Millie. It was Nora.

"Hi, gang," Nora said in a cheery voice that was every bit as contrived as the relaxed poses of her associates. She slid into a vacant chair.

Luddy Poole's face eased until it could almost pass for friendly. "And where is Mrs. G.?"

"Ask me no questions. On her way, I'm sure."

Tim Rourke stared at her with a look of informed suspicion. "Who else is coming? Who are the very vacant chairs for?"

"Sorry. Same answer."

"Come on, Nora." Rourke's knowing smirk made it obvious he didn't believe her . . . not for a minute.

"Tim, baby," Nora said, "on this flight, we go down in flames together . . . if we crash."

There was a monumental pause. Then Sim Crumb spoke. "Look. We all agree she's a classy lady. Millie Gardiner and Joan Kroc . . . patron saints of San Diego. Class acts. So why doesn't she play to type . . . do good works . . . give charity galas? She's a sponsor of the San Diego Symphony . . . a benefactress of La Jolla Auxilliary of Scripps Memorial Hospital—" He shut up as the door opened and Millie Gardiner entered . . . looking like a well-groomed teacher in a beige turtleneck dress and slouchy camel hair jacket. "Hello, Mrs. G.," he said heartily as she took the vacant chair next to Nora.

Millie and Nora exchanged a wordless greeting.

"Hello, Tim." Millie surveyed the room, sensing the air

of expectancy . . . like a first night audience waiting for the
curtain to rise. "Everyone is here and accounted for. Good.
I'll spare you any further suspense. I'm here to tell you my
new idea—"

"We heard," Tim broke in glumly. "You applied to the
FCC for a license. Channel 18 becomes a superstation."

Millie was poker-faced. "An interesting idea." She started
to laugh. "Also preposterous. But since you've wasted time
trying to guess my intentions, we'll waste more time and play
a game. Guess again. Which of you has the pipeline to the
oil?"

"I heard you have a hot new program idea," Pat said tim-
idly.

"Better. Take three giant steps forward. What's the idea?"

Pat shrugged. "The rumor says it's upscale."

"Warmer. Take three more steps. Clearly, the water cooler
has a leaky faucet. Tell me your source, Pat . . . so I can cut
off their ba—their sacred parts. The show is upscale. Also
mass. Culture with sex appeal. In minutes my idea will arrive
with my granddaughter, Ali Gardiner." Millie sat in the
chair, drumming her fingers lightly on the table. "No burning questions? Any of you?" Silence lay around the room
like dust.

Sim labored to remain composed. "Why wait? Tell us
about it now."

"You give up so soon? Why not consider our options . . ."

Tim frowned. "Knowing you, it's not sports. ESPN and
the networks have a lock on sports. Unless it's horses and
racing . . ." He looked at Millie's amused face. "NBC has
the triple crown signed for years. Breeding horses? No. The
FCC would never okay the video. Not of a stallion mounting
a mare." Tim rubbed his chin. "It's not news. We have two
hours of news five nights a week. We use CNN tapes for
national news. And our local team is hot. What else is there?
And will it work in America's TV room?"

Sim picked up. "It's not a music show. MTV gets the best
music tapes. Besides, our audience is mixed. It goes for rock,
jazz, polkas, country music, Mexican and Mozart. We can't
satisfy them all."

"Right so far," Millie said . . . her smile hadn't lost an
iota of amusement. "It's not sports, news or music. I'll give
you a hint. You might say it's human interest . . . of sorts."

"I got it!" Pat stared across the table at Millie. "You've come up with a new approach to talk and news shows. Geraldo Rivera co-anchored by MacNeil/Lehrer."

"No! Oprah Winfrey and Diane Sawyer!" Luddy was not to be outdone. "Lots of woman appeal."

Millie laughed. "No. Not a news and talk show."

"Maybe an upmarket kid show? The Muppets doing Shakespeare."

Millie nodded toward Donna Zabriskie. "You're warmer. Donna, take three giant steps. You're catching up with Pat."

"Good Lord, Mrs. G.! A kid show? Shakespeare?" Sim choked.

"No. Not kids. Not Shakespeare. But Donna is on the right track."

Luddy's mouth tightened with anger. "Which of our ambitious syndicators got to you directly . . . bypassing me? MCA? Viacom?"

"Cultural sex is not their style," Pat said. "Probably Lionheart. They're upscale. They feed the BBC to public television. 'Mystery Theater'—"

Millie cut in. "Nobody bypassed you, Luddy. It's not a syndicated show."

"You made a deal for a special movie package? With Paramount? Or Davis Entertainment?" Luddy asked.

"No. It's not a movie package. But you're closer. You're now tied with Donna."

Luddy sucked in his breath. Sim rubbed his forehead.

"We give up," Luddy said at last. "What is it?"

Millie exposed her cards slowly . . . one at a time. "It's plays . . . theater." Millie's voice conveyed an unapologetic air of delight. "We will videotape plays as they're staged in a theater. Downstairs in Studio A."

Sim could hardly get the words out. "Here at the station?"

"That's what I said. Studio A was designed by top lighting and sound engineers. It deserves to be used for more than 'Dandy Lions' and other children's programs. Or local news about the latest drive-by shooting."

Nora was businesslike. "Millie, taping a play for television is a very ambitious undertaking."

"I'm ambitious." Millie studied her nails.

Nora said, "We can do it, technically, but we don't have the theatrical expertise . . . the actors, the director, the producer, the set and costume designers. My God! That's just for openers.''

"We will have to hire the talent." Millie was serene.

Tim Rourke tried a diplomatic approach. "Look, Mrs. G., I love theater. But on television? Jesus! The cost will be out of sight."

"Tim's right." The idea had caught Nora's imagination, but she wanted to be objective. "The cost-to-return ratio won't thrill you."

"Time won't be cheap. Rehearsals will take big chunks of time. It'll cut down the personnel we put into other programming," Sim pointed out.

"I said we won't use station personnel. The director will bring in his own people." Millie saw how much they hated the idea, and—at the same time—tried not to object too strenuously. Did they think she'd fire someone for disagreeing? Maybe. It had been known to happen.

Suddenly Luddy Poole erupted. "Just tell me, Mrs. G.— for my own peace of mind—did some fast-gun producer get to you with this Terrytoon? CBS Entertainment? Lorimar?''

"No, Luddy. It's my idea. No one got to me."

Nervous silence filled the room. Everyone—except Nora— was convinced that Millie Gardiner had freaked out. Nora waited for the other shoe to drop. Where was Ali? The other shoe . . .

"What play do you want to produce?" Sim finally asked. "And where will you get the performers?"

"It's not one play . . . it's a series of plays. The working title of the show is 'Night of Stars.' It will be a television play of the month."

Luddy's face had a pained, pinched look. "Mrs. G., try to remember. Channel 18 is an independent station . . . not a network affiliate. We must pay cold, hard cash for every program we air. Until the cable networks took over, people couldn't even find us on the dial. They still can't in southeast San Diego . . . no cable there. For us to mount a live dramatic play. Damn! It'll break the bank!''

"Bankrupt us!" Tim was winded.

Millie let them stew for a few moments. Then she said, "True. It's expensive. So I, not the station, will foot the bill for the first play."

The air in the room cleared. Everyone took a deep breath.

"This is how I see the program. On the first Thursday night of each month Channel 18 will present 'Night of Stars.' It will be a play chosen by an actor or actress of international reputation . . . a genuine star playing a part he or she has chosen to play."

"Like who?" Luddy kept his voice neutral. "What actress or actor?"

"Like Anjelica Huston. Bruce Willis. Dustin Hoffman. Tom Hanks. Michele Pfeiffer. Jack Nicholson. Tammi Meredith. Sean Connery. Harrison Ford." Millie waited . . . watching.

"Have you contacted these performers?" Tim swallowed.

"Yes. Ali Gardiner—I mentioned her earlier—has been my envoy."

"Has anyone agreed?" Sim's voice was awed.

"Some have . . . others are considering it."

At that moment the door opened and Ali entered the room followed by a man and a slim girl with cropped hair. Everyone recognized the girl . . . the fabulous Tammi Meredith. Barely thirty, Tammi Meredith had clawed her way up the Hollywood ladder to certified stardom. At first glance she seemed a slightly refined version of a farm girl, but the camera's eye was more discerning. In close-ups one saw a face lovingly sandpapered to a razor-sharp fineness by a master craftsman. With an off-center intensity in her penetrating brown eyes . . . something fey . . . childlike. Lean and leggy in faded jeans, a loose sky-blue sweater hiding her famous breasts, the mass of honey-colored hair cut short . . . she could pass for fifteen. An ingenue vamp . . . just rid of her baby fat. Ali, radiating self-satisfied gaiety, was on her right. Ken Savage, Tammi's husband-manager, on her left. If Tammi Meredith was all bright sunlight and flowers with the merest hint of corruption, Ken Savage was dark night . . . a blatant corruptor of the innocent. He was dressed entirely in black . . . black shoes, black slacks, a black shirt . . . even carried a black briefcase. Black suited him . . . matched his dark eyes, black hair and the dark blotches under his eyes. They fit together . . . Tammi and Ken . . . a team. Their alleged excesses were featured monthly in the *Enquirer,* the *Globe* and other tabloids sold at the supermarket checkout counters.

"Welcome, Tammi . . . Ken," Millie said. "Good to have you here. Hello, Ali."

Ali nodded, saying nothing. Usually she sought the spot-
light . . . fought for it. Not today. Nora considered, half
amused, what it would cost her to remain in the background
. . . even for an hour.

"Glad to be here, Mrs. Gardiner. If I wasn't here I'd have
an identity crisis." Tammi gave a gutteral, sexual giggle and
sashayed to the vacant chair at Millie's left. "I know that
sounds trendy, but it's true. It makes up for the canned vegetable soup dinners of my childhood."

Savage sat to her left . . . Ali next to him.

"I've been telling the staff my program idea."

Tammi treated the Channel 18 employees to her funny,
lopsided smile . . . the smile was one of her trademarks . . .
it appeared at least once in every film. "It's a wonderful idea
. . . a breakthrough. I hope you all love it. And me. But if
you don't . . . well . . . I'm used to rejection. It goes with
the territory." Throaty giggle again. "I can give you reasons
you can't think of to reject me. But don't. I'm so pleased to
be part of the series' kickoff . . ."

"Why?" Tim asked, awed by her presence.

Tammi paused, raked her hand through her hair, a look of
doubt clouding her brown eyes. "I haven't figured that out.
I'm not sure why I do lots of things. Ken here . . ." She
fluttered her eyelashes at her husband. "He says it will be
good for me at the box office. Television reaches lots of people. If they like me . . ." Giggle. "But that isn't it. I don't
think . . ."

"Then what is?" Pat Yokum pressed, trying to sound
friendly.

Meditative. "I guess I'm looking for something . . . looking so hard I almost didn't come today. I was throwing up
all night . . . a touch of flu." Ken handed her the cigarette
he'd been smoking. She took a puff and handed it back. "No,
that's not true. It wasn't the flu. I mean . . . Fuck it! I mean,
my fucking nerves are shot! I want to do this play so badly."

"What is the play you want to do?" Luddy's voice surprised himself. It was both hoarse and shy . . . a kid just off
the farm chewing on a blade of grass.

"It's a play I saw long ago . . . in Belleville. That's in
Missouri, where I grew up. The local playhouse did it. That
play changed my life. I decided to become an actress . . .
not a veterinarian. I love animals, but the play changed that.

It's like destiny that I've got the chance to do it now. Because Mrs. Gardiner said I could do anything I wanted.''

Her audience was mezmerized. Only Millie—watching with detachment—evaluated the actress's performance. Tammi was auditioning. Her reading was good . . . even touching.

"What is the play?" Sim repeated.

"The title is . . ." Dramatic pause. *"I Remember Mama."* Tammi took in the look on Tim's face. "You never heard of the play, did you? Irene Dunne was in the movie. She played Mama.''

Tim shook his head. So did Luddy. And Sim. And Pat.

Nora clapped. "Bingo! I expected a *Romeo and Juliet* riff. *Mama* will play very well on television.''

Donna the cognoscente agreed. "We did it in college."

Sim cleared his throat. "You realize the idea of filming a play is risky. It's not a sitcom . . . or a mystery. Suppose it bombs? Won't it hurt you at the box office?''

Chin quivering. "If it does . . . well . . . I don't care. I'm never sorry for anything I do. I'll never be sorry about this.''

Everyone was impressed with her earnestness.

Tammi anguished. "My mother worked her tush off to support the family. She dropped dead one morning at the water cooler . . . in the plumbing company office where she worked. So maybe I've got a mission . . . to give this play to her . . . to tell her I remember Mama too.''

Ken opened his briefcase and handed her a slim volume.

"I'll read the opening lines for you. Maybe you'll understand what I see in it. I play the daughter, Katrin.'' Again she gave them her famous lopsided smile and began to read. Her voice changed and now she sounded fifteen. . . .

"For as long as I could remember the house on Steiner Street had been home. Papa and Mama had both been born in Norway, but they came to San Francisco because Mama's sisters were here. Nels, the oldest and the only boy—my sister, Christine—and the little sister, Dagmar.'' She raised her eyes and stared at those seated at the table. When she continued, she didn't glance at the script . . . she knew the lines by heart. "It's funny but when I look back, I always see Nels and Christine and myself looking almost as we do today. I guess that's because the people you see all the time stay the same age in your head. Dagmar's different. She was always the baby—so I see her as a baby. Even Mama—it's funny, but

I always see Mama as around forty. She couldn't always have been forty. . . ." Tammi smiled at the hypnotized audience. "Besides us, there was our boarder, Mr. Hyde. Mr. Hyde was an Englishman who had once been an actor and Mama was very impressed by his flowery talk and courtly manners. He used to read aloud to us in the evenings . . . but first and foremost, I remember Mama . . . I remember that every Saturday night Mama would sit down by the kitchen table and count out the money Papa had brought home in the little envelope . . ." Tammi paused, one eyebrow arched in question.

While she'd been lost in her performance, the door had opened quietly, and a man now leaned against the doorjamb listening . . . watching . . . an observer by training and temperament. Although he was just over six feet tall, somehow he gave the impression he was a giant. He was angular . . . rangy. His skin—a weatherbeaten tan and red . . . the result of having worked for too many years under a hot tropical sun—was stretched tightly over his long bones. His clipped black hair, bony forehead, high cheekbones and long square jaw blended with his weathered face. He wore a maize-colored work shirt, chinos and butter-colored boots. When Tammi Meredith came to the last sentence, he applauded loudly, startling everyone. Seeing him, Nora's heart skipped. He glanced at her for a second and smiled.

Tammi Meredith suddenly sat up very straight.

"Jordan! How was I?"

"Fine, Tammi. Who coached you?"

"I did," Ken said.

"You're good, Ken. Ever consider directing?"

Ken's expression relaxed . . . it was almost good-natured. "No. Tammi has a monopoly on my talents . . . such as they are."

"Can I do it?" Tammi sounded like a scared kid.

"I wouldn't have let you do it if I didn't know you could. You'll be wonderful."

Millie broke in. "Hello, Jordan." She glanced around. "Let me introduce Jordan Banska . . . executive producer of 'Night of Stars.' He'll choose the director for each play, supporting cast, camera crew, technical people. And direct plays that interest him."

Millie went on to describe the details of Jordan Banska's

role in the project. And there was a slow exhaling of breath at the table . . . swallowing . . . low gasps. For the first time in their lives, the Channel 18 staff had come face-to-face with the Big Time . . . they were intimidated. Nora heard nothing. The sight of Jordan made her giddy.

Luddy gave up his fight. "Okay, Mrs. G., I'm convinced. I only hope we can convince advertisers . . . and get ratings."

"We will. But what I want first is a contract from a cable network. Nora, you hear? TNT, TBS, WWOR."

Nora nodded, dazed. Too much was happening. Jordan was back . . . older than she remembered. More weathered, battle-scarred . . . changed . . . but underneath, the same Jordan Banska. The seamed texture of his skin, the rueful lines around his mouth, were all too familiar.

"You think a cable network will go for this?" Sim came up for air.

"I do. Don't you? You don't think we'll get a bite?"

"Mrs. G., I just hope the cable operators are ready for a diet of serious theater."

"It won't all be serious. There'll be comedies too. Listen to me . . . all of you. I know the philosophy. If some viewers fall in love with a show, other viewers must hate it. For every action there's a reaction. So the wise men say, a show that is moderately liked—but not loved—is safest. It will draw the widest audience. It's the theory of the 'least objectionable' programming. This is not such a show. Some viewers will love it . . . others won't. My gamble is there'll be many more lovers than haters. Jordan, come sit down and tell my staff how you see the series."

Jordan selected the chair next to Ali. He pushed it away from the table so he could stretch his legs. When he was comfortable, he began to talk. After that first smile, if he noticed Nora at all it was as if by accident . . . or simple courtesy. Not even Ali—bubbling with questions—could hold his attention. Only Millie and Tammi and Ken got Jordan's full concentration. Nora had always known that someday she would see him again. For years she'd prepared for it mentally . . . practicing her speech. Now it was too late . . . there was nothing to say. What might have been was a long time ago. What there was now was a business arrangement. In the course of the meeting, Millie appointed Nora executive co-

ordinator between the project and the station . . . adding to
her duties as national sales manager. Ali was to act as Millie's
personal emissary to Hollywood and/or Broadway. "I expect
my granddaughters to work together on this project," Millie
said. Nora noted that, thanks to Millie, Ali and she were
going to see a lot of each other. Millie finished with a warning . . . everything about the project was to be treated as top-
secret, confidential business.

When the meeting ended, Tammi, Ken and Ali left with
Jordan. Jordan paused at the door. Then he turned back to
say something more. He studied Nora in an odd, professional
way . . . as if he were a camera judging the length of her
nose, the shape of her mouth. His look made her own eyes
blur. He seemed to reconsider, turned away and closed the
door. The Channel 18 crew got up to leave. Millie asked
Nora to stay.

Millie and Nora had a brief, meaningless conversation
about what had happened . . . what would happen . . .
Nora's responsibilities. Then Millie asked, "You're curious
why I didn't tell you about this project sooner?"

"I'm human. Humans are curious."

"From the start I knew I would ask Jordan to be executive
producer. I thought if I mentioned him you'd have had strong
opinions . . . pro or con. Until I'd firmed up my own
thoughts, I didn't want to hear your opinions . . . they'd only
have muddied the waters."

"He's a good choice. The best." Nora's tone was carefully
neutral.

Millie gave her a searching look. "You can work with
him?"

"Easily. You're afraid I still care for him?"

"Do you?" There was nothing in Millie's voice beyond
genuine concern.

Nora spoke quickly . . . hoping to escape her grandmother's eyes. "He's history. Mark is now my significant other."

"Fine. Then working together will be easy." Millie let
Nora think she'd thrown dust in her eyes. "I want a successful show."

"If the actors come along so will the audience." Nora
swallowed her pride. "I see why you're using Ali. She's a
charmer. She'll charm the pants off—" Nora laughed awkwardly. "I mean . . ."

"I know what you mean. She can be charming." Abruptly Millie's face became a closed door . . . hiding a fleeting concern. Nora had seen the expression before when Ali's name happened to come up. Now she had a sudden intuition. Millie knew more about Ali than she said . . . things so personal she'd told no one . . . not even her.

"Then you like my idea?" Millie asked, changing the subject.

"Very much. Culture that's commercial."

Millie rose and walked to the door. "I counted on your vote." In the corridor, she kissed Nora lightly on the cheek and left. Watching her walk away, Nora wished she had a prayer wheel. She bargained with fate. She couldn't say, "Tell me about Ali and I will . . ." Will what? It made no difference. Millie wouldn't accept her offer. She had once said, "Nora, it's the way it is. We patch as patch can. Life is a patchwork quilt . . . not a cycle of song." Nora gave a wry smile . . . all true. Life wasn't a cycle of song.

This made Nora think of Jordan. Does love really ever end . . . even when it goes wrong?

Millie left the building, thinking about Tammi. Once she had been that young . . . younger. Perhaps if her world had been the way Tammi's world was now, she might not have married Max . . . not given up Milos. These days long-buried events would come back as if they happened yesterday. Memories skipping about out of order. Not all good memories . . . some bad . . . Her first meeting Milos . . . and her last . . . that short, happy, unhappy time. Her exhausted father, who had patience, courage and dignity through the awful months of the trek . . . her father, who could be fooled by the smallest of favors. Images and sensations were pouring through her. The first tall buildings she ever saw . . . the Hollywood Hills . . . the frantic chaos on the set with the lights and cameras and people and Millie Thorne, frightened and hurting. And Dr. Schwartz . . . the sharpest memory of all. She wished she could tell him she'd beaten the odds . . . she'd won. So many pictures and sounds mixed up in time, suspending her sense of reality.

Juan opened the car door and Millie stepped into a morning of sixty years ago.

PART 4

Millie
1923–1948

Chapter 7

"NOW I lay me down to sleep. I pray the Lord my soul to keep . . ."

Kneeling beside the old pickup truck, Millie recited the only prayer she remembered . . . the prayer her mother had taught her. Her father watched . . . the one time in the day when his cracked, compressed lips relaxed into a smile. She smiled back. Then, wrapping her blanket around her, she pretended to sleep. Her father turned away and surrendered to misery . . . misery that drove him like a dry leaf before the wind. Each night he asked himself the same wretched questions: Why did I lose the farm? What will become of us? And each night he was forced to settle for the same answer: I don't know . . . I just don't know.

Millie waited. In time his breathing grew regular. Under the wide and starry skies she sent up a small second prayer.

"Please, God . . ." Her lips barely moved; she was afraid she might wake him. "Please, God, make it rain. You can . . . if you put your mind to it. Make it rain, God, so the corn will grow again. And we can go home. . . ."

Many nights passed, and she prayed and she prayed. She was stubborn, but one night she understood. Just like the sheriff who nailed the foreclosure sign on the tree and the doctor who didn't make her mother well, God was saying no to her. Still she prayed. God was kind . . . God was good. How could he say no to her? He could. It didn't matter how hard she prayed, nothing would change. God was saying no to her. It was a lesson she'd never forget.

She got used to sitting quietly—day after day, mile after mile—in the old pickup . . . bouncing along the crumbling blacktop roads. They were not going home. Ever! They were going to California. Mostly their food came from the temporary soup kitchens that dotted the countryside. A gully by the side of the road was their toilet . . . a stream that hadn't completely dried up was their bathtub. When they came to a migrant camp, they would stop to rest and gossip and dream with the other migrants. They all had the same dream . . . to get to California . . . the golden state where the land was alive with fruits and vegetables. California . . . where jobs waited for them. They had to believe in California . . . they'd lost everything else. So, like a river, the stream of old cars and trucks carrying the families from the dust belt flowed westward across the continent.

One night Millie's father stopped at a camp where an old man sat by a fire and strummed a guitar. Some of the songs he sang she didn't know. But one she recognized . . . it was one of her father's favorites.

"As I walked out in the streets of Laredo
As I walked out in Laredo one day,
I spied a poor cowboy all wrapped in white linen . . ."

At that point Millie joined in, singing in a low voice . . . as if singing to herself. But when they reached the last line— "For I'm a poor cowboy and I know I must die"—her throat went dry and she couldn't go on. The song was sad, but that wasn't the reason.

The morning they were leaving the camp the old singing man didn't wake up. Millie knew he was dying . . . a plant that had its roots cut through. Like her daddy. As they drove away, Millie tried not to think about it.

A month before the mountain passes were snowed in for the winter, Millie and her father sputtered into the San Joaquin Valley. California! They'd made it. So had tens of thousands of other families from the dust bowl. To the well-fed California farmers, living in white frame houses, they were Okies . . . no matter where they came from. Okies weren't human. Okies were good only for picking grapes, apples, lettuce . . . for a few pennies a basket. That is, if they were lucky. If they weren't lucky . . . well . . . the sick and the weak didn't survive.

Millie's father was lucky. At sunrise each morning he joined the men gathered in front of the Castelli farm hiring shed. He held Millie's hand and waited. Jude Castelli, third-generation Italian-American, and the owner of the biggest lettuce farm in the valley, personally decided who would—and who wouldn't—work in the fields that day. Castelli rode his horse through the crowd holding a long bamboo pole. A tap on the shoulder told a man he was selected. Each day lucky Andy was tapped.

Millie said nothing, but she didn't think they were so lucky. She and her father shared a cot in a wooden shack thrown up for field hands. There were no windows and the only air came from the one small door. When it rained, water dripped from the tar paper roof and seeped under the walls. The dirt floor became sticky mud. A ditch with a sprinkling of lime along the bottom was the toilet used by Millie and the women. On still, hot days the stench was so awful she could hardly breathe. There was no schooling . . . the nearest school was three farms away. But the most terrible thing about the lettuce farm was the chain-link fence that penned the workers in the camp at night . . . like cattle. Inside the fence, her father sweated and strained for pennies to buy food. Outside the fence, there was freedom of a sort. The freedom to steal or go hungry and die. Still, Millie would stand for hours with her face pressed to the fence, staring at a blue sky so full of light it almost blinded her. Remembering her mother humming in the kitchen, thick ears of yellow corn, and birds way up . . . dancing in the air. She would gladly change places with the birds . . . except then she'd have to leave her father.

Winter passed, spring came, the grass grew. So did Millie. She grew four inches. She turned eleven. Several months later, she began to bleed. Between the cramps and the blood, she believed she was dying. Blood trickled down her thighs as she huddled in the shade of the shack. Her heart pounded with fear . . . her head ached. Andy hadn't thought to tell Millie about menstruation. Then a passing woman saw what was happening and explained to the terrified child that she wasn't dying. She was growing up. Jude Castelli noticed the same phenomenon. The blond child who always stood with her father was becoming a beautiful young girl. He'd hoped that would happen . . . which was why he'd tapped Andy Thorne's shoulder with his bamboo rod in the first place.

Jude Castelli was forty-five . . . a tall, thin man with shiny black hair and a sense of his own superiority. A man who felt he was made of essentially finer stuff than the other farm owners in the county. Reviewing his personal balance sheet, he saw nothing but assets . . . a respected family name, a fine education, one of the largest landholdings in the valley, plus a beautiful wife and many children. Castelli looked like a man who enjoyed food and wine and women and slept well at night. Actually this wasn't entirely true. His beautiful wife, Gina, was stupid . . . good for nothing but childbearing. So he consoled himself with the daughters of the migrant families. The younger ones—thirteen, fourteen, fifteen—were juicy little devils. He liked young girls. Unspoiled. Clean bodies. Empty minds. He filled their bodies and their minds . . . they were his protégées. The notion that he was a teacher appealed to his sense of superiority. He gave girls a liberal arts education . . . very liberal. Sex. History. Sex. Music. Sex. Literature. When he grew bored with a protégée, he gave her money to leave the county. Not a single girl ever complained.

As Millie ripened, Castelli's interest grew. He determined to give her the benefit of his knowledge . . . she would be his next protégée. With this in mind, he had Gina buy Millie a few simple dresses. He introduced her to good music and literature. She must listen to the Saturday afternoon Metropolitan Opera broadcasts. She must read newspapers and books in his library. One hour each day Millie sat in the Castelli library struggling with books and newspapers. When she came across words she didn't understand, she looked them up in the big Oxford Dictionary on the stand in the middle of the room. If there was a story she didn't understand, Castelli would explain it to her. He followed Millie's education carefully. Soon she'd be old enough to enjoy the benefits of a higher education . . . but there was time.

Castelli waited because he was a cautious man . . . proud of his status in the valley. Neighboring landowners smiled knowingly when he picked himself a pretty migrant girl . . . they might do the same. But they wouldn't smile if he picked a child . . . California farmers tended to be self-righteous. It was important to avoid gossip if he wished to be invited to their homes for the harvest parties and dances. So Millie continued to spend nights in the shack with her father . . . the only difference was they now slept on separate cots. While Castelli waited for her to mature into young womanhood . . . to look—if not actually be—sixteen.

Millie accepted what Castelli offered . . . the good food, the clean toilet, the baths in his house, the clothes, the music, the books . . . everything . . . including the friendship of Castelli's wife. Gina Castelli was a sweet-tempered woman who didn't have it in her to be suspicious of either Millie or her husband. She had what she wanted . . . children, a fine home, a handsome husband. Most of all, she enjoyed being happy. Since Jude was her husband, it made her happy to think he was a kind, generous man. She believed in Jude without understanding him . . . not understanding her husband was indispensable to the housekeeping of her life. Gina liked Millie. She thought the youngster was pretty and willing. Millie helped her in the kitchen and in cleaning the house. As for Millie, she remembered how God had said no to her . . . how the doctor had said no to her mother . . . how the sheriff had said no to her father. Jude Castelli said yes. She knew Castelli's yes wasn't for free . . . for a migrant worker's daughter nothing was free. Jude Castelli said yes for a price . . . a bigger price than housecleaning and cooking. She would pay the price . . . that much she knew. What she didn't know was when the bill would come due.

It took two years. By the time Millie was fourteen, the bone structure that would last all her life was in place. Her hair was a flaxen yellow. Her features were flawless. And her figure—what Castelli could see of it—was breathtaking. She had the long limbs, rounded hips and high breasts that certain Greek sculptor of the classical period had preferred. Every movement had an untaught grace. But there was something else . . . a sensual aura surrounding her. Whenever she walked by—her legs moving to some unheard music—men whistled. She knew why they whistled . . . she knew what they wanted. She smiled without smiling. It was exciting to be wanted by men. What would it be like to want a man the same way?

Castelli's interest in Millie worked for her father and his baskets of lettuce. In the morning, the foreman offered ten cents for each basket harvested to the men Jude Castelli selected. But at sunset—when time came to pay—he often found reasons to pay less. A picker had bruised the lettuce . . . or there weren't enough heads in a basket . . . or he had no excuse. "Too damn much lettuce," he would roar. "Today we pay five cents a basket. Take it or get off the farm." But the foreman always found Millie's father's baskets to be full . . . his lettuce never bruised. The foreman had offered ten cents a basket . . . and ten cents a basket was the price he paid . . . to Andy Thorne.

A few men fought against this unfair treatment. One was Ewen Campbell—a gnarled farmer from Oklahoma—who tried to organize a union. Millie's father listened to the organizers. He admitted they made sense. But he didn't join the union. Unions weren't American . . . they were a foreign invention. Hard as their life was, most of the migrants agreed with Andy. Campbell's meetings were sparsely attended.

Still, the farm owners like Castelli thought Campbell was a menace. Dangerous. Unions meant strikes . . . the lettuce wouldn't be picked. Lost crops meant lost money. A farmer who lost money could lose his farm. One afternoon, the two sides faced off at the Castelli farm. The union men stood on the dirt in front of the house. The farmers lined up on the porch.

"Communist!" Castelli shouted from the porch. "Campbell, you're a lousy, stinking Commie. Leave my men alone or . . ." He gestured with his head toward the sheriff and a half dozen deputies itching to crack heads. "You'll wish you were back in Oklahoma eating Oklahoma pig shit."

"Shove it up your ass, Castelli," Campbell shouted back. "We're unionizing!"

The men shouted some more obscenities at each other.

"What we want is fair treatment, you bastard," Campbell howled.

"Fair treatment? I'll show you fair treatment." Castelli nodded to the sheriff. "They're all yours." With the farmers following, he stalked into the house.

Brandishing clubs, the deputies charged into Campbell and his union members.

Millie and her father had been watching from different vantage points. Millie, in a dress Gina Castelli had bought her, stood in the shack door . . . eyes wide with fear. Bad things were happening. Her father was standing off to one side . . . watching.

The union members outnumbered the deputies six to one, but they scattered. Millie's father didn't run . . . he wasn't in the union . . . why run away? The deputies looked for someone to hit . . . Andy Thorne was the nearest target. When the first club hit his arm, he looked more surprised than hurt. Automatically, his raised hands became fists. To the red-faced, sweating, frustrated deputies, it looked as if he would attack them. Six beefy young deputies brought their clubs down on the thin, thirty-nine-year-old man . . . driving him to his knees. A kick in the ribs knocked him to the ground. The deputies took turns hitting him over the head, in the ribs, in the kidneys. Except for the grunts of the deputies as they swung and jabbed their clubs and Andy Thorne's gasps as air was forced from his lungs, the beating went on in an eerie silence. Most of the people watching from the house wanted to stop the violence. But they didn't . . . they were paralyzed by the terrifying brutality.

Hair flying, Millie hurtled from the shack and barreled into the deputies. "Stop it," she screamed. "Stop it! He's my daddy." Her fists were flying in all directions . . . a few of her blows actually landed.

A beefy deputy picked her up and held her in the air. "Hey. Look what we got here, guys. The Commie's daughter . . . wearing her little dress. . . ." His laughter was savage. "Ain't she a pretty one? No Commie should have such a pretty kid. Ain't right . . ."

"Leave her alone, Lenny," another deputy said.

"She's a Commie's kid. Me first. Then you can all have her. Over by the fence where it's quiet. . . ."

Two shots sounded. The deputies swung around, reaching for their pistols. And froze. The sheriff and Jude Castelli were standing a few feet away . . . their guns were pointed toward the sky.

"Put the kid down, Lenny." When the deputy didn't do it fast enough, the sheriff stepped forward and rapped him on the side of the head with the barrel of his gun.

The deputy dropped Millie and staggered back. "Why'd you do that, Earl?" he mumbled.

"Because you're stupid." The sheriff spit the words out. "You beat the shit out of one of Mr. Castelli's best men. Maybe you killed him."

"Lenny," Jude Castelli said, his voice flat, "if my man is dead, you better leave the county." He was as angry as he sounded . . . but not at what had happened to Andrew Thorne. The deputy had threatened Millie . . . threatened to ruin a garden he'd spent two years cultivating. He watched as Millie crawled on her hands and knees toward her father. She stared at the blood spurting from his neck, oozing from his head, running from his mouth and nose . . . coloring the soil around him.

"All you all right, Daddy?" she asked, her voice a broken whisper. She tugged at him with all her strength, lifting his bloody head and cradling it against her. "Say something, Daddy. Please!"

Andy didn't answer.

Jude Castelli joined Millie. "Get up, man," he said.

What remained of Andrew Thorne didn't move.

"Daddy!" Millie wept. "Don't die. . . ." Her eyes were fixed on his face. "Please, Daddy . . . please . . . don't die." When Andy didn't answer, she began to tremble. A sudden, overwhelming pain struck her head and she collapsed over her father's body . . . her face was buried in the warm and sticky pool of his blood. It was as if she had been flung headlong into a bottomless pit. Millie fell and in falling knew her world had ended . . . for a second time.

Millie was unconscious when Castelli pried her arms from around her father and moved her away from him. He knelt and felt Andrew Thorne's pulse . . . he shook his head.

Lenny backed away, then turned to run. Before he'd taken three steps a shot rang out. Lenny stumbled . . . caught himself and stood still. He was a badly wounded animal . . . too hurt to run . . . too frightened to fight. He sagged to his knees. A stream of bright red blood spread from his thigh, soaking into the brown soil.

Jude Castelli slipped his gun back into its holster. "Earl," he said to the sheriff, "your deputy killed my man. Get him out of here. You understand me, Earl?"

"Yeah, Jude," Sheriff Earl Grimes said.

Castelli lifted Millie up and carried her into the house. As he walked he muttered to himself, "Damn Communists. Nothing would have happened if it wasn't for the Commies!"

With her father dead, Millie went to live full-time in the Castelli house. She was almost like one of the family . . . sort of a poor relation. She continued to help Gina with the cooking and housecleaning. And she also took care of the children . . . three boys and a girl. Gina was pregnant again. Dreamy Lucia, the girl, was Millie's favorite. And Millie was

Lucia's favorite . . . the child followed Millie around like a puppy. A year passed while Millie waited for Mr. Castelli to present his bill. The night after her fifteenth birthday he did.

Millie paid in full. To her surprise, payment was easy. The girls in camp said the first time would hurt. The next time would be better . . . they swore it got better and better. Millie didn't agree. It didn't hurt and it didn't get better. It was nothing. Over the next year, Jude Castelli and she would meet in one of the many bedrooms in the farmhouse. Or in a hotel room in town. Or on the back seat of his Cadillac. Millie soon discovered a great joke about sex . . . one Castelli didn't teach her. Because the joke was on him. He wanted her to enjoy the sex . . . as he did. It made him feel manly. And it made her laugh in private how easily she could fool him. She'd moan and groan and cry, "Yes . . . yes . . . yes!" Castelli heard what he wanted to hear . . . believed what he wanted to believe . . . and was satisfied.

By 1942 the country was at war . . . most of the young men were drafted and the demand for lettuce went through the ceiling. Jude Castelli was getting rich . . . not land rich . . . rich like having more cash in the bank than he knew what to do with. He spent a tiny portion of his new wealth on amusing Millie . . . he showed her the local hot spots. But at sixteen, Millie knew there was a bigger world beyond the one bounded by the lettuce farm and the few tiny, nearby villages . . . Buttonwillow, Lost Hills, Rio Bravo. The great cities to the south—San Francisco, Los Angeles—were as foreign to her as Charles Dickens's London. She dreamed about city lights, beautiful dresses, warm rooms in the winter . . . and waited for still another year. Then something happened that forced her to make a decision. She missed her period. When she missed a second period, she guessed she was pregnant. I'm not ready, but it's now or never, she told herself. The house was fast asleep as she dressed quietly, packed her favorite clothes and a few things she needed into a suitcase. In the kitchen she filled a canteen with water . . . she could live for days without food but not without water. The wooden floors kept her secret . . . no board squeaked as she tiptoed into the library. She knew where she was going. Millie's memory was remarkable . . . she remembered everything, many things she'd rather forget. Now she recalled the Thursday afternoons when the Wells Fargo armored truck delivered the weekly payroll. The cash was deposited in the safe in the library, behind the painting of Mr. Castelli. There it remained until Friday, when the foremen, the guards and the field workers were paid. Standing in front of the painting, she thought about Mr. Castelli. What she owed him. What he owed her. Then she moved the painting and gazed at the safe. Once when she was fifteen—before he noticed her remarkable memory—Castelli had let her stay in the library when he opened the safe. As he turned the lock he recited the numbers out loud. Millie heard the numbers and remembered them. Right to thirty-two . . . turn left twice to six . . . right to forty-nine. She turned the handle and the door swung open. Millie took out one thousand and seventy-four dollars. She left a note . . . her balance sheet.

Dear Mr. Castelli:
You gave me a home and taught me about music, literature and art. I owe you for that. You also brought the men here who killed my father. You owe me for that. You had sex with me five hundred and thirty-seven times . . . I kept track of each time. A good whore—I was a good whore—charges two dollars a time. You owe me one thousand seventy-four dollars for sexual services. I'm not charging you for my father. It would cost you more than money. I took one thousand seventy-four dollars from the safe . . . for the whoring. Good-bye, sir.

Millie Thorne

Millie's plan was to walk or hitch a ride to Bakersfield, the nearest big city. There she'd buy a train ticket to Los Angeles. In Los Angeles she'd find someone to help her with the baby. But she was jumpy. She didn't know what Mr. Castelli would do once he read her letter. On the first day, she hid in the drainage ditch beside the road every time she heard a truck coming. By the second day she realized she had to take a chance . . . she was hungry and her water was running low. Trucks—ones from out of state—were the safest bet. She walked along the dusty road and tried hailing an out-of-state truck. Several trucks passed by before it struck her she was being a fool. She found an apple grove and, after munching two apples, she took off the blue dress with the Peter Pan collar . . . Mr. Castelli liked the dress because it made her look twelve. She packed it away and slipped on a pair of denim shorts and a shirt. Now she looked her age. The first truck passed . . . screeched to a stop . . . then waited for her.

The driver called from the cab, "Where you going, girl?"

"Bakersfield." Millie smiled. "Can you give me a lift?"

"Sure. Hop in."

In Bakersfield the driver presented his bill. Millie paid it. The five hundred thirty-eighth time was like the five hundred thirty-seven times before. The driver was a little younger than Mr. Castelli, stronger, a bit rougher, but as easy to fool. When she moaned and groaned and said "Yes . . . yes . . . yes," he believed her and he felt good.

The next morning he asked, "Where you going from here? Maybe I can take you part of the way?"

Millie thought this over. She was worried about Mr. Castelli. The farther away she got the better.

"Los Angeles," she said.

"I'm going to L.A. It's a good place for you. You ought to be in pictures . . . you're pretty enough."

"You think so?"

"I think so. You could be a star."

"I'd like that." Why not? she thought. Why not try to be a movie star?

"Come on. I'll give you a lift. To Hollywood."

Millie shrugged. What were a few more times feeling nothing after five hundred and thirty-eight? "Okay," she said. "Let's go."

And they did.

As for Jude Castelli, she need not have worried. When he read Millie's note he was angry for a few moments. Then he laughed. In a way he was glad . . . he had been a little afraid of her. Sometimes he had the feeling he didn't understand her. And for a year now he'd been eyeing Martha Ryan, the thirteen-year-old kid of a field hand. Because Millie wasn't a child anymore . . . she was a woman. If he wanted a woman, he'd fuck Gina. Or a whore . . . if he felt in the mood. "Fair's fair," he murmured. He'd have given her something close to what she took. Then he frowned . . . she'd beat him to the punch. That girl was too smart for her own good. Martha Ryan would be a welcome change.

* * *

When Millie and Larry arrived in Los Angeles, they said good-bye the way friends say good-bye. Millie liked Los Angeles. It felt familiar . . . like the camp. Below the Hollywood Hills were miles and miles of flat land with tiny houses and half-paved roads. The air hung hot and heavy over the flat land and smelled of smoke and sweaty people and unwashed animals. It reminded her of nights she lay in the shack beside her father and smelled the sweat of the unwashed field hands making love. Some of the chattering, laughing people looked familiar too . . . she saw lettuce and apples and grapes in their faces. They were country folk. But there were other faces . . . from far away . . . with histories she couldn't imagine. She quickly found a room in a boardinghouse on Sunset Boulevard.

"Ten dollars a week and no men overnight, Miss Thorne," the fat landlady said.

"Okay."

"Two weeks in advance."

"Yes," Millie said. "Could I use the bathroom, please?"

"Sure." The woman pointed to a door at the end of the corridor.

Millie shut and locked the door. She needed privacy to take twenty dollars from the roll of bills pinned into her panties.

"Here's the two weeks in advance," she said to the landlady.

The landlady smiled. "Dearie. That trick won't fool anyone. Take my advice. I don't know how much money you got, and I don't care. But if it's more than this twenty dollars, put it in a bank. Don't keep your cash in your panties."

Millie said nothing.

"Suit yourself. Just don't forget, every time you drop your panties, you'll drop your money. One of your customers might get the idea you ought to pay him instead of the other way around."

"I'm not a whore."

"I know. You're an actress. You're all actresses." She patted her broad hips. "I'm an actress too. I was . . . once. Before I got fat. Now my kid's acting in the movies. Baby Gustave. Ever hear of Baby Gustave?"

"No," Millie admitted.

"That's okay. He's not very good." She grinned. "I'm Sheilah Carr . . . you can call me Sheilah."

"I'm not an actress, Sheilah . . . not yet anyway. But someday I'll be a star."

"That's nice. Which studio have you decided to be a star at?"

"Whichever one will take me."

"That's the first sensible thing you've said since you walked in the door. Come along. I want to show you something."

Millie followed the woman to the front door.

"Over there," the landlady said, pointing across Sunset Boulevard. "That dump is called the Garden of Allah. I don't know why, but a bunch of writers and directors live there . . . good writers and directors . . . some are even successful. Tomorrow morning go over there. Look around."

Millie hesitated.

"What's the matter, dearie? Too shy? You can be a lotta things and be a star, but one thing you can't be is shy."

"I'm not shy." I won't be, Millie promised herself. "But I'm busy tomorrow morning."

"Too busy to become a star?"

Millie smiled. "I have to find a bank. When I drop my panties, I don't want to drop my money."

"Ha!" Sheilah howled and slapped Millie on the back. "Good girl. You may get lucky. Who knows? Crazy things happen in this town."

Millie and Sheilah had many cups of coffee. They talked about the different movie studios . . . about the rules of the game. And finally about Millie being pregnant.

"Jesus!" Sheilah exploded. "How the hell did you get yourself knocked up?" When Millie told her, she grimaced and asked, "Do you want an abortion?"

"No," Millie said. "I want my baby."

"You can't raise a baby in this town and become a star."

"I know."

"There is one thing you can do. Maybe I can help."

Millie looked at her questioningly.

"Adoption. You can give the baby up for adoption. I know a shyster—a lawyer—named Tom O'Hara. Tom arranges these things . . . for a fee."

Millie chewed on her lower lip. Adoption? That meant giving her baby away . . . never seeing it again. "I don't know," she said.

"There's something in it for you," Sheilah insisted. "Whoever adopts the baby will pay your bills for the next six months . . . including the lawyer's fee, the doctor's bill and the hospital costs."

Millie said nothing.

"What choice do you have," Sheilah asked, "if you want you and your baby to survive?"

Frightened and desperate, Millie finally agreed. She would give her baby up for adoption.

Sheilah took care of everything. The only nonmedical people who knew were Sheilah, Eddie O'Hara, the adopting couple—Jim and Harriet Sloan—and Baby Gustave, who didn't count.

Millie gave birth to a healthy daughter. She was allowed to see her baby once . . . only once. When the baby was taken from her arms, she wanted to sob . . . but the tears wouldn't come. God had said no to her again.

Millie was young and resilient. Her muscles quickly regained their strength. She was fitted for a diaphragm, and her movie education continued. She was a quick study. It took her three months and sleeping with four men—an agent, a casting director, an assistant director and a cameraman—to get her first screen test. She neither liked nor disliked the sex, but she gave a great performance. She did it—as she did everything—well. So well that some of the men believed her. Those who didn't admired the performance. The agent got her the screen test. When Millie saw the screen test, she grimaced.

"You're a great piece of ass, kid," the agent said. "But you can't act worth shit. You got no silver nitrate magic."

"What's that?" Millie asked.

"It's . . . uhm . . . like, wow! The girl leaps off the screen. You don't. Tell you what, kid. I'll get you work as an extra and . . ." He grinned. "We'll have a quid pro quo arrangement."

"What's a kwidprokwo arrangement?"

"It's Latin. It means I do this for you, you do that for me. . . . Tit for tat."

I'm the tit, Millie thought. She shrugged. "It's about paying bills. I always pay my bills."

"Good. That's what it's all about, kid. You got it."

Millie didn't give up. But four screen tests and many men later, she was nowhere. She didn't understand why her screen tests were so bad . . . why the girl on the screen wasn't her.

Off the screen, men continued to whistle at her. She worked days as an extra, and when she walked from the soundstage to the commissary, the grips, stagehands, electricians whistled and applauded. If she gave them a treat, wiggling her bottom as she passed, she could cause a near riot. One such day, walking by the studio office building, she was stopped by a perspiring young man wearing glasses and carrying a clipboard . . . a pencil was tucked behind his ear.

"You," he said. "What's your name?"

"M-Millie Thorne," she stammered.

The young man wrote down her name. "You're the girl they whistle at?"

"I . . . I . . ." Millie had heard that troublemakers were barred from the lot. "I won't do it again."

"What won't you do again? Walk?"

"No. I . . ." Millie didn't know what to say.

"Come with me." He took her arm and pulled her into the office building.

"Where are we going?" Millie gasped.

"He wants to see you close up. He's been watching you for two weeks."

Millie was too frightened to ask who "he" was.

The young man opened a door and pushed Millie into a large office. "Wait here." He closed the door behind her.

"You may as well sit down," a bored woman said. "He's busy. You'll have to wait. I'm Zelda Riggs, his private secretary."

"Th-th-thank y-you."

"Do you always stutter?"

"N-no. I . . ." Millie took a deep breath. "I'm confused."

"Everyone in Hollywood is confused. It's a natural state. Now sit down. I have to get his letters typed or he'll kill me."

Millie wished she knew who the "he" was. She could ask. She should ask. She didn't ask.

Minutes later the door to the inner office opened and a tallish, thin man carrying a clipboard appeared. He was pale

. . . pale skin, pale blond hair—almost white like hers—a thin hawk-shaped nose topped by brilliant blue eyes and blond eyebrows.

"I haven't finished the letters, sir."

"That's all right." His voice was deep and he had an accent. Like Cary Grant, Millie thought. But she didn't think he was English. "You're . . ." He consulted the clipboard. "Millie Thorne."

"Yes, sir." Millie was determined not to stammer.

"You're the girl who caused the fuss on Stage 11?"

"I'm sorry, sir."

"What did you do?"

"Nothing."

"You just walked and the men whistled."

Millie made a helpless gesture.

"Walk for me."

"I . . . I don't understand."

"What is there to understand? Get up and walk. You know how to walk. I've seen you walk myself."

"Yes, sir." Millie rose and walked across the room.

"No! That's not how you walked outside." He turned to his secretary. "Hold all calls, Zelda. We'll see if we can get this child to walk the way she walks for the stagehands. You . . ." He crooked his finger at Millie. "Come with me."

Millie followed the man into his office. Who is he? she asked herself.

"Walk!" he commanded. Millie took a few steps. He shouted, "Stop! No grip would whistle at that." He thought for a moment. Then . . . "Take off your clothes."

"What!"

"Your clothes, girl. Your clothes. Take them off." When Millie stood paralyzed, he shouted, "Damn it! I'm not going to rape you. I've seen your screen tests. They're terrible. I think I know why, but I want to be sure. Take off your clothes. You can put them on the chair."

"B-b-but suppose someone comes in?"

"So what?" He rolled his eyes toward the ceiling. "Look! You want to be a star? Right?"

"Yes."

"Then do it."

Millie turned away and undressed stiffly. Despite her acute embarrassment, she worried about the tiny red ridges her garter belt left on her thighs. When she was down to her bra and panties, she glanced over her shoulder. He was sitting behind his desk reading something . . . a script? Millie knew she had a good figure . . . every man she'd been to bed with said she had tits like Lana Turner and an ass like Betty Grable. Why wasn't he paying attention to her?

As though he heard her thoughts, he looked up. "I don't have all day. Take off your bra and panties or get dressed and get out."

Millie unhooked her bra. She then slid her cotton panties over her hips and stepped out of them. An odd thought crossed her mind. She was glad she never wore dirty panties.

"Okay. Turn around."

Millie faced him. Her right arm was crossed over her breasts and her left hand partially shielded her crotch.

"Jesus! You look like the girl in *September Morn*. Stand up. Straight. With your hands at your sides." He watched as Millie followed instructions. "Now walk across the room."

Millie felt stupid. She didn't know what she was doing . . . she didn't know why she was doing it . . . she didn't know what he wanted her to do. Stiff-kneed, she clumped from the chair to the far wall and back.

"Worse than before. Does the word *relax* mean anything to you?"

"How can I relax with you looking at me?"

"Are you trying to tell me that no man ever looked at your naked body?"

"No. But . . ."

"Aaaah." He rubbed his forehead. "I see. They were fucking you. So that made it all right for them to see you naked. I'm not going to fuck you so that makes it wrong for me to look at you. Is that it?"

Millie flushed. A red glow suffused her breasts . . . it rose to her shoulders, her chin, her neck, her forehead.

"Now we have September Morn blushing. Okay. Suppose I call in Eddie . . . he's the boy who brought you here. He says he gets an erection just watching you. He'll fuck you and then you'll walk for me. Will that help?"

"Noooo." Millie collapsed in the chair. Don't cry, she told herself.

"Good girl. Tears will make your eyes red and puffy. We'd have to postpone the test."

"What test?"

"Your screen test. Once you walk for me, I'm giving you a screen test."

Something clicked in Millie's mind . . . fury replaced fear. Another screen test meant another bill. What the hell! He'd been playing a game with her. This was the screen test game, and she knew the rules . . . she was a pro at that game. Millie sat up . . . she slapped her hands against the leather-covered arms of the chair. "Walk. That's what you want. Watch me." Millie swiveled her way across the room . . . her revolving hips could have churned butter.

He applauded. "Better. Much better. Now again. Wait a minute." He stood up and went to the far wall. "I'm your lover. I'm waiting to make love to you. Come to me."

Millie moved toward him.

"Yes. That's it. Walk to your lover."

When Millie reached him, she stopped. She stood help-lessly confused . . . her arms dropped to her sides. Inside her body was a high-pitched sound that only she could hear and feel.

"Walk to the chair and back," he said.

Millie sashayed across the room and back.

"That's it. You've got it!"

"Got what?" Millie gasped.

He touched her chin gently . . . stroked it . . . ran his fingernail around the edges of her lips. "If the camera loves you, you're going to be a big star." He quickly stepped be-hind his desk. "Get dressed. I've got a soundstage and crew—costume, makeup, sound, lighting, camera—waiting. It'll cost a fortune, but we'll make the best goddamned screen test this town's ever seen."

"But don't you want to . . ."

"Of course I want to. But first you fuck the camera . . . then I fuck you. Now move!"

On the way to the soundstage, he explained to Millie what was wrong with her screen tests. "It's the goddamned Hays Office. Everyone in this town is scared of Will Hays. Sex is out . . . Andy Hardy is in. The boys who did your screen tests didn't want you to look too sexual. So they smothered you with the wrong clothes, the wrong makeup, the wrong dialogue. I saw one of those tests. You wore a fur coat that hid your body and a big hat that covered your hair. And you read lines you didn't understand to an actor who wasn't listening.

"You're not afraid of the Hays Office?"

"Afraid?" He thought about that for a moment. "I'm not afraid, but I'm not stupid. Hays has drawn a line . . . I won't put one tiny toe over that line. But if you know what you're doing, then there's still room to play games."

In a dressing room, the wardrobe mistress handed Millie a large, brightly patterned square of cotton. She told her to get undressed and she'd show her how to wrap the cotton around her.

"What is it?" Millie asked.

"It's called a sarong. Women in the South Seas wear them . . . below the waist. In the film, the sarong will cover your breasts."

"For the Hays Office?"

The wardrobe mistress nodded.

Makeup came next . . . bronze makeup.

He was waiting for her on the set . . . sand and palm trees and water combined to give the illusion of a tropical island. He studied her and nodded. "Fine. Now, walk from there"—he pointed to a mark that was out of camera range—"to there. The last palm tree. It will get windy . . . very windy. And it will rain . . . hard. When you can't stand against the wind and the rain, hold on to the tree."

"What do I say?"

"Nothing. Just hold on. Ah . . . one more thing." He brushed his finger against her bronzed chin, being careful not to mar her makeup. "Think of the palm tree as your lover . . . as me. You're going to make love to that tree . . . to me."

Millie felt so wet between her legs she thought her period had come . . . two weeks early. She only hoped the blood didn't spoil her leg makeup.

"Go," he said. "When I say 'Action,' walk across the sand to the tree and hang on."

Millie waited. She heard the magic words: "Lights. Camera. Action." She walked toward the tree. The wind grew stronger. The water poured down on her. Every step was an effort. Her sarong was plastered against her body . . . her nipples pushed against the fabric. Finally she reached the tree. She stood, her legs apart, her feet gripping the sand.

The wind and the rain forced her to step back. She recovered her balance. Her hair blew back behind her. Without being aware of it, she was smiling . . . a strange smile . . . an inviting smile. Then she had to hold on to the tree as the wind and the rain pounded her. She wound her arms around the tree . . . her legs were on either side of it. Gripping it with her knees, she moaned as she made love to the tree. She didn't hear him say, "Cut. That's a print." The abrupt end to the wind and the rain shocked her. Although there was no longer a need, she clung to the tree. It was over too soon. She hadn't . . . She hadn't what?

He pried her arms loose and held her at a distance. "Yes," he said. "Wonderful."

Millie blinked. She looked around. The wardrobe mistress, the makeup man, the stagehands, the lighting director, the grips, the entire crew were applauding.

"Harry. How long will it take to develop the test and print it?"

"Two hours. I don't want to screw this up."

"You'd better not," he said. "Come with me, Millie." He led her to the dressing room, shut the door and locked it. "Take that off," he said. As Millie unwrapped the sarong, he took off his clothes. He raised her face to his . . . she began to tremble. He kissed her . . . her nipples grew hard . . . the white-blond hairs on her arms stood straight out. Her eyes were closed, her mouth open . . . her tongue searched for his ears . . . his mouth. When he caressed her between her legs, she opened to him. Then they made love. He thought to take her. He couldn't . . . she took him. The ruthlessness with which she used him astounded him. She's a sexual anarchist, he thought. As capable of anything as he. When she climaxed, a shiver passed along her spine . . . she came in a sudden freshet against his sex. Again and again he felt her. Milos had known women who flooded the sheets. This was something else. He could hold back no longer . . . groaning with pleasure, he climaxed.

They rested on the dressing room floor for a while. Then Millie raised herself on her elbow and looked at him . . . a shy, embarrassed look. "Uhm . . . I . . ."

"What is it?"

"Uhm . . . Can I ask you . . . ?" She took a deep breath.

"Can I ask you . . . what's your name? I keep thinking of you as 'he.' "

"You don't know who I am?"

"I'm sorry. No one told me."

He started to laugh. He laughed so loud and so long the tears ran down his cheeks. "That's the funniest thing that's happened to me in years," he sputtered. Laughter again contorted him. "You really don't know who I am." Finally he said, "I'm Milos Banska."

"Milos Ban—Oh my God! You can't be."

"Why not?"

"There's Cecil B. deMille, John Ford, Darryl Zanuck . . . a few others, and Milos Banska. You're a legend. I thought you were dead."

Milos frowned. "I'm not. I've been living in Switzerland. The war"—he hesitated—"and other matters kept me there."

"You haven't made a film in years."

He smiled. "I know. I will now. I'm not dead."

Millie touched his penis. "No! You're very alive."

"And I'm back, and you'll star in *Monsoon*. That's my new film. You play a South Sea island girl."

Later they took a shower together . . . to wash off body makeup and smile with joy at being together. They looked at each other and spoke to each other as if they'd been lovers for years. Knowing whatever there was to know about each other's body and heart. They made love again. And again Millie responded in a way Milos had never experienced. Afterward he thought, You poor kid . . . you'll never be able to fake an orgasm. Moans and groans won't do it.

Monsoon made Millie Thorne a star. And Galaxy Productions a fortune. Millie's picture was on the cover of every major movie magazine . . . the Millie Thorne look—rain-slicked, dyed black hair and vivid sarong—crowded the beaches from Santa Monica in L.A. to Jones Beach in New York. Hedda Hopper, Sheilah Graham, Luella Parsons filled their columns with stories about her. Milos Banska took her everywhere . . . the Clover Club—a small restaurant with illegal gambling upstairs—the Directors Guild dinner dance at the Coconut Grove, the Brown Derby and the Trocadero Restaurant. Milos knew everyone . . . stars and studio heads. Louis B. Mayer and Clark Gable, Jack Warner and Norma Shearer.

One day they went to the Santa Anita Racetrack. At the club-house Milos and his friends placed bets. Millie thought the bets obscenely large. The biggest gambler was a tall, loose-jointed, dark-haired young man . . . handsome enough to be a movie star.

"Millie," Milos said, "this is my old friend Max Gardiner. Max, meet Hollywood's newest star . . . Millie Thorne."

"I know Miss Thorne. I've seen *Monsoon* three times." He paused to collect his thoughts. "Miss Thorne . . ."

Millie smiled. "Call me Millie. All my friends do."

Max stood still . . . his chin lifted a little . . . his eyes on her face. "Will we be friends?"

Millie gazed at the handsome young man. The best of life seemed to surround him like a halo. "Why not, Mr. Gardiner?"

"I'm Max to my friends. But will we be good friends, Millie?"

Millie understood. The way he said it meant, "Will we be lovers?"

Max plunged on. "If Milos, our film genius, neglects you, I'm in the book. Under G. Please call me . . . or I'll have to call you. I'm good on the phone. Meanwhile . . ." He gave Millie a lopsided grin. "There are races to be run. Jock Whitney has a horse in the next race, Milos. He says the horse is ready. Want to join me?"

"No." Milos looked up briefly from his handicapping sheet. "Whitney's horses are never ready."

Max Gardiner brushed his lips over the back of Millie's hand. "Court etiquette states a man should never kiss the hand of an unmarried woman. You are unmarried?"

"Yes," she said.

"You must forgive my lapse in etiquette."

"I forgive you," she said.

"Thank you. One last request. Please remember my name." Then he loped off in the direction of the betting booths.

Millie watched him go . . . her face sober. She wasn't deceived by the emperor's new clothes. She saw him as naked and shivering in the cold. God, what need, she thought. Why? She asked Milos, "Who is he?"

"Max? He's the scion of the Gardiner family. He's had everything a human being can want."

"Maybe more than anyone can bear."

Milos gave her an odd look. "You have sharp insights. But he's brave . . . physically. Actually, he's a war hero. He was a bomber pilot . . . wounded three times and three times he brought his plane home safely. Finally the air force gave him an honorable discharge. He's been awarded every medal except the Medal of Honor. He won't get the Medal of Honor because in 1940 his father called Franklin Roosevelt 'That man in the White House' to his face and backed Wendell Willkie for president. The Gardiners own office buildings, apartment houses, oil wells, a shipping line, pieces of several railroads, and land . . . miles and miles of the good earth. Still, you may be right. Sometimes I think that, for all his wealth, Max was not born under a lucky star. . . ."

Millie asked, "What does he do? Where does he work?"

"What does Max do . . . now that he's no longer trying to kill himself? Let's see. He sleeps with women. Drinks. Gambles. Collects paintings. Plays polo. Has a horse farm somewhere in San Diego. Oh, yes. He gives money to worthy causes."

"He doesn't work." There was a hint of contempt in her voice.

Milos said, "He doesn't have to work."

"You're rich. You work."

"I'm rich enough . . . not the way the Gardiners are rich. But I must work . . . for my own sake."

"I wish he worked," Millie murmured.

Milos said dryly, "That may be his problem. There's nothing he loves enough to work at . . . or for."

Millie didn't see the momentary disintegration in Milos's face. It was as though his eyes, his nostrils, even his mouth, were moving in different directions at the same time. Then his features composed themselves. His face was again the face Milos Banska showed the world.

Millie fell in love with Hollywood—one moment a sleepy village and the next a frantic city—almost as much in love as with Milos. But being a movie star in Hollywood was hard work . . . the lights, the heat and the tension on the set gave her headaches. Gradually the headaches grew stronger and lasted longer. She swallowed too many aspirin, which upset her stomach. But she never missed a day, and she showed up on the set each morning knowing her lines and prepared to work. At Milos's insistence, she rented a house in the Hollywood Hills. It became her bolt hole . . . her escape. The place where her head never ached . . . where she and Milos were together. Friends as well as lovers, they laughed and quarreled, joked and made love. But loving Milos was no escape . . . they were too much alike. She was as strong as he was . . . he was as proud as she. And both were as vulnerable. In a way, this was their bond. This deep and silent awareness of being the same . . . strangers and afraid. Sometimes at night, thinking how she loved him, Millie's heart pounded. "God help me," she prayed.

Inevitably the evening came when he told her the truth about the years when he'd made no movies . . . a truth she already knew. She'd wrapped up her second picture, *The Innocent Voyage,* and returned from a month-long, exhausting national publicity tour. There were days on the tour when her head never stopped hurting. The limousine deposited her at her house, and to her delight, she found Milos waiting. They kissed and made love. Afterward they had drinks on the deck overlooking Los Angeles and talked about her future.

Feeling brave and full of pizzazz, Millie took a risk. "Forget my twinkling stardom. Marry me, and I'll give you lots of kids. I'd rather have kids and be your wife than be a star."

Milos looked grave. "Are you proposing?" Millie nodded. "I'm flattered, dear, but I can't."

The pizzazz went out of Millie. "Can't or won't?"

Milos gazed at the lights of the city . . . they seemed to grow dim, as though a sea fog had blown in to blanket his happiness. He'd known from the beginning the question was coming. He'd searched for a way out. But there was none. Nothing was left but the truth.

"Can't." He said the word flatly, without emphasis. "I love you . . . I don't want to lose you. But I can't marry you."

Millie had learned well the lesson of the camp . . . to be stoic when disaster struck. "I didn't think you could. I was testing."

"I'm married—" His voice broke.

"I know."

He smiled grimly. "I'm not surprised. There are enough gossips in town to tell you."

"And where there's gossip sometimes there's fact."

"Do you know the facts?"

"I'd rather you tell them to me."

His voice was rough with anger at himself. He spoke slowly, choosing his words with care. He told her how he'd been in Austria before the war . . . how he'd seen what the Nazis did . . . how he helped many Jews get to Switzerland. And how the Swiss interned the Jews . . . made them work on road gangs. He told what happened to one Jew in particular . . . Anton Schmidt, who once sang in the Vienna State Opera. "Anton was a tiny man with bird bones, little strength and a beautiful tenor voice. He died in the labor camp, leaving a twenty-year-old daughter, Hannah Schmidt. Hannah was a beautiful girl . . . also with tiny bones and little strength. We fell in love . . . I married her."

He bowed his head. He looked distraught, dispossessed. He reminded Millie of the migrants—refugees too—on the border between nowhere and nowhere. Eventually he spoke again.

"Our marriage got her out of the labor camp. We had a son. His name is Jordan. The birth was very hard, and the time in the labor camp completely wore her out. She wasn't strong . . . as you are. She developed tuberculosis. Now she lives in a sanitarium outside Zurich."

Millie thought about the women on the lettuce farm with tuberculosis. . . .

"I can't bring her to America . . . she needs the clean, dry Swiss air. She's no longer able to lead a normal life. Or be a normal wife. But I can't ask for a divorce." Milos's recitation reeked of despair. "If the shock didn't kill her, the Swiss authorities might. They could put her back in a labor camp."

"But she'd die. . . ."

With resigned cynicism Milos said, "The Swiss still think Germany could win the war. Switzerland is a neutral country . . . Switzerland has always been a neutral country, neutral with a tilt in the direction of the winner. Such a government can easily get rid of one sick woman. She's safe only if she's married to me . . . an American. America might win the war. Either way, the Swiss win."

"Where's your son?"

"He's being taken care of by a governess. The Swiss have fine sanitariums and equally fine governesses."

The sound of the front door chimes startled them.

"Jesus! I forgot. Damn! I'll send them away." Milos sprang up.

"Send who away?" Millie asked.

"Max Gardiner and a woman. I forgot. I said we'd go to dinner with him. I'll say you're too tired."

"No. I'm not too tired." Millie didn't want to be alone with Milos . . . not tonight.

The chimes sounded again . . . Milos answered the door. Moments later Milos, Max and a girl invaded the terrace.

Millie didn't know the girl, but she knew her type. She'd seen hundreds like her—young, pretty, ambitious, willing to do anything for the big break. Girls not as lucky as she'd been . . . or as talented. If being whistled at showed talent.

Max made the introductions. "Millie, this is Lorna Baldwin. Lorna, Millie Thorne."

"Nice to meet you, Miss Thorne. I loved you in *Monsoon.*"

Millie could read the girl's mind. Why you? Why not me? Before Millie could say thank-you, Lorna left to worship at the feet of Milos Banska.

"Oh . . . Mr. Banska . . . you're a genius. I adored *She.*" Millie watched, bemused.

A voice broke her reverie. "Where have you been? I've been looking for you." Max Gardiner was staring at her.

Millie smiled. "On a publicity tour for *Innocent Voyage.*"

"I meant where have you been all my life?"

"Please, Max. No fan magazine clichés."

"All truisms are clichés. I've been looking for you all my life."

It was true. Max Gardiner knew that everyone admired and envied him. Only he knew a strange fact . . . something was very wrong with him. He had everything he wanted . . . so much that he'd forgotten how to want anything. For him the world had become an empty place. Then he met Millie and his world grew harmonious. It was no longer empty . . . he wanted something.

Millie sighed. "Max, the studio needs you. You could write love stories. Now where do we go for dinner? You're our man about town. We count on you for decisions."

"There's a new restaurant in Malibu . . . the Dolphin. The seafood should be good. I've made a reservation. We'll go there."

During the longish drive to Malibu, Max thought of Millie sitting with Milos in the back seat of his Packard convertible. The car was expensive. So was his suit . . . his boat . . . his plane. He could afford to buy anything he wanted . . . except Millie. He couldn't buy her . . . or own her. She was beautiful, and she was steel . . . like his father. He had had everything . . . he sensed she'd had nothing. He was soft. She'd be his strength. He wanted her.

After only two months' rest, Millie was rushed into a new film, *Bad Girl*. Milos was in Mexico putting together the cast and crew of his own new film . . . to be shot on location in Guadalajara. Max filled in for Milos, taking Millie to polo matches in Santa Barbara, to dinner at the Trocadero, to Laguna Beach to look at California artists. They lunched at the Malibu Inn and Max went swimming. Millie played in shallow water . . . she didn't know how to swim. One evening Max took her to meet his father, the first Max Gardiner. The Gardiners' home was a mansion in Pasadena surrounded by acres of lawns and paths and flower gardens. Every room was hung with paintings. Millie gazed at the paintings . . . Rembrandt, del Sarto, Botticelli . . . Picasso, Degas, Monet, Manet, van Gogh . . . an incredible collection. Silently, Millie gave thanks for the education Jude Castelli had given her.

"They belong in a museum," she said.

"When my father decides to give up the ghost, I plan to turn this place into a museum."

"Where will you live?"

"I bought some acres and a house in Rancho Santa Fe." Max took in Millie's puzzled frown. "I like it. It's near the ocean a little north of San Diego . . . next to the Fairbanks Ranch."

"Is that where Doug Fairbanks and Mary Pickford used to go when Hollywood got too hectic?"

"That's where." Max checked his watch. "Time to meet the old man. I warn you, my father is eccentric . . . damn near Byzantine. Also the source from which all blessings flow."

Millie's expression became reverent. When one meets a Source for the first time, one must be properly awed.

Max Gardiner, Sr., greeted Millie genially. But under the surface charm were a pair of judgmental eyes . . . appraising, calculating. The Source was a leaner, acrid version of his son. It was as though somehow he had reduced himself to the bare essentials . . . skin, bones, sinews and a brain. Over dinner Millie enthused about the paintings . . . Max Sr. credited his son with the collection. Millie was enchanted with the house and the grounds. Max Sr. credited his dead wife with decorating the house and designing the formal gardens. Millie complimented the silver place settings . . . Max Sr. credited Paul Revere. Millie rhapsodized about the bluefish . . . Max Sr. credited the estate manager who saw to hiring the proper chef. Feeling desperate, Millie said flatly she liked the Los Angeles weather . . . Max Sr. had no comment. Millie's Max—her noisy, talkative, hyperactive Max—said nothing and drank glass after glass of wine.

After dinner, Max Sr. led the way to the library. He offered Millie a brandy.

"No thank you," Millie said. "Today I wasn't needed on the set. Tomorrow I am. At six A.M. Bright-eyed and bushytailed."

"You watch how much you drink?" Max Sr. asked.

"I have to."

"Max doesn't. Do you like the horse races at Santa Anita?"

"Yes. The horses are beautiful."

Max Sr. smiled. At least Millie took the curve of his mouth to be a smile. "Do you bet on the horses?"

Millie snorted in disdain. "No. I work too hard to throw my money away on the races. But I like watching horses run. . . ."

"Max likes to bet. He tells me you're a star . . . a movie star?"

Millie caught his irony. "Think of me as a small star on a small planet in a small solar system. Not the Orion Cluster or the Milky Way."

Max Sr. again smiled . . . broader this time. "But you make a lot of money?"

"More than I ever dreamed I'd make." She looked around the library. "And considerably less than you've made."

"Forgive my rudeness, my dear, but . . . how much *do* you make?"

"Dad! That's enough."

"It's all right, Max. I'm sure your father has his reasons for asking. Galaxy just renewed my contract. I make two thousand dollars a week."

"You will earn more next year."

"I may."

"Good. That agrees with what I've been told. I prefer successful people. They envy me less. Now let's sum up our talk. You don't drink much. You don't gamble. You don't need money. You have nothing in common with my son. Why do you want to marry him?"

"Marry Max!" Millie struggled to regain her composure. "I don't want to marry Max!"

"Max says he wants to marry you. Max is rich and will be richer. He's handsome. I believe he can marry any girl he wants."

"Max . . ." Millie turned to Max, who was leaning against the fireplace mantle. "Tell your father that I don't want to marry you." Her anger was softened by pity . . . pity for Max, who had everything and wanted what he couldn't have. And pity for herself . . . she too wanted what she couldn't have.

"Let me explain, Father," Max said softly. "Millie is in love with Milos. Everyone knows it so I'm not telling secrets."

"Milos is a fine man. Speaks five languages. A good chess player."

"I am in love with Milos . . ."

"My dear," Max Sr. said with utmost patience, "I know and respect Milos Banska. You may love him but you mustn't wait for him to marry you. That would be a sad business. Not because he's already married . . . women have loved married men since some idiot came up with the idea of marriage. You mustn't wait because he's Milos Banska. Between his career and Hannah and his son, Milos has enough to think about. He has no room for you . . . or your children."

"I have no children." Millie had long ago learned how to lie and smile as she lied.

"Not now. But in time you will want children. Max is good with children . . . he's never grown up himself." Max

Sr. nodded in his son's direction. "Millie, I'll be frank with
you. Since my son is so taken with you, I've had you investigated. Nothing is known about your prestudio years. I like
that. You're discreet. But much is known about your instinct
for movies . . . not just being a star. You know a film must
make a profit or the studio won't be able to finance new films.
You have a good business sense. So I appeal to your business
sense. Max has everything to offer. And you have everything
to gain. Think about it." He yawned. "Now, if you'll excuse
me, I'm tired." He rose and went to Millie. He took her face
in his two hands, raised it and kissed her lightly on the forehead. "Marry Max, child. He's the right man for you and
you're the right woman for him." He chuckled. "After all,
you have nothing in common. Good night."

Millie watched the old man leave the library. It struck her
that Max and his father had been speaking lines from a script
they'd memorized the night before. On the way home, she
asked, "Now what was that about? Your father had me investigated?"

"Of course. He knows how I feel about you. And getting
him behind me was the best way I could think of to ask you
to marry me. If I'd just up and asked you, you'd have laughed
at me. No one laughs at the old man."

"I love Milos and you want to marry me?" It made no
sense.

"Yes. I don't expect to take his place. You love him in a
way you will never love me. But . . ." He grinned. "That
leaves us room to maneuver."

"I wouldn't be faithful to you."

"I don't expect it. I won't be faithful either. That way you
won't feel guilty. And I won't be heartsick. Actually, that's
the beauty of it. Neither of us is capable of being faithful to
anyone for long."

"I've been faithful to Milos."

"I know. I said that was different. . . ." He groped for
words. "What you feel for Milos is beyond love . . . or sex.
I'm no poet, but I think your loving Milos is like a passion
of the soul." He paused. "It won't happen again."

No, it won't, Millie said to herself.

"And tonight you start your new life. You'll be unfaithful
to Milos. It's time."

"Tonight? You expect to . . . ?"

"I expect to make love to you."

Millie said nothing. She knew that her silence was itself an answer. But she no longer saw her way. Until Milos, she'd made love to pay her bills. What would it be like to make love to a man to whom she owed nothing . . . not clothes and food . . . not a ride when she needed one . . . not a screen test . . . not even love . . . nothing?

The idea grew within her. "We'll see, Max."

Max was content . . . he knew a yes when he heard one.

When they made love, Max held her in his arms . . . he was light-headed with desire. Millie responded with a fervor that astonished both of them. Her wantonness excited him to a pitch he'd never known . . . their orgasms were like a sudden thunderstorm.

The filming of *Bad Girl* continued at a furious pace. Milos was still in Mexico. Millie enjoyed the attention Max lavished on her. Some nights they made love . . . other nights she had a headache. Like a bad dream, the headaches had returned . . . stronger, sharper than ever. Then one day it happened. In the middle of a scene, she was raised by a giant hand and flung against a wall. Slowly returning to consciousness, she found herself lying in a strange place. She was lost. But after a few moments she realized she was lying on the lounge in her dressing room. Through a haze she saw the studio doctor looking down at her.

"Don't move," he said. "Just tell me what happened." When Millie explained that she'd had a headache—worse than any before—the doctor looked grave. Then he said, "I want you to see Dr. Ralph Schwartz today. He's a specialist in neurophsiology. His office is in Beverly Hills."

"I don't have an appointment. And I am all right," Millie said.

"I hope so. You're too valuable to the studio not to be all right. I'll call Dr. Schwartz. He'll see you today."

Millie nodded. The pain was beginning again.

When Millie left Dr. Schwartz's office, she drifted to the Beverly Wilshire. She needed a drink. She felt like she was walking on a narrow, high ridge . . . on either side the drop was straight down. To keep from falling—to face the future . . . if she had a future to face—required she keep her nerve.

Her success was no defense against fate. She might as well still be in the migrant camp.

Sitting in the dark bar nursing a brandy, her mind was full of scraps of the past. Gina making pasta. Lucia tugging on her leg. Her father on his knees picking lettuce. The old singing man in the camp. Out of the darkness of years, the song floated into her mind. She sang softly to herself. . . .

Then beat the drum slowly and play the fife lowly,

Play the dead march as you carry me along. . . .

She didn't go on. She was too conscious of the strange turns of life . . . the cheats of hope. The cold quietness of Dr. Schwartz's words stilled her. He'd said there was nothing to be done. As for the future, he would make no predictions. Given her condition, an inoperable aneurysm in her brain, she might die tomorrow . . . or next month . . . or live to be a hundred. There was no way to know.

Millie motioned to the waitress and asked for a phone. She dialed Milos's private number. Maybe he'd returned and hadn't had a chance to phone her. No answer. She dialed his office number. His secretary said he was hip-deep in chaos in Mexico. Millie listened and understood more than was said. She would never marry Milos. But it made no difference. No matter what happened between them, something lay beyond it . . . something that would never die or lessen in intensity. It came home to her now with supreme sharpness that Max had understood too. This idea fortified her will. She hung up and dialed him.

He answered on the second ring. "Millie?" He was puzzled. "Where are you?"

"In the bar in the Beverly Wilshire."

"Why aren't you on the set?"

"They're shooting exteriors. Max, your father was right."

"My father's always right. It's the family curse."

"He said I'd want babies . . . I do. I'll marry you . . . if you'll have me. And we'll have a baby."

"If I'll have you? How soon can you marry me?"

"In a week we wrap up *Bad Girl.*"

"Fine. That takes care of next week. But what about to-night . . . tonight is a good night to make a baby. Come to dinner at my apartment . . . at eight."

"At eight." Millie hung up. A powerful feeling of love came over her. Love in the past, love in the present. Its force was in the air all around her. Her father's love for her mother . . . for his farm. Her love for them both . . . for Milos . . . for her lost baby. She looked up to the heavens. "God," she whispered, "this time I'm not asking you for a favor so you can't say no. I'm telling you where I stand. I will not die! Not today or tomorrow or next year. I'll have children. My children will have children. And their children will have children. When I'm a great-grandmother, I'll discuss dying with you . . . maybe." She left the bar and walked out into the sunlight . . . refusing to be afraid.

PART 5

Mark
1992

Chapter 8

MARK TRIED to reach Nora . . . missed her three times. She'd checked out of the Bel Air by the time he called. When he called Channel 18 she hadn't yet arrived. The third time, Sheri said she was in a meeting with Mrs. Gardiner.

"And you'll never guess who else," Sheri whispered.

"Who else?"

"Tammi Meredith . . . the movie star! And her husband, Ken Savage. They say terrible things about him. He's . . . he's . . . Well, you know. Indecent."

Mark grinned at the longing in Sheri's voice . . . if only Savage would be indecent with her. It occurred to him he'd overlooked a good thing in Sheri. He smacked his forehead with his palm. Nora's secretary! Stupid!

Sheri gushed on. "And the director Jordan Banska. I love his movies . . . *Desperate Journey, He, She* . . ."

What the hell is Banska doing at Channel 18? Mark wondered.

"He's won three Academy Awards."

Banska! Nora had talked about the SOB. Were they lovers? "Sheri, girl, why has Tinseltown set up shop in Channel 18?"

"Jordan Banska's directing a play for us. Imagine."

Mark cleared his throat. "Sheri . . . *por favor,* don't tell Nora I called. She sounds busy. I'll see her tonight."

"You're so considerate, Mr. Stern," Sheri said.

"I am. 'Bye, Sheri." Mark hung up. Jordan Banska! Shit! Millie was right . . . high time he and Nora got married.

That evening Mark drove home at the legal speed limit. He needed time to clear his head . . . reorganize his priorities. He'd postponed getting married for months. Because— he grinned at the rearview mirror—San Diego was bachelor heaven. Girls called him all the time. He could knock off a quickie after the market closed and tell Nora he was working out at the club. Lisa was his latest. She didn't give a flying fuck about Nora . . . about the Gardiners. Mark rolled his eyes. He'd always known that sooner or later he'd marry Nora. Now it was sooner. Compared to the sex appeal of a ten-million-dollar account, Lisa, baby, had nothing to offer. Hail the bride! Here comes the groom!

How to explain his sudden urge for connubial bliss? He'd told Nora a lie . . . a beaut. But plausible, even heartrending. He'd lost their honeymoon money buying Ultrasonics, Inc. Crap! The money was safe in an account in his name at First Interstate. He thought of it as "fall back" money . . . should he ever need something to fall back on. Mark considered his lies. They gave him no qualms. They were all believable. That was the first rule of successful lying. Tell only believable lies. Meaning lies that were ninety-five percent true. And the untrue five percent must be plausible. Take the Ultrasonics lie. He told Nora that Reiner & Co. took the company public. That was true. He said the CEO died in an automobile accident the next day. Also true. Then the stock went down the toilet. Was that ever true! The five percent lie was saying he lost money in the stock. He never owned a share of Ultrasonics. Watching his mother blow the grocery money on penny stocks had taught him the hard way . . . never risk your money on a new issue. That was for the suckers. Now he needed another plausible lie.

Nora's car was in the garage when he drove in. Getting out of his car quickly, he pressed the automatic garage closer and crossed the small concrete courtyard to the front door of the house. The house had redwood siding and was built on a long, narrow, sloping piece of land that ended at a cliff. The plot's contour had forced the architect to invent a unique layout . . . reversing the way most houses are designed. The top floor contained a large living room and deck, a dining area, a guest bathroom and a generously sized kitchen. Down one flight of stairs were two bedrooms and a bathroom. Mark and Nora used one of the rooms as a library/TV room and the second as a shared office. The master bedroom and bath took up the entire ground floor. Sliding glass doors led from the master bedroom to a grassy area surrounded by bushes. The tiny lawn ended where the cliff dropped off to the beach and ocean fifty feet below . . . straight down. Mark had erected a wooden fence . . . low enough not to block the white water view and high enough to prevent accidents when they sun-bathed and played leapfrog . . . naked. Nora loved the house. He liked it, but he envisioned something grander . . . when they could afford to buy instead of rent. Entering the house, he laughed. He had it . . . his next lie. What a funny twist. It would work. It was logical. He was content.

Mark greeted Nora with a smile, kisses and knowing ca-resses.

Breathless, Nora asked, "What's up? I'm gone one night and you're sex-starved? Don't tell me you want to f.f. not e.f.?"

"Right. Fuck first . . ."

Nora felt between his legs. Her mouth became a greedy circle. "Ready when you are, MS."

Mark was tempted, but Nora's surprise warned him. Stick to routine. "On second thought, I'm a man of habits. Lets e.f.—eat first."

Through drinks and dinner and clearing the dishes, he limited himself to asking about Nora's meeting in L.A. and telling her about his canny trades for customers. All went swimmingly until Nora sideswiped him.

"By the way," she asked, "who is your friend Stanley Tseng?"

Mark's mouth tightened. "Who mentioned Tseng?"

"Ali . . . the other night at Millie's. She met him in Paris. Flew with him to Fiji. Said you introduced her."

"Stanley Tseng is Arthur's client. Sometimes I execute his buy and sell orders . . . if Arthur's out of the office," Mark sputtered. "Tseng is a big trader . . . Hong Kong money. Moves in and out of companies faster than I sign my name. He was in Paris. She was in Paris. Probably he picked her up in some bar. Maybe he mentioned Arthur. Remember, we managed her money . . . when she had money."

"Hong Kong money? Is he Chinese?" Nora tried to con-centrate on what Mark was saying while part of her brain struggled with a flashing picture of Fiji. She'd never been there. Where had she seen the blue water?

"Not Chinese. I think Korean. But his passport is Swiss . . . a true internationalist."

Nora brightened. "Now I remember where I saw Fiji!"
Abruptly she stopped talking. She had to think about Fiji . . .
think about the time she waited in Mark's office to pick him
up for dinner and he was closeted with Arthur. Sitting at his
desk, mooning, she'd idled through the scattered papers on
his desk. Under a report was a postcard from Fiji. She didn't
turn it over. It was probably from one of Mark's clients. Now
she asked herself . . . from Tseng? Or Ali? Or who?

"What are you talking about?" Mark sounded peeved.

"Nothing."

Mark dropped a plate.. It was Limoges. Nora had inherited
twelve place settings of Limoges porcelain china from her
mother. It splattered on the kitchen floor. "Damn! Sorry. It
slipped out of my hand."

Nora forgot Fiji . . . forget Stanley Tseng. She loved everything her mother had left her. Together they gathered up
pieces.

"Give them to me," Mark said. "I'll have the plate re-
paired."

Nora shook her head. "It's in too many pieces." She managed to smile. "We'll have to be more selective. We can only
invite eleven to dinner."

"I'm sorry."

"I know you are." Nora swept the shards onto the dustpan
Mark held. Mark then dumped them into the garbage pail.
When they finished, she asked, "You're jumpy. You don't
drop dishes, Mark. Is Arthur biting you?"

"No. I hardly see him. I've been thinking about us."

"About our getting married?"

Startled, Mark almost forgot his lines. "How'd you
know?"

Nora put down the dish she was drying. "We didn't get married because you lost our honeymoon money in a dumb stock.
Now you found the money because the stock—Ultrasonics—
bounced back. Is that why you want to get married now?"

Mark swallowed. "Who told you about Ultrasonics?"

"Tim Rourke. He switched his account from Smith Barney
to Reiner. Howie Flagg's his broker. Howie put Tim into
Ultrasonics. He said Arthur put Humpty-Dumpty together
again. Sold the company to a firm listed on the New York
Stock Exchange. Howie said he made a bundle on the stock's

comeback. The whole firm did. Except you. He said you wouldn't touch the stock. That's crazy . . . isn't it?''

Mark was outraged virtue. "I own twice what Howie does."

"That's what I told Tim. You own a chunk. I made a bet with myself that we'd get married. Pronto. Now that you made back our honeymoon money." Nora ran the tip of her tongue over his lips. "Let's make love."

Mark smiled and crossed the living room to the deck overlooking the ocean . . . trying to regain his composure.

Nora joined him, putting her arms around him. "Listen, foolish heart," she murmured. "Are you hearing wedding bells?"

Mark turned Nora around so she stood in front of him. He cupped her breasts and pushed against her buttocks. She leaned her head back . . . resting it on his shoulder. He nuzzled her ear. He could feel her breathing grow rapid . . . feel her hard nipples press against the palms of his hands.

"Let's make love," she panted.

Mark laughed nervously. "I made back every cent I lost on Ultrasonics. We have enough money for—"

"Our honeymoon. You don't have to convince me."

For an instant Nora frowned. A strange idea raced through her mind. Growing up with Barron Gardiner for a father, she had a sixth sense for a performance . . . when someone was putting on an act. Tonight Mark was pulling a con job . . . had been from the moment he'd entered the door. The kisses and caresses when he liked to eat first. The dropped dish. The stumbling around because she had his punch line. It shook him that she knew he'd made back the honeymoon money. He was giving a performance. Her anxiety about Mark and her love waged a short, silent battle. Love won.

"Come with me to the Casbah. . . ." Nora took Mark's hand.

He hung back. "I'm serious. Let's get married."

"I hear you. Ultrasonics . . . honeymoon money . . ."

Mark didn't know what to think. Nora had zapped him . . . given him back his perfect, plausible lie word for word. Exactly what he meant to say, she'd said. Weird.

"Will you marry me?"

"You bet." Nora smiled. "In sickness and in health." She slipped her arms around his neck. "We'll get blood tests and go to the City Hall at Vista . . . closer than San Diego. Civil ceremonies are the new thing. Big weddings are passé.''

More eeriness. Kissing her, he thought how her words echoed Millie's. He stepped back. ''We need a best man and a maid of honor.''

''I'll get mine. You get yours.'' She paused. ''Yours is Arthur?''

''Yeah. Arthur. But don't you get Ali,'' Mark snapped.

Nora felt a sharp twinge of anxiety. The idea of Arthur and Ali unsettled her. She disliked herself for what she was thinking. She dismissed it. ''You don't like her. I do. And she asked to be my maid of honor. If she isn't, she'll be offended.''

Mark made a wry face. ''How did she know we were going to get married?''

''She didn't. She's been pumping for us to elope to Vista.''

The Ali Cat strikes again. For a moment Mark said nothing. Then . . . ''All right. Arthur and Ali it is. You satisfied?''

''Satisfied,'' Nora said, uneasy and unsatisfied. She'd discovered she wished Mark hadn't agreed.

Mark tried to calm his nerves. The future was now . . . rosy with promise. Ali didn't matter. Only two things mattered. Jordan Banska. That name did nothing for his peace of mind. The second was . . . what the hell was it? He couldn't remember.

''By the way.'' He put on a teasing voice. ''Your onetime lover, Jordan Banska, was spotted at Channel 18 today.''

For an instant Nora looked strained . . . stalked. Then her face cleared. ''We never were lovers . . . unfortunately. He thought I was too small a fish—too young—and he was married then. So he threw me back. How do you know about Jordan?''

Mark leered. ''I have spies everywhere. What were Jordan Banska, Tammi Meredith and her husband doing at Channel 18?''

''You tried to reach me and Sheri told you?''

''Right! You were in conference. The station was lousy with glitz. She said something about the channel producing and televising a play.''

Briefly Nora outlined Millie's project. Mark stared into space, thinking. ''It won't come cheap. Can you sell it?''

"I can sell anything. Doors open for me. If they don't, I walk through them." Nora spoke with more confidence than she felt.

Mark rubbed his chin. "Fascinating idea. But what if it pulls a nothing rating?"

"As you hope." Nora's tone was caustic. "I'll bet you'll light candles that it bombs. Imploring the Lord. 'You up there, sir. One big bomb please, so Millie will lose millions.' Then Millie will be discouraged and decide to sell the station."

"How can you think me capable of such dirty prayers? Me, a lamb in wolf's clothing?"

Nora laughed. "Darling, I know you. To know you is to love you. But as far as business is concerned . . ." She gave a seductive sigh. "Enough business. I have a lovely idea . . . right out of the Kama Sutra. Give me three minutes in the bedroom alone." She left the kitchen.

Mark glanced at his watch. "Three . . . no more." When he finally started down the stairs he heard music. What was it? By the time he reached the master bedroom floor, the music was loud. Familiar. Damn! He couldn't place it. Entering the bedroom, he forgot the music. Nora lay on the bed, naked . . . her eyes closed . . . her lips parted . . . her legs spread apart. She was touching herself. Mark gasped. Nora heard Mark's gasp, opened her eyes for an instant and moved voluptuously as she continued to caress herself.

"Come, my husband," she crooned. "They're playing our tune."

For an instant Mark was becalmed. Nora reminded him of someone . . . who? Forget it. Nora would be his wife. Nothing must interfere with the marriage. Not Howie Flagg! Shit! That was the second thing that mattered! Flagg! Ultrasonics! The bastard! He'd like to kick his ass clear across the Coronado Bridge. His clothes became a trail from the door to the bed. He kissed Nora's mouth, her nipples, her belly. That SOB Flagg could fuck up his marriage . . . his life! Then he entered Nora, slowly moving in and out . . . in and out . . . their excitement rising together. He heard the music . . . he recognized it . . . Lohengrin's wedding march. He had to do something about Flagg. Then he climaxed.

The next week, Mark and Nora took their blood tests and got a marriage license. The civil ceremony was in the mod-

ern, impersonal Vista courthouse . . . legal, if chaotic. Nora
wore beige silk. Ali was maid of honor, in shimmering blue
silk. Mark wore a navy blue business suit. Arthur wore gray
seersucker. Dorothea Reiner, Arthur's wife, invited herself
to the wedding. She wore something white by Saint Laurent.
Standing in the back of the room, watching, she could have
been the bride.

Nora glanced around the room trying not to laugh. The
walls and ceiling of the wedding chapel were covered with
paintings of vivid flowers and a blue sky with fleecy white
clouds. Perched on the clouds were pink cupids wearing what
looked like diapers. Modesty, modesty, everywhere is modesty . . . even in heaven. The modest cupids were shooting
arrows at the altar. A rose arbor was painted on the wall
behind the judge.

Unfortunately, the face of the judge who was marrying
them was pulled out of shape by a new set of dentures. Either
they were poorly fitted or he had not yet grown accustomed
to them. As a result he kept putting his finger into his mouth
to adjust his dentures all through the reading of the marriage
vows. Nora and Ali behaved like schoolgirls. The judge's
dentures and the diapered cupids were too much for them.
They struggled to control spasms of laughter. Nora's hilari-
ous giggles almost smothered her "I do."

Afterward, the wedding party drove to the Valencia Hotel
in La Jolla and met at the "Library" for a champagne lunch.
The room was paneled in dark oak. Bookshelves and maroon
velvet settees lined two of the walls. The other two walls had
picture windows fronting the ocean. The room could seat
fifty. They were only five. Still, Arthur had reserved the entire room. He'd arranged everything, including a private bartender and a gourmet menu. Nora ordered *salad Nicoise* and
swallowed one bite. Mark, on the other hand, demolished a
plate of *petits filets de boeuf.* Ali and Dorothea both ordered
troute amandine . . . both toyed with their food. Arthur had
crepe suzette and a blueberry soufflé. Like Mark, he ate it
all . . . washing it down with a second bottle of Dom Perignon. As Arthur drank, he grew more exuberant . . . his
gestures broader, his voice louder. He took over from the
bartender and poured refills of champagne. It struck Nora he
refilled Ali's glass more than anyone else's. They stared at

each other constantly. Ali's eyes were all over him . . . inviting him to jump on her bones, as Pat Yocum would say. Nora was glad everyone was slightly drunk . . . especially Dorothea, who apparently noticed nothing.

Among the five of them, they finished eight bottles of champagne. Arthur drank the most . . . Dorothea was the most smashed. Eventually she got sick and Nora escorted her to the powder room. A good soldier in her wedding finery, Nora held Dorothea's head while she heaved and threw up into the toilet bowl. Afterward Dorothea stumbled to a sink, rinsed her mouth with tap water and dabbed her face with wet Kleenex. Looking into the mirror she fumed, "Damn him! He insults us with juvenile lechery."

Nora winced. Dorothea wasn't as drunk as she seemed. "Arthur is seeing the world through a champagne mist," she soothed.

"In a pig's eye it's the champagne. He's watching her like a cat watching a bird. I've seen Arthur operate before . . . more times than I care to count."

"You're imagining it, Dorothea. Arthur's playing host. Being convivial. Mark can't. He's too busy eating and drinking."

"Convivial, my ass," Dorothea said wearily. "I know my Arthur . . . the congenital philanderer. It's in his blood. I have reports from the detective I hired. I know every bedroom he's occupied . . . with or without clean sheets."

Nora could think of nothing to say.

"The one thing I thank Arthur for is consistency. I always know what he's doing." Dorothea massaged her forehead. "Why don't I trust her?" The words spilled out of her mouth. "Your Ali?"

"I don't know." Nora choked. She knew damn well why, and she was ashamed of her disloyal thoughts. She only hoped Dorothea knew nothing about Ali's schoolgirl fling with Arthur.

"She isn't really beautiful, but she has a kind of charm." There was bitterness in the set of Dorothea's lips.

"Yes," Nora said. "She is charming. You'll end up liking her very much. Everyone does."

"Don't be absurd, Nora. I will not end up liking her."

Dorothea sat down in a chair in the powder room. She

stared at herself pensively in the mirror. "I've a feeling I know her. Her family. Who is her mother?"

"Amanda Gardiner. Amanda married my uncle Hiram."

"Aaah . . . Millie's son?"

"Millie's son. Hiram is Ali's stepfather."

"Now I remember. Her mother was killed in a skiing accident."

"In Davos."

"So the Gardiner family is behind her. What a pity." Dorothea took a tube of lip gloss from her purse and applied it skillfully to her lips.

"I don't understand you, Dorothea." This was a woman from another generation, but a woman Nora had known many years. A friend of her father's—when he was alive—a friend of Millie's now . . . of many of Nora's cousins and aunts . . . a family friend.

"What is it you don't understand?"

"If Arthur has always had women, why worry about Ali?"

"Oh, Nora. You are a child. Can't you see that her act is almost foolproof? I wish she was trashier." Dorothea blotted her lips.

Nora combed her hair and applied lipstick. Then she turned to Dorothea, now slouching in the chair. "Please don't worry about Ali. I know for a fact she's not interested in married men." Nora had reminded herself with relief of Ali's list of objections to back street affairs. She hoped Ali remembered her own list.

"I wouldn't make book on that." Dorothea's voice was hoarse. "I watched her today . . . she's given him the go sign."

"The champagne has gone to your brain. . . ."

"Nora, please. I know Arthur. I know Ali's type. It's too bad, but she's a better breed than the trash he usually chooses. She's not cheap."

"She's not cheap."

"She's not crude."

"She's not crude."

"She gives new meaning to the word *cunt.*"

For an instant Nora said nothing. "I can't imagine Ali—"

Dorothea interrupted. "I can. It's funny, isn't it, how things happen? I go to a wedding and Ali Gardiner, who I never

met before, waltzes into my life and every instinct warns
me . . . Go to red alert.''

Nora's relatives had thought Mark showed respect by
agreeing to postpone the wedding date when Nora's father
died. So their objections to the small wedding were by and
large smothered. And Millie's approval cut off the dissidents
at the pass.

"Truly, Angie," Millie said, "I think the small wedding
was appropriate."

"Do you? Even Lolly and Jenny were surprised. Nora is a
Gardiner. We always welcome a new member of the family
with a big wedding party. . . ."

"You have years to welcome Mark. By the way, I'm giving
a dinner party for those of us who weren't at the wedding.
You can toast the happy couple with me."

"Oh, Millie! How exciting!"

"I am sorry Mark's mother and sister won't be coming. I
sent them invitations, but Mark says they never leave New
York."

"That's strange," Angie said.

Stranger than you know, Millie thought. They cashed in
the plane tickets I sent instead of returning them. That was
something she didn't tell either Mark or Nora.

At home in Queens, Shirley, Mark's sister, smiled at the
invitation and put it in her scrapbook . . . along with the
other item about Nora Gardiner Stern. She wasn't ready to
call in her marker. But the day would come. . . . Indeed, it
would come.

One afternoon some weeks after the wedding, Ali called
Mark. Mark took the call, cautious and curious.

"Mark, this is a wedding present call. I want to give you
and Nora something special. But I can do nothing until you
tell me about the new house you're buying. Nora says you're
thinking of one in Solana Beach."

"Solana Beach is a possibility."

"I love North County. The ocean at your doorstep . . . it's
so good for the soul. But isn't Solana Beach expensive?"

"What isn't expensive today? We're looking all over
North County . . . from Rancho Bernardo to Carlsbad. No-

thing's settled.'' Millie had not yet opened her account at Reiner & Co.

"Keep me posted. I want to surprise Nora with something splendid.'' There was a tick of silence during which Mark almost heard Ali shift gears. "And, Mark,'' she said in an intimate whisper, "I've a problem I'd like to talk to you about.''

"What kind of a problem?'' Mark asked warily.

"It's really a financial question. I need help. Have dinner with me tonight. You mustn't dine alone every night. It's bad for your digestion. And I promised Nora I'd see you one evening.''

As usual, Ali was one step ahead of him. She'd checked and found out Nora was in Chicago for three days. Kellogg's had sneezed at a San Diego time buy on Channel 18. Kellogg's' ad agency was anxious about catching the flu. If the agency stayed anxious they might cancel the buy . . . and Channel 18 would catch pneumonia. Nora explained that she was expected to pump everyone full of vitamin C.

Mark said, "My digestion's fine. Give me a thumbnail. Maybe I can give you an opinion over the phone.''

"I can't do it over the phone,'' Ali insisted. "And I'd like you to see my apartment. Then you can take me out to dinner. And I can swear to Nora that you had a decent dinner one of the nights she was away.''

Mark was in a muddle. He didn't want to get within arm's length of Ali. Still, the best way to keep informed on an enemy is by staying in touch. That's why we have diplomats, he told himself. "All right . . . dinner. Where do you live? Nora told me, but I forgot.''

"3536 Seventh Avenue. It's called Coral Tree Plaza . . . twin high-rise buildings in Hillcrest. I won't bother to give you directions. Just open to page sixty in the *Thomas Guide*. You'll find Seventh Avenue. I'm in the high rise on the left— the east building—on the tenth floor. Look for my name and number on the bulletin board outside the front door. Push the number and I'll buzz you in. Can you make six-thirty?''

"Plus or minus.'' Mark knew he was taking a risk. This could be a Venus's-flytrap, but he'd learned the drill long ago. That weekend in East Hampton when Nora had first introduced him to Ali.

* * *

Nora was summering at Millie's compound. Ali was in East Hampton while her stepparents spent the summer on the coast of Spain. Or Portugal? Estarreja . . . was that it? Or San Sebastián? Nora wasn't sure. Hiram rented the cottage on the Simone estate for Ali's summer vacation. Nora explained that the Simones were related to the Gardiners. Who isn't? Mark thought. And since Ali was entering her senior year at Bennington, Amanda agreed she didn't need a live-in housekeeper to act as a chaperone.

The second week in July Nora escaped from Martha's Vineyard. She lied like a trooper. She told her father, Millie, and the visiting entourage that she was spending the week with Ali in East Hampton. The truth was she was spending the week with Mark in his non-air-conditioned, no-ocean-view walk-up on West Sixty-fourth. The plot was to spend the weekend with Ali at her cottage. Ali had a guest room cooled by ocean breezes.

"Ali is my best friend," Nora said. "We've been best friends forever. Not like you and me. . . . You, I love. You must meet Ali. You'll love her. She'll love you." Nora assured him they would all live together happily ever after.

Mark smiled cynically. For a second he wondered if his virtuous Nora meant a ménage à trois? He! What she was doing was testing the waters. Trying him out on Ali—the freest thinker in her family—to get a reading. To see how much opposition she might have to face when she told her family she was marrying a poor boy from Queens.

Mark decided Ali's cottage was the classiest summer rental he'd ever seen. A white frame cottage surrounded by carefully tended rosebushes; inside, the personal touches that Mark soon learned to associate with Ali. Fresh flowers everywhere . . . a pair of tasteful prints signed in pencil by Miró . . . a Dufy watercolor . . . photographs of famous relatives or friends of the family . . . an antique cigarette case . . . needlepoint pillows . . . a Chinese screen.

On Saturday evening Mark's assignment was barbecuing a two-inch-thick porterhouse steak. Standing on the lawn staring at the sky, he heard ice clinking and a lilting voice. Ali joined him.

"I'm delighted finally to meet you, Mark. You are everything Nora said." She arranged herself like a happy kitten beside him and gazed up into his eyes with an impish smile.

"I told Nora I'd back you to the death. But you won't need it. You'll be a shoo-in with the family. With Millie."

"Right. I'm Mr. Nice Guy. What's not to like?" Mark exuded more confidence than he felt.

"I'm so pleased." Ali's voice was full of impending drama.

"I'm glad you're glad."

Her eyes fixed on him as though he were a distant horizon. "I am glad. I like you so much."

A deaf man would have heard more than she said as her mouth shaped the words, seen more in her sparkling eyes as they teased him, read more into her lips as they unfurled in a tantalizing smile. Mark's adrenaline shot up.

"In fact, I like you so very much it's a pity Nora found you before I did," Ali said softly, slipping her free hand through Mark's arm and pressing her soft breast against him. Mark barely moved. Automatically he glanced toward the house, where he could see Nora through the dining room window . . . setting the table.

"I'm an old-fashioned good girl, Mark," Ali confided. Her hazel eyes narrowed. "I never poach on a friend's territory. But you're so damned attractive! Mmmm. If you weren't spoken for by my baby cousin, I could be tempted to forget my principles."

The weekend was beginning to involve too many twists and turns. Mark wiggled out from under by saying, "I'm glad about your principles."

"So am I . . . most of the time. It's a shame, but that's how it is. I've a hunch we'd make beautiful music together, but I can never sleep with you." Then she squeezed his hand briefly and slipped her arm out of his. "Principles are boring, but at least we can be friends."

Mark maintained a virtuous silence. When he found his voice, he said, "Right. Friends."

"We'll just have to make do. Occasional lunches. Like good friends have. Occasional dinners." Her voice promised more.

"Nora would love dinner," Mark blurted out.

Ali thought about this. "We'll have dinner with Nora, and we'll have dinner without Nora." Her smile was mischievous. "We may have things to say to each other that we'd rather Nora didn't hear." Then she shrugged her shoulders. "But for now, Mark, my pet, how is the steak coming?"

The hairs on the back of Mark's neck quivered. "I'm about to turn it."

"Very good. The corn is in the pot. The salad is ready. It will all time out beautifully." Ali stood on tiptoe and pecked his cheek. "I am so pleased we met." She licked her lips and smiled. Then she turned and started toward the house.

Mark stared after her, mesmerized by the wiggle of her dancer's buttocks beneath the skintight French jeans. He blinked. What he'd been subjected to was a virtuoso performance complete with appropriate gestures . . . guileless eyes . . . a provocative smile. He gave thanks for the protective presence of Nora. Nora? Should he tell her about the conversation? No! Let it drop. Then the words *lunch* and *dinner* floated into his consciousness. It won't happen, Mark promised himself. No way! He'd have a previous appointment that he would make the minute Ali called. If she called. Suppose she didn't call? Christ! What was he thinking?

Ali didn't call. Weeks went by. Every time the telephone rang, Mark's tension rose. It was a customer. A co-worker. His boss, John Eckstein. Nora. Everyone but Ali. Then came the last week before Labor Day. Nora was zonked into the compound on the Vineyard . . . arranging her father's birthday party. She apologized profusely for not inviting him. Too soon. But she swore they'd dance at her father's next birthday party. That's when Ali called.

"Mark . . ." Her lilting voice floated over the wire. "I'm driving in from East Hampton. I have to see the dentist. Let's do lunch today."

"Who is this?" He knew damn well who it was.

"Don't be silly. It's me." Still no name. "Tomorrow I fly to the Vineyard to help Nora with party fixings. It's Uncle Barron's birthday. You know. Barron is Nora's father."

"I know." Mark was furious at her arrogance, her maddening confidence he would know her voice. Certain he was waiting for her call. Fuck her! "I can't have lunch today."

"You must. I need your help." Her voice dropped an octave. "Mark! Please!"

"I have a lunch date."

"Break it."

"It's with an important customer."

"Say you're sick."

"I can't be sick. I trade thousands of shares for him."

"Okay. You're not sick. You have a terrible emergency. Your mother's sick. You do have a mother?"

"I have a mother."

"Please, Mark. You must! I need a man's advice . . . a man's point of view. An unbiased man who isn't sleeping with me . . . who has never slept with me . . . who isn't hoping to. . . ." She started to laugh. "You aren't hoping to sleep with me? Are you, Mark?"

"No! I am not!"

"There! That's what I mean. I need the advice of a man with character. Who has nothing to gain or lose sexually by his advice." Her delivery was perfect.

"Ali, I don't see how—"

"Mark, you are a darling." Ali knew when to rake in her chips. "Why don't we lunch at the Chateau? I'll meet you at one—"

"At eleven forty-five. Before the crowd crowds in. I can take an hour. No more." He hung up and walked to Dudley Ryan's desk. "Dudley, old buddy, can you take my calls for an hour? My sister's in town, and she insists I take her to lunch so she can talk about her rape. She was raped in a movie theater watching *Rambo II* . . . or *III*. I can't keep them straight. Now she's pregnant . . ."

Dudley gave him a bored look. "If you'll cut the crap, I'll take your calls. Go get laid. And give your sister my number."

Ali toyed with her salmon, sipped her white wine. Her voice was low-key, crisp . . . her head tilted . . . her eyes big and shining. Mark tried to concentrate on his shrimp and on her problem. It was hard. Her body language was unbelievable.

"Okay. You got a lousy grade in art history . . . your major."

"Awful! I don't usually care about my grades . . . as long as I pass. But this is different. I deserved an A. I worked for it. And I know more about art history than most museum curators. Professor Slocum, the skunk, gave me a C-minus. Amanda—she's my mother—will have a hemorrhage."

"You told me that your skunk, Professor Slocum, is head of the department? He should be able to judge your work."

"He didn't. He's crazy."

"Come on. Maybe you can't take tests."

"When I want to, I do beautifully on tests."

"You had an attack of amnesia."

"I wasn't high on pot . . . or drunk, if that's what you mean. I answered every question perfectly . . . facts, dates, painter, brush style, the name of the model, the apprentice who stretched the canvas. But he gave me a C-minus. Why?" Her eyes narrowed.

"I don't know why."

"I'm trying to decide if I should go to the dean—the dean's also a man—when school opens. And protest."

"On what grounds?"

"On the grounds that I deserved an A. If I let that bastard get away with C-minus now, he could pull the same stunt next semester. I'm taking another course in art history. He's the professor. Then what do I do?"

"I repeat. I don't know."

"Slocum's acting like a cad."

"A what?" Mark laughed. "A cad? Ali, you sound like a character in a 1920s novel. So he gave you a lousy grade. That doesn't make him a cad."

"It does. After all, we were lovers."

Mark stopped chewing. He swallowed the piece of shrimp slowly and spoke even slower. "You and your professor were lovers?"

"Attractive women always have sex with their professors. It's a quid pro quo. Good sex . . . good grades. The trade-off is almost as old as . . . well . . . as an eye for an eye." Her words were heartfelt. "What isn't quid pro quo is my grade. C-minus."

"Maybe the sex wasn't so good . . . like a C-minus?" Mark couldn't resist the crack.

Ali was inflamed. "Mark Stern, that's stupid. If you weren't practically engaged to Nora, I'd show you . . ." Her mouth tightened. "I'm the best lay in Bennington. If you want a sample—strictly off the record—let's get out of here and . . ."

Mark got the message. He had to think of something. He did. "Is that the Slocum who was nominated for a Pulitzer?"

"The same. Also he's a consultant to the Met. A Knight of the Papal Guard. A rat!"

"And he gave you a C-minus. . . ." Life in the fast lane was complicated.

"After sleeping with me. Honestly, Mark, I am good in bed." She fluttered her eyelashes. "We did it twice a week. Sometimes three times."

"That often? Slocum must be in his sixties."

"I turned him on."

Mark was convinced. She turned him on. He thought about this as he reeled out his idea. "Okay. You were eager. You pressed all the right buttons. You blew him . . . that blew it. Don't you see what happened?"

"What happened?"

"Slocum outguessed you. He covered his ass." Mark gave Ali a sympathetic look. "Do a 'for instance.' You're Ali. I'm Slocum. We're in the dean's office. You say, 'I've been sexually harassed. I had sex with Professor Slocum because he insisted. He said if I wanted a good grade—like an A—I must sleep with him.' "

"I'd never put it that crudely. I'd be more subtle."

"Subtle yes, subtle no, Slocum'll deny it. He'll gallantly claim that you, you poor girl, have lost your mind. He would never force his attentions on you. To be truthful, he had to fend you off. Your wild infatuation. Until you began making unseemly advances, he felt like a father toward you. That kind of crap."

"The bastard! He insisted."

"Sorry. You'll never prove who was sexually harassing whom." Mark sounded the note of authority. "He can say, 'Alison says she slept with me to get a good grade.' "

"He insisted. So I did."

"Great. Then I say—I mean me as the dean—I say, 'Did you get a good grade?' "

"No!"

Mark grinned. "Exactly Slocum says, 'I did not sleep with you, Alison. As proven by the fact that Alison did not get a good grade. I'm a man of honor. If I had done something so foolish as to sleep with Alison, she would have gotten a good grade.' The dean nods his head in agreement. He has his own delicious memories of lovely young women in search of good grades. You did not get a good grade. Case closed. End of discussion." Mark took a sip of wine and smiled at Ali. Smugly.

Ali opened her mouth. Closed it. Finally she said, "Right. Thank you for the lesson. I may change my major to modern art."

"You're welcome. And I agree. Next semester keep away from old lechers." It was time to end the lunch. He stood up. "You stay and have dessert. I've got to get back to the office. My buy and sell orders are steaming. I'll get the check."

"Don't bother with the check." Ali's best smile was back. "Lunch is on me."

"That's silly."

"I owe you. You taught me something. The student always pays." She tilted her head. "I liked the way you looked at me while I talked."

"Oh?"

"Oh, yes. You have a dirty mind, Mark Stern." She started to laugh. "When we have dinner, you can pick up the tab."

For the rest of the week, Mark struggled with the question of whether or not to tell Nora about his lunch. He wasn't sure, and he wanted to be sure before saying anything. On the Tuesday after Labor Day, Nora returned from Martha's Vineyard. He still hadn't decided. Nora decided for him.

"Ali said you were so helpful a couple of weeks ago," she murmured as she played with his hair.

"I did my best. I'm glad she thought I was helpful."

"She raved about you."

"Is that good?"

"It's great. She swings weight with Amanda. Who swings weight with Hiram. Who swings weight with Millie. Better to have Ali on your side than against you."

Nora was right. Aaah, Ali. A complicated mix of sugar, spice and things not very nice. The enigma next door who was nobody's dummy. He was the dummy. What was he thinking? That she wouldn't tell Nora? Maybe she looked like a classy broad, but when the oohs and aahs stopped, you saw something else . . . an alley cat with claws and teeth. And a ravenous hunger. Mark promised himself the next time he saw Ali Gardiner and Nora wasn't with them, he'd tell Nora all about it . . . before Ali did.

At 6:35 Mark stepped from the elevator on the tenth floor and looked around.

"This way, Mark," Ali called. She was waiting for him in the open doorway to her apartment . . . wearing a pink mini dress with a halter top that fit like a swimsuit. As she turned away, Mark's eyes were trapped by her rear. He remembered the weekend in East Hampton when they first met, and he sighed. All these years later Ali still had tight, muscular, dancer's buttocks. Already nervous at seeing her without Nora, he was more so at the siren sight of her.

After offering him a scotch and soda, she insisted on showing off the condo.

"I haven't finished furnishing . . . I haven't the money. But I've filled in with a few things I brought back."

Mark looked around. The condo was impressive . . . at least two thousand square feet—larger than most houses—with a spacious living room and spectacular views of Balboa Park and the bay. But it was barely furnished . . . the second and third bedrooms were empty.

Mark finished his drink as they finished the tour . . . perfect timing. Ali offered a refill.

"No thanks. I made a reservation for seven at Stefano's. It's around—"

"The corner." Ali sparkled. "A neighborhood hangout. The manicotti is divine." She gave Mark an appraising look. "So are the cantinpalo sausages. The sausages are almost as large as . . ." She licked her lips and sighed. "Let's go. I'm starving."

Feeling a tense mix of relief and disappointment, Mark followed Ali. Whatever was on her mind, it wasn't sex . . . not at the moment anyway. When they reached the restaurant, a crowd was waiting for tables. Ali was enough of a local celebrity to be welcomed by the maître d'.

"Aaah . . . Miss Gardiner!" he exclaimed. "Mr. Stern didn't tell us you were joining him tonight. One moment, please." He scurried off . . . returning almost immediately. "Your favorite table is ready. Please follow me." Mark trailed Ali and the maître d' between tables noisy with laughing, chattering diners and up a half flight of stairs to the main dining room. Mark noted that "Ali's table" was in the front of the restaurant.

"Would you like a drink?" the maître d' asked.

"Yes. A glass of wine," Ali said.

The maître d' handed Mark a wine list. "I suggest number forty-three. You like that wine." He smiled at Ali.

Mark glanced at 43. A Barefoot Creek white zinfandel . . . fifty-two dollars a bottle. Ali could still spend money. What the hell! He'd find a way to put the meal on his expense account. "Number forty-three will do . . . not too chilled."

Mark and Ali chatted. The condo was perfect . . . so convenient. The garage had three levels. Ali's two parking spaces were on the top level near the elevator. The view was . . . The waiter brought the wine.

"Forty-three sir." He poured a little into Mark's glass and waited.

Mark sipped the wine and nodded. The waiter poured the wine and left.

Ali grinned mischievously. "Having thrown away millions, I'm now a working stiff. But Aldo was worth it . . . in a way. He was such fun in bed. Latins are not lousy lovers."

"Mmm . . ." Mark smiled. What was he supposed to say? Was that a come-on or a lead-in to the reason for the dinner? He waited. It was neither. It was the Aldo story. Mark had heard the Aldo story from Nora. Like it or not, he would hear it again.

Eventually the waiter came. Ali ordered angel hair pasta with a red sauce. Glancing at her defiantly, Mark selected fettuccine with shrimp and a side order of cantinpalo sausages. Ali smiled archly at the sausage order while continuing her Aldo story. Half listening, Mark wished she'd get to the point. In due time the pasta was set in front of Ali. Mark's fettuccine and cantinpalo sausages followed.

Before beginning to eat, Ali said softly, "Dennis, my landlord, is selling my condo. He offered me first crack at buying it."

"Will you buy it?"

"He wants heaps of money." She sipped her wine slowly.

"How much?" Mark decided the dinner was to solicit his advice on the condo . . . to buy or not to buy.

"Two hundred thousand. The mortgage is one hundred thirty thousand. I need seventy thousand cash. It's a steal."

"Mmm. Nice layout. Good building. Convenient. It's worth the money. Buy it."

The waiter poured the last of the wine. "Would madam like another bottle of number forty-three?" Mark was about to bark, The hell she would, when the waiter added, "Compliments of the house."

"I'd love another bottle of wine." Ali smiled graciously and the waiter left. Twirling her fork to pick up the pasta, she murmured, "Mark, dear. As you know better than most, I don't have seventy thousand dollars."

Mark's fork and the sausage he'd speared froze midway between plate and mouth. "Ask your stepfather for it. Hiram Gardiner can write a check for seventy thousand—or seven hundred thousand—and not bother to enter it in his checkbook." His fork unfroze and continued to his mouth. He chewed contentedly on sausage, forgetting whom he was talking to.

They ate in silence. When the second bottle of wine arrived, Mark toasted Ali and her new condo. Ali clinked glasses, smiling. Pleased with himself, his advice, and euphoric from wine, Mark smiled back. He remembered pleasures past . . . the years B.N. . . . before Nora.

Ali put her glass down gently. When she spoke her tone was caressing. "Mark, I can't ask Hiram. He could but he won't lend me a cent. He's never forgiven me for throwing away the money Amanda left me. He insists I earn my keep before I buy a condo." Saying this, Ali devoured the last of her pasta.

Mark gathered his forces. "Okay. Scratch Hiram. Ask another relative. Millie? Or won't she because Hiram won't?"

"Exactly. And no one else in the family will for the same reason." Ali gazed at him appealingly.

"Well . . ." Mark put on his business hat. "If Hiram won't lend money and the family won't, apply for a bank loan."

"I did. Wells Fargo turned me down. I don't have a real job yet and I sold my authentic antiques in London at Christie's. Remember . . . I furnished a villa. I don't have collateral, nothing to justify a loan. I'm broke." Her smile was shy.

Mark didn't smile back. In his world, when people like the Gardiners were broke, they bought one less house . . . or sold the yacht. Then there were people like the Sterns. When they were broke, they were dispossessed. He knew Ali had drained her account at Reiner & Co., but was she broke the way Gardiners were broke . . . meaning she was tight for immediate cash? Or was she flat-ass broke . . . Stern-type broke? He was getting the impression she was Stern-type broke.

"How can you buy the condo if you're broke?"

Ali's eyes were fastened on Mark. "It's worth the price. You said so yourself."

Mark had the nasty feeling she was weighing him, judging how to use him to her advantage . . . if not his. "Yes. But you don't have the money. It's the buy that got away. There'll be others."

Ali tilted her head. In a tantalizing voice she said, "You could lend me the money, Mark. We're old friends. We could be better friends. . . ." She took a sausage from his plate and licked it. "Good friends."

Mark hurtled to a conclusion. She was propositioning him. The image of having sex with Ali and her dancer's ass got to him. He breathed deeply to calm himself. Stupid! He had to stop the proposition before it was made—or stupid or not—he might take her up on it. Christ! He'd been wanting to since that first weekend. "You're an attractive woman, Ali," he confessed, "but you're Nora's best friend. . . ."

Ali sucked on the sausage before biting through it and sliding a piece into her mouth. Mark cringed. Ali munched and smiled. "It's a sausage, Mark . . . just a sausage." She stroked the remaining piece of sausage with the tip of her tongue, then put it all in her mouth. "Mmmmm . . ." She chewed lasciviously. "Dear Mark, there's nothing about me worth seventy thousand dollars. I give it away for free too often. I even once offered it . . ." She fluttered her lashes. "You could lend me the money."

"You're crazy!" Mark snorted. "I don't have seventy thousand!"

"Nora said you've been saving money for your honeymoon. But you didn't go on a honeymoon so you must have some money."

Mark had trouble speaking. When he got the words out he was in shock. Outraged. Furious at himself for having dinner with Ali in the first place. For not guessing that a quagmire was waiting.

"Nora and I pooled our money . . . it's now our buy-a-house fund. Have you talked to Nora about this?"

"Of course not." Ali's tongue wet her lips. "Mark, dear,

I only talk to you. We understand each other. We could be such good friends. . . .''

"I don't have any money!" he snarled with frustration. "And I can't take a cent out of our house fund."

"Mmm. Nora would notice. But don't you have a private account? A secret one Nora doesn't know about?"

Mark choked. Ali was a hound dog chasing a fox. "No, I don't have a secret account!"

"How unlike you. Well, I prepared for that. I'm going to make it easy for you to lend me the money."

"If you can make it easy for me, why not take the money yourself?"

"I can't. You have an advantage I don't. You're a stock-broker. You have clients who let you handle their money." Ali's smile was tantalizing.

Mark felt the danger. He mustn't buy Ali's sizzle. There was no steak on that platter. "Ali, if you're thinking I can borrow money from a client, you're wrong. I can't. If I told a customer I needed a loan, he'd lose confidence in me."

"You don't need a loan, Mark. I do."

"What the hell are you driving at?"

"I need your help. So I'll make it worth your while to lend me the money. Not by sleeping with you . . . although that could be an extra. I'll give you a new client . . . a big, new client."

"Who?" Was she thinking of Millie?

"And this big, new client will give you full power of attorney over his account."

It's not Millie.

Ali spoke slowly, chewing on each word as though she were eating grapes with seeds and must be careful. "When you acquire his account—which runs to millions—you can borrow enough to lend me what I need."

"That's misuse of client funds."

"Why misuse? You're only borrowing the money. You can pay it back with—"

"No!" Mark exclaimed.

"Pay it back with the commissions you make churning the account. I know you, Mark Stern. You will churn the account."

"Who are you thinking of?" Mark asked in a dry voice.

Ali gave him a conspiratorial smile. "Dr. Abe Lombard.

You know Dr. Abe . . . Millie's personal physician . . . a cousin of sorts. We had dinner last week. He complained about his broker. With proper guidance, he'll switch to you.''

The prospect of a big account—free of Millie's watchful eye—ran through Mark's blood like warming brandy. "How much does he have in the market?''

Before Ali could answer, the waiter approached. They both ordered espresso, skipped dessert and waited for the waiter to leave.

Then Ali said softly, "About five million.''

"That much?''

"That much and it's all yours. Abe's five-million-dollar account for a seventy-thousand-dollar loan to me.''

Mark wrestled with his eagerness. "If I borrow from Abe's account, I'd be stealing. It's grand larceny. You go to jail for that. Jail is a rotten experience. I don't want the account.''

"You must take it, Mark. I've already recommended you.''

"Without asking me?''

Ali shrugged. "You're always pitching the family for accounts. If you refuse Abe, he'll be upset. It'll start talk in the family.''

Mark waited. This wasn't the end of it.

"And if you take the account and don't lend me the money, you'll regret it. I'll wait a week—maybe two—then tell Millie what you did to me.'' She gave him a small smile.

"What I did to you?''

"Once, when Nora was out of town on business, you invited me to dinner. I accepted . . . we *are* family. Dinner was pleasant. But when you brought me home afterward, you asked for a nightcap. I'll hold back the tears as I explain how you tried to force yourself on me . . . to rape me . . . you beast.'' In a sexy, sotto voce tone she murmured, "As if you would ever need to rape me. Anyway, I kicked and fought wildly, but you were too strong. You tore off my dress. At this point I think I will sob. If you hadn't been drunk, I'm sure you would have'' her look was both amused and lustful—"had your way with me. How exciting. Anyway, I managed to get you out the door . . . slammed and locked it.''

Ali sighed and said in a schoolgirl voice. "What do we do, Grandmother? How do we protect Nora from that monster? That's you, Mark . . . the monster.'' Her tone flattened. "Take me seriously, Mark.''

Mark did. He knew Ali. And what's more, he wanted Abe's five-million-dollar account that was hanging out there . . . a ripe peach begging to be plucked. "You win," he said. "If Dr. Abe asks me to handle his account, you get the money for your condo."

"You are a darling. I could hug you. Nora's so lucky to have found you. I thought so the first time I met you in East Hampton." Ali's face beamed with goodwill.

Mark blinked. Ali had trapped him once before . . . shame on Ali. Now he'd allowed her to trap him again . . . shame on him. He'd never again see her alone. "It's best you not mention this dinner to Nora," he said.

"Mum's the word." Ali glanced about the room to see if anyone at a table might know them. "Call me tomorrow. I'll make an appointment for Dr. Abe to see you. My number is 398-7878."

Mark penciled the number into his address book . . . to be erased when this arrangement ended. "One more thing, Ali . . ." His voice had a cold, sharp edge. "If you really want that condo . . ."

"Dear Mark, what one more thing?" Ali's mask of goodwill vanished. In its place was an Ali Gardiner Mark had never seen. Manipulative, vain, arrogant . . . also frightened and childish. Not as tough as he thought.

"You work on Millie's TV series. Keep me posted on how it goes. Gossip . . . dirty linen . . . who's doing what to whom."

Ali relaxed. "That's easy. Won't Nora tell you?"

"Yes. What she knows. But she hasn't your gift for looking under rocks. And she won't sleep with the boys. You will. You'll be my spy at Channel 18. Say yes, Ali."

"Yes."

Later that evening, Mark sat at his desk making notes on the dinner. He thought about Ali. He knew her. But she didn't know him. He'd let her think she had him by the short hairs. But if the shit hit the fan, he'd tell Nora that Ali had wanted him to steal for her. He'd refused . . . she'd blackmailed him. Nora would believe him. Millie would believe Nora. He'd have the proof. The canceled check for seventy thousand dollars he'd give Ali for the condo. Mark made more notes on Ali and Dr. Abe . . . code name, Coyote. The name fitted. Ali Cat was like a coyote. As for himself, the dinner proved that his lust for Ali—as well as his scruples—came in a poor second to his lust for money. Mark shrugged. So he wasn't a saint.

Two days later Dr. Abe showed up at Mark's office. He brought with him a list of his portfolio.

Ali had been right. Dr. Abe did have stocks and bonds with a current market value of about five million dollars. His last broker had him in safe income producers . . . utilities and basic industries . . . 3M, GM, GE, IBM, and so on. All low-beta stocks. Dr. Abe liked the dividend checks low-betas provided but he was antsy for more action. He'd heard about high fliers . . . high-beta stocks. He courteously explained to Mark their meaning. High-beta stocks soared when the market soared. Low-betas barely moved. Mark did not mention that beta stocks were his lifeblood. In at 6:01 . . . out at 9:00 . . . back in at 11:30 . . . out again at 12:59. Four trades and four commissions in one day. If Dr. Abe wanted high-betas, he'd get them. Mark made only one proviso.

"To do that kind of trading, I need your power of attorney. So I can turn on a dime without calling you."

"My advice would be useful. I'm a sophisticated investor."

"I'm sure you are, but I can't handle your account any other way. High-betas go up and down on the whiff of a rumor. About a palace revolution . . . interest rates . . . an endangered species. The instant I smell trouble I must be free to pull you out . . . or put you in. If I can't reach you— say, you're with a patient and you don't want to be disturbed—it could be too late. We might miss the move."

"Ali thinks very highly of you." Dr. Abe sounded as if Ali's opinion mattered.

"I'm good," Mark said immodestly. "When my customers follow my advice, they sometimes make killings."

Dr. Abe said, "I want to make a few killings."

Dr. Abe gave Mark power of attorney. Once the papers were signed, Mark explained that Abe would get a monthly statement telling him how much money Mark had made for him.

After he left, Mark rubbed his temples. Fantastic! He'd make huge commissions churning Abe's account. Much more than Ali's seventy thousand. He might even make the fool some money.

A few weeks later, Mark arrived home to find Nora waiting, drinks waiting, news waiting. He barely had time to sit down.

"Ali did it again . . . landed butter side up. Guess what she did?"

Mark stretched out. "Okay. What's new on the Ali Gardiner front?"

"She bought her condo. Where'd she get the money?"

Mark passed it off. "Hiram. Where else?"

"Not a chance. Hiram was against her buying a tent until she earned money. How'd she do it?"

"A bank. Banks are looking to make loans on condos."

Nora traced the outline of her lower lip pensively. "Banks are not her style. And she asked no one in the family for a loan."

"How much did the condo cost?"

"Two hundred thousand."

Mark dismissed the Ali questions with an airy, "She had some money squirreled away. She inherited three million."

"She told me she blew it all."

"Maybe not quite all."

Nora rose to go to the kitchen. "I'm going to check the family. I'm curious where the money came from."

"If you're so curious, ask her."

"I can't. She'd be offended. It's intruding. Besides, sooner or later she'll tell me. She can't keep a secret."

Mark sipped his drink and smiled. He knew better. This was one secret Ali would keep. He'd mailed her a photocopy of his canceled check. With a short note warning her what would happen if she ever indulged a whim to tell Millie or Nora or anyone who bankrolled her.

Chapter 9

THE TWO-ROOM-AND-BATH cottage occupied by Dorothea Reiner—complete with a moon deck for nighttime contemplation of a woman's place in the universe—was one of the forty-two identical cottages in Spa Pacifica . . . the reclusive, expensive, widely revered health spa. Although jaded clients referred to the spa as "the fat farm," at least once a year those who were rich enough came from the four corners of the world to Lindbergh Field in San Diego. There they were met by the Spa Pacifica limousine and driven forty miles north to the spa. Only a few decades ago, the sixty acres owned by the Spa Pacifica were rugged clay mountains and steep ravines covered by cactus and dry golden brush. But an army of laborers—aided by bulldozers, backhoes, compactors and levelers—had rounded the mountains and filled in the ravines and changed the arid, ugly land to lush gardens, artificial lakes, streams that bubbled (thanks to concealed pumps), and gently rolling hills. Once the landscaping was complete, the forty-two cottages, a dining room and recreation room, a gymnasium and luxurious spa and other athletic facilities were constructed.

The Spa Pacifica had the feeling of a children's summer camp in Shangri-la. And considering the air of serenity that enveloped the landscape, it might well have been that fabled place . . . reserved for the blessed few. Meaning those who could afford to spend thirty-eight hundred and forty dollars . . . the minimum cost of a one-week stay at the spa. But for the few clients who, among equals, were more than equal—those who demanded the freedom to come and go at will—a house was set aside . . . at half the weekly rate . . . a mere one hundred thousand dollars a year . . . to be paid in advance. Millie Gardiner and Dorothea Reiner were among the more equal.

Having spent two weeks being pampered by daily massages—both Swedish and Japanese—mud baths, pore-cleansing facials, manicures and pedicures—as well as indulging in light exercise—low-impact aerobics and paddling about the pool aided by small inflated balloons—Dorothea was anxious to leave. She had not had a single drink in two weeks—not even a glass of wine—and the cuisine at Spa Pacifica was a disaster . . . fresh juices and vegetables, a variety of yogurts, cereals heavily laced with bran, and herbal tea. She paced around her luggage while swearing silently at her chauffeur. Where the hell was he? Her irritation evaporated when a limousine stopped at the entrance and Millie Gardiner got out of the car.

Millie was staying for a week. Her cottage at the spa was her bolt hole . . . where she dug in when she didn't want either to see or to hear from anyone. For the last week she'd been wakened by raging headaches . . . jagged bolts of pain. The attacks lasted only seconds, but these were the symptoms that had sent her to Dr. Keller originally. They left her shaken, holding her breath . . . waiting for the next attack. Now she needed freedom . . . to be alone with her fear. To consider the possibility that her health was deteriorating at an increasingly rapid pace . . . that her time on earth was growing short . . . shorter even than she had imagined when she stood on the sidewalk in front of Scripps Memorial Hospital.

Nora had called the other day to tell her the wonderful news . . . she was pregnant. Even as she congratulated Nora, she knew she was in a race . . . a life-and-death race. Would she live long enough to see Nora's baby born?

"Millie!" Dorothea holloed. "I was going to call you to congratulate you. You're the patron saint of San Diego. Your television idea is the most exciting thing that has happened here in years. It will bring theater to everyone . . . free. And with box office names like Al Pacino . . . Michele Pfeiffer . . . Tammi Meredith, even Arthur—who is fixated on sports—will watch."

The words drew Millie's undivided attention. "I'm glad you like it. . . ."

"Like it! I love it! It's using television as the media should be used."

"Thank you." Millie gave Dorothea a probing look.

"News does travel fast. Who mentioned the program to you
. . . at whose party?"

A strained embarrassment came over Dorothea. "Arthur
did. One morning at breakfast. Was he telling tales out of
school?"

"I wonder who told Arthur."

"Didn't you? You two often speak about financial matters." She laughed awkwardly. "I know he's not your only
financial adviser. There is Hiram and Warren Whatshisname.
Barret . . . Baffet . . . something like that. But Arthur and
you talk all the time."

Millie's smile was spare, meticulous. "I haven't mentioned
the program to Arthur. How did he find out about it?"

"I don't know. Does it matter?" Although Dorothea had
no idea why, she was embarrassed.

"Yes, it matters. I'd like to know."

Grasping at straws, Dorothea made a connection. "Probably Mark Stern told him. Nora must have told Mark."

"Probably." Millie studied Dorothea . . . a hard, direct
gaze that had no interest in simple politesse. As she turned
away, she said, "We must lunch, Dorothea."

"Of course. 'Bye." Dorothea's relief at Millie's departure
was palpable. She resumed circling her luggage. Now where
was that idiotic chauffeur of hers?

That week the market was quiet. Up three points one day
. . . down five points the next. The volume . . . zilch. Less
than one hundred thirty million shares one day . . . about
one hundred fifty million the next. What trading there was
was institutional. Customers' men like Mark seldom got a
whiff of the action. It was distant thunder . . . they heard the
sound coming from over the horizon but never saw the lightning. Mark'd made a few small trades for his accounts but
nothing to write home about. Millie's money was still gathering interest she didn't need in a Reiner & Co. money market account. Why the hell hadn't she arranged to transfer the
money to her new trading account . . . to him? The day was
so quiet Mark thought of taking a long lunch, or—and this
showed how bored he really was—scanning a Reiner & Co.
analyst's report. A hand touched his shoulder.

"Mark Stern," a woman said. "The man I was looking
for."

Mark spun his chair slowly . . . arrogantly. Then he swallowed and jumped to his feet.

"Mrs. Reiner . . . I mean . . ."

"My name is Dorothea. Mark, I was at your wedding."

"Sure, Dorothea. What are you doing here?"

Dorothea looked understatedly expensive in a beige nubbed silk pants suit and a silky black turtleneck. Her only jewelry was a diamond-and-sapphire brooch pinned to the lapel of her jacket. On her head was a dashing black bowler with a small multicolored feather in the band.

"I was planning to lunch with Sara Miller . . . an old friend. She's a vice president at the Merrill Lynch office on B Street. But one of Sara's important clients showed up . . . I was bumped. Why don't we have lunch? My treat?"

"I'd love to," Mark mumbled, "but it's still the middle of the trading session . . . it's only three o'clock in New York. I never leave my desk during the—"

"Never say never. Arthur just left for a massage. He says the market's in the doldrums. I'll bet you haven't written five tickets all morning."

Mark was intrigued . . . she knew the lingo. He laughed. "You'd lose, but I won't bet I'll write a seventh."

"So we'll lunch." She nodded toward the next cubicle. "If you ask Jim Collins nicely, he'll cover for you."

Jim looked up from his CRT and grinned, flattered that the boss's wife knew his name. "Live it up, Mark. I'll stand guard."

"Right on, comrade! I'll eat for both of us."

Mark and Dorothea started toward the door.

It turned out that Dorothea had made a reservation at Flo's, a trendy restaurant in the Gaslight District. As they walked and chatted, Mark wondered what Dorothea had in mind. His filling in for a broken lunch date didn't ring true. She and Mark were shown to a prominent table . . . one of a half dozen tables reserved for the restaurant's most important clientele.

Dorothea ordered a martini . . . Mark, a dry sherry. Mark chatted up a storm about business. What the rumor mill rumored about the next takeover attempt . . . which CEO would be the next to try an LBO . . . the recent Chapter 11 bankruptcy of an overleveraged retail chain. None of it earthshaking or reeking of inside information. Still, it fascinated

Dorothea. She ordered a second martini . . . Mark sipped his sherry. Daytime drinking played havoc with his thinking. They ordered and continued their random talk about the market. When they were served, Mark concentrated on his lasagna stuffed with stewed duck. He ate . . . he didn't talk. If Dorothea had something to say, he would give her every chance to say it.

Dorothea ate her Venetian-style liver with diced onions and sipped her martini. The glass was empty before she finished eating. Mark could see her inwardly debating a third. The need for a clear head won. Dorothea finished her liver using water—not gin—to wash it down.

"Tell me," she said with splendid disinterest, putting her knife and fork down. "Do you like working for Arthur?"

Loaded questions called for non-answer-type answers. "Best job I ever had. Arthur knows the market inside out."

"He says you're a comer. That's why he works late with you so often. He wants to teach you all he knows. . . ."

The lasagna went dry in Mark's mouth, but he continued to chew. Arthur Reiner hadn't spent five minutes with him . . . not in the morning, nor at noon, nor night. What a damn fool thing to tell his wife without warning him first. He glanced at Dorothea and was brought up short. She seemed to be laughing at him.

"Arthur has been very helpful."

"Arthur is famous for being helpful."

The conversation reached a choke point. Mark hoped he still sounded natural. "You must know I'm handling one large account . . ." He cleared his throat. "I'll soon be handling another. I need all the help I can get."

"Yes, you do." Dorothea was all sympathy. Then, catching the waiter's eye, she said, "Two coffees, please. Black." She ordered without asking Mark if he wanted coffee . . . or how. "And no dessert," she added. After the waiter left, she said, "I hope you don't mind missing dessert. Any dessert worth eating is a mine field of cholesterol. As Arthur's wife, I'm an authority on cholesterol."

"I rarely eat dessert. In fact, I rarely eat lunch away from my desk."

"You're a good man, Mark Stern. Loyalty to the hand that feeds you is an admirable trait."

Dorothea fell silent, leaving Mark to wonder who Arthur

was fucking when he was supposed to be teaching him the market. As if there was a question. That middle-aged lecher and Ali Gardiner . . . two lovebirds playing you show me yours and I'll show you mine. Mark remembered the scene at his wedding. There was Ali giving Arthur the eye. Whistle and I'll spread my legs. You do know how to whistle? Apparently Arthur knew how to whistle.

When coffee came, Dorothea seized the check and paid with a fifty-dollar bill. Mark understood the cash ploy. When her credit card statements came at the end of the month, there would be no printed evidence of their lunch for Arthur to see by chance. As for his mentioning the lunch, she'd decided he wasn't a fool. It occurred to Mark that, in some ways, Dorothea Reiner was as clever as her husband.

"By the way," Dorothea said as they left the restaurant, "did you tell Arthur about Millie's new project at Channel 18?"

Mark started to say "You mean Millie's Mania." Then his guard went up. " 'Night of Stars'? Sure. I mentioned it. Nora told me. I thought he'd be interested."

Dorothea remarked in an offhand way, "He was . . ."

They parted at the entrance to the Reiner Building. Riding the elevator to the twenty-second floor, Mark reviewed the lunch. Arthur's secret life . . . a nest of Chinese boxes. On the not-so-secret side, there was the matter of Ali. On the more secret side, there was Arthur's informer at Channel 18. Who was it? Mark recalled his reaction when he told him Millie's plan . . . a shrug . . . indifference. He already knew about it. This recognition set off an alarm in Mark. Who told Arthur? Who else was in on the buyout? Ali? No! She reported to him . . . or else. Whoever it was had to be cut in for a piece of the action if Millie sold. If some snitch was cut in, his slice—not Arthur's—would be less. The idea infuriated him. Who was the bastard?

The next day Mark began a routine he followed faithfully for a month. Once a week—after leaving the office—he drove to Hillcrest and parked on the corner of Seventh Avenue and Pennsylvania. From there he could see the circular cul-de-sac at the end of Seventh Avenue, the guest parking area and the entrance to Ali Gardiner's high rise. Although he allowed himself only a half hour of watching, sooner or later he was confident he'd catch Arthur leaving the building. The more he knew about Arthur's extramarital sex life, the better. In Mark's mind, life imitated Wall Street . . . one never knew when inside information might come in handy.

One afternoon Arthur left the office at exactly two-thirty . . . at the close of trading on the Pacific Stock Exchange. He was carrying his tennis bag as if planning to stop at the La Jolla Beach and Tennis Club for a game. Playing a hunch, Mark canceled a late afternoon client appointment, making it for the next day. A personal problem, he told his irritated customer. At four o'clock he left the office for his post in Hillcrest. Once parked in his usual spot, he surveyed the scene. There was a car waiting in the cul-de-sac . . . a white Cadillac limousine parked at an angle that made it impossible for him to read the license plate. Still, he was sure it was Arthur's limo. "Maybe." He exhaled slowly. Maybe today he'd hit the jackpot.

The air was warm, and with the window open he relaxed listening to a CD of Bonny Raitt. Out of nowhere, a short, fat man appeared and leaned against the side of the car. His thin hair was held in place across his forehead by hair spray, and he wore a dark, shiny suit that had been to the cleaners too often. Mark's instinctive reaction—honed by his having survived in the playgrounds of the New York Public School System—was to get the hell out of there. With one hand he reached for the ignition key to start the engine and with the other for the handle to raise the window.

"Easy does it, buddy," the man said. "If I wanted to take you out, I could have done the job from across the street. And I'm not a crackhead out after your wallet."

Mark raised his eyebrows. Except for the man's California accent, this could be taking place on almost any street in Queens. "What do you want?" he asked.

"I'd like to talk to you."

"About what?" The man was too polite for Queens.

"First, can I bum a cigarette? I swore off last month. It's shitsville."

Mark didn't smoke, but he wasn't fanatic about others smoking. He kept a pack of cigarettes in the glove compartment for clients who smoked. "Sure," he said, opening the compartment and handing the man a pack of Marlboros. "Keep the pack . . . they'll go stale anyway."

"Thanks. You saved my life." As the man lit the cigarette, Mark studied his face. He had a thick, lumpy, high-bridged nose and a scar down his right cheek. Mark would have no difficulty picking him out of a police lineup.

"Lousy habit, smoking. One day I'll kick it."

From the look of satisfaction the one drag gave him, Mark doubted his willpower. On the way to surgery for lung cancer, he'd try to bum a cigarette from the intern.

"Anything else?" Mark asked, wanting to be rid of him.

"Yeah. Tell me why you're parked here. I spotted you last week." He pulled a small spiral notebook from his coat pocket. "Tuesday afternoon . . . the week before, Wednesday. You on a job too?"

"A job? What are you talking about?"

"Cut it out." The fat man exhaled, blowing the smoke out of his nostrils. "You're tailing someone. So am I. Probably the same guy."

It dawned on Mark that the fat man was a private detective, and he thought Mark was a detective too.

"Maybe we should work together? I guess the broad didn't trust you or me to do the job right. So she hired us both."

Mark had a flash of insight. "You're working for Mrs. Reiner and you're following Mr. Reiner?"

"Right on. You too?"

Mark started to laugh. "No. I work for Mr. Reiner . . . not Mrs. Reiner. I'm following him to satisfy my curiosity."

The man dropped the cigarette to the pavement and meticulously stamped on it. "Blackmail is a nasty business."

"I'm not out to blackmail him," Mark exploded indignantly. "I said I was curious . . . that's all . . . curious."

The man grinned. "Right. You're curious. And you're Jake, and I'm the Fat Man. Is that your squeeze up there with Reiner?"

"No. Just a friend."

"Sure. A friend." He grinned and lit another cigarette as he watched the building entrance. "I wouldn't have bothered you, but I needed a smoke. And I can't leave to buy a pack. . . ." He inhaled again. "Plus I was interested in you. . . ." He paused. "Look, I'll make a deal with you. You don't tell Mr. Reiner about me, and I won't tell your wife about you and your squeeze." He pointed to Mark's wedding ring, which was clearly visible. "I've got your license number. I can find out who you are, where you live and who you're married to in about one hour's work. Capish? We work together . . . no trouble. We don't . . .'' He shrugged.

Mark revised his original estimate of the detective. Smarter than he looked. And who could tell when he might have use for a smart private eye? ''You got a deal.''

The detective smiled and nodded. ''Shake,'' he said.

They shook hands. Then the man faded into the shadows of a doorway across the street. The only evidence that he was still there was the glowing tip of his cigarette and a brief glimpse of his face as he lit a fresh one.

Promptly at five o'clock, Mark saw the chauffeur pick up the car phone, have a short conversation with someone and hang up. In five minutes the chauffeur started his engine. He then got out and opened the rear door. Arthur Reiner scurried across the sidewalk—still carrying the bag with his tennis racket—and stepped into his limousine. As the limousine passed Mark, Mark ducked so Arthur couldn't see him. When he straightened up, the car was gone.

Mark grinned. Arthur was getting into Ali's knickers. And he was so cavalier about it he used his chauffeur to drive him to her place . . . as though he didn't care who knew. Okay! Now he knew. His grin faded. So what? What use could he make of the information? Should he confront Arthur? No! What was in it for him? Feeling no obligation to keep his word to the detective, he considered warning Arthur that Dorothea was having him tailed. A possibility . . . but again, no! What was in it for him? Arthur wouldn't shake his hand and say, ''Thanks, friend. I'll watch my step.'' Hell no! Not Arthur. He'd more likely ask what the fuck was Mark doing in front of Ali's apartment in the first place? He might fire him for butting into his private life. He couldn't warn Arthur. And he couldn't mention the stakeout . . . or meeting the detective . . . to Nora. How could he say, ''I parked up the block from Ali's building waiting to catch Arthur with his pants at half mast.'' Nora'd want to know why . . . the answer was tricky. Dorothea hadn't confided in him . . . she'd given him a hunch, just a hunch. Why tell Nora anything? There was no reason to bring her into this, not yet anyway. He'd wait for the right moment . . . when the info would buy him something. Knowing Ali, there was bound to be a right moment for the trade-off.

Mark had an anxiety attack a week later when Nora mentioned she hadn't spoken to Ali in days. She'd called once, but Ali hadn't returned her call. Mark worried that something was wrong . . . very wrong. The detective had broken his word and told Dorothea about him. Dorothea had landed on Arthur. Arthur had warned Ali. Now the ménage à trois thought it a good idea to put the Sterns on ice for a while . . . if not forever. Mark said nothing to Nora about his fears. He waited for Arthur to make a move. Arthur did nothing. All Mark could do was wait Arthur out . . . and sweat . . . and twist in the breeze. Which he did.

Mark sweated bullets for two weeks waiting for hell to break loose. Then one afternoon, as he was packing his briefcase to leave, Arthur called him into his office. Here it comes, Mark thought. He was half into the room before he saw that Arthur was deep in conversation with a big, massively built man . . . if the man lived on Ultra Slim-Fast for several months, he might break under three hundred pounds. What was Arthur cooking up with Lew Dobbs?

When Arthur saw Mark standing in the doorway, he motioned him in. "Sit down, Mark," he said. He gestured to one of two Mies van der Rohe chairs facing his desk . . . Lew Dobbs was seated in the other. From the low seat, Mark had to crane his neck to look up at Arthur. He wondered how Lew Dobbs felt about looking up at Arthur. Lew, six-foot-six in his stocking feet, rarely looked up at anyone. Mark's pulse slowed. Whatever else was going on, Arthur and he were not about to have a head-to-head . . . not in front of an important client like Lew Dobbs.

"How you cutting it, old buddy?" Dobbs drawled.

When Mark first met Dobbs, he, like most people, was taken in by Dobbs's I'm-just-a-dumb-country-boy act. Dobbs's black jeans—ordered from Sears, Roebuck's tall men's catalog—were tucked into hand-tooled, silver-embossed, black patent leather boots. His red plaid flannel work shirt—also ordered from a Sears catalog—and red string tie didn't go with his made-to-order black suede jacket with silver buttons . . . each button was as big as a silver dollar. His black ten-gallon hat rested against the nape of his neck

. . . held in place by a leather cord that was knotted under his double chin. Dobbs's size, his bizarre combination of polyester, silver, and suede, and his lazy, folksy way of talking fooled people into thinking that he was a slow-thinking, lumbering oaf who had hit it lucky in something . . . oil was the usual guess, but no one knew for sure. Dobbs was regarded as the Helmut Kohl of the TV industry . . . the target of every bright, fast-talking, fast-thinking hustler from New York to Dallas to Los Angeles with a TV channel for sale. They were convinced they could talk rings around him and think rings around him . . . they'd have a signed deal and a check and be relaxing in their Jacuzzis before he figured it out. That the channel he'd bought—for which he'd overpaid—was a genuine, bona fide dog. They were wrong. Somehow—the way Helmut Kohl's slow, relentless pressure led to the unification of the two Germanys—the slow-talking oaf, Lew Dobbs, quickly turned their dogs into cash cows.

Mark's answer reflected the respect he felt for the Jolly Texas Giant. "I'm very well, sir. It's nice to see you again."

"I hear you got hitched. You catch yourself a lively filly or a brood mare?"

"A little of both," Mark said. "Nora's two months pregnant."

"Congratulations. Getting your gal pregnant can be lots of fun . . . for both of you. But having a baby is women's work. Good thing too. No man would want the job."

Arthur looked up from a report he'd been scanning. "Let's drop the baby talk. It's a bore. I asked Mark to join us to go over the deal. Since he's going to be carrying the ball for the firm, I want to bring him up to speed."

"I can understand that," Dobbs said. "What I don't understand is why Mark? Why not you?"

"I . . . uhm . . . I . . ." For an instant Arthur stumbled. Then he said, "I have a deal here in San Diego I have to put to bed. It's taking a lot of my time."

Mark looked up at Arthur. The only deal Arthur was bedding was Ali.

Lew Dobbs gave a hoot—a Texas-size hoot. "Any chance on my getting in on the deal you're bedding?"

"This isn't your style deal," Arthur said impatiently. "If you're looking for female company, I can set something up for you."

Dobbs waved him off. "Never needed a pimp before . . . don't need one now."

Arthur was not offended. "Okay. Let's get down to your deal. Mark, did you ever hear of the Group H stations?"

"No."

"Group H owns three independent UHF TV stations in New Mexico and Arizona. Small markets, but Lew wants to buy them."

"Are they for sale?" Mark asked.

"Well, son. They weren't. But I had a nice meeting with the owner . . . nice little guy. Turned out he was open to a nice sales pitch."

"What did you offer him?"

"Besides this?" Lew's huge hand became a sledgehammer-sized fist. He laughed at Mark's startled reaction. "Only joshing you, son. I offered him money . . . heaps of money . . . more money than he thinks the stations are worth."

Arthur pushed the report he'd been reading across the desk. Mark recognized it as one of Reiner & Co.'s analyst's reports. He had no interest in the analyst's opinion about the future of independent TV stations . . . between the growth of superstations like TNT and CNN and the huge VCR market, Reiner & Co.'s entertainment analyst had been predicting for five years that the market value of TV stations would decline. He'd been right. In 1988 buyers were paying up to fifteen times a channel's cash flow. By 1991 the multiple had dropped to ten. Mark went directly to the financial statements . . . Group H's cash flow had gradually dropped from a peak of five million in 1986 to a little over two million last year.

"How much are you paying for the stations?" he asked.

"I made the little guy an offer he couldn't refuse . . . thirty million for all three channels."

"Thirty million!" Mark exclaimed. "That's way out of line."

Lew Dobbs shrugged. "Easy come, easy go. He gets what he wants . . . money. I get what I want . . . Group H."

"Then you think the price is fair, Mark," Arthur said.

"More than fair."

"Good. Because we're going to write an 'opinion letter' to that effect," Arthur said.

Mark looked first at Arthur and then at Lew Dobbs. "I don't get it," he said. "Who are we working for?"

"Group H, son," Dobbs said. "I don't need no 'opinion letter.' They're a public company . . . they do."

Mark scratched his head. "Let me get this straight. You're a client of Reiner & Co. . . . you pay us an annual retainer to find good TV properties for you. You're buying Group H. And we're supposed to write an 'opinion letter' for Group H . . . one that says you're paying them a fair price."

"You got it right, son." Lew chuckled.

"Which means that we're also working for Group H . . . Group H will be paying our fee on this deal. Can we take money from both sides, Arthur?" Mark asked.

"We can and we will," Arthur said. "All we're doing is certifying that Lew is paying a fair price. He is, isn't he?"

"More than fair," Mark mumbled.

"Good. In about two months, you're going to Phoenix to meet with Victor Ashland . . . he's the CEO of Group H. You'll look around the facilities, you'll study the books, you'll talk to the personnel. And when you're done, you'll hand Victor the Reiner & Co. 'opinion letter.' The next day you'll sit in on the closing and Victor Ashland will hand you a check made out to Reiner & Co. for five hundred thousand dollars, our fee for representing Group H."

Mark did a quick mental calculation. "That's double the Lehman Formula." He was awed.

"It's the Reiner & Co. formula," Arthur said calmly.

"Ashland agreed to this?"

Lew Dobbs jabbed Mark's jaw lightly with his sledgehammer fist. "I told you I made him an offer he couldn't refuse."

Mark blinked. Even the playful tap felt like he'd been hit by a log. "Yeah," he said. "I see what you mean." He wondered if Victor Ashland had accepted Lew's offer because it was so good or because he was afraid not to.

"Son," Lew said, "how you doing with Millie Gardiner? I want Channel 18 pretty badly . . . it's going to be my flagship station."

"Millie doesn't want to sell," Mark said.

"I told you about her idea to produce great plays for television," Arthur said.

"That's my notion of a real lousy idea. Now if she'd got it into her head to do a country-and-western program, I'd be kind o' worried. Still . . ." Lew scratched his bald scalp.

"She's a stubborn lady. She might just make it work. Must be some way to persuade her . . ."

Mark looked at Dobbs out of the corner of his eye. The Jolly Texas Giant mask had slipped. The face Mark saw wasn't friendly, wasn't jolly. It was ice-cold and menacing. Then the mask was back in place. Jolly Lew hoisted himself to his feet. For a man of his size and bulk, the ease with which he rose from the low chair was remarkable. "We've done all we can for today. I'll keep you informed about Group H, and you—I mean you, Mark—you keep your eyes peeled for a way to persuade Mrs. Gardiner. There's always a way." He stopped at the door and turned. "I almost forgot. Give my best to your wife, Mark. She's Millie Gardiner's grand-daughter . . . that ought to count for something." He waved to Arthur and shut the door behind him.

When Mark started to rise, Arthur motioned for him to remain seated.

"Have you figured out your share of the firm's fee?" Arthur asked.

"Is the percentage the same as I get on commissions?"

"Yes."

Mark's smile was tempered by confusion. "You're going to pay me two hundred thousand dollars for flying to Phoenix and going through the motions for two days? You could easily make that trip yourself and save the money."

"I told you I have a deal cooking here. . . . I don't want to leave it."

Jesus Christ, Mark thought. He's paying one hundred thou-sand dollars a day to fuck Ali. That makes her the highest-priced whore in California, including Hollywood.

"Now that I've done something for you," Arthur said, "you can do something for me."

"If I can." Mark suddenly realized Arthur wasn't offering him two hundred thousand dollars just to fly to Phoenix.

"What were you doing on Seventh Avenue in Hillcrest a week ago?" Arthur's tone was deceptive, conveying mild cu-riosity.

Mark considered his options. The truth was impossible. He'd be fired. To gain time, he answered the question with a question. "How did you know I was on Seventh Avenue?"

"I saw your car. There's not another green Aston Martin in San Diego . . . the steering wheel's on the right-hand side of the car. It was you. I've been busy or I'd have had you in the next day.''

"It was me." Mark kept his voice steady. "But I don't count. Do you know there was another man on the same street watching you?"

"No. Who was he?"

"A private detective . . . hired by your wife to follow you. By now he must have reported to Dorothea."

"A private detective . . ." Arthur rubbed his chin reflectively. "That's curious. Dorothea's known about my women for years. She never cared before. Why now?"

"Maybe she takes Ali seriously."

Arthur shook his head. "Dorothea is too smart for that. Ali's no different than the others. A little classier . . . from a better family. Hiram and I went to school together. But Ali's not important and Dorothea knows it. . . ." He continued to rub his knuckles against his chin. "Unless she wants the information for a reason?"

"What does she want from you?"

"Nothing. She was born with everything she wants or needs. That's always been the rub. I can't give her anything she doesn't have . . . or can't buy with her own money."

"Except yourself," Mark said under his breath.

Arthur had sharp hearing, because he gave Mark a strange look. Softly . . . wistfully, he said, "I gave her myself at first. Then I suppose I did start divvying it up. When she found out, that changed things. She hasn't wanted any of me in a long time." In a stronger voice, he asked, "You're sure about the detective?"

"Positive." Mark risked adding, "I gave him a pack of cigarettes so he wouldn't have to leave his post." He waited for Arthur to return to his original question . . . what he was doing in Hillcrest in the first place. He'd come up with a whippy, on-the-nose, answer.

"Do you know the detective?"

"I don't even know his name."

"Then why give him a pack of cigarettes?"

Mark went for the opening . . . he enjoyed using his talent. And if there was one thing he did well, it was tell a convincing lie.

"Twice this month I spotted this guy hanging around the building. He was obviously waiting for somebody. Then one day you left the office early to play tennis. I was also leaving early to see a client. As I came out of the building I saw this clown get into his car and follow you. That made me suspicious so I tagged after the two of you to Seventh Avenue . . . to Ali's condo. But I couldn't stop . . . my client was waiting. About a week later, the same thing happened. This time I was able to wait. That's when you saw my car.''

"Why didn't you tell me?" Arthur asked in a flat voice.

"I didn't know what to do," Mark said plaintively. "On one hand, I'd discovered something that was none of my business. On the other hand, I knew I should tell you about the detective. But, frankly, I didn't want to stick my neck out.''

"What'd you think I'd do? Can you?"

"It's a positive maybe."

"Why the hell is Dorothea having me followed? Why this sudden interest in my sex life?" Arthur was thinking out loud. "She never did that before. . . .'' Then he came back to himself. "Mark, it was a mistake not to tell me what you knew. Next time trust me to do the right thing." He adjusted the Windsor knot of his tie and stared thoughtfully at Mark. "I think I owe you one for spotting the detective," he said quietly. "I was going to make you the offer in six months, but why wait?"

Mark blinked. What was he talking about?

"You're handling big accounts. You have an instinct for the market. You make good money for your clients and the firm. You're a born trader. When you go to Phoenix, you'll be acting as an investment banker. Beside me, you'll be the only investment banker in the firm. So it's time we made you a partner." Arthur enjoyed the imperial "we." "One percent of the firm's stock goes with the partnership. And a share of the firm's profits at the end of the year. What do you say, Mark? Do you want to be a partner in Reiner & Co.?''

"Hell, yes!" Mark exclaimed.

"Then it's settled. With the partnership goes a private office and a secretary. I'll have my girl do a memo to circulate through the office. There are papers to be signed. Once that's done, you'll be a partner." A calculating look crossed his face. "Nora and Millie should be proud of you."

"I'm sure they will be." It pleased Mark what a little judicious lying had accomplished. Arthur believed every word of his story because he wanted to believe it. Otherwise, he'd have had to fire him. But thanks to Dr. Abe and the prospect of Millie's account, he was too valuable an asset to be fired.

"Back to the wars," Arthur said. "You have any clever ideas as to what to do about Millie and Channel 18?"

"No. But I'll think of something."

"Think hard, Mark. Think very hard. Dobbs wants that station, and what Lew Dobbs wants, Lew Dobbs gets . . . one way or another."

"The way he got Group H?"

"That's one way. There's no law against spending too much money to buy something you want badly . . . if you can afford it."

"Is it all his . . . I mean, the money? The way he throws money away, it's almost like he's playing with Monopoly money . . . or OPM."

"It's his money," Arthur said quickly. "And don't forget, when push comes to shove, he always makes money."

Mark rose from the low chair and held out his hand. "Partner," he said. The tradition of a handshake to cement a deal remained strong on the Street . . . East Coast or West Coast.

Without hesitation, Arthur shook his hand. "Partner." He smiled. He was still smiling as Mark floated from the office.

PART 6

Nora
1992

Chapter 10

"I'M MAKING it, kiddo! I'm really making it," Mark shouted, slamming the front door and hurtling into the kitchen.

"Making what? Ouch!" Nora yelped . . . nicking her finger on the carrot knife. She blew him a kiss.

Mark threw out his chest and pounded it. "Me Tarzan . . . you Jane. I am king of the jungle!"

"You're mixing up gorillas and lions. What's happened?"

"I have finally received the appreciation I so justly deserve . . . if not the adulation." He applauded himself. "Arthur Reiner has shown unusual acumen. He's made me a partner."

"Oh, Mark!" Nora cried, dropping the knife into the sink. She flung herself into his arms. "How marvelous!"

"Don't let it go to your head. I'm only the king of a little jungle, a foothill. I've miles to go to reach the peak."

"You'll go all the way . . . right to the top. I know you."

"You love me . . . you're prejudiced."

Nora smiled at the note of satisfaction in his voice. He was lit up with hope . . . already thinking, like a chess player, of his next move . . . and two moves after that. Mark was the most ambitious man she'd ever known, and she'd grown up in a family full of ambitious men and women . . . except for her father. "When did you get the news?"

"I was about to leave for the day when Arthur called me into his office."

"Tell me. . . ."

"I am telling you. We had a big meeting with Lew Dobbs—"

Nora interrupted. "About Channel 18."

"No!" Mark was exasperated. "About Group H . . . three TV stations in Arizona and New Mexico. Lew is buying

Group H and Reiner & Co. . . ." He smiled. "In this case, me, is representing Group H in the acquisition. Guess what my share of the fee will come to." Excitement made his voice shrill.

"I can't," Nora said quietly. She looked at her husband. She was well aware that Mark didn't always tell her the truth, not the whole truth anyway. But she was too much in love with him to think he would tell her a flat-out lie.

"Try," Mark insisted. "Pretend you're on a TV game show and try to win the grand prize."

"Okay. Fifty thousand dollars."

"Nooo." Mark drew out the word. "Try again."

Nora shook her head. "This is a silly game."

"Two hundred thousand dollars," he crowed.

Nora stared. "Arthur Reiner is paying you two hundred thousand dollars . . ." She took in a breath. "Why? For what?"

"For representing the firm at the closing."

"Has this got anything to do with Grandmother Millie . . . or Channel 18?"

"Absolutely nothing!"

"And his making you a partner has nothing to do with either Grandmother or Channel 18?"

"Absolutely nothing! Damn it, Nora. I come home with great news and all you think about is Millie and that lousy TV station."

"I'm sorry, darling. Maybe it's because I don't like Lew Dobbs."

"You don't know him."

Nora grinned impishly. "I guess not to know him is not to like him."

"Would you like to meet Lew? He's really something."

"No thanks. It's easier to dislike a person you don't know than one you do."

"That's my Nora . . . always ready to give a rat the benefit of the doubt." Mark paused. "Maybe having Arthur as my best man helped." He paused again. "The weird thing is I think he likes me."

"Why shouldn't he like you?"

"Why should he? I'm not part of his crowd. You know what a snob he is. I didn't go to Choate . . . or to an Ivy League school. I'm not social . . . my clients aren't social.

They're nouveau rich . . . not oldveau rich. But I guess I squeeze through. My sister is on the NYU faculty . . . not a waitress at McDonald's.'' Mark studied Nora for a long moment. ''You're my best social credential.''

''Forgive me my sins.'' Nora laughed. ''I'm glad my family has done you some good. It worked against me at the station.'' She clapped her hands. ''Let's have a split of champagne to celebrate.''

''Let's,'' he said. He went to the refrigerator. They always kept several splits of champagne chilled . . . for good luck.

After toasting each other, they sat on the couch happily sipping champagne. At last Nora said, ''The gods have decreed that we celebrate. To pay homage for good fortune.''

Mark was deep in his own thoughts . . . thinking about Arthur and Dorothea and Ali. He was relieved that Arthur wasn't being a damn fool. The Ali Cat was only a good lay, nothing more.

''Mark,'' Nora repeated. ''Wake up! We owe it to the fates to celebrate.''

Mark came back into focus. ''Rght! My birthday's in two weeks. Let's have a birthday party.''

''And we'll know in our heart of hearts it's also for the partnership.''

''So will Arthur. We'll have to invite him.''

''I would hope so,'' Nora said. ''Let's make up a guest list. No more than twelve. We'll have a buffet. I'll get Ilsa to help with the menu . . . do hors d'oeuvres and serve. We'll have a bartender and a waiter.''

''The last of the big spenders.''

Nora scrambled from the couch and went downstairs to the office. Picking up a pad and a pen from her desk, she returned and sat beside Mark. They tossed names back and forth like Ping-Pong balls. Holding some, discarding others. Finally they settled on some of Nora's co-workers from Channel 18, two of Mark's clients and their wives whom they liked, two couples who were old friends and knew everyone. Arthur and Dorothea. Millie . . . if she'd come. Dr. Abe . . . if he'd come. When Nora reached Ali's name, she hesitated . . . she remembered her conversation with Dorothea in the powder room at her wedding lunch.

Finally Mark spoke. ''You're thinking of Ali?''

''Yes.'' Nora wished she'd told him what Ali had said about

married men . . . at the same time she was glad that she hadn't. "We can't have a party and not have her."

"I can. It's my birthday. I sure as hell can have a birthday party without Ali. Try me."

"We have to have her. Since she started working on Millie's project, she's often at the station. She'll hear about it and be offended. She is my oldest friend."

"She's nobody's friend. Suppose she makes a pass at Arthur? I saw them at the wedding playing footsie with their eyes." He didn't add, Now he's fucking her.

"Given your imagination you should be a writer."

"With Ali's help, I may consider doing my autobiography. *How I Murdered Ali Gardiner.*"

Mark's stubbornness forced Nora to stand on her principles . . . her belief in Ali must be defended, as she'd always defended her father. Squaring her shoulders she took a position. "You're pigheaded. We must have her."

"We must not. If you had any sense you'd dump her." Then, quixotically, Mark capitulated. One way or another, he'd handle the Ali Cat. "Okay," he said. "With a proviso. She comes with a date."

"Three dates," Nora said, relieved the strain had passed.

"One date will do," Mark said.

"Case closed." For an instant, Nora wished Mark hadn't agreed. The stakes were so high and the penalty so severe . . . if her trust in Ali was misplaced.

Millie was on the top of Nora's list, but she didn't expect her to accept the invitation. Years ago Millie made it clear to the family that she was not available for bridge games, lawn parties, cocktail parties or formal dinners. Her point was if she said yes once, she'd be swamped with invitations. She had other people to see besides relatives. So she'd have to say no most of the time. The result would be disappointment, hurt feelings, jealousy . . . even anger at her. Best to say no to everyone.

After Millie did the expected, she made an unexpected suggestion.

"Nora, your house is very nice, but it's not that large. Abe and I are going to New York for several weeks. There are three plays and the Met is mounting a new production of *Otello* that I want to catch. Why not give the party at the Farm? You could use the patio and the space around the wading pool. Oscar and Rosa will tend to everything . . . including Mark's birthday cake. The party will be my birthday present to Mark."

"That's a wonderful idea, Grandmother. I'll talk to Mark and let you know."

"Mark will agree. Believe me, Nora, he will agree."

When Nora told Mark of Millie's offer, he agreed. He more than agreed. He literally jumped in the air and clicked his heels. He was going to have a birthday party at the Farm in Rancho Santa Fe. The poor boy had made good . . . with a vengeance.

Rancho Santa Fe in October . . . the burnished sunset over the hills . . . the lights coming on in the Farm . . . the drinks and hors d'oeuvres waiting and the flowers arranged around the wading pool. It might have been a real estate advertisement meant to increase the price of Rancho Santa Fe homes . . . as if the houses in the Ranch weren't already expensive enough.

Guests arrived and had a drink. Then they stood around like toy soldiers . . . staring, on guard against strangers, speaking only when spoken to by a familiar face. Nora and Mark—like goodwill ambassadors—worked their butts off promoting mirth and merriment . . . mixing and mingling . . . introducing one group to another. People had second drinks . . . the liquor worked wonders. The drinkers loosened up, drifted around, settled into couples or cliques. The Sandersons and Wolfsteins—talkative and traveled—found each other. Both couples had recently been fishing in Alaska and were in love with the landscape and the folk art. Then there was the Channel 18 clique. Luddy Poole was at the center, holding court with his co-workers and their wives and Pat Yocum, who came alone. Babs Poole, Luddy's wife, made it clear that television talk bored her out of her mind. There was nothing worth seeing on television . . . there never had been . . . there never would be. The group smiled indulgently—Babs was the boss's wife—and went on drinking and schmoozing. They knew Luddy and Babs had a marriage made in hell.

Dorothea Reiner's brisk, commanding "Hello!" rang out as she strode onto the patio. Arthur's cheery "Hi there" added to the feeling of well-being in the air. Dorothea kissed

Nora on the cheek as Oscar took her cashmere wrap. She was wearing a sunblaze of diamonds on her left shoulder. Nora had inherited what remained of her mother's jewelry . . . the pieces her father hadn't sold or hocked and never reclaimed. Her taste didn't run to ostentation, but face-to-face with Dorothea, she was glad she had taken the pearls, a yellow gold bracelet and a diamond ring out of the safe-deposit box. A little something in the way of glitter.

The chatter rose several decibels. People milled around the wading pool in the center of the patio. Oscar and Rosa sidled through the groups . . . taking orders .. refilling glasses.

On her way to the hors d'oeuvres, Nora was interrupted by Lola Gillebaard, the wife of one of Mark's clients. Lola was chock-full of tributes to Mark's talent as a broker. Nora accepted the accolades . . . while at the same time she listened with one ear to the heated back-and-forth among her co-workers at 18.

Tim nagged Luddy. "Damn it! When do we go into production? The great heartrending drama, *I Remember Mama,* has been circling the landing field for months."

"Schedules have to match up." Luddy's voice was professionally neutral. "Tammi Meredith is in the middle of a picture. Jordan Banska is about to start a new film . . . in Poland. Frankly, I wish he'd cast Mama before he leaves for Warsaw. But I don't think he will. Things like that."

"Mrs. G. told me to open a special Channel 18 account at the downtown branch of the Bank of America," Sim Crumb remarked. "For the 'Night of Stars' project. But statements go directly to her, so I don't know if she's funded the show yet."

"What the hell is Norakins doing?" Pat Yocum cut in. "Sitting on her butt . . . that's what. There's not even been an opening pitch to Ford or Budweiser . . . or any major advertiser. Nothing! What does she do with her time?"

"She has nothing to sell, Patti Cake," Tim said impatiently. "She won't have anything to sell until there's something on tape . . . at least a couple of scenes."

"Norakins can't sell worth shit," Pat griped. "With or without a tape. We bust our balls for a paycheck, but not dear, sweet Norakins. She doesn't bust anything. She's Mrs. G.'s granddaughter"

"You ain't got no balls, Patti Cake," Tim Rourke said in too loud a voice. He ignored his wife's elbow in his ribs. "You can strap on a dildo and play let's pretend with your girl friend, but you sit when you piss. Don't forget that little fact of nature. And if you don't quit the Norakins shit, you'll find yourself collecting unemployment insurance . . ."

Nora had had enough. She'd introduce Lola to Dorothea and get away from Pat's Norakins. Damn! The nape of her neck was turning red. Norakins! That had been Pat's name for her when she first started at the station. What a fool she was . . . she'd thought Pat now respected her.

Dorothea and Lola had Spa Pacifica in common. While listening to them recount its joys, Nora saw Arthur join the Channel 18 group. A nice-to-meet-you conversation began between Arthur and Pat. Nora watched. If Tim was right about Pat and her girl friend, Arthur was wasting time. Arthur smiled and said something. Pat shook her head . . . twice. Arthur smiled a second time—this time it lacked conviction—and turned away. He clinked glasses with Tim. Nora liked that. At least Tim was on her side . . . she hoped.

Mark watched Arthur and Tim chatting at the bar as they waited for refills. He wished he could read lips. What were they saying? One of that crew was Arthur's informer. Which one? Tim? Then Arthur wandered away and Mark lost interest.

Nora took a deep breath. Ali was standing in the French doors leading to the terrace. Her right arm was linked with Jordan Banska . . . her left with Tammi Meredith. Ken Savage brought up the rear. Nora felt a surge of anger. Was Ali moving in on Jordan . . . or Jordan on Ali? She dismissed the question. None of her business . . . either way.

When Jordan spied Nora, he slipped away from Ali and walked toward her. With his body angled slightly forward, he looked like an ambulatory exclamation point. Still, even though he wore old jeans and a denim work shirt, people gave ground . . . clearing a path for him to reach her.

"Nora!" Jordan said in his whiskey-hoarse voice. "It was sweet of you to ask Ali to bring us." He waved in Tammi's and Ken's direction. "We thank you for the generous invitation."

Nora swallowed hard. "Yes . . . I'm glad . . . I mean, we're glad you could make it."

"We? That's right. You're married. Congratulations. Still . . ." He smiled as only he could smile. "We do have very bad timing. I'm divorced . . . again. And you're all grown up . . . I wouldn't have to throw you back. But now you're married."

"I'm not only grown up and married, very soon I'll be growing out." She took in his quizzical frown. "I'm pregnant."

"That's wonderful. It calls for a drink. Come!" He took her elbow and guided her to the bar. "I feel foolish, but I don't remember what you drink."

"You didn't forget . . . you never knew. You never bought me a drink. You said I was too young to drink."

"You were."

"I wasn't."

"You were, but you're old enough now." He turned to the bartender. "Take that glass"—he pointed to a Manhattan-size glass—"and fill it with gin. No ice. Just gin. Nora? What do you drink?"

"A white wine."

"There you are. Damn you, Jordan!" Out of nowhere, slinky and seething, Tammi Meredith joined them. Like Jordan she wore jeans and an open-throated denim shirt, but her jeans and shirt—made by her personal tailor—fit like a second skin. "I had to mortgage my body and soul to that low-life, Marty Skenk, to get a long weekend off the set. The bastard doesn't give a flying fuck about my soul, but he is one eager beaver to collect on my body. So what happens? You get too sloshed to fly the plane to Puerta Vallarta."

"Dear Tammi. I will not be too sloshed to fly the plane. I have it on good authority from the *National Enquirer* that I have a hollow leg."

Tammi gave him an innocent ingenue smile. "Take note, Banska. If you don't make it to Mexico, you don't make *I Remember Mama*. At least not with me you don't."

"Tammi. You're being unreasonable. That's not like you."

"What the fuck gave you that asshole idea? I am god-damned unreasonable . . . when I want to be. And if I don't get to the villa tonight, you'll find out how unreasonable I can be." Without a pause, she said, "Bartender. I want a large scotch and ice and a club soda." She grinned at Nora. "The club soda is for Ken. He has an ulcer, and he never drinks water. He claims fishes fuck in it." Her grin grew broader. "That's my specialty. I give great head—you can check that out with Jordan—and large, bleeding ulcers. *Ciao*, Nora." Holding a drink in each hand, she undulated across the room.

Nora watched Tammi for a few seconds. Then she turned back to Jordan. "Tammi's right about your drinking. If you expect to fly a plane, go easy on the gin."

"You, too," Jordan said teasingly. "I can't believe you're Barron Gardiner's daughter. I really miss him. We used to drink all night and sober up racing my powerboat."

Nora's face was bleak. "I remember. That's how he killed himself." She tried to keep her voice steady. "He didn't sober up in time to know when to duck."

Jordan put his half-finished drink on the bar. "I heard something, but I never got the details straight. I was in Africa at the time . . . making *Memsahib*. When I got back, it seemed too late to call."

"He tried to break the nighttime speed record around San Diego Bay. But when he cut between a dinghy and a yacht, he never saw that they were passing bags of cocaine back and forth on a nylon line. The thin line sliced through his neck. The Coast Guard found his head three days later. It had washed ashore thirty miles south . . . almost at the Mexican border."

"Oh, sweet Jesus."

"I had to identify the head. When I saw it, I threw up. Suppose you stop drinking, collect Tammi and Ken, and get your asses out of here. I'm running out of disaster relief."

Jordan's face was drawn. "I'm sorry, dear. I only came to see you. I'm sorry I brought back bad memories."

"You didn't bring them back. They never go away. Sometimes I wake up shaking . . . I see Daddy's head floating in the ocean. Do you know what a head looks like after three days in the water?"

Jordan finished his drink with one swallow. "I can imagine. I think it's time—"

A woman's high, shrill voice interrupted them. "Mr. Banska. I always knew I'd meet you someday."

"How are you, Babs?" Nora smiled gamely. "Jordan, this is Luddy Poole's better half, Babs Poole."

The plump Clairol blonde in mid-life crisis was all over

Jordan. "You don't remember me, do you, Mr. Banska? You spoke at a seminar at UCLA . . . films versus television as an art form. Luddy and I—I mean Luddy Jr.—took the series together. You signed my notebook. I still have it."

"I hope you enjoyed the lecture."

"You know, Mr. Banska, years ago—when I was a teen-ager—I took a course with your father, Milos Banska." Jordan's face was expressionless. "Luddy and I—I mean Junior—argue all the time about which of you is the better director . . . you or your father." She simpered girlishly. "Luddy—I mean Junior—is going into film directing. He's taking courses now at UCSD. If you could possibly help—"

"Mr. Banska," Sid Wolfstein interrupted, "I read about your big game hunting in Africa. Ever think of fishing in Alaska? That's a real big-time sport."

Jordan smiled and sipped another drink. He glanced at Nora helplessly. "Thanks for the tip. Now if you'll excuse me . . ."

"Mr. Banska. Nora, why didn't you tell me Mr. Banska was coming? Oh, never mind. Mr. Banska, I give a big party at my ranch up the road . . . when the Del Mar racing season opens." Dee Bronson, a tall, bosomy redhead joined them . . . followed by her short, breathless husband. "I invite turf club members and all of the famous jockeys. Of course, there are Hollywood celebrities too. Last year, Shelly and I had two hundred and fifty people . . . I think. Oh, Mr. Banska, would you be the guest of honor at my next party . . . when Del Mar reopens in July?"

"I'd love to, Mrs. . . . Hmmm . . . You tell Nora and she'll be in touch with me." Moving swiftly, he broke away from the group, dragging Nora along with him. "I'm going while I'm still alive and well. Tell Tammi and Ken to meet me at the car." He gulped down his drink. "I'll talk to you when we have more time and privacy." He glanced around like a wary fugitive. "We have to set below-the-line budget costs, casting, production dates . . . things like that. Millie said you're the production coordinator so I'm coordinating with you." He squeezed her hand. "You all right? You look pale."

Someone was calling, "Mr. Banska. Mr. Banska."

"I'm okay," Nora said. "You better run for it."

Jordan kissed her lightly on the mouth. "In memory of

what we missed," he said smiling. Then he turned and ran. Appearing out of nowhere, Tammi and Ken Savage followed. Nora never knew by what psychological shortwave they got the message to leave. In no time, the three vanished from the patio. Nora was so focused on the mystery of celebrity telepathy she didn't notice Mark had joined her.

"What the hell were they doing here? Who invited them?" Mark was barely able to disguise his anger.

"Jordan came because . . ." Nora racked her brain . . . why had they come? "Because Ali invited him. You made me promise to tell her to bring a date. Tammi and Ken tagged along."

"If he's Ali's date, why did he leave without her?"

"I don't know, and I don't care."

"You should care." Mark glared at Ali, who had materialized behind Nora. Rather than lose his temper publicly, he disappeared into the party.

"Nora, darling, what a wonderful party," Ali said, taking Nora's arm and towing her along. As they slowly circled the pool, hellos and how-are-yous? flew about in the air.

"Lola Gillebaard! You look wonderful in red. How is Muffin? If she grows any faster you can give her your castoffs," Ali said.

"You like this old thing?" Lola glanced down at her dress. "It was Benny's Valentine Day present last year."

"Let's hear it for Benny." She turned to a large, plump man with a white goatee, a head that was too small for his bulk, and pleasant features with the kind of openness that tells you nothing. "Benny, I hear that Marvin Davis offered you a spot. Would you consider leaving Wainwright and Scott to work with a raider?"

"I take the Fifth," Benny said.

"You can tell me." Ali twinkled as though he should love her prying.

"No comment," Benny insisted, smiling back.

"I detest secrets that I'm not in on," Ali said, full of mischief.

So it went. Ali had something to say to everyone, including the group from Channel 18. She spoke with gaiety and intimacy, willing to be impressed and at the same time speaking her mind without thinking twice.

"I'm hungry," Sim Crumb complained.

"Have some more hors d'oeuvres," Ali suggested as though she really cared what Sim did.

The conversation quickened and the voices grew louder with each drink, typical of a cocktail/dinner party. Lynn Wolfstein was talking about a friend who was having an affair.

"What's the woman like?" Ali asked with a chuckle.

"Madly glamorous," Nora heard Lynn say.

"In that case the wife has nothing to worry about. It's not the madly glamorous to watch out for when hubby works late. It's the frump of a secretary who is a frenzy of buried passion." Ali's eyes lit up. "Wouldn't you agree, Dorothea?" she asked, moving away from Nora and the center of the group to Dorothea. Dorothea had been standing off to one side, watching. Ali linked her arm through the older woman's. "Wouldn't you agree that it's the seemingly drab, little, hardworking type who can do the most damage to a happy marriage?"

Ali's actions struck Nora as bizarre. Was she actually trying to butter up Dorothea?

"I've never given it much thought," Dorothea said.

"That's fortunate for you. Too many women waste time worrying about their husbands' fidelity. When their husbands should be worrying about their fidelity."

"I worry," Arthur said, joining them.

"Go away, Arthur," Ali said. "We are having a quiet female chat. Nothing a man would understand." Her eyes glowed with disrespectful pleasure as she took Dorothea's arm and urged her toward the colonnade . . . away from the crowd.

"Men can be so ridiculous," Nora heard Ali say. "Sometimes I think they're another species."

"Or less evolved than women," Dorothea said. This was a game two could play.

Their conversation grew more animated. Ali and Dorothea completed a turn around the colonnade and then returned to the bar by the pool. Arthur interrupted them a second time. They stared at him as though he had broken into a lover's rendezvous.

"Go on," he said. "I'm riveted."

"Arthur, scat," Dorothea said authoritatively. "You are superfluous."

"Ladies! Please! I know you are having a heart-to-heart woman talk. Women fascinate me. I much prefer their gossip about people to the boring discussions about business, politics and sports that men call conversation."

"Amuse yourself, Arthur . . . you know how to amuse yourself very well. Join the party. Why don't you push someone into the pool?" Dorothea said. "Or better, jump into the pool yourself."

"Don't be unkind, Dorothea. I simply want to be with you ladies."

Ali gave Arthur a social smile. "Arthur, be a dear and find Oscar and freshen our drinks," she said. "When you return, we can take a turn around the pool together."

"You're a born politician, Ali," he said, smiling. "Exactly like Hiram."

"Why shouldn't I be like Hiram? I've studied him for years. Learn from the best, that's my motto."

"I collect mottos." Arthur grinned at Ali, then left to find Oscar.

While he was gone, Nora joined Ali and Dorothea.

"Delicias in the Ranch? I like it. It's a lovely setting," Dorothea said. "What time?"

"Let's say one," Ali said.

Nora listened to the luncheon arrangement with mild amazement. The tone between Ali and Dorothea had the warmth and camaraderie that implied greater intimacy to come. What had brought on this season of harmony? How had Ali managed it? What had she said? Then Nora spotted Rosa bringing out another platter of hors d'oeuvres. The conscience of a hostess took over and she left.

The high point of the dinner was the drop-dead birthday cake . . . three brandy-soaked, diamond-shaped tiers iced with white fondant, topped by the front page of the *Wall Street Journal* imbedded in Lucite and decorated with white ticker tape and pale blue Wall Street "tombstones." The tape and the "tombstones" were edible . . . the *Journal* was not. Oscar cut the cake, and everyone—even Babs Poole, who was always on a diet—ate at least two wedges.

For the rest of the evening Ali and Dorothea mingled and flirted, laughed, ate and drank. Occasionally they would pause and whisper to each other. Clearly they were growing more and more chummy. Once Nora nudged Mark to show him what was happening. Mark grunted and shook his head. Nora shrugged and smiled confidently. The party rolled on . . . peaked . . . and wound down. Tim and Eileen Rourke were the last to leave. When Mark helped a very drunk Tim into the passenger seat of his car, Nora could finally relax and take credit where credit was due. Her faith in Ali had been vindicated, at least as far as Arthur was concerned. Ali was still Ali . . . her charming, scheming, opportunistic, unreliable friend. But she wasn't interested in Arthur. For the moment, that was all that mattered.

Getting ready for bed that night, Nora crowed over her triumph. "Happy birthday, Mark," she called out from the bathroom. "Now, sing my praises."

"For throwing a great party?"

"For my remarkable instinct for mingling and mixing people."

"It worked very well . . . except for Jordan Banska and Ali."

"Except for Ali! Ali was my greatest triumph. She was smooth as silk with Dorothea. That won't hurt you one bit with Arthur."

Mark was silent as he took off his shoes. Than he shook his head. "You are an innocent. Dorothea and Ali . . . Christ! That's about the worst thing that could have happened."

Nora opened the bathroom door and stared at Mark. "Why? They got along beautifully."

"Too beautifully. Ali's up to something."

"Like what?"

"I don't know, but I have a hunch."

"What kind of hunch?"

The silence spun out. Then Mark said, "I once took a course in the Italian Renaissance. Ali could have been a member of one of the great Italian families . . . the Borgias, for example. Like Lucretia Borgia, she wears a poison ring."

"You think Ali will poison Dorothea? Don't be silly."

Mark grimaced. "Ali won't poison Dorothea. She'll poison Arthur . . . after she breaks up his marriage."

Nora crossed the bedroom and stood in front of Mark, her hands on her hips. She rarely raised her voice . . . now she did. "Ali didn't speak two words alone to Arthur. Or give him one winning smile or write her telephone number on his business card . . . or on a paper napkin.''

"Arthur can find Ali without any help."

Nora slipped between the sheets. She closed her eyes while Mark took over the bathroom. But as she listened to the buzz of the electric toothbrush, she suddenly became angry and shouted, "With millions of men all over the world chasing Ali, why should she choose Arthur?"

Mark said nothing until he climbed into bed and turned off the lamp. He lay on his back staring at the ceiling. Finally he spoke, and in the semidark of the bathroom night-light, his voice had an eerie ring. "Because, of the millions of men all over the world chasing Ali, very few have Arthur's millions."

"Some do."

"Some do. But they don't have Arthur's other credentials."

"Such as?"

"A history of heart disease in his family."

"Stop it, Mark," Nora said in a low voice. "You give me the creeps."

"Sorry. But look at it practically. Ali loves money . . . lots of money. She also loves her freedom. And she has two genuine talents. One is finding rich men."

"What about Aldo? He wasn't rich?"

"I'm not sure there ever was an Aldo. And if there was an Aldo, he was a learning experience. She hadn't yet found her true calling . . . her second talent. A talent that has only now begun to blossom."

"Okay. What's her second talent?"

"Inheriting," Mark said firmly. "I have a few clients who've done very well in the field."

Though the house was pleasantly warm, Nora felt chilled. "Where did you get such an awful idea?"

"Where Ali's concerned, from you."

Nora was aghast. "Me?"

"Remember her stepmother."

"Amanda died in a ski accident . . . an avalanche. There was nothing sinister about it."

"As far as anyone knows. Except that Ali inherited three million dollars."

"She'd have gotten the money anyway . . . on her thirtieth birthday."

"But she couldn't wait. So she inherited the money when she was twenty-two. And . . ." he added thoughtfully, "I think the time will come when that avalanche won't seem so accidental." He paused. "I don't believe Arthur has many years left. One day he'll drop dead on the tennis court. That's why I was so anxious to become a partner. I had to make partner before Arthur dies."

"You sound as conniving as you say Ali is."

"I am. That's why I understand her. Believe me, Nora. If Arthur leaves Dorothea for Ali, we'll be reading his obit sooner . . . not later."

Nora listened to the soothing sound of the surf. It didn't help. At last she got out of bed.

"Where are you going?" Mark asked.

"To get a sleeping pill. Don't say anything else."

"I won't. It's just that I hate being an accessory to murder."

The next morning Nora dressed rapidly and rushed through breakfast. For once she felt relieved that Mark had left earlier. She didn't want to hear any more about the short, unhappy life of Arthur Reiner. As she double-locked the house door she heard the telephone ring. She started to turn back . . . then stopped and continued to the garage. Just as she arrived at her office, her telephone rang. She stared at it. Where the hell was Sheri? If that was Ali . . . On the fifth ring she picked up. "Hello?"

It was Ali. "Nora! I missed you this morning. Oh, Nora, it was a wonderful party. Wonderful!"

"I thought everyone enjoyed themselves."

"I didn't think you'd get to the office before noon after that bash. But when I telephoned your house, you were up and at 'em." There was a question in her voice.

"I had a breakfast meeting with Pat Yocum," she lied.

Ali felt Nora's restraint. "Well . . . I had a wonderful time. And so did everyone else."

"That's nice. What can I do for you?"

Ignoring Nora's coolness, Ali jumped in feetfirst. "Nothing. I just wanted you to know that Dorothea and I will become bosom buddies. I threw a barrel of oil on troubled waters."

Nora's curiosity shot up. "How did you manage that?"

"I told her a fantasy she couldn't resist."

"What fantasy?"

"The oldest one in the world. That my stepmother, Amanda, said Arthur was a philanderer."

"You didn't."

"I did. I told her that Mumsie claimed he was congenitally unfaithful, but he would never, never leave Dorothea."

The air whooshed out of Nora's lungs in an almost audible gasp. "She must have loved that."

"She did . . . she really did." Ali chuckled softly. "I said Amanda claimed Arthur would never leave Dorothea because no other woman measured up to Dorothea in bed."

"You didn't!" Nora smothered her startle.

"I did."

"Did Amanda say that?"

"Of course not. When it came to sex, Amanda never thought about other women . . . only men."

Nora laughed in spite of herself. "She was faithful to Hiram in her fashion."

"Absolutely. I had Dorothea eating out of my hand."

"You wretch."

"Now you sound like your old self."

"I am my old self."

"Hmmm. You sounded so strange when we started talking."

"I am strange. It's my morning persona . . . after a night of almost no sleep. I'll be human by noon."

"Fine. I'll call you this afternoon late, and we can gossip."

Nora took stock of that possibility and found it disagreeable. "I'll be in a work session with Tim Rourke all afternoon. And because of last night I'm working late tonight. I've got to get ready for a big marketing meeting next Monday. I'll call you tomorrow afternoon."

"I'll be in Los Angeles for two days . . . talking to CAA . . . ICM . . . William Morris. About Millie's project. I'll call you when I get back."

"Power lunches. Nice work if you can get it. Call me. . . ."

* * *

On top of his usual business, Mark had put in a profitable month moving Dr. Abe and other clients in and out of a half dozen stocks . . . thirty trades in all. He guessed right on twenty-one out of the thirty trades, which meant that his customers made money. Of course, he made money on all thirty trades . . . over three thousand dollars. Win, lose or draw, Reiner & Co. always collected its commission. When he arrived home, he found Nora and Millie in the living room having drinks. Instantly he lost interest in the three thousand plus dollars he'd earned. Nora was seated in a deep leather chair while Millie sat on the hard-backed wooden chair reserved for her.

"Mark," Millie said, "glad you're home. Nora and I decided to have a meeting here . . . about my project . . . the one I hear you call Millie's Mania. Reminds me of Fulton's Folly."

Mark couldn't sink through the floor so he laughed sociably. "Bad joke. I'll never make a stand-up comedian."

"That's true. Come sit down. We finished our shop talk and went on to more personal matters . . . your wedding present."

"It's a wonderful idea." Nora's face glowed as she looked up at Mark. "Wait till you hear, Mark . . . you'll love it."

Mark made a supreme effort to remain calm. He said, "Oh . . . I'm sure I will."

Millie put down her drink and went through the elaborate procedure of selecting a cigarette from a thin silver cigarette case, inserting it into her jade holder, and lighting it.

Nora pulled on the lobe of her ear. "Arthur Reiner told Millie you're a natural trader . . . you have an instinct for the Street. That's why he made you a partner."

"I do my best," Mark said with a show of modesty.

"Apparently your best is better than most," Millie said.

"Thank you." Mark could no longer contain himself. "What is it? I mean, the present."

Millie smiled at Nora. "Tell him."

"Millie's not satisfied with the way Raymond Welsh handles her risk capital portfolio. She'd like you to take it over."

"What!" Although still sitting in his chair, Mark slowly levitated. Millie was coming through.

Nora turned to Millie. "He's done very well for Paul Pratt and Leslie Kelly and the Bretts."

"They told me." Millie gave Mark a quizzical glance. It said, Nora didn't mention Dr. Abe's account.

Mark prayed Millie remembered that although the wedding ceremony said "For richer, for poorer," it did not say he had to tell Nora the details of how they got richer.

Millie didn't drop the candy in the sand. "Well, Mark . . . tell me. Do you like my present? Do you want to manage a ten-million-dollar account for me?"

"It's a nice piece of business," Mark said carefully.

"It sure is," Nora said. "Reiner & Co. will get the commissions on all the trades you make for Millie." She turned to Millie. "You know, Mark keeps forty percent of the commissions."

"I know," Millie said with a smile. "I expect Mark to make a great deal of money trading the account . . . and make my ten million grow like Topsy." A look of pleasure crossed her face. "I've plans for this money—"

Nora interrupted, full of happiness. "That's the point, Mark. Millie's come up with a wonderful idea. The ten million plus the money you make for her will go to our children—"

"My great-grandchildren." Millie smiled.

Mark stared at Millie in total admiration. She had played a trump card. How could Nora ever say no to such an offer? For the first time he dared to tempt fate by doing a rough mental calculation on how much money he'd make on Millie's ten million. If he turned over the ten million, say, three times a year—three times wasn't churning the account—he'd be trading sixty million a year . . . figuring both the in and out trades. Reiner & Co. averaged about a one percent commission on each trade. That came to six hundred thousand dollars. And he got forty percent or . . . Wow! Two hundred thousand dollars a year. The numbers made him dizzy.

"And the first should be bowing in in about six months," Millie said.

"Millie! Ssssh! It's a still a secret. Only Mark, you and Dr. Sussman know. I told you in the strictest confidence."

"Of course you did." Millie and Nora smiled at each other. They both understood. Millie would tell the family. Nora was relieved, thinking of the calls she wouldn't have to make . . .

they'd call her. "As soon as Nora gives birth, I'll be setting up a living trust for the baby. The money will go to my great-grandchild after my death."

"You're not going to die," Nora stated firmly.

"Everyone dies eventually. Some sooner and some later." Millie crushed out her cigarette. "Now I'll be going."

"So soon?" Nora asked.

"Yes. The chairman of the Rancho Santa Fe Polo Club executive committee called a meeting for six o'clock. I'll barely make it." Millie stood up. There was no meeting at the club, but Nora and Mark had a lot to talk about . . . she'd be in the way.

Chapter 11

IT WAS Friday . . . mid afternoon . . . the freeways were in gridlock. Too many people were trying to get home early to the Southern California good life . . . swimming in their heated pools, playing tennis or golf, jogging on the beach while the daylight lasted. That afternoon Mark worked late . . . Nora worked late. Neither was enjoying the good life. Both were frayed . . . frazzled . . . battle scarred.

Mark had a pissing contest with Arthur on the matter of going long on the Dow for Dr. Abe's account.

"But, Mark, it's a high-risk move," Arthur cautioned.

"He wants high-risk moves . . . that's why I got the account. I made him a bundle going long on oil futures."

"And you almost gave him a heart attack. I hear he was on the phone every fifteen minutes."

"Dealing with Dr. Abe's heart attacks goes with the territory." Mark was matter-of-fact.

"Okay. He's your account . . . it's your call. If he calls me to complain, I'll say he's absolutely right and bounce him back to you."

"If he calls you, don't take the call."

"Stop it, Mark. He's too close to Mrs. G. for me not to take his calls. That reminds me. The Lew Dobbs Group H deal closes in three weeks. Who's covering for you while you're in Phoenix?"

Mark grinned. "You are. My clients won't trust anyone else."

"Oh, Jesus! Mrs. G. . . . Dr. Abe Lombard. Damn it!" Arthur grimaced. "Go away, Mark . . . while I still like you."

Mark gave Arthur a mock salute. *"Ciao*, boss," he said as he left.

On her end, Nora had a run-in with with Tim Rourke about a thirty-minute infomercial called "Updating Men."

"Saints be praised," Nora sounded off. "We have the Rufus Halsey Cure for Baldness . . . Impotence . . . Obesity. Tim Rourke, I call down the curse of Saint Paddy on you. May the snakes return to Ireland. Rufus Halsey is pitching snake oil. And you, a lad from Country Kilkenny, want to run this stupid drivel."

"New evidence proves that . . ." Tim's Irish smile was impish.

"New evidence proves shit! Doctored doctors . . . doctored evidence . . . false and misleading advertising. Where are your ethics, man?"

"In my wallet, baby. It's survival time. In case you've forgotten, the country's in a recession. The car dealers have cut their ad budgets . . . including the guy who claims the only dog on the lot looks like Lassie. Also the shampoo groupies . . . gone are those beautiful broads with the long, fluffy hair. You think they're working the strip in L.A.? And the fiber freaks? What's happened to the American nightmare . . . constipation? Even the perfumes are pfft! Where are Passion and Obsession? Nowhere . . . that's where. They've given up on earlobes . . . on nipples . . . on belly buttons. The point is—in case you haven't been following me—Channel 18 needs to sell more ad time. Infomercials bring in big bucks."

"They also tell big lies."

"So who doesn't?" Tim glared at Nora. "Go away. We are running Rufus Halsey's infomercial . . . end of story."

A furious Nora slammed out of Tim's office. She spent the rest of the day making a series of futile calls to ad agencies. The time buyers were out, or on the phone, or in a meeting. She'd try again tomorrow. If she could pick up something reputable, she'd force Tim to deep-six Halsey's cure for baldness . . . impotence . . . unemployment.

By the time Nora and Mark got home, they were too tired to either cook dinner or eat out. So they telephoned an order for two small pizzas to Pizza Trends. Over Nora's protests—Mark's cholesterol was borderline high—Mark ordered a pizza with the works . . . double cheese, sausage, mushrooms, pepperoni and anchovies. In self defense, Nora had a vegetarian pizza . . . mushrooms, onions, bell peppers, black olives and no cheese. When the pizzas arrived, they opened a couple of cans of beer and turned on the TV. They were munching away watching "Mystery Theater" when the phone rang. It was Ali. Nora disappeared into the second-floor office. By the time she returned, Mark had finished his pizza and was into his second can of beer. "Mystery Theater" was over.

"What did your girlhood chum have to say? She's always a mine of misinformation."

"Dorothea and Arthur and Ali went to an opening at the Museum of Contemporary Art in La Jolla. Dorothea and she adored Yusef Chamoon's paintings. Arthur was bored out of his mind."

"Is that all you talked about . . . for almost an hour?"

"We talked about people. Love. Her future. Ours . . ."

Mark sat up straighter . . . his paranoia rampant. "Hold it right there. What did you say about our future."

"I didn't say anything . . . she did." Nora nibbled on her cold pizza. "Guess who she saw earlier this evening?" She sipped her warm, flat beer. Mark stared at her. "Come on, Mark. Try it. You'll hate it. It's someone we know and love."

"Not your uncle Hiram? He's not . . . Millie? What has Millie—" He stopped. Nora was shaking her head. "Eric Smollens . . . the rich kid she fucks. We don't know him that well."

"She only sleeps with Eric"—Nora bit off a piece of pizza, chewed on it, and dropped her bombshell—"when she's not sleeping with Arthur."

Mark swallowed wrong . . . he coughed violently. For an instant he thought he would choke on the beer. After Nora slapped him on the back several times, he stopped coughing. He said, "I'm glad she has other interests . . . besides my boss. Don't say I didn't warn you."

"She sleeps with Eric . . ." Nora finished her beer before remarking, "But she's in love with Arthur. It's different."

"Right! He's the love of her life."

"Quit it, Mark." Nora felt nauseous. "It wouldn't have happened if Dorothea hadn't asked Ali to make sure Arthur had a few decent meals while she was doing low-impact aerobics at Spa Pacifica. Ali made dinner for Arthur one night and . . . well . . . One thing led to another."

"So it's all Dorothea's fault?"

"It's nobody's fault. They just clicked. These things happen." Nora tried to stifle her dismay.

Mark didn't. He'd won a bet with himself . . . that Ali would go public sooner rather then later. Still, this was sooner than he'd expected. "How long have you known about the romance of the decade . . . the Liz and Dick of the nineties?"

"A few days." Remembering Ali's tearful telephone confession, Nora winced. "The day after Arthur told her you were watching her building. . . ."

Mark took his time absorbing this piece of information. "Nice of Arthur to keep her posted," he said at last.

"He saw your car parked near her building. When he talked to you about it, you said you just happened to be there . . . by accident . . ."

Watch yourself, Mark thought. Arthur was playing some kind of game. True to form, the asshole hadn't let him in on it. "Right. It was an accident."

"I've been waiting for you to tell me why you followed Arthur," Nora said quietly.

"I didn't follow him. I told you it was an accident. I was seeing a client in Hillcrest—"

"Mark, that's bullshit! Don't tell me you just happened to be parked in Hillcrest near Ali's condo? If Arthur believes that, he's a bigger fool than I realized. I don't believe it. Not for a minute. You were spying on them. Why?"

Mark reminded himself that a believable lie must be ninety-five percent true. "Game, set and match to Nora Stern." He smiled. "Yeah. I was spying on them. You know I've had this itchy feeling about them ever since our wedding. Then I got itchier when you said Ali and Dorothea had become great friends. They have about as much in common as I do with Jordan Banska." He ignored Nora's tight mouth. "So I played a hunch. One night I was seeing a client in Hillcrest . . . Ben Gillebaard lives in Hillcrest. For the hell of it, I drove by the Coral Tree Plaza . . . where the Ali Cat lives. And what do you know . . . there was Arthur's limousine. And where Arthur's limousine is parked, Arthur can not be far behind. So I parked and waited."

"Why do you care if Arthur and Ali are sacking out? You can't blackmail Arthur."

"Forget blackmail. Arthur Reiner is the Reiner of Reiner

& Co. I want to know as much as I can about the last of the red-hot lovers.'' His voice became hard. "And believe me, my palms sweat at the idea of your Ali Cat spreading for my boss. Think about it, Nora, Ali met Arthur through us. What if Dorothea feels vindictive? Being a partner won't save me from unfriendly fire. I could be whipsawed between those two eagle scouts.'' Mark studied the tips of his shoes. A good lie, he thought. Barely a lie at all . . . not even five percent untrue.

"She says she's in love with him,'' Nora said wearily.

"That follows. Sex is just Ali's opening strategy. Next . . . she's in love. Ali is like a general with a life mission. Marry money . . . serious money . . . available money . . . the kind of money that can be inherited quickly. Like Arthur's money.''

"Mark, stop it!''

"Sorry. Just pointing out the facts. She'll be expecting an expensive wedding present . . . a silver something. And I don't mean silver plate.''

"Ali can't marry Arthur . . . he's married to Dorothea . . . has been forever.'' Nora's voice became hopeful. "Apparently Dorothea doesn't know about them. That's a good sign.''

Mark considered his options. Arthur had not told Ali about Dorothea's detective. A shrewd decision. He'd play the same game.

"Apparently she doesn't know,'' he said cautiously. "Not yet anyway.''

Nora stopped nibbling her cold pizza. "I think that you think Dorothea will find out.''

"Ali will make sure she does.''

"You may be right. She doesn't like back street affairs. She says they're stifling . . . you can't go anywhere together.''

"She's just a poor, caged Ali Cat . . . mewing and vulnerable.''

Nora didn't look at Mark. She was struggling with her own lie of omission . . . the memory of Ali's chitchat about her college fling with Arthur . . . and her promise to keep off the grass. So much for Ali's promises.

"I was a fool to trust her. I should never have invited Arthur and her to the same party.''

"Apology accepted." Mark was generous to a fault. He enjoyed a good gloat. "What the hell! They were bound to find each other. Two deprived sex junkies in search of a quick fix." His face lit up with a gargoylelike smile. "I have a thought for you. Suppose Dorothea doesn't care?"

"If you mean she doesn't care about Arthur's fucking around, you're right. But if you mean she doesn't care about the marriage, forget it. She's a true believer in marriage." Nora half wailed, "And it'll be my fault if Arthur asks for a divorce."

"Mea culpa. Mea culpa. You sound like my mother. She's guilty about everything. The spotted owl. Losing the rent money on a penny stock. The salmon. Blowing the food budget on another penny stock. The redwoods. The one time she hit a winner, she was guilty because she lost her nerve and cashed in when the stock hit one dollar. The Halloid Company—later known as Xerox—went a lot higher. Take off the hair shirt, Nora. Arthur will not ask for a divorce."

"I know Ali. She gives no quarter."

"I know Dorothea. She'll fight to the death."

Nora gave him the ghost of a smile. "Let's make a bet."

"Sure. I'll bet Ali comes out with egg on her face."

"And I'll bet she'll win in a walk . . . I mean a walk down the aisle." She crossed her fingers. "Please, God. Let me lose."

"You will. What's the prize?"

"The winner picks it."

"Okay. So now we sit and wait for the milk to curdle." Mark gave Nora a long look, then he folded his arms across his chest. "By the way, when the Ali Cat bared her soul to you, did you read her the riot act . . . tell her where to head in?"

"No . . ." Nora flushed. "I should have. I didn't."

Mark unfolded his arms. "Good. I'm glad you didn't blow. Diplomacy tells us . . . jaw, jaw, jaw. Not war, war, war. The best way to keep informed about an enemy is to go to lunch with her, go to dinner with her . . . even go to bed with her. If girl-to-girl sex is your style."

Nora slumped on the couch . . . smiling a crooked smile. She'd been thinking exactly the same thing.

* * *

Nora slammed down the phone. She'd been on a telephone marathon . . . called every major ad agency that she'd ever done any business with. The net result was zero. Not a single agency had agreed to increase its advertising on Channel 18. The excuse was always a variable on the same themes. Ad budgets were cut back . . . Channel 18 is an independent station . . . your shows are network reruns, old movies and programs of local interest. The buzz of her intercom roused her.

"Yes, Sheri?"

"Mrs. G. wants to see you now . . . before the meeting. And she says you should bring Donna's brochure with you."

"Tell her I'm on my way." Before leaving her office, Nora tucked the 'Night of Stars' promotion piece under her arm.

Millie's office was at the far end of the corridor, at the juncture where the two arms of the V-shaped building came together. Unlike the other Channel 18 executives, Millie had no private secretary. If she needed anything done, she used Sheri. Since there was no one at the desk in front of Millie's office, Nora knocked on the door and then entered the office.

Millie looked up. "You have Donna's presentation. Good. What do you think of it?"

Nora always told Millie the truth. This was no time for sugar coating. "It's clever. But there are too many blanks. Not only the cast members and crew. It's the advertisers . . . the playbill/brochure has no advertising. Who is going to advertise on the program?"

"That's your job . . . to sell the time slots. I asked Luddy and the others to join us, but first I wanted to hear your ideas. How do we attract advertisers?"

"I've been thinking about that. We don't go for advertisers. We start by selling a superstation. Once we can promise an advertiser national distribution, I think enough will bite. And if we strike out with the superstations—none of them will buy the show—I'll call Danny Darroch and we'll see what we can do with the national advertisers."

A knock on the door interrupted them.

"Damn!" Millie said. "There's nothing worse than people who are punctual when I'm running late. We'll pick this up later. Come in," she called out in a loud voice.

The door opened and Luddy Poole, followed closely by Tim Rourke and Pat Yokum, spilled into the room.

"Sit down, please." Millie gestured toward the conference

table. When everyone was settled, she said, "Nora, show everyone what Donna has come up with." She waited until Luddy, Tim and Pat finished studying the brochure. Then she said, "The floor is open. Comments, please."

Luddy and Pat were enthusiastic. They took turns saying what they assumed Millie wanted to hear.

"A good piece of work," Luddy said.

"It makes a statement." Pat sounded eager.

They went on.

Finally Millie held up her hand. "Enough. Tim, you're pretty quiet," she said. "Don't you like the playbill?"

"Donna hasn't reinvented the wheel. Maybe it'll work. But . . ."

"But what?"

"But there are a lot of blank spaces for advertisers. And we have no demographic studies on who wants to see plays on television. The yuppies . . . the Gray Panthers . . . the couch potatoes? Who? We don't know which advertisers are right for the program. Nora's going to bust her butt . . . Sorry, Mrs. G." He coughed as Millie motioned for him to continue.

"Anyway, I think the playbill idea for a brochure is good. But it's putting the cart before the horse. We don't need a brochure now . . . we need to pinpoint our audience."

"We know our audience," Millie said. "It's the same audience who watched Dustin Hoffman in *Death of a Salesman.*"

"*Death of a Salesman* didn't get a double-digit rating," Tim observed.

"It was shown on public television. Nielson doesn't rate public television," Nora said.

"A cable network will schedule a play starring Tammi Meredith," Millie said. "Right now my granddaughter Ali Gardiner is in Los Angeles talking to Mel Gibson's agent. Gibson did *Hamlet.* Maybe he'd like to do another Shakespearean role."

"Can we get Gibson?" Pat asked.

"We can try."

Pat glanced slyly at Nora. "Shouldn't you be out selling 'Night of Stars' right this minute? It would be a lot easier to get Mel Gibson if we had Ford and Kellogg's lined up."

"I like it," Luddy said. "We can test the waters before we spend any more money on *Mama.*"

"I think you're off the wall," Tim said angrily. "Nora has nothing to sell . . . except this." He held up the playbill/brochure.

"What do you think, Nora?" Millie asked. "Can you sell 'Night of Stars' to the Ford ad agency from this brochure?"

Nora hesitated and then said, "I don't know. I do know it would be easier if I had fifteen minutes of Tammi Meredith in *Mama* on tape."

Millie slapped the conference table with the flat of her hand. "We don't have Tammi Meredith, so I did the next best thing. I had Manny put together a show for you. Come with me." She led the group from her office to a nearby screening room. When everyone was seated, she spoke into a microphone. "Are you ready, Manny?"

"Ready, Mrs. G."

"Run it."

The lights dimmed and the Channel 18 executives watched a thirty-minute short. It consisted of a series of scenes from film versions of plays . . . in part the scenes consisted of Richard Burton and Elizabeth Taylor in *Who's Afraid of Virginia Woolf,* Rex Harrison and Audrey Hepburn in *My Fair Lady,* Laurence Olivier in *Henry V,* Wendy Hiller in *Major Barbara,* Vivien Leigh in *Caesar and Cleopatra.* Nora counted twenty scenes . . . each scene was riveting.

When the film ended, Millie said, "Thank you, Manny." She brought the lights up and swiveled her seat to face the Channel 18 staff. "What do you think of that as a selling tool?"

Luddy was quickest off the mark. "It's great," he said.

Pat chimed in, "Christ! Even I could sell the series after showing those scenes."

"Whoa, dobbin," Tim said. "That stuff is under copyright. We can't use any of it."

"We can with the studios' permission," Millie said.

"They'll never give their permission." Tim was adamant.

"They already have." Millie gave him a small smile.

"Incredible!" Tim gasped.

"Not incredible. Friends in high places."

Tim wouldn't give up. "You want Nora to lug around a can of film to every appointment?"

"I'll carry a videotape cassette," Nora said. "Channel 18 has the technical facilities to transfer the film to tape."

"One more time, everyone. Should Nora try to sell 'Night of Stars' to the advertisers? Now? Or should she wait until we've finished *Mama*?"

"I say she goes now," Luddy said.

Pat nodded. "I agree. Nora can do it."

At least she didn't call me Norakins, Nora thought.

Tim stubbornly held out. "It's too soon. We're a year away from production. Your half-hour film was great, Mrs. G. But Channel 18 had nothing to do with those films. And I don't think Jordan Banska directed any of them. Nora will be selling hot air . . . smoke and mirrors . . . nothing tangible."

"Nora?" Millie said. "What do you think?"

Nora had a hunch the whole meeting was an exercise in make-believe . . . and Millie thought so too. But that was nobody's business. "Let's go with it," she said.

"All right. That's it," Millie said. "Everybody, back to work. Nora, stay with me. We have details to work out."

After the Channel 18 people had left, Millie said what Nora had expected.

"Tim is right. We had nothing to do with those films. We won't get credit for them. Actually, the demo was a dog-and-pony show . . . to smoke out the pros and cons. Who is for 'Night of Stars' . . . who is against it. Luddy and Pat agreed to your pitching the show now . . . they hope you'll fall on your face. And I'll drop the whole idea. Tim is against it because he's smarter. He knows it's premature. Even if you make no sales, I won't drop the project. So he'll be all for my going ahead . . . until we tape the entire play. And I've spent a few million producing it. Then, if it bombs, he believes I'll drop the project. What it comes down to is they're all against the project."

Nora recognized the shrewd workings of Millie's mind. She couldn't have given a more precise analysis. "I agree," she said. "But I have another reason for wanting to test the waters now. I want to hear the negatives from the broadcasters . . . beside the standard argument that the show's too highbrow. Then—when I try to sell the show for real—I'll know how best to pitch it. The demo gives me an excuse to sound out the boys."

Millie smiled her approval. "The more we know, the better. And nothing ventured, nothing etcetera.'' She stood up and gave Nora an affectionate smile. ''Two minds are better than one . . . or some such nonsense. Meeting ended.''

Nora was preparing to leave the station when her private line rang. When she picked it up, a small voice said, ''Nora?''

Nora hardly recognized the voice. ''Ali?''

The small, uncertain voice continued, ''Nora, we must talk.''

''I thought you were seeing agents in L.A. Mel Gibson's—''

''I was . . . Something came up.'' Shy laugh. ''Or someone.'' Nora waited. ''Anyway, could we meet? I'll explain when I see you.''

''I have to get home. Where are you?''

''At the lower-deck bar of the *Ruben E. Lee.* That's not far out of your way . . . is it?''

''No. It's only minutes off the freeway. I'll be there as soon as I can.''

''I'll wait for you.'' Ali's tone was heartfelt. ''I knew you wouldn't let me down.''

''Think of me as Old Faithful.'' Nora hung up . . . she stared at the phone. Did Ali actually believe she'd be a patsy again? She did.

When Nora arrived at the *Ruben E. Lee,* she parked her car and walked across the gangplank leading to the Mississippi riverboat that had been converted into a restaurant and bar. Ali was seated at a booth at the side of the room, sipping a scotch and looking pensively out the window at the water and the San Diego skyline.

As Nora slipped into the seat opposite her, Ali faced her and said, ''I need your advice, Nora . . . desperately!''

''About what?''

''I have to make a decision.'' They exchanged looks. ''About—I loathe the word *affair,* but that is the right word— about our affair. The situation with Arthur is becoming untenable.''

Nora felt a shortness of breath. ''Dorothea?''

''Yes. Arthur's always had women. Evidently Dorothea has always known about them. But somehow I'm more important to Arthur. He cares for Dorothea immensely. I care for her too . . . she's a very dear friend . . .''

"You've an odd way of being a friend."

"Oh, Nora, you're wrong. I've shielded Dorothea as long as I could," Ali said quietly. "But I won't be able to much longer. Arthur's talked of our getting married. He wants to divorce Dorothea. I've stopped him so far."

After a long silence Nora asked, "Do you want to marry him?"

"I haven't let myself think of it." Ali gave herself a little shake. "But I've known that sooner or later I'd have to decide." She continued in a tremulous tone. "Sooner is now. I want to marry him very much, but I wish . . . I wish I didn't have to face it so soon."

"Why soon?"

"Because people—our friends—are beginning to suspect. I've caught some odd looks. You know. The curious face with the unspoken question. Sometimes when we go out—Arthur and Dorothea and I—we have dinner in a restaurant or go to a movie. I see it on the faces of friends. It's intangible . . . the tiny pursing of a woman's lips . . . a slight narrowing of a man's eyes. What surprises me most is that I notice the looks at all. People have always talked about me. I can't say—can I—that I haven't given them cause?"

"You have been visible."

Ali put her drink on the table and brought her hands to her face. "What makes it worse is that Arthur is not well. . . ." Her voice was muffled. "He knows he hasn't many years to live. Degenerative heart disease of some kind . . . he won't talk about it." She folded her hands in her lap and raised her face, the charming face all smooth and shiny with tears . . . braced for the act of self-sacrifice. "He wants to be happy while he still has time. He says I make him happier than he's ever been in his life. That's why he wants to marry me."

"And you want to marry him?" Nora was businesslike. This was worse than she'd expected.

"Oh, Nora, yes! But it won't be easy." Ali's voice begged for understanding. "What do I do after he's gone? I love him so much. How do I dispose of my leftover life? Maybe forty years or more. Arthur's spoiled me for all the green, money-grubbing young men . . . and the rich, aging widowers with their Lifecycle machines. I couldn't bear a professor with pretensions or a beautiful actor who freaks out on coke. Am I behaving like a fool, Nora? Tell me I am. Tell me I should say, 'No, Arthur, no!' Help me, Nora. Help me help myself.''

Nora didn't know whether to laugh or cry at Ali's dramatics. At last she said coolly, ''You have a problem. By the way, what about Dorothea?''

''Yes! What about her? I owe her so much.''

''Will she give Arthur a divorce?''

''Yes. She told me she's met a young man . . . a musicologist of some sort.''

''That's convenient.'' Nora frowned. ''Then I suppose it's settled. Tell Arthur to ask for a divorce.''

''You think I should? You really think it's all right?''

''I think it's all right.''

''I was afraid you'd see it that way. As usual, you're right. I'm so emotional I've forgotten how to make decisions. Thank you . . . you always understand.''

Nora almost lost her temper. Diplomacy. Diplomacy, she reminded herself. Keep in touch with the enemy. Yes, Ali, she thought. I understand you . . . too well.

That evening over drinks Nora told Mark the news.

Mark shook his head, astonished. ''Arthur is getting old. He's thinking with his prick.''

Nora was full of self-reproach. ''She targeted him at the wedding.''

''And played potsy with Dorothea for six months.''

''The best I can say for myself is that she called me first. At least we're prepared should Dorothea set off any fireworks.''

''She had to call you first. Arthur knows we know.''

Suddenly Nora felt chilled. ''Did you deliberately let Arthur see your car?''

Mark raised an eyebrow. ''No. But I would have if I'd thought of it. In any case, I'm glad he saw the car.''

''As I said, you're as bad as Ali.''

''I'm much worse. You're lucky to have me to protect you.''

''And who will protect me from you?''

His smile was real. ''I'm yours. You're mine. You don't need protection from me.''

Nora stared at Mark. But instead of the Mark she loved,

she seemed to see many other things. Eventually she said, "I hope not. I'm not sure I could handle it."

Mark studied her coolly, objectively. "You'd figure out something . . . you're Millie Gardiner's granddaughter. The blood runs true. . . ."

Dorothea got a quick divorce and asked for neither alimony nor child support for their son, Roger. Nora decided the divorce was what people call a "good divorce." As opposed to a "messy divorce," with the bitter legal battles over who gets custody of the children or who gets the paintings or the house or the sailboat or the Royal Doulton place settings for twenty-five. It occurred to her that the Reiners' divorce was a "good divorce" because neither was in love with the other . . . and neither needed the other's money.

The only serious opposition to Arthur's marriage to Ali came from Hiram Gardiner. It was unexpected and vehement. Hiram called the marriage obscene. He pointed out that Arthur and he had been classmates . . . Arthur was old enough to be Ali's father. Ali pleaded for understanding. Hiram refused. He was sick and tired of trying to understand Ali. He would not give the bride away. In fact, he would have nothing to do with the wedding, not one damn thing.

A week after Hiram and Ali agreed to disagree, Arthur called Mark into his office. There was a red velvet box on the conference table. "Open it," Arthur suggested.

Mark did as requested and blinked. Set in the red velvet box was a huge square-cut diamond engagement ring . . . platinum with twin diamond baguettes. Mark knew nothing about diamonds, but he did know this ring was large and expensive. He held the ring up to the light . . . the diamonds sparkled with a life of their own.

"Beautiful," was Mark's opinion. "This should make it up to Ali for Hiram's narrow-mindedness."

"Ali's forgotten Hiram," Arthur said blandly. "That's an eighteen-point-five-carat ring."

That evening Mark told Nora, "Who am I to argue with a man who has bought his fiancée an eighteen-point-five-carat diamond ring?"

Given Hiram's objections, Arthur and Ali gave up on the idea of a big wedding . . . there'd be too much gossip about

Hiram's refusal to give the bride away. They settled for the Vista City Hall and a judge. Except for Dorothea, the cast of characters was the same as for Nora's and Mark's wedding . . . only the roles had changed. The bride wore white with a bang . . . white palazzo pants with yards of ruffles and a lacy white bodice and a white veil. As Mark and Nora drove to the wedding brunch at the Valencia, Mark asked, "Did Ali wear white to prove to Arthur she was a virgin bride?"

PART 7

Nora and Mark
1992–1993

Chapter 12

LIKE OTHER men who had grown up knowing that they would have to wear the same pair of pants for several years— even if, eventually, the pants barely reached their ankles— Mark took meticulous care of his clothing. Each of his suits and jackets was kept in its own clothing bag to protect it from moths. His ties hung from a stainless steel tie rack . . . the ties that went with his blue and gray suits were on the left and the ties he wore with his brown and beige suits were on the right. His shoes were also divided according to the suits with which they were to be worn, and each shoe rested in a separate pocket of the cloth shoe caddy that hung on the back of the closet door. What amused Nora the most was the precise arrangement of Mark's underwear, socks and shirts . . . everything was compartmentalized and color coordinated for easy selection . . . depending on whether he was wearing a suit from his blue/gray collection or his brown/beige collection. Her own lingerie . . . lacy panties, Jockey shorts, bras and undershirts were crammed together in a bureau drawer. When she fumbled through the drawer searching for something, all she knew for sure was it would be clean.

Mark packed with the same care that he kept his clothes. He folded a pair of pants on the bottom of his suitcase so they wouldn't crease. Next came his tie . . . also folded so it wouldn't crease. Then the jacket was folded inside out with the shoulders fitted in such a way as not to crush the tiny amount of padding . . . Mark had learned the technique from an old-time Brooks Brothers salesman. His shirts, underwear and handkerchiefs followed. The suitcase was almost packed . . . there remained space for a bathrobe, his socks, shoes and his toiletries.

Mark abruptly looked up from his packing. "Somehow she conned him . . ." He waved a shoe in the air.

Nora laughed without humor. "You object to happy endings?"

"Who's happy? Are you happy? Am I?" He placed the shoe against the side of the suitcase.

"You thought she was a fool." Nora handed him the other shoe.

"Yes. But her own special kind of fool. She's tough . . . she has imagination and wiliness. A fool with a purpose. How did she get Arthur to marry her?"

"I wish I knew. I am not her private secretary. She doesn't keep me apprised of her troop movements." Nora handed him two pair of socks.

"Was it blackmail?" Mark shook his head. "How the hell could she blackmail Arthur?"

"Maybe lover boy was smitten." Nora was sweet reason. "Now tell me, will Lew Dobbs meet you in Phoenix?"

"Come on, Nora. Ali must have told you something . . . you can tell me. Am I not your favorite husband?"

"You are . . . and we are having a lover's quarrel. I am bored with the Ali hype. It just makes me mad. So let's drop it. Will Dobbs . . ."

Mark slid the case containing his toiletries into the space he'd left for it. "Dobbs will. At the closing. He's the buyer. I don't understand you. Despite everything she's done, whenever Ali Cat's name comes up, you head for the hills." Nora met him at eye level and his voice slowed to a halt. "Okay . . . skip it. Let's talk about Michelle." He patted her stomach. "Or Michael. How do you feel?"

Nora handed him his robe. "Stop worrying about me. I'm fine. After work today, I'll go to the club and swim laps. Tomorrow I'll jog three miles on the beach . . ."

"With your sore legs and your aching back? You're nuts. Please take maternity leave soon."

"Why? I'm strong as an ox. Dr. Sussman agrees. I'm supposed to be uncomfortable. My back is supposed to hurt. My legs too. And don't forget my hemorrhoid."

"You'll be okay while I'm away?" Mark asked with nervous pride.

"Well, hardly lean and mean. But . . . okay. And in four months it's over . . . he or she arrives."

Mark fidgeted while closing his suitcase. He suddenly asked, "Tomorrow you're meeting with Jordan?"

"With Millie and Jordan." The animation drained from her face. "A four o'clock meeting at the Farm."

"I'm sorry you couldn't sell the program." He made sympathetic noises.

"So am I. But it was a long shot. Very long."

"You did the best you could. You can't win 'em all."

"I didn't even place or show. It was worse than I expected," she said dryly. "And you're glad I blew it."

Mark had difficulty meeting Nora's eyes. "You know how I feel. I think 'Night of Stars' is lunacy. Why is Jordan going to be at the meeting? It's Millie's business . . . Channel 18's business. Why isn't he boozing it up in Ireland or making a film in Africa?" He set his suitcase on the floor.

"I don't know. Miss Kratz telephoned yesterday that he was joining us. Millie invited him."

Mark slipped on his jacket. "Will you have dinner with him later? Or will you eat at the Farm?"

Nora smiled. Watching his face was like seeing an X ray of his psyche. "Dear heart, what are you . . . my protocol officer?"

He grinned. "No. Just a standard-issue jealous husband."

"Relax. Our love and togetherness reigns." With a quick, almost shy gesture she raised her lips. "Kiss me."

Mark took her in his arms carefully . . . not holding her tightly for fear of hurting the baby. This constant self-policing was doing a number on his sex drive. He brushed his lips against her hair as she buried her face in his shoulder.

"Sorry, honey. Sometimes I act like an asshole."

Nora opened her eyes and looked up at him. She pressed his hand against the swell of her breast.

He tensed. "There's no time . . . the plane leaves . . ."

"I know," she said, biting her lip. "Just so you remember."

Mark drew back a little and, bending over, kissed her hard. Bravely. As lovers they possessed a past. As husband and wife their future had only begun. Their kiss was a pact and a reassurance.

When they broke for breath Mark picked up his suitcase. "Wish me luck with the closing. With Dobbs. With Group H. . . ."

"Amen! Good luck with Group H. Break a leg with Dobbs."

"Will you love me if I fail?" Mark teased.

Nora's gaze was haughty. "In the words of the immortal Bob and Ray—"

Mark burst out laughing. "Write when you find work."

"Hang by your thumbs."

They both laughed.

"I'll call you tonight from Phoenix," Mark said. Picking up his suitcase, he started up the stairs. The airport shuttle service was due any minute.

When Mark arrived at Sky Harbor Airport on the outskirts of Phoenix, there was a pleasant surprise waiting for him . . . a very pretty blonde in a gray chauffeur's uniform. She was holding a large white card with "Mr. Mark Stern" printed in bold black letters. Mark stopped in front of the girl. "I'm Mark Stern."

"My name is Gigi. I'm Mr. Ashland's chauffeur. He asked me to meet you and drive you to your hotel. Where are you staying?"

"At the Airport Holiday Inn."

"With your permission, sir, I would like to cancel your reservation. Mr. Ashland arranged for you to stay at the Camelback Tennis Ranch in Scottsdale. It's convenient to Group H's headquarters."

"I see."

The chauffeur's voice became intimate. "Mr. Ashland has reserved our company bungalow for you. The bungalow has a small pool and a Jacuzzi . . ." She smiled. "Also absolute privacy."

Mark looked hard at the girl. The come-on was blatant, too good to be true.

"I've been assigned to you while you're here . . . to make sure you're not bored at night."

It was true.

"You checked your luggage, sir?" Mark nodded. "Then you just follow me. I'll cancel your reservation at the Airport Holiday. Then we'll collect your luggage and drop it off at the bungalow."

Mark nodded . . . and nodded . . . and nodded.

* * *

Mark allowed Gigi to take care of everything. On the way to Group H headquarters, Gigi talked about the bungalow. "We lease it all year 'round. We get many important visitors . . . advertising executives and station reps . . . sometimes they bring their wives. Mr. Ashland believes making VIPs comfortable is good business."

"Right," Mark said.

Gigi pointed down the road. "There it is," she said. "Group H headquarters."

Mark shook his head as though to clear away a mirage. "In Arizona did Kubli Khan a pleasure dome decree," he chanted. "Drive slowly, Gigi. I don't want to miss a thing."

Group H headquarters stood on top of a small mountain of rock . . . about two hundred feet high. Engineers had blasted off the peak to create a flat area. Then they'd floated a slab of concrete that extended well beyond the edge of the mountain and was supported by concrete columns that angled down from the slab and were anchored into bedrock. On top of the slab was a one-story round concrete building—corporate headquarters—and a good-size parking area. The driveway to the headquarters wound up and around the mountain like a corkscrew and was also supported by concrete columns that angled into the bedrock. The safety railing at the outer edge of the driveway was made out of stainless steel that was formed to spell "Group H, Group H, Group H" more times than Mark could count. The complex was an architectural triumph, a monument to one man's ego and an enormous waste of corporate assets. With this huge nonprofit making capital expenditure on the books, no wonder Group H's cash flow had dropped from five million to two million in only a few years.

When Gigi stopped the car at the entrance to the building, Mark was met by another young woman. She said, "Welcome to Group H, Mr. Stern. My name is Bobbi Weeks. I'm Mr. Ashland's private secretary. Mr. Ashland asked me to show you around the facility. He'll join us later in the executive dining room."

Mark took in the girl's conservative dress for success, tan suit, tan blouse, and sensible low-heeled brown shoes. If Gigi was for fun and games, Bobbi Weeks was all business. He followed her along the circular corridor that went clear around the building. Although the outside wall was glass and the hot

Arizona sun was beating down on the glass, inside the building the temperature was comfortable.

"You must have quite an air-conditioning system," Mark
said.

"We do. Without air-conditioning, this building would be
unlivable."

"I wouldn't want your electric bill."

The secretary shook her head. "Yes you would. It's zero.
All our electricity is supplied by solar energy. The panels are
on the roof."

"I'm impressed."

Bobbi Weeks spent the rest of the morning guiding Mark
through the building . . . the private offices, the secretarial
pool and the single production studio . . . the studio was
barely large enough to run a local news program. It struck
Mark that the building was a glorious white elephant. He
wondered how Lew Dobbs planned to get rid of it. Finally
they joined Victor Ashland in the corporate dining room.

"Mr. Ashland, this is Mr. Mark Stern," Bobbi Weeks
said.

"Nice to meet you, Mr. Stern," Victor Ashland said. He
held out his hand.

Mark shook it. "My pleasure, Mr. Ashland."

Victor Ashland was a dapper man with long, wavy, silver
hair, parted low on one side and combed to cover a growing
bald spot. His blue suit was stylishly European . . . slightly
pinched waist and flared skirt with a double vent. His blue-
and-white candy-striped shirt had a solid white collar and was
set off by a bright red tie.

"Please call me Victor."

Mark smiled. "Of course, Victor. I'm Mark to my
friends."

"I hope you didn't mind my changing your reservations.
The Camelback Tennis Ranch is very pleasant . . . far nicer
than any local hotel."

"The bungalow is perfect." Mark was determined to match
the client's gracious manner.

"I put Gigi and the limousine at your disposal. There's not
much nightlife in Phoenix, but you may want to look around.
I promise you Gigi knows where—how do you young people
put it?—where the action is."

"I'm sure she does, but I'm a homebody," Mark said.

"I'll probably have dinner and fall into bed. Tomorrow's a big day."

As they ate, they talked about Group H . . . its past, present and future. Mark was soon convinced that Ashland believed he'd cut a very good deal with Dobbs. And Lew believed he'd pressured Ashland into selling. Interesting. They couldn't both be right. He didn't care who got the better of whom . . . as long as the deal closed and Reiner & Co. collected its check . . . and he collected his piece of the action.

When they'd finished lunch, Ashland excused himself . . . he had work to complete before tomorrow's closing.

Mark spent the afternoon going over the corporate books. In the process he learned why television stations are bought on the basis of cash flow, not profit or loss. There were so many capitalized assets. Corporate headquarters, movies bought for multiple showings . . . with some rights still remaining, network shows Group H had bought when the series went into syndication . . . with many episodes still to be shown. Given the capitalized assets, a television channel's balance sheet was meaningless. By the time he finished, his eyes were bleary. But as far as he could see, there was no reason for the deal not to close.

He stood up and stretched. The head bookkeeper, Laura Conn, joined him. "Thank you, Mrs. Conn," he said. "You keep an excellent set of books . . . very current."

"We do our best, sir. Shall I tell Gigi you're ready to leave?"

Mark nodded.

"Go out that door. Turn right and keep walking. Gigi will meet you in the lobby."

Gigi drove Mark to the Camelback Tennis Ranch. When they arrived at the bungalow, she parked the limousine in the rear of the building, where it couldn't be seen from the road. Without asking, she followed Mark into the house. Mark stood in the center of the living room . . . wondering what would happen next.

"You look a little frazzled, sir," Gigi said. "Would you like a drink?"

"Yeah." Mark looked around. There was a well-equipped bar in the corner of the room.

"What's your pleasure, sir?" Gigi asked.

"Is there Crown Royal?"

Gigi quickly produced a bottle in a purple cloth bag. "Crown Royal."

"In a glass. No ice."

"Do you mind if I have one also?" Gigi asked.

"Be my guest."

"We're both Mr. Ashland's guests," Gigi reminded him as she handed him his drink.

Mark walked to the French doors and sipped his drink. The pool and the tiled Jacuzzi were only a few steps from the doors. Although there was still a little daylight left, the underwater lights were on . . . Mark could see steam rising from the hot, bubbling water in the Jacuzzi. "I wish I'd brought a bathing suit," he said.

Gigi joined him. She stood so close her hip brushed against him. "I told you the Jacuzzi's real private. You don't need a bathing suit."

"Want to join me?" he said, his tone carefully casual.

"I kind o' figured that was the idea."

"What will you wear?"

"Same as you." She grinned.

In the bedroom, Mark stripped off his clothes and arranged them neatly over the back of a chair. When he turned to face Gigi, he saw her carefully hanging her chauffeur's uniform in the closet.

"These are my working clothes," she explained. "Mr. Ashland insists that everyone at Group H look neat as a pin at all times." She then faced Mark and posed, smiling . . . she was holding something in her right hand.

Mark whistled. Gigi had a spectacular body . . . lots of tits and ass and no waist. She was tanned all over, her wispy pubic hair only slightly darker than the hair on her head . . . she was a natural blond. He thought of Nora . . . her body thickened by the pregnancy. Making love to Nora had become a chore. Lately he'd begun to fantasize he was fucking another woman, one who wasn't pregnant. But he'd never fantasized a girl with a body like Gigi's. He'd been on the wagon since the marriage. This was a hell of a way to fall off.

Gigi grabbed several towels, opened the French doors and walked slowly to the Jacuzzi . . . Mark followed her. Just looking at her revolving ass gave him an erection. Gigi dropped the towels on a chair, and they stepped into the Jacuzzi. Mark sat on the tile ledge and lowered himself until the hot water covered his shoulders. Gigi ducked under the water . . . Mark felt her kiss his prick, then suck on it. He groaned . . . he was about to come. Gigi suddenly stopped and bobbed to the surface.

"You're too fast for me, sir," she said, brushing her hair from her eyes. "I got to get ready for you." She moved a few feet away and knelt in the water.

The steam was so thick Mark could barely see her. "What are you doing?" he asked.

"Getting ready," Gigi said.

"You're masturbating?"

"Sort of. The water jet is doing me." She looked at Mark and grinned. "Would you like it better if I played with myself . . . so you could watch me?"

"No." Mark grunted. His voice was thick with excitement. "Maybe later. Just hurry."

"You are eager. What's the matter? Not getting enough at home?"

"My wife's pregnant." In Mark's mind that explained everything.

"I'm almost there," Gigi panted. "Wait." She ducked under the water. Mark felt her fumbling with his prick . . . she rolled a condom up it. That's what she'd been holding in her right hand. When she surfaced, she said, "I practice safe sex. So should you."

"I do."

"How do you want me?"

"Any way you like it."

"From behind. You go in deeper from behind."

She knelt on the tile ledge and guided Mark into her. Mark was so aroused he came in seconds.

"Damn!" he exclaimed. "I'm sorry."

"It's all right. You just relax. We got plenty of time." Gigi removed the condom and set it on the edge of the Jacuzzi . . . next to a packet of unused condoms. Then she crouched again over the jet and after only a few minutes let out a shrill whinny as her orgasm came. "That was okay," she murmured as she joined Mark. "Be better with you inside me."

They leaned against the side of the Jacuzzi and caressed

each other. Mark was soon hard. Gigi rolled another condom
over his penis and lowered herself onto him. She said, "Stay
still. I'll do everything."

Mark felt the walls of her vagina tighten and loosen and
tighten again as she rode him. Having already had one orgasm, he was able to maintain control. He stared at her face
. . . her eyes were half closed, her lips parted . . . she was
so aroused she was unaware of his cold appraisal. "You really like fucking," he finally said.

Gigi opened her eyes and stopped moving. "Yeah. And
I'm good at it."

"You sure are."

"Look, sir . . ."

Mark began to laugh . . . he laughed so hard he damn near
lost his erection. The idea of a girl calling him sir while
fucking him was too much. "Knock off the 'sir' routine. My
name is Mark."

Gigi shrugged. "It's like this, Mark. Some girls are good
with their brains . . . Mr. Ashland pays for their brains . . .
they're producers, program directors, promotion directors.
Other girls are good with their hands . . . Mr. Ashland pays
for their hands . . . they're secretaries, bookkeepers, computer operators. I'm good with my cunt . . . Mr. Ashland
pays for my cunt . . . I fuck. At Group H you do what you
do best."

"You are the best," Mark whispered.

"I am."

Her vagina seemed to dissolve into a thousand tiny mouths
. . . each sucking him . . . swallowing him . . . melting
around him. There was something animal about the way she
made love. They came together . . . Gigi whinnied again—
louder and more shrill than before—and Mark groaned at his
release.

Then—as before—they leaned against the edge of the Jacuzzi and played with each other. Finally Gigi said, "I like
you, sir—"

"Mark. Remember. I'm Mark."

"Okay. For tonight you're Mark. I like you, Mark. I really
do. But right now, I got to go to the bathroom."

Mark shrugged. After two orgasms he could use a break.
It occurred to him that he'd promised to call Nora in the
evening. While Gigi was in the bathroom, he'd call.

They dried each other and entered the house. Mark waited until Gigi closed the bathroom door before dialing home. The phone was picked up on the first ring . . . Nora had been waiting for his call. "How's the heir to the Stern fortune?" he asked.

"Getting bigger every second. When are you coming home?"

"Tomorrow, I hope. There are a couple of things to be straightened out before we close."

"Are you as lonely as I am?"

"Lonelier." Mark hoped he sounded sufficiently lonely. "Cheer up. You're going to be the proud mother of Baby Stern."

"Sorry. I am depressed." Nora's misery spilled out in a rush. "I didn't think I'd actually make a sale at WWOR. But I did think I'd get a positive maybe. Or at least an opinion . . . an attitude. I got nothing . . . *nada.* Larry Pomerado had no opinions . . . he can't think unless he sees a show on the tube. What happened to his left brain?"

"I know, honey. You already told me . . . and told me. Think positive. Think about the baby."

"You think about the baby. Being pregnant is not a cakewalk. Everything hurts . . . my back . . . my legs . . . my ass. I miss you."

"I miss you too. We'll cuddle like crazy when I get back. Which reminds me. Tomorrow, you keep Banska's hot, clammy hands off you. He's a movie director. He'll fuck any body that's still warm."

"Are you saying nobody would touch me in my condition? Nobody but a sex-crazed freak? Am I that unappetizing?"

"Come on, Nora. You know I'm not saying that. You're being hypersensitive—"

The bathroom door opened. Gigi stood in the doorway . . . looking surprised.

"Damn! The waiter's at the door with my drink. Nora, honey, I want to touch you. I can hardly wait to get home. Look. I'll call you tomorrow. With a little luck, we'll close in the morning. Then I'll be home in time for dinner and . . . Well, I'll show you how much I love you tomorrow."

"I love you too. Close that deal. 'Bye."

Mark hung up the phone and gazed at Gigi.

"I'm sorry," Gigi said. "I figured you'd be uncomfortable

talking to your wife with me in the same room, but I thought you'd finished. I didn't mean to interrupt.'' Her nipples were hard . . . her eyes shone in an extraordinary way.

"Stop talking and come to bed,'' Mark murmured.

Gigi lay on top of him. She rested her full weight on him . . . her breasts, her belly, her pudendum crushed against him. Mark rolled her over and entered her . . . she wound her legs around his back . . . pulling him deeper into her. When they'd both come, she kissed him . . . it was the first time they'd kissed. She then stretched out beside him, and holding hands like an old married couple, they drifted off to sleep.

When Mark woke, Gigi was gone. There was a note on the pillow next to him and a chocolate mint in green foil. "Thank you, Mark. It was wonderful. I'll be by for you tomorrow morning at nine sharp.'' The note was signed "Gigi Cantrell.''

The next morning Gigi deposited Mark at the entrance to Group H headquarters. "Good luck, sir,'' she said. "If you're in Phoenix again, call me. I liked showing you the best Phoenix has to offer.''

Mark flushed. "I'll call.''

"That'd be real nice.''

Mark sensed she didn't believe him. Despite her high sexuality—or maybe because of it—she probably didn't get much repeat action. Men might be intimidated by her . . . worried they couldn't get it up often enough to satisfy her.

"I'll be picking you up after the meeting . . . to take you to the airport.''

"Thank you,'' Mark said.

"You're welcome.'' She smiled and drove away.

Bobbi Weeks was waiting to guide him to the Group H conference room. Mark, Victor Ashland, and his lawyer sat on one side of the long, narrow table. Lew Dobbs, accompanied by two lawyers, sat on the other. The debate was polite—everyone spoke in well-modulated tones—but Dobbs and Ashland did some pretty good head knocking. The meeting broke for lunch, during which everyone talked about golf, tennis and the weather . . . then the closing resumed. By late afternoon there was only one item left . . . the employment contract for Ashland. How many years at what salary and, last but not least, who had final authority for running Group H? Dobbs and Ashland could not agree. Mark's palms grew moist . . . this was a deal breaker.

In the middle of the heated argument, Lew Dobbs abruptly excused himself . . . he had to make a personal phone call. Bobbi Weeks led Dobbs from the room. Mark stared at Dobb's broad back. That personal phone call routine was a business ploy . . . when an executive had to check with his superior. Was Dobbs checking with someone to get approval? But Dobbs was the boss . . . wasn't he? He didn't need anyone's approval for anything . . . or did he? If Dobbs wasn't the boss, who was? Mark was still chewing on that one when Dobbs returned. He put a new proposal on the table. After some compromising so no one's pride was too badly bruised, Ashland and Dobbs agreed. In essence, Ashland traded off final decision-making power for more money and a longer employment contract. After that, everyone relaxed. There was nothing more to do except wait for Bobbi Weeks to make the changes in the agreement. Then the papers would be signed and witnessed. Dobbs would hand Ashland a certified check for thirty-five million dollars, and Ashland would transfer the ownership of Group H to Lew Dobbs. Last but not least—in Mark's mind—Ashland would hand him a check for five hundred thousand dollars.

Chapter 13

AT FOUR o'clock—as planned—Nora drove to the Farm to meet Millie and Jordan. When she stopped at the gate, Juan told her that Mrs. Gardiner was waiting for her at the stables. The stables? Nora frowned. Why? Then she smiled ruefully. How could the bearer of evil tidings complain? She thought again about her meeting with Larry Pomerado at WWOR . . . she'd chosen WWOR because it was located in New York City. New York, Broadway, the Great White Way, Theater with a capital *T*. Where else would she have a better shot at arousing interest in a TV series of great plays? If 'Night of Stars' wouldn't sell in New York, it wouldn't sell anywhere.

"So you're Nora Gardiner," Larry Pomerado said as he stood up and held out his hand. They shook hands. "I hear some interesting rumors about Channel 18 and your grandmother. Do I have it right? Millie Thorne Gardiner is your grandmother?"

"She is."

"And she owns Channel 18?"

"She does."

"And you're peddling an idea she has for a TV series?"

"I am."

He grinned. "When I was a kid I had a real crush on her. I saw her at least five times in *Monsoon*. Tell me something. It used to bug me . . . you know how kids are. If she was so in love with Milos Banska, why didn't she marry him? Yeah . . . I know he was married. But movie people play musical marriage. They marry and divorce and remarry and redivorce. I bet he'd have gotten a divorce if she'd been willing to marry him. I know I would have."

Nora shrugged. "I don't know why she didn't marry him.

236

She never told me. I wasn't even born at the time she knew Banska.''

Pomerado smiled. "Too bad. Someday I'd like to meet her . . . the gorgeous Millie Thorne." His smile faded. "How does she look now? People get old . . . especially beautiful women.''

"Grandmother is older, but she still looks wonderful.''

"Good for her." When he sat down, there was a dreamy expression on his face. Then he abruptly changed the subject. "Sit." He gestured to a chair facing his desk. "Tell me about your show. I read the brochure. There isn't much to go on besides Banska, Tammi Meredith and Cathy Leslie.''

"I know. That's why I brought this." She opened her attaché case and placed the videotape cassette on Pomerado's desk.

"What is it? A pilot?''

Nora smiled encouragingly. "Not quite. An appetizer. Just play the tape.''

"Why not?" Pomerado crossed the office and inserted the tape into his VCR. He watched as scene after scene exploded on his king-size TV set. When the tape finished, he removed it without rewinding it. "That's nice. What are you telling me?''

"Those are examples of great plays that were made into great movies . . . with great actors. They were very successful. That's what 'Night of Stars' is all about . . . making great plays into great television . . . with great stars. The TV series will be just as successful as the movies were.''

"Maybe. Maybe not. Your timing is lousy. The cable industry is not recession proof. Can you guarantee double-digit ratings?''

"No. But I can guarantee a great show.''

"And I can't buy a pig in a poke. It's an interesting concept, but interesting concepts are a dime a dozen. When you've got a pilot on tape—one complete play—two or three would be better—come back.''

"Do you think it's too highbrow?''

"I don't know. These days highbrow and lowbrow cohabit.''

"How about the stars? I think they'd pull an audience.''

"Sometimes, yes. Sometimes, no. Depends on the material.''

"Don't forget the Broadway connection.''

"Lots of towns have streets called Broadway. Nothing special about that."

"Larry . . . off the record. What do you think of the idea? Do you love it . . . or hate it?"

"I don't love it and I don't hate it. I don't think anything until I see a tape of a show. I loved 'Star Trek' . . . I was right. My son loved 'Twin Peaks' . . . he sold me on the show . . . we were both wrong . . . it bombed." He smiled at the ceiling. "But I'll tell you what. If your grandmother has prints of her old movies—*Monsoon, Innocent Voyager, Bad Girl*—I'll pay through the nose for them. And run them first opening I get. Those oldies are great. About them I have opinions."

Nora stood up. "I don't think she has prints, Larry." She returned the cassette to her briefcase. "I'll be back."

"You're always welcome," Larry Pomerado said as he escorted Nora to the door. "I'm a Millie Thorne fan. So's Elsie, my wife."

Thirty acres of the Farm were devoted to the care and feeding of horses . . . Max Gardiner had had Arabian horse fever. In his time there was a stable with enough stalls for five Arabian stallions. Millie had added to the original stable, and a second stable was built . . . far enough from the first stable so that a mare in heat wouldn't drive the stallions wild. Seven Arabian stallions with legendary bloodlines—their progeny had won many Class A show championships—were kept in the enlarged original stable. Beside the Arabians, three hunter jumpers and two hackers occupied stalls in the second stable. Two trainers, two exercise boys and four grooms were on staff to feed, groom and exercise the horses daily . . . and muck out the stables.

Nora drove along the winding dirt road. When she reached the stables, she saw one of the exercise boys riding Heat Wave, an Arabian stallion, around the exercise ring. Millie, in boots, jodhpurs, and a white shirt, sat on the white wooden fence between Sara Kratz and a trainer. Nora blinked. Why was Millie in jodhpurs? It wasn't her style to wear riding britches at a business meeting. Where was Jordan . . . waiting at the main house?

"Hello." Millie waved as Nora slid out of the car.

Nora waved back. When she neared Millie, she said, "Jordan's not here."

Millie shook her head. Sara Kratz answered for her. "Mr. Banska's not coming. I reached him an hour ago. He's checked into the Grant. I explained that Mrs. G. was leaving this meeting to you and him." She smiled at Millie . . . a dog waiting for a pat of approval.

"I don't understand," Nora said to Millie.

"Nothing to understand." Sara, the palace guard, took over. "Mrs. G. was riding all morning . . . she overdid it. She's tired."

"I really am beat." Millie glanced at Nora with an abstracted expression. "Give me the bottom line. What happened?"

"As you know, I didn't expect to sell WWOR. But I did think I'd get a reaction . . . negative or positive." She ran through the details of the meeting, concluding with, "Pomerado's a fan of yours. If you have a print of any of your films, he's in the market."

"That's nice."

"There's more of the same. I also went to TNT—"

"Spare me the details. You know my plan. You and Jordan decide how best to proceed. If we have to fly blind, we will."

Nora felt an unnatural alertness. Millie's reaction was out of character. She always wanted the blow-by-blow details. No one decided anything for Millie Gardiner.

"But I don't know your plan," Nora protested. "Only bits and pieces. Ali hasn't kept me posted on whom she's contacted . . . who's agreed . . . and agreed to what? I've no idea what you've budgeted for the series, how many shows you project . . ."

"Nothing's set in concrete. Jordan and you can work it out."

"We could be way off the mark . . . spend more money than you want to—"

"You can fill in Mrs. G. another time," the unflappable Sara Kratz interrupted. "Mrs. G. is not available today."

Nora gazed at Millie. Her boots were polished to a high sheen . . . her jodhpurs crisp . . . her shirt fresh. No hairs strayed around her forehead. No hint of sweat . . . hardly like someone who had been riding all morning. Then it struck Nora. Millie, the actress, was wearing a costume for a part in a play called *Daily Ride*. Sara Kratz, the prompter, was feeding her lines. It was a performance . . . and a lie.

"You could audit the meeting . . . just listen. Then if we go off half cocked, you can stop us. Jordan can drive up from the Grant. When it's over, we'll both leave. This meeting's important to the success of—'' She broke off. Millie's face wore a dry, pinched expression, and Nora retreated with a half-ashamed nod. "Okay," she said. "We'll handle it."

There was a moment's silence. Their eyes met. "Thank you." Millie attempted a smile.

"You're welcome," Nora said. Her throat felt dry and tight. More than anything, she longed to ask Millie what was wrong. But she couldn't. Millie would be both offended and furious at the intrusion. "I'll talk to you tomorrow." She turned to leave.

"Tomorrow," Millie echoed.

Driving into San Diego, Nora thought about her grandmother. During the last year there had been a subtle change in Millie. Sometimes Nora was certain she could date the shift from Cathy Johns's telephone call . . . Cathy seeing Millie at Scripps. Sometimes she wasn't sure. Had it begun then or was that merely the first time she'd noticed it? Millie had always kept her own counsel. She enjoyed keeping secrets, even from those she loved the most. But this was different . . . it was a withdrawal from intimacy . . . from her. The withdrawal was sad, even reluctant. But it was withdrawal just the same. Something was very wrong. What was it?

Nora handed the keys to her car to the garage attendant at the Grant Hotel, accepted the claim check and pushed through the doors that led to the refurbished lobby. The main lobby was as elegantly furnished as a Louis XV drawing room . . . a judicious placement of Louis XIV, Louis XV and Louis XVI chairs, sofas, tables and lamps. Several huge crystal chandeliers hung from the high ceiling and the waxed wooden floors were covered by a number of oversized D'Aubusson rugs. If she had a criticism, it was that everything looked too new. The hotel had a long history . . . years when it had flourished and a year when it had been forced to file for protection under the bankruptcy laws. The furnishings had no history . . . not enough guests had sat on the chairs, spilled drinks on the rugs, put cigarette burns in wood. For all its elegance, the room was ice-cold. The double doors to the bar were on her left. Nora entered the wood-paneled bar and stopped . . . her eyes ranged the room looking for Jordan. No Jordan. The maître d', recognizing her, smiled and led her to a small marble-topped table next to the far wall. She sat on the banquette, ordered a glass of Chardonnay and made an effort to compose herself. Her short meeting with Millie had been unexpectedly hard . . . draining.. This meeting with Jordan was equally important and now even harder. For a moment the room blurred before her eyes. She saw only the slanting rays of light from the street and the motes of dust, dancing. The wine came and she sipped it . . . while her mind laid out pieces of her past like a series of stills from a movie. Her father, Barron . . . Jordan . . . the summer she met him.

An auction of horses was being held. Nora remembered the three of them sitting on the fence of a corral watching two stallions fight, prancing on their hind legs and lashing out with their hooves until a half dozen grooms wrestled them apart. They cheered as three unbroken ponies galloped around the field . . . hooves pounding. She liked the sight of their manes flying.

Then they wandered around the grounds, looking at the many pens, noting that several colts wore "sold" ropes around their necks. Jordan stopped at a stall where a beautiful palomino gelding was standing quietly with a "sold" rope around his neck.

"Do you like him?" Jordan asked.

"Who wouldn't?" she'd answered reverently.

"I told you she'd like him." Jordan grinned at her father.

Her father's eyes were suddenly liquid. "He's yours, dear. A sweet sixteen birthday present. A Thoroughbred hunter jumper . . . cost a fortune. Didn't he, Jordan?"

Jordan's grin became a smile . . . a detached smile. He looked at her father with a concern he tried to hide. "A fortune . . ."

Suddenly she knew Jordan had paid for the horse. For a few seconds, she couldn't breathe. Then she flung her arms around her father. "Daddy! I'm so lucky I'm your daughter!"

"I'm lucky I'm your father. You even look a little like me." He put his hands on her shoulders and held her off, studying her face with comic seriousness. "Doesn't she, Jordan?"

"A little. Enough to prove the bloodlines. But more like Millie."

"No! I look like Daddy!" She glared at Jordan! Their eyes met for a second, and held. Something within her realigned, settled. Then she looked away.

"You're your father's daughter, all right," Jordan said. "What will you call your new horse?"

At a loss for words, she felt herself blush. "I don't know. I have to think."

For the rest of the afternoon, she was only dimly aware of faces and voices and the sound and smell of horses. All she knew was that she loved Jordan . . . and the love was futile.

It could have all happened yesterday rather than twelve years ago . . . the memory was so vivid in Nora's mind. She sipped her wine and waited, trying to compose herself and at the same time wishing she could leave. Glancing uneasily at the entrance she tensed . . . Dorothea Reiner was standing beside the maître d'. She was scanning the room. Nora had a childish impulse to hide under the table . . . it was too late.

"Nora!" Dorothea called out. In seconds she slid into the chair facing Nora. "We meet again. How pleasant. My appointment is late. We can have a cozy chat."

"Yes." Two spots of color rose in Nora's cheeks.

"Now what shall we chat about?"

Nora felt a nervous desire to laugh. "I like your outfit."

"I do too. Forget clothes . . . they're a bore. Let's dish the dirt. Incidentally, you don't look that pregnant."

"I look pregnant enough. And I'm only in my fifth month. I don't want to think about what I'll look like in four months. I'm sorry, but I've heard nothing dishy in a long time."

"Then let's chat about our mutual friend, Ali Gardiner Reiner."

Nora tried on a smile. "I don't know what to say." She licked her lips.

"She's restored my faith in the national ideal . . . looking out for number one." There was a malicious glint in Dorothea's eyes.

The remark jolted Nora. "Well . . ." She cleared her throat. "Ali is a survivor."

"She is indeed. She uses vitamin E soap and eats a low-fat diet. She means to live forever . . . with or without Arthur."

"I never thought she'd fall in love with him," Nora said defensively.

"Don't be childish, Nora. It isn't becoming. We both know about real life. In real life, there's no such thing as love . . . for anyone over twenty-five. There is chemistry . . . and companionship. But primarily there is money. Ali doesn't love Arthur. She loves Arthur's money. A rational position, I'd say." Dorothea was half laughing. She was not an outraged ex-wife.

"You sound pleased," Nora said.

Dorothea looked at Nora levelly. "I'm not displeased. Why should I be? My illusions weren't shattered. My trust wasn't betrayed. That happened ages ago. Oh . . . I admit I did seethe a bit at first. One grows accustomed to one's possessions. Even possessions one no longer wants. Then it struck me I was bored with Arthur . . . my over-fifty teenager . . . the eternal adolescent. So I gave him to Ali for potty training and child guidance."

"You're impressive, Dorothea. The way you agreed to the divorce without any of the usual fuss," Nora said admiringly.

Dorothea gazed at her with amusement. "You have it wrong, dear. I agreed to nothing. Arthur agreed to the divorce. I asked him for it."

"You asked Arthur for the divorce?"

"Of course. He was stunned. It took him the better part of a fifth of scotch to get it through his head that I meant it."

"Arthur didn't want the divorce?" There was disbelief in Nora's eyes.

"Of course not, silly. You look so surprised."

"I am." Nora choked.

"Why would he want a divorce? Men are creatures of habit. Arthur likes to keep his summer suits in one closet . . . winter suits in another . . . his slippers on the right side of the bed. He likes knowing where everything is."

"So does Mark," Nora said.

"It was fascinating to watch it dawn on him that I meant it. At my age I take my amusement where I can."

Nora's mouth fell open . . . she was a fish out of water gasping for oxygen.

"I really should thank Ali for convincing me it was time. After all, unlike your Grandmother Millie, I may not live forever. And I owe myself some years of pleasure."

"Ali convinced you?" Again Nora gaped.

"Yes. She'd do very well in sales. Insurance. Real estate. Cars. Snake oil. She must take after her biological father. Nora, stop gaping. She did not weep and beg me to divorce Arthur."

"She didn't?"

"Of course not. She staged a seduction—not of Arthur— of me. The more I got to know her, the more I realized we could co-exist peacefully. After a few luncheons and drinks and dinners à trois, it struck me that Arthur and she were destiny's children. The wannabe femme fatale and the most gullible man to strut about naked since the emperor tried on his new clothes."

Nora was too flummoxed even to say, Go on. But Dorothea needed no urging.

"Beyond that, I realized she'd make an ideal stepmother for my son, Roger. Ali would feel no responsibility for encouraging the boy. He thinks he can paint . . . he can't. She'll keep her distance and her hands off him. She probably loathes children and that's fine. She makes an ideal stepmother."

"She does?"

"Of course she does. You still don't understand. Look. Arthur is as greedy as Ali. You can't believe for a moment that he would want a divorce. Divorce the Kellman millions? Never!"

"I thought he fell in love . . . ." Nora's own head was spinning.

"Fell in love with Ali? Don't be silly," Dorothea said impatiently. "This year he enjoys having sex with Ali. Next year . . ." She shrugged. "We'll see. Nora, you're a woman of today. Don't let your faith in Mark stop you from learning how to read a balance sheet. I own what I own. Arthur owns what he owns. Actually we each own twenty-six percent of Reiner & Co. And the partners own the balance . . . forty-eight percent. When Mark was made a partner, he was allowed to buy one percent of the company."

"I know." For Nora the conversation had taken on the

zany quality of a dream. "So you asked Arthur for the divorce . . ."

"I just told you I did. Arthur showed no true maturity. The sad truth is, money calls to money . . . like moose to moose. He pleaded—"

"He didn't want to marry Ali?"

"Of course not. What sane man would? But I wanted a divorce and I wanted Arthur married. He's safer married. So, with my blessing and insistence, he proposed to our nymph."

Nora took a deep breath.

"Arthur needed a lot of convincing. Actually he wanted it in writing. I refused."

"Refused what? He wanted what in writing?"

"My permission for him to marry . . . he wanted a written agreement. That's his business head. But in the end he agreed he didn't need it."

"A written agreement that you allowed him to marry Ali?"

"Yes. It was totally unnecessary. We had a verbal agreement. My word is my bond. So is his. In business matters we are both honorable. So he had nothing to worry about. He'll still have my vote in all matters concerning the firm." Her smile was weatherproof.

"I understand." Now Nora did. There was an intimate silence . . . both women were lost in their own thoughts.

Dorothea spoke first. Laughing, she said, "Do you know how Ali persuaded me to ask for a divorce?"

"No." By now Nora knew that she knew nothing.

"Her imagination. Ali gave me that cock-and-bull story about her mother. Quoting Amanda as saying that although Arthur was a philanderer—which he is—he would never leave me. And why? Because no woman could measure up to me in bed."

Nora winced, remembering Ali's words.

"Rubbish!" Dorothea scoffed. "Arthur and I haven't been near each other's genitalia in years. We can't stand each other's erotica and exotica. But Ali's story showed so much tasteless flattery and true ingenuity that it occurred to me she might be a family asset. She could prove useful in many ways in Arthur's business deals. She could entertain the visiting firemen . . . in ways that I wouldn't."

Nora gaped again.

At that moment Jordan Banska arrived at the table.

"Nora! Sorry I'm late."

Nora looked up at him . . . a tall, hawklike stranger standing next to her. A stranger she'd known all her life.

"Hello, Jordan. Jordan, this is Dorothea Reiner. Dorothea, Jordan Banska."

Dorothea gave Jordan an appraising look. "You're *the* Jordan Banska . . . the motion picture director?"

Jordan smiled.

"And you and Nora are old friends?"

"Very old," Nora said quickly. "We grew up together. What I mean is . . . well . . . I grew up with Jordan. He was a close friend of my father."

"I see. A friend of your father. Excuse my indelicate fantasies," Dorothea teased. She rose from the chair and waved to a bearded gentleman at the entrance. "How nice. I see that my friend has arrived. A German banker. He was not a friend of my father . . . very few Germans were." She gave Jordan a three-hundred-watt smile. "Lovely meeting you, Mr. Banska. If you're ever at loose ends in San Diego, you must call me. I'm in the book. Dorothea Reiner. R-E-I-N-E-R." She smiled at Nora. "Of course, our conversation is our little secret." Nora nodded. "Good." She smiled again at Jordan and left, waving her hand to catch the attention of her German banker.

Jordan slid into the seat. "Who is Hamlet's mother?"

"The ex-wife of the king. A family friend."

"That ex-queen is an authority on ear poisons." He gave Nora a long look . . . his eyes so firmly fixed that she had to struggle to look away. "And how are you? Gloriously pregnant?"

"Gloriously." Once—in another life—she thought she could never have enough of his long looks.

"And happy?"

"Very happy . . . and a little frightened." She studied her drink. "Having a baby is an awesome responsibility. I'm saying good-bye to my childhood."

"Welcome to the adult world." He gave her a wry smile. "One needs children if one wants to found a dynasty. I'm sorry I never had any."

She looked at him with surprise. "You are?"

"Yes."

Nora considered Jordan's words. Were Mark and she

founding a dynasty? She'd never thought about a baby in those terms. Did Mark? There was a living creature inside her . . . part Mark, part herself. No part belonged to Jordan. What could she say? Then the reason for their meeting came to her rescue. "We're not here to talk about babies and dynasties . . . we're here to work out the details about 'Night of Stars.' " She laughed nervously.

With a quiet smile Jordan agreed. "That's true . . . more or less."

"You want to know about my enthusiastic reception at WWOR and TNT?"

"Tell me what happened." His tone was soothing, encouraging.

"I bombed out. Larry Pomerado at WWOR wasn't enthusiastic. He didn't clap and stomp his feet. He didn't boo. He didn't anything. But he did . . ."

Long ago Jordan had learned the art of the pause. It took him a while to say, "But?"

"But he wanted to talk about Millie Thorne. Is she still beautiful? What does she look like now?"

"You could have said, 'Like me.' "

"I wish that were true. I don't look like her. Well . . . maybe a little. He also wanted to know why Millie and your father never married."

"Because my father was already married . . . to my mother. Still, Millie and he were lovers," Jordan said with a splendid detachment.

"I know."

He gazed at her with sympathy, listening with his eyes. "Pomerado had nothing else to say about 'Night of Stars'?"

Nora thought of all the phrases she had rehearsed for just this moment. Of all the calming explanations and comforting upbeat excuses she'd make. The "show me" attitude was standard . . . better than nothing . . . better than an outright rejection. But his eyes took her in . . . she settled for the hard, unvarnished truth. She cited the weak economic climate and underlined Pomerado's question—"Can you guarantee double-digit ratings?" And his finally saying he had to see a pilot before making a commitment.

Jordan heard her out. He nodded. He smiled. But he offered no opinions as to what he thought of her trial balloon. She searched his eyes for the smallest sign of scorn. There was none. "So that's the way the Jell-O shimmers," she ended. "No yeas. No nays."

"They have to see a pilot," he said to himself.

"One pilot . . . if we're lucky. If not, two . . . maybe three." Nora wished to be thoroughly conscientious. "And Millie foots the bill."

"The pilot will cost four to five million." Jordan was as careful as Nora to place his cards—face up—on the table. "I'll do a final budget when I know exactly who's doing what. Then we—"

"Show them to Millie. . . ." Nora suddenly gasped. "Jesus! I have a terrible cramp. I can't breathe." She doubled over, her hands pressed between her legs. She felt a gush of wetness through her dress. Blood. Fluid. She didn't know. "Oh God! It hurts. It's happening."

"What's happening?"

"The baby. Noooo!" Her insides were being shredded . . . she could hardly talk. "It's coming, Jordy," she gasped. Unthinking, she used his long-ago nickname.

"Now?" he asked, feeling an unfamiliar panic. "It's too soon."

"Much too soon. I'm losing my baby. Help me, Jordy."

"How? I've never had a baby."

Nora laughed . . . holding her stomach.

"What's funny?"

"You. I always laugh when the pain gets too awful. The hospital, Jordy. Take me to the hospital." She doubled over, her face pressed against the marble top of the table.

He tried to ask an intelligent question. "Which hospital?"

"Scripps in La Jolla. No. Scripps is too far. UCSD Medical Center on Dickenson . . . get a taxi . . . the driver will know."

When Jordan helped Nora stand, he saw a stream of watery blood running down her legs. And a small pool of blood on the floor. "Jesus!" he shouted as he lifted her in his arms. The blood continued to ooze from between Nora's thighs . . . soaking his jacket. As he hurried from the bar, he caught a glimpse of Dorothea Reiner, her eyes wide with curiosity and fear. By sheer luck, a cab let a passenger out at the door. Jordan grabbed the cab.

"UCSD Medical Center on—"

"Dickenson," the driver said.

"It's an emergency. Hurry."

Jordan held Nora in his lap as the car sped through downtown San Diego . . . red lights, orange lights, green lights . . . it made no difference. The cabbie kept his hand on the horn. By the time they reached Hillcrest, they'd picked up a police escort. Intuitively the driver of the police car knew this was a genuine emergency, not a drugged-out cabbie on a spree. The wail of his siren added to the din. Up Fourth Avenue . . . across University. There was a dip in the road. The taxi bottomed out and bounced. Jordan's head hit the ceiling, stunning him for a second. Through it all, Nora continued to whimper, "I've lost my baby. I've lost my baby." A left on Washington Street and a right on Front Street . . . they were going the wrong way on a one-way street. The cars coming at them quickly moved to the side of the road. The cab skidded to a halt at the emergency entrance. Cradling Nora in his arms, Jordan got out of the car. He staggered toward the door. Before he could reach it, the door opened and two orderlies pushing a gurney hurried to meet him.

"What happened?" the first orderly asked.

"I think she's having a miscarriage," Jordan gasped.

The second orderly lifted Nora from Jordan's arms and placed her on the gurney. "She's unconscious," he said. "She's lost a lot of blood."

As they entered the hospital, the first orderly said, "We'll get her to Obstetrics. Got to stop the bleeding." He glanced at Jordan. "Man, you're a mess!"

"Forget about me."

"Clean yourself up. The men's room is on the right as you enter the building. Then check with Admitting. They're going to need information. Who are you? Who is the woman? Does she have insurance?"

"I'm Jordan Banska. She's Nora Stern . . . Mrs. Millie Gardiner's granddaughter. Mrs. Millie Gardiner," he repeated.

"Oh, shit! Eddie," the orderly called out, "this one goes to the eighth floor . . . move it!"

"The private . . ."

"Yeah. It's Mrs. Millie Gardiner's kid . . . the charity broad. Don't you ever read the papers? Move! Arlene," he shouted to the woman at the admitting desk. "Page Dr. Schmidt. Tell him there's an emergency in eighth-floor sur-

gery . . . a miscarriage . . . fifth month, I'd guess. Stat!''
The elevator door opened and the orderlies quickly wheeled
Nora onto the elevator.

The doors closed, leaving Jordan Banska standing in the
lobby. He hurried to the men's room and washed as much of
the blood as possible off himself and his clothes. He then
went to the admitting desk. The plump, middle-aged, black
woman was matter-of-fact.

"What's the name of the patient?"

"Nora Stern. Mrs. Nora Stern."

"Is she your wife?"

"No. My name is Jordan Banska. Nora is an old friend of
mine."

"I see. Has her husband been notified?"

"No. He's out of town."

"Ah. Does Mrs. Stern have medical insurance coverage?"

"She must."

"But you don't know?"

"I don't know. Look . . . What's your name?"

"Mrs. Arlene Ziff."

"Mrs. Ziff, does Mrs. Millie Gardiner mean anything to
you?"

"No."

"And you don't know who I am?"

"No. Should I?"

Jordan was disconcerted. He'd lived too many years in
closed circles where everyone who mattered knew Jordan
Banska . . . or wanted to know him. For a moment he was
uncertain how to proceed. Then he said, "No. Forget it. I
will take responsibility for all the costs."

"That's nice. And who'll take responsibility for you?"

"This will." Jordan flashed his wallet from the breast
pocket of his ruined jacket. He handed Mrs. Ziff an American Express Platinum Card. "I can charge half a million
dollars on this card. Run it through your machine."

"We don't take American Express. Do you know how to
reach Mrs. Stern's husband?"

Jordan thought about that. "I can try."

"You do that . . . after you sign the admittance papers."

As he filled out the forms, Jordan worried about Nora.
She'd lost so much blood. He handed the signed papers to
Mrs. Ziff—he was now responsible for all Nora's medical

bills—and took the first elevator to the eighth floor. He followed the corridor until he found the nurses' station. "Mrs. Stern?" he said to the attending nurse. "She was admitted a little while ago . . . a miscarriage. How is she?"

"Dr. Schmidt is with her now . . . he's head of OB-GYN . . . he's doing whatever can be done. The visitors' room is over there." She pointed to an alcove with a few tables and chairs off the main corridor. "You can wait there."

"Mrs. Stern may need a blood transfusion. I think we have the same blood type . . . O positive. If she needs blood, I'll give it."

The nurse looked at him and nodded. "I'll tell Dr. Schmidt." It wasn't necessary for either of them to mention the danger posed by the possibly AIDS-contaminated blood supply.

Jordan sat for a few minutes before he was composed enough to call Reiner & Co. Someone at Mark's office would know where he was.

Signing the papers took longer than Mark had expected. By the time he pocketed the five-hundred-thousand-dollar check made out to Reiner & Co., it was almost nine P.M. On the way out, he was stopped by Bobbi Weeks.

"Mr. Stern. A Mr. Jordan Banska called about a half hour ago. He said to tell you your wife had a miscarriage. She's in UCSD Medical Center."

"What! Why the hell wasn't I told?" It took an effort for him to keep from shaking the girl until her teeth chattered.

"I had strict orders not to interrupt the closing . . . except for a genuine emergency. Mr. Banska said she was receiving the best care. Women often have miscarriages. In my judgment there was no emergency . . ."

"You know where you can stick your judgment." Mark's face was flushed with rage.

"Drop it, Mark," Lew Dobbs said, urging Mark along the corridor. "There's no point getting pissed at the girl. Even if you knew an hour ago, what could you do? You're in Phoenix and your wife is in San Diego."

"She should have told me." Mark hurried to the lobby . . . Gigi was waiting. "The airport, Gigi," Mark said. "My wife's had a miscarriage. I have to get home."

"You sure do, sir," Gigi said. Mark had barely time to

close the door before the car started. It rocketed around the corkscrew driveway and out onto the road. "You want to stop at the Camelback Ranch and pick up your bag?"

"No. Don't have time."

"That's okay. I'll pack for you and send it to you . . . UPS."

"Thanks." Mark pressed his fingers against his forehead.

"It'll be all right, sir. My sister's had three miscarriages. It's no big deal."

"Yeah."

"I was sort o' hoping you'd stay over. Last night was fun."

"It was great!"

"With you gone, I got no excuse. Tonight I gotta show Mr. Dobbs a good time." She made a face. "He's so fat." Her expression smoothed out. "I guess what I do is no different than any other job . . . you have good days and not-so-good days."

Mark's brain was a maelstrom of confused images. Nora in the hospital with Jordan Banska hanging over her . . . Gigi naked, panting, crouched over the hulking Lew Dobbs . . . Damn it! He had to get Gigi out of his mind. She was a whore . . . a whippy one-night stand. That was all. He loved Nora . . . he loved their baby. What baby? Nora had lost Baby Stern. Shit! He might lose Millie's account. . . .

By the time Mark got to the hospital it was almost midnight. When he reached the eighth floor, he found Jordan Banska waiting in the visitors' area. His clothes were crusted with dried blood that had turned brown, and he looked pale and exhausted.

"Jordan," Mark gasped. "Nora? Is she all right?"

"She will be. She's very lucky."

"Lucky! She lost our baby. That's your idea of luck?"

"You can have other babies. I meant, she dilated enough to expel the fetus. Dr. Schmidt didn't have to operate. The rest was like a D & C. Schmidt called it a dusting and cleaning."

"That's not funny."

Jordan shrugged. "Anyway, I'm glad I was available."

"So am I," Mark grudgingly admitted.

"I mean, Nora lost a lot of blood. She needed a transfusion. We have the same blood type, so I—"

"You gave Nora blood?"

"It's the custom these days. Using your own or a relative's blood. A precautionary measure. I'm not a relative but I am an old family friend."

Mark wanted to say, are you sure your blood is safe? He didn't have the nerve. "What room is Nora in?"

"It's that way." Jordan pointed to the right. "Ask the nurse."

Mark went to the nurses' station and asked to see Nora. "I'm Mark Stern . . . her husband," he said to one of the two nurses.

"She's asleep," the nurse said. "I'll let you look in, but my orders are not to disturb her. She needs to rest. You know you owe Mr. Banska quite a lot."

"He gave Mrs. Stern blood," the other nurse said.

"Three pints. If he wasn't such a strong, healthy man, Dr. Schmidt would never have permitted him to give three pints of blood," the first nurse said, adding, "He intimidated the doctor into letting him."

"Yeah. Right. What room is my wife in?"

"Eight-oh-five. Follow me."

When the nurse opened the door to room 805, she held a firm grip on Mark's arm. Nora was lying on her back . . . she had an IV tube attached to her wrist. To Mark she looked awful . . . everything about her seemed to have shrunk . . . her cheeks were hollow, black circles rimmed her eyes, her breasts were flat, her belly that only yesterday bulged with life was concave . . . sterile.

"Will she be all right?" he whispered.

"Well . . . er . . . yes." The nurse hesitated. "Five months is late to have a miscarriage . . . plus her Fallopian tubes are messed up. Scar tissue. But except for that, Dr. Schmidt assured Mr. Banska that your wife's plumbing was in A-one shape." She smiled. "The doctor uses vivid language."

"Vivid!" Mark snorted. "When can I see Dr. Schmidt? I don't give a f— I don't care what he told Banska. I want to talk to the doctor myself. I'm the husband . . . not Jordan Banska. Got it?"

Chapter 14

FOR SEVERAL days, Nora ricocheted wildly between numbed, silent grief and semihysterical tears. She'd lost their baby . . . she'd failed Mark. They would never found a dynasty. On the surface, at least, her morbid thoughts soon faded. But the miscarriage had left deep psychological doubts. What kind of a woman was she? Would Mark continue to love the woman who had lost his baby? Still, her physical recovery was mercifully short . . . and unmercifully harassed. By her family, friends and business associates. Laden with flowers, Mark visited her early every morning before going to the office and every evening after work. Jordan—exercising his usual tact—timed his daily visit to miss Mark. He also brought flowers. And Millie appeared at least once a day . . . equipped with bouquets of fresh-cut roses, a painted-on smile and cheerful words. Each senior member of the staff at Channel 18 made the obligatory call . . . and each carried an armful of flowers. When their flowers were deposited next to Millie's, Mark's and Jordan's, Nora's room looked like a funeral parlor, which in a way it was. Her baby had died. Also, scar tissue had blocked one of her Fallopian tubes. According to Dr. Schmidt, while it was not impossible, it would not be easy for her to become pregnant again. The medical report upset Mark. Nora had lost the baby . . . Millie's great-grandchild. He was sure he would lose Millie's account. He was wrong. Millie sensed his fear and assured him, privately, that the account would stay put . . . for a while, anyway. The only close friends who did not visit Nora in the hospital were Ali and Arthur Reiner . . . the happy couple were touring the bazaars of the world. The day before Nora was scheduled to be discharged from the hospital, Mark brought her a letter from Ali. It was postmarked Hong Kong.

During the month Nora recuperated at home, she received several letters from Ali and Arthur . . . each from a resort more glamorous and outré than their previous stop.

The Reiners' honeymoon was hectic . . . exotic. Ali and Arthur toured the Far East in style . . . meeting friends, partying in Hong Kong . . . then to Macao . . . pausing for a quick breath at a friend's beach villa in Colane. The big spenders from Taiwan and the gambling casinos in Macao attracted Arthur. For Ali gambling was an acquired taste. Still, she wrote that she adored Macao . . . she could shop and party till dawn. When exhaustion set in, it was off to Africa for a ten-day stay at the Chobe Game Lodge, located in the Chobe Game Preserve. Ali wrote that she thought it a romantic honeymoon spot . . . Liz Taylor and Richard Burton had remarried there. Going on to Europe, they spent the remainder of the summer on the Spanish Riviera. In September they flew home from Paris.

There seems to be a time in the tide of a man's fortunes when he is content . . . at peace with his condition . . . all doubts brusquely dismissed. This was Arthur's time. He loved Ali and Ali loved him. He forgot it was Dorothea who had coined the marriage. He believed it fated . . . a meeting of twin souls. Mark told Nora that Arthur was merry as a hummingbird in the office . . . always bitching about something, yet actually carefree. For the first time in Arthur's life he did not worry about his future . . . what was there to worry about?

Arthur and Ali considered living in Rancho Santa Fe, then La Jolla, then one of the coastal communities in North County. Unexpectedly they settled in Coronado. It was villagey yet statusy . . . a quick zip to Reiner & Co. in downtown San Diego . . . convenient for the theater, the opera, the symphony . . . also the charity balls at the downtown hotels. It was a short limo ride to the galas in La Jolla or Rancho Santa Fe. Arthur bought Ali four adjoining town houses in a condominium at a total cost of four million two hundred thousand dollars. Walls were torn down, new walls were put up, several spiral staircases were added. What resulted—with pricey, professional guidance—was a stunning architectural statement . . . a ten-thousand-square-foot triumph. The entire condo—except for the garage, the servants' quarters, the kitchen, storage rooms, and the three guest

rooms—had long stretches of glass wall facing San Diego
Harbor and the city skyline. When Ali gave Nora a guided
tour of the completed renovation, Nora was consumed by the
flip side of envy . . . pure awe.

The ten thousand square feet Ali had to play with moti-
vated what Nora called "a world-class spending spree." Ali
had hand-painted tile floors in some rooms . . . in the master
bedroom, the tile matched the bedspread. The vestibule, the
hall, the dining room, the living room and the library floors
were black Carrara marble with red and yellow veins . . .
the effect was dramatic. Warm Mexican saltillo tile was used
in the floors of the kitchen, butler's pantry and bathrooms for
a homier feeling. The twenty-five-by-fifty-foot living room
was eclectic . . . a study in contrasts, a mingling of cultural
traditions. French and Italian antiques hobnobbed with contemporary furniture. Several cubist-inspired chairs and a pair
of sleek olive-colored leather sofas complemented an early-
seventeenth-century Genoese corner cabinet and an
eighteenth-century lacquered commode. Hanging on the
white walls throughout the condo was a potpourri of costly
art . . . an eighteenth-century Dutch painting, two French
Fauvists—landscapes by Derain and Monet—American landscapes by John Singer Sargent and Frederic Remington, a
Harnett fantasy of Americana, and works by California artists
such as McManus and T. J. Dixon. Victorian needlepoint
rugs as well as a Tabriz, Ardabil and other Oriental carpets
were scattered over the tile floors. The furnishings cost Arthur more than the four combined condos. If spending money
was the way to live happily ever after, Ali and Arthur were
well on the way to eternal bliss.

In the first year of marriage they dined at the standard
gourmet restaurants . . . Mille Fleurs, Rainwater's, Mr. A's.
They also had ethnic yens . . . Khyber Pass for Afghan food,
Sibyl's Down Under for Australian dishes. But they seldom
visited local Mexican eateries . . . preferring to hop down to
Tijuana or fly to Cabo San Lucas or Mazatlán for the real
thing. Nora wondered how Arthur survived the pace . . . he
didn't have Ali's iron constitution. Still, he did survive and
apparently thrived.

As a couple—but more often Ali alone—they were regularly noted by trendy magazines. Ali was as devoted to high
visibility as any rock star. She was photographed by *San*

Diego and *Ranch & Coast*. Both she and Arthur were spotlighted by *Town & Country* as typical of the new, elegant, West Coast life-style. *Architectural Digest* did a spread on their condo. *Vanity Fair* included them whenever they showed up in Manhattan for a bash featured in *Vanities*. *Sunset Magazine* did Ali's kitchen. One columnist wrote about Ali, ". . . a swank and smart socialite addicted to A List parties. Her style smacks of social climbing. . . ." Reading it, Ali shrugged and paraphrased Disraeli, "It's not what they say that matters, it's that they say something." Much was said about Ali.

Nora watched curiously as Ali scaled the social heights . . . it had the same fascination for her as watching a trapeze artist do somersaults in midair. The Reiners made substantial donations to the San Diego Opera and Symphony. Ali was tireless in support of select charity galas . . . the Candelight Ball, the Jewel Ball, and the Monte Carlo Gala for openers. All the while angling for a box at the Charity Ball . . . the top of top-drawer San Diego affairs. Millie had a box . . . it followed that Ali should have one too. Ali demanded status . . . the status Millie Gardiner had . . . Joan Kroc had . . . Helen Copley had.

Yet despite her devotion to the social climb, Ali made time for Nora . . . on the telephone. More was impossible. Nora worked. Ali had engagements. Nora sympathized. Mark didn't. He bad-mouthed her. His smile was nasty.

"Ali is no cuddly toy. Madam Borgia is covering her bets. If you inherit Millie's millions, you're a friend in a million. . . ."

Nora lost her temper. "You call her a con artist, but you drool over an invitation to one of her evenings."

"You bet your sweet ass I do. They're Arthur's evenings too. That's where I hear about deals . . . mergers, acquisitions, LBOs. I'm in the loop."

"With the Big Guns."

"Big Guns are my specialty. Plus I pick up clients. . . ."

Nora, Pat, and Bruce Bevins—the producer of the Channel 18 news—sat in the screening room watching a rerun of the local news half hour . . . a series of shots of painters at work.

A hippy blonde in optimistically tight jeans smiled and said, "You see, I own this painting by a serial killer. It's awesome . . . thrilling. I'm trying for the same killer impact.''

Cut to a plump man with a gargoyle smile. "Honestly, yesterday a lady said, 'Excuse me, but is that a real painting? My eight-year-old could do that. . . .' ''

A man in a seedy velvet waistcoat and striped trousers was painting a thousand-dollar bill. "One of my friends uses words in his paintings. Like *tacky!* and *diddly doo.* My granddaddy, John Haberle, he painted greenbacks. Did it so well the T-men told him to quit it. Said they could pass as counterfeit. I've inherited his talent—''

The screen went black . . . the room lit up. Nora turned to Pat and Bruce.

"That's what I mean. News with local color. The San Diego Art Festival. Or the one called Taste of Main Street . . . that six-block party in Encinitas with seven hundred people eating shrimp pizza, chocolate raspberries . . . hanging out. Local news with flair. . . .''

"Like the one on the sunset balloon flights over Del Mar?'' Bruce asked. "With the sailor proposing . . .''

"Like that. I got Mark up in a balloon,'' Nora said. "My birthday present. They taught him how to make the damn thing go up and down.''

"Did he freak out?'' Pat asked.

"He didn't. I did. My stomach did anyway. Then he wanted us to try free-fall. Which brings me to the next event.''

Bruce brooded. "The Bid for Bachelors.''

"A display of shitty taste,'' Pat remarked.

"It's for charity . . . it's already oversold. And you're elected, Pat.''

"To bid on a bachelor? Me? You're kidding. Why not Sheri?''

Friendly concern. "She's the wrong age. You'll love it, Pat. Cameras will grind . . . immortalizing you . . . and him.''

Suppressed fury. "I can't afford it. It costs money.''

"Channel 18 will back your bid . . . up to three thousand. To buy you your Frog Prince . . . and be a photo op.''

Bruce yelped, "Nora! Our budget! Rhett Butler paid one hundred fifty dollars for Scarlett. Three thousand is—''

"Chalk it up to inflation. The Bid for Bachelors preview is next Monday evening. The auction's the following Friday evening. You have all the info, Bruce . . . time and place. Meeting adjourned.''

After Nora left, Pat moaned to Bruce, ''I hate it! I won't do it! It's a fuckin' low punch.''

''Patti Cake, baby, your income could drop if you're fired.''

''The bitch!'' Pat had a gift for outrage.

''You want that promotion?''

''It won't happen. She's Millie's granddaughter.''

Bruce sighed as if he were about to Miranda-ize an amateur criminal. ''Pat, please consider who might be there.''

''Who?'' Pat's open mouth formed a circle.

''Lew Dobbs. The man who wants to buy Channel 18. If he does, and if he likes you . . .'' A significant glance.

''Yuck. I understand he looks like a defensive tackle. Why's he going?''

''Angie Pratt—she's related to Mrs G.—chairs the charity. Angie's husband, Paul Pratt, is one of Lew Dobbs's asshole buddies. So Dobbs is going. Now what about you?''

The standoff was over. ''I hope I don't throw up.''

Back in her office, Nora took a call from Ali. ''We must have lunch.'' In the small, teary voice Nora knew so well, Ali added, ''Please . . .''

''When? I'm busy until . . . uhm . . . Thursday.''

''Fine. Where? You pick. Convenient for you.''

Ali's quick accommodation warned Nora. What did she want? ''Let's do Epazote? At one o'clock. You'll have a margarita.''

''I hate trendy places . . . also chips and salsa.''

''The salsa isn't hot.''

''I love it hot. I prefer Mexican food in Mexico.''

''We are not all free spirits like you and Arthur. They'll doctor your salsa with chili. Or you can order tamales. Tacos. All kinds of fillings . . . shrimp, shark, *carne asada.*''

Ali sighed her agreement.

They sat at a table on an outdoor terrace. Ali sipped her margarita. Nora had white wine and waited.

At last Ali began. ''There's no one else I can talk to . . . I'm so unhappy.'' One of Ali's many talents was to weep on demand . . . she delicately wiped a tear from the corner of her eye.

"What's the matter?" Nora asked. "Are you sick?"

"Not sick in the body." Ali munched greedily on the fresh chips that she hated. "I'm sick in the soul . . . the spirit."

"Why?"

"I love Arthur, but marrying him was a mistake."

"You're supposed to be the happiest couple in San Diego."

Ali gave Nora a smile . . . an inspirational smile, the kind of smile you bring up courageously through pain . . . through tears. "Are you aware that Arthur is a compulsive philanderer?" she suddenly blurted out.

"No kidding. Come on, Ali. We talked about it often enough. It's a nervous tic. But he's crazy about you."

"That's true."

The smug confidence in Ali's voice puzzled Nora. What was this all about?

"But a leopard doesn't change its spots," Ali grieved. "I'm soul-sick."

Nora was not Barron Gardiner's daughter for nothing. She was a connoisseur of crap . . . and this had the ring of quality crap. She asked, as if she didn't already know, "Honestly, do you give a damn?"

"No!" From tears and smug confidence, Ali plunged headfirst into indignation. "But he's so bloody indiscreet. Some nights I smell her perfume."

"What perfume do you smell?" Nora tried not to laugh.

"Chanel No. 5. That's what." Nostrils flared. "I use Shalimar."

"Naturally." The conversation had taken a comedic turn. "And you found lipstick on his collar that wasn't your color?"

Ali's eyes widened. "On his handkerchief. When I sorted his laundry for the laundress. How did you know?"

"Because the whole thing sounds like a bad soap opera."

"It's not a soap opera. I am hurt . . . hurt and jealous. I thought when he married me he'd change. He didn't." She lowered her voice. "Once a cocksman, always a cocksman. I want to get away."

Nora tried not to laugh. "You want to divorce Arthur?"

Ali sucked on her cheeks with pouted lips. "I want to be free . . . to begin again . . ."

"With another man? You're kidding." But even as Nora said it she knew Ali wasn't kidding.

"If there was one." Ali stared at the tablecloth. "But there isn't."

Their eyes met in silent communion such as is sometimes granted to old friends.

"It's hard finding someone as rich as Arthur," Nora remarked casually.

Ali had the grace to blush. "True. And I am addicted to money. How can I give up Arthur's millions? I see the cynical look on your face. Nora, am I being a hypocritical prig?"

"You sure are. You never stuck to the rules yourself. . . ."

Relief cleared Ali's face. "Maybe I wanted you to say that. Say sensibly that I must go on. Even if I have to take a lover myself. In fact . . ."

This had a familiar ring. "Don't tell me about it," Nora said.

Ali gave her a knowing smile. "You've heard nothing." She signaled the waiter for another margarita. In an abrupt shift of subject, she asked, "Nora, when are you going to buy a house? You ought to soon. Arthur says real estate is coming back."

Afterward Nora thought about Arthur's infidelities. Why had Ali talked about them? Or about taking a lover? It made no sense. She'd bet an Eisenhower silver dollar that Ali, herself, was an authority on adultery. So what was the lunch all about? She didn't know. Unless there was someone just over the horizon, and Ali was building a constituency in the family. But who?

The quintessential California restaurant . . . picture windows revealed one of California's great natural wonders, the Pacific Ocean. Art by San Diego painters—Francois Gilot, Garret Greve, and others—on the walls. The chef had prepared a California nee Pacific Rim buffet with shrimp stuffed with crabmeat, seafood pasta, rotisseried beef. Monday evening, at the Bid for Bachelors preview, a twittery, overflow crowd, mixing well-dressed men in dinner jackets and face masks—the products to be auctioned—and equally well-dressed women in crotch-high, décolleté evening dresses—the bidders—strolled about eating grilled ahi tucked into tacos . . . pesto pizza . . . drinking wine and beer . . . chatting it up. Pat cruised the room . . . shuttling between groups.

"Lew? What's your last name, Lew?" Pat studied the ID tag on the man's lapel. "Lew what?"

Lew took in her silky blond hair, the valley between her breasts, and two of the longest legs in captivity. "Why?"

Pat flashed a smile. "I'm with the FBI. There's a warrant out for Lew . . ."

"For sex crimes?"

"I can't say. Where you from?"

"La Jolla. Good address. Bid high on me and I'll tell you my last name. What's more, I come with the best personally designed date package on the list."

"Like what?"

"Like a get-acquainted brunch, overnight in a four-star hotel—separate rooms, if you insist—three theatrical performances, Sunday brunch, and a symphony matinee . . . all that plus a limousine to chauffeur me and my fortunate buyer around."

"Sounds marvey. Be right back." She hurried to the entrance of the restaurant, where Bruce and the Channel 18 mobile news unit were set up.

"It'll make a good news clip," Nick, the cameraman, observed. "Eligible single men recruited for charity . . . auctioned off to the highest bidder."

"Like the three big ones we sponsor Pat with," Bruce complained. "Plus those seats at the sell-off for a hundred bucks. Pat, pick a star type like Tom Cruise. A guy who fucks the camera . . . gives great interviews. Not a vet or an ecologist. There's a Top Gun pilot here. Maybe—"

"Brucie, baby. Cut the shit. Where is he?"

"Where is who?"

"The Big D from Dallas. I found two Lews from La Jolla."

"What can I say?"

"Lew Dobbs. Dallas. The Lew lineup in there is La Jolla."

"Sorry, Patti Cake. Never met the man. I read about him in the papers . . . the *L.A. Times,* the *San Diego Union.* One of them mentioned him. Check the ID tags."

"I did. First names only. No Big Lew from Big D."

"Try anything with *L.* Maybe Lew's his nickname."

"There's a Lawrence . . . a Leonard. Which one is Dobbs?"

"Beats me. Maybe you can spot the Big L when they sa-

shay down the runway." Bruce grinned. "Supposed to be
built like a defensive lineman."

"I know," Pat said . . . her stomach clenched.

"Why the masks?" Jed, an assistant director, asked.

"They don't want their current squeezes to bid on them."
Nick chortled.

"Damn it! Which one is Dobbs?" Pat frowned and moved
back into the male-female fray . . . looking for an XT and
XXL size.

"By the way, Leonard . . . what's your last name?"

A husky voice whispered in her ear. "Pat Yocum! Surprise, surprise! What's a nice les like you doing here? You
going straight?"

"Lenny!" Pat paled, recognizing the voice. "Leonard Gerard! For Christ's sake! Is it really you?"

"It's me all right. What happened? You and Juno split?"
He grabbed her shoulders.

"Stop it, Lenny. Juno and I are business as usual."

"So why are you here bidding on bachelors?" Rubbing his
nose against hers, he said, "I knew you were bi—"

"I am not!" Pat said, jerking her head back.

"Yes, you are. You're bisexual. AC/DC. I always knew it.
Pat, I'm crazy about you, always have been. I'm broad-
minded. If you wanna change your style now and then . . .
what the hell! You can do your thing with Juno."

"Come off it, Lenny. I know you too. Since when do you
give a damn about any woman, including me? Land's sake,
boy. Your little ol' friend Christal with the gorgeous muscles . . . Christal baby will spank you when he—or is it
she?—finds out about this escapade."

"Christal approves of this escapade. He says I should see
what a real woman is like . . . I'll appreciate him even more
after the experience."

"I pity the real woman who wins you." Pat gave him a
mean grin. "Unless she's into KY jelly and butt fucking."

Lenny was hurt. "Pat, I can make it with a woman any
day . . . I've done it twice before. . . ." He reared up. "But
since we're making points, can you make it with a man . . .
a man, sweetie . . . all of him, not just his mouth?"

Pat hissed softly. "I can be just as heterosexual as any
bimbo in this room. Now let's drop it."

Leonard smiled. "I promise I won't tell if you won't. Our

heterosexual outing will be our secret . . . providing you bid
on me. High as it goes. Understand?'' Through the mask his
eyes gleamed. He was curious what would happen when they
hit the sack . . . who would do what to whom. ''What's more,
I have a great package arranged. Five days in the Caribbean
at a top hotel. And to make me even more desirable than I
am, I'll pay you back whatever your bid costs you.''

Pat's eyes were not starry. ''How come you're suddenly so
rich?''

''I'm not. My cousin, Lew Dobbs, is. He got called back
to Dallas. You know how it is . . . business before pleasure.
So I'm a stand-in. . . .'' An owlish look. ''You know he's
out to buy your station?''

''He is? I didn't know . . . Mmmm . . .'' Interest mounting. ''I've never been to the Caribbean. You know what,
Lenny?'' She lightly traced his lips with her forefinger. ''I
think we're on the same wavelength. We're both closet het-
erosexuals. . . .''

So it came to pass that Pat Yocum and Lew Dobbs's cousin,
Leonard Gerard, became intimate . . . much to Juno Pole-
ski's and Christal McGurdy's indignation.

Nora noted that Ali seemed more at peace with her marriage and concluded that she had definitely added variety to
her sex life. Conversely, Arthur was less at peace. One day
it struck Nora that, quite unnoticed, Arthur had changed. He
was like a candle melting down . . . no longer good-humored
. . . laughing easily. He had an air of brooding resignation,
depression. Like someone who is fatally ill and knows there
is nothing to be done. In the spring he wanted to get away.
Ali suggested Fiji . . . her second-favorite island. Arthur had
never been to Fiji, but the island had been highly touted by
Stanley Tseng, an important client. So, the Regent on Fiji it
was. Upon returning, Ali told Nora she adored the rattan
furniture, the handwoven fabrics and the woven straw mats
. . . and the men. ''To be more accurate,'' she added with a
sly grin, ''only one divine man on this trip.''

That summer Nora and Mark bought their first home . . .
the same house they'd rented for the years they lived in North
County. The house cost a cool million dollars, and the four
hundred thousand in cash they put up stripped their savings.
Although the house was not as grand as the one Mark had

once envisioned, he was buying into his dream . . . he owned a million-dollar home. So what if he had a six-hundred-thousand-dollar mortgage? Everyone owed money on their houses . . . debt was the American way of life. For Nora the purchase was more complex. Since losing the baby, something had gone out of their sex life. Maybe it was her fault. Since the miscarriage, she'd become unsure of herself . . . of her sexuality. But Mark's attitude hadn't helped. They didn't have sex as often, and there were times when she felt a part of Mark was standing back and judging her performance, comparing the way she made love to someone else . . . another woman? But there was no other woman, she was sure of that. It occurred to her that buying the house might bring them closer. The sex would get better, and maybe—if she got lucky—she'd get pregnant. Mark would love to own a house and have a son.

One evening they made love . . . for whatever reason, the sex was better than it had been in months. Afterward they had drinks on the patio. Feeling euphoric, Nora shared an inspiration. "Ali called today. Don't make a face. She had the same idea I've had. This is the third time she's mentioned it. Arthur's for it too. They're waiting for us to give a house-warming party."

"We could . . . I guess. We owe invitations to half my partners."

"How about ten congenial partners . . . plus spouses . . . plus the literary lights up the block. The painters we like. Thirty people. We can't invite Millie . . . she's at the Vineyard."

"Better figure on forty. Add Chuck Tysen and his latest mopsie. He's shopping for a new broker."

They settled on forty-four . . . a small, intimate group from Ali's standpoint . . . an army division to Nora. Naturally the Reiners were on the list.

Then Nora had a brainstorm. "Let's invite Tammi and Ken. The play's going into rehearsal in a few months. I think of them as co-workers. They can drive down from Malibu."

"Include them out," Mark said. "And do not invite Jordan."

"I can't invite Jordan. He's reading scripts in Malaysia or trekking somewhere in Nepal."

"Or getting drunk on a freighter to Singapore. That boy

has a hard life. I thought he was kissing ass at CAA, ICM, and William Morris. Playing footsie with agents for Millie's project. Didn't he replace your dear departed Ali Cat . . . now one of the idle rich?''

"That's right. Tim didn't work out so Jordan said he'd take over. Right now all new productions are on hold . . . till *Mama*'s completed.''

"Good! Forget Tammi . . . forget Savage.''

"Why? They'll add glamour.''

"They're a collective pain in the ass. You'll need applause trucked in. Besides that . . .'' Mark sipped his scotch.

"Besides what? What am I missing?''

"We must invite the Reiners . . . both of them.'' An ultrapatient tone. "We can't have Arthur without the Ali Cat.''

Mark and Nora had a brief, wordless struggle of wills. Nora won. "We'll have Tammi, Ken and the Reiners . . . both couples.''

Mark sucked in his breath and shook his head. "Here's to you, Lady Macbeth, and to your next murder.''

Nora ignored him, leaving the patio to get a pad and pencil. When she returned, she perched on a recliner and started planning the housewarming. For minutes there was no mention of the guest list while she estimated the liquor and food needed.

Mark broke the silence. "Okay. Listen. I've been watching Arthur. He's suddenly looking his age . . . twenty years older than before he married Ali. Maybe he still makes it in the sack, but I wouldn't want to match him against Savage. Savage is younger, tougher . . . with an eye for anything that twitches. Knocking off Ali would be easy for him . . . like shooting fish in a barrel.''

"Ali met Ken before she married Arthur. No sparks. Why now?'' Nora continued adding figures.

"As you said, that was B.A. . . . before she married Arthur. When she was desperate for a stake. Ken is not one to depend on for a grubstake.''

"Plus Ken is show biz . . . not Ali's type. Plus she's not his type . . . she isn't show biz. They have nothing in common.''

"He's male. She's female. That's enough in common.''

"Tammi will be here too,'' Nora said, glancing up.

"Exactly my point.'' Mark's tone was ominous. "If something happens, you're going to be up that smelly brown creek without a paddle. Millie expects a production of *I Remember Mama*. You could blow your star . . . the whole enchilada. And if Arthur gets pissed off, he could fire me. Since he married Ali, my partnership hangs by a thread.''

His stare was so implacable, so mulelike, it jolted Nora. She had not forgotten Ali's "falling in love" with Arthur . . . or their lunch and her heartbroken crap about her "sick spirit" . . . or the "divine" man in Fiji. She hesitated. Then she shook her head. Ali wouldn't dare . . . not with Ken Savage. "Mark, I hear you," she said. "But Ali's a survivor. She won't bite the hand that feeds her . . . Arthur's hand. The guest list is set. I stand pat.''

"With your feet planted firmly in midair. Why don't you slit both our wrists? We'll die together. A love pact.''

The evening was sultry and warm. The guests arrived early . . . some in Mercedes, others in Jaguars, Fords, Jeeps, Buicks, Pontiacs, Cadillacs, one Excaliber—and one couple actually came on foot. The men were more or less casual— with and without jewelry—but showered, barbered and fragranced to a fare-thee-well. The women were more shimmery . . . hormones alert, jewelry formidable, breasts implanted, chins remodeled, classy rhytidectomies.

Penny Moffat, a painter wearing a new nose and chin and sprayed-on sparkle that began in her hair and ended at her bare feet, asked in a husky voice, "Where's Ali?"

"Be here any minute," Nora reassured.

"Nora, I'm hyper. When I started I had doubts. Was I up to a portrait of Ali? Her sheer impact . . .''

"You're doing Ali's portrait?"

"It's my masterpiece. In form . . . in color . . . it's unique. The essence of Ali. It reveals her indomitable spirit.'' Penny's voice expected applause.

"I look forward to seeing it." Nora gulped. "The bar's over there.'' She nodded toward the bar set up at the far end of the room and hurried to greet Ann Randall, the journalist, decked out in a white sequinned stretch jersey bodysuit that clung like a second skin. Ann's smile was toothy . . . her cleavage seismographic . . . her implants had implants.

"Where's Ali? My boychic accidentally erased our interview from the tape. We need another recording session.''

"What interview? What tape?"

"Oops. Sorry. My bloop. She wanted to surprise you. Well, it's out now. I'm ghosting her diary . . . her memoirs. We're working from taped interviews."

"I bet it's interesting." Nora swallowed.

"Interesting? Fuck interesting. She's riveting . . . the underage, unwanted, abused daughter of Ma Perkins. Tight pants and boobs . . . a teenage cock teaser . . . always in heat. But she asks no quarter and gives none. She makes it against all odds. None of that self-serving, sentimental slop you see in most autobiographies."

"Ali? What odds? Who's Ma Perkins?"

"A figure of speech. She's no ingenue done in by the fuckin' world. She's taken her licks, but she's tough. She bounces back. When I finish polishing the manuscript, I'll have a best-seller." Ann always took full credit.

Nora nodded, remembering that to Ali the unpublicized life—real or fictional—wasn't worth living.

"She'll bounce in any minute," Nora said, moving to greet their next-door neighbor, who had danced with Bob Fosse and wore lacy lingerie remade by her dressmaker into a mini-dress that left her billowing breasts—all hers—threatening to spill out from her bodice.

"Nora, you must clear the center of the room later. Ali and I need the space for our act."

"What act?"

"Our dance routine. I've been giving her dancing lessons . . . tap and modern. We'll buck-and-wing it. Ali's a born trooper."

"You're joking." Even as Nora said it she knew she wasn't. The evening was a revelation. "Ali dances?"

"And how! If she'd started as a child, she'd be a cross between Ginger Rogers and Twyla Tharp. She's gifted. I'm introducing her around. She's itching to work in theater."

"I can hardly wait to see your act. The hors d'oeuvres are over there," Nora said, seeing Tammi Meredith enter looking serenely sexy in something strapless done with thousands of fake pearls, a white velvet stole sequinned and shining across her shoulders, her arm linked possessively with Ken's.

"Hello, Nora."

Nora drew herself up for the welcoming. "Hello, Tammi. Hi, Ken. I'm glad you could come."

"Wouldn't miss it for the world." Tammi gave Nora a practiced smile. "Is Ali Reiner here?"

"Not yet." Nora almost winced. "You remember her?"

"Vividly. We met at Channel 18 . . . before she married. Then we bumped into her at Musso and Frank's . . . schmoozing with Swifty. Ken thinks she's interesting."

Nora chewed on that revelation. "She'll be here soon," she said lamely. She glanced at her guests in glitter and bead shine and herself in lacy mauve pants with halter to match . . . and felt her throat tighten. She had a strong premonition a tidal wave was coming . . . and an instinct to run for her life. Mark had been right.

Ali arrived—Arthur trailing—a huge pink camellia in her hair, wearing a strapless slip dress in a sequinned mélange of color. She threw Nora a kiss, calling, "I love your house-warming," and scooted to the terrace to talk to Ann Randall. She was instantly surrounded by people—mostly men—almost disappearing from sight. Ali's charm oozed out of every pore, perfuming everyone at the party. The women reacted with grudging admiration. Nora watched frozen as Ken picked up Ali's scent . . . her musical laughter called to him . . . it bombarded the men vying for her attention. They'd come expecting good drinks, food, a casual flirtation, conversation out of the pages of *Vanity Fair* or *People*. What they got was a star blazing on the terrace. Madame du Barry would have run for the hills. The party moved into high gear as the men tried edging Ken out.

The decibel count rose . . . Nora's heart sank. Ali and Ken moved to the far end of the terrace, deep in conversation . . . allowing no interruptions. Ali was as taken with Ken as Ken was with Ali. He might be saying the most banal things in the world, yet Ali's eyes were fixed on him reverently. Show biz or not, they were each other's type.

Feeling helpless, Nora welcomed the distraction of Hilda, the caterer, signaling for a conference regarding the mozza-rella rolled with prosciutto, eggplant with goat cheese, lamb souvlaki—a Greek specialty—plus stuffed calamari, mee krob, tacos with pork, brandied scallops, tempura chicken . . . an international menu. Once Hilda-and-help began setting up the buffet, Nora returned to the party. Checking the bar, she saw Tammi chatting up a storm with Arthur Reiner, the first of a lineup of men waiting for Tammi's smile. But after Arthur, Tammi played the field. She flirted with one, tantalized another, drifted around followed by admirers. She was looking for someone. Nora perspired . . . she knew who. Ali and Ken had vanished.

Nora started to turn on the outside lights to flood the small ground-floor patio. What stopped her was instinct. Where was Ali . . . where was Ken? Arthur was drinking alone at the edge of the terrace. In his sharply creased white slacks, white open shirt with an ascot, navy blazer and deck shoes, he looked deathly ill. Mark approached him like someone approaching a sickbed. He tried to engage him in conversation, but Arthur wasn't talking. He was quiet and withdrawn . . . his eyes flitted from person to person, searching for Ali. At the other end of the terrace, Tammi was being tipsy and coquettish with Pat Moffat's live-in lover . . . with Ann Randall's wandering husband . . . with any available man. The moon was rising. In minutes the food must be served, the outside lights lit. Arthur and Tammi were still at the party, meaning Ali and Ken were too. But where?

Nora knew where. Unobtrusively, she edged out of the circle of the party. She tiptoed down the stairs and entered the master bedroom. Without turning on the lights, and making no sound, she stood at the open French doors leading to the small patio. The night was dark . . . she could see nothing. But she could hear everything. From the bushes ringing the patio, she heard what she had been afraid she would hear . . . heavy panting . . . moaning.

Then Ali's voice. "You're so hard! Again!"

Ken's voice. "With you I'm reborn. I could go all night."

"Come in me now."

More panting . . . more heavy breathing . . . more moans. Nora could imagine the scene. Quietly she backed out of the dark bedroom and returned to the party. Luckily the guests were at the buffet tables foraging for food. Nora labored to remain composed. She whispered to Mark, "Keep Arthur occupied. And Tammi."

Mark asked grimly, "Ali's skinny-dipping?"

"Downstairs. On our patio. Fill you in later." Nora headed for the light switch. End the orgy before all hell broke loose. Furious, she snapped on the Malibu lights. Adulterers, go to red alert . . . pull up your pants!

It worked. Within minutes Ali and Ken appeared, holding

drinks. Not a hair on Ali's head out of place, not even the camellia. But she had the lax look of a contented, well-fed—or well-fucked—Ali Cat. They joined Mark and Nora, who were in the kitchen arguing about when to put out dessert.

"Great view you have out back," Ken said jovially to Mark. "Bet you and Nora enjoy it."

"Bet you did too." Tammi swayed into the kitchen.

Ken pecked her cheek. "We use our view, kid."

"I want to go home, lover boy."

"The party's only begun."

"For you the party's over," Tammi said in a furious voice. "I know. It was a primal event full of wonder and awe. A miracle . . . a revelation . . . a solar explosion in the mind . . . the spirit. I've heard it. I want to go home." Tammi started to laugh, a hair breadth away from hysteria.

"Okay, babe. We'll go beddi-bye," Ken said soothingly.

Tammi gave Ali a hard look. "Did he breathe into your ear . . . whisper about the doors opening into corridors of light? Tell me . . . in what holy realm of spiritual communion did you fuck? Some hideaway by the ocean?"

"We looked for the Big Dipper." Ali was sweet dignity.

"Maybe we'll stay." Tammi smiled at Ali. "You and I have so much to talk about. Now we have Ken in common. And he is common. We'll drink to him." Tammi weaved out of the kitchen toward the bar.

Ali smiled at Ken sympathetically. "She's had a bit much to drink. Take her home, Ken." Her voice was intimate as the rustle of sheets. Then she gave them all a dazzling smile and left the kitchen. Nora heard her laughter . . . unrepentant, unembarrassed . . . fucking Ken Savage was a whoopee.

Nora watched her for a minute. This was not the time to tell Ali where to head in . . . once and for all.

Ken said, "Tammi's not been feeling well. I shouldn't have risked coming."

"And coming, and coming, and coming," Tammi said, reappearing.

Ken put his arm around her. "I apologize for my bride. The kid's never held her liquor well."

"Don't you dare apologize for me . . . you shithead! Listen to me and listen to me good. We go home now or I'll teach that amateur tart not to compete with a professional."

She glanced around the room. "Arthur Reiner will do for openers. Then I'll—"

"Okay," Ken said quickly. "Good-bye, Nora. It's been fun."

As Nora followed them to the door, she heard Tammi say in a loud voice, "Remember the last time you got me pissed? I made you jerk off in a corner while I took on five jocks. I can do better. If you don't—" Tammi slammed the door in Nora's face.

Mark tapped Nora's shoulder. "Hollywood." He hummed "Hooray for Hollywood." He stopped humming. "I wonder what they'll do for an encore."

"Shut up, Mark," Nora hissed. Then she walked slowly into the living room. Ali was surrounded by eager men . . . Arthur stood on the fringe watching with a harrowed face, carrying his cross up the hill.

After the guests had gone—Ali and Arthur left with arms linked—after Hilda and her helpers had cleared and gone, Nora gave Mark a full report on the debauch behind the bushes.

He wasn't surprised. "Do you know what that carnival of passion may cost us?"

"Arthur might ask you to resign. Your presence might be an embarrassment, an awkward reminder of . . ."

"Yeah. And suppose Tammi quits? Millie wouldn't fire you?"

"No, but . . ." Suddenly Nora was stung by an old fear of looking like a failure to Millie . . . as her father had. Of having to borrow money from Millie . . . as her father had. Of Millie's deciding she was rash, unthinking . . . as her father had been. Indiscretion was Barron Gardiner's autograph. Exposing Ken to Ali was a classic indiscretion. At last she sighed. "But she will be disappointed."

"If Tammi quits, who else do you have?"

"No one." Nora thought about the negative reactions Tim Rourke had gotten from the agents he'd contacted. Which was why Jordan had taken over. Even with Jordan Banska producing and directing the shows, they weren't trampling over each other to commit to 'Night of Stars.' They took a wait-and-see attitude . . . they'd wait and see what Tammi's ratings were.

"Will that deep-six 'Night of Stars'?"

"Could be," Nora said with bitter distaste. "I don't look forward to telling Millie . . ."

Mark spoke with careful fairness. "Look . . . what's done is done. Tammi hasn't quit yet. If she does, maybe you—and your boy, Jordan—can hold the project together. There's enough time."

"Jordan might. But . . ." Nora changed the subject, not wanting to admit she had a bad feeling that Millie didn't have enough time.

Ali telephoned Nora later in the week at the office to say what a wonderful time she and Arthur had. She blithely went on to mention how appealing she found Ken Savage.

". . . the most attractive man I've seen in years. My fantasies should be censored. How can you work together without climbing into bed with him?"

Nora detected Ali was probing. "I manage," she said dryly. "Maybe I have a low sex drive."

"I don't. I'd love to spend a weekend with him. On some island painted by Gauguin." She giggled. "Scratch that remark. What a way for Mrs. Arthur Reiner to talk."

Nora couldn't control her anger. "Stop the shit, Ali," she snapped. "It's me . . . Nora . . . I know you too damn well. This is exactly the way I expect you to talk. Remember . . . you filled me in on your yens over margaritas."

"I did, didn't I? Oh dear . . . how childish of me." Ali's disembodied voice was full of fun.

"You seemed to want my permission to fuck around. Did you have Ken Savage in mind at the time?"

"He had crossed my mind. . . ."

"Well, I don't approve! Just because Arthur fucks around—"

"All the time!"

"And you do too. You're evening the score . . . in fact, going him one better."

"I'm a straight shooter." Ali giggled. "It's appropriate."

"Maybe. But what's not appropriate is putting Ken Savage on your tit-for-tat list. That moonlight revel in the bushes was tasteless."

"Now, Nora—"

Nora cut her short. "Now, Ali! It was stupid and irresponsible. When you screwed Ken you traded Millie's project for a lousy orgasm. Suppose Tammi gets pissed and quits the show?''

"It wasn't lousy, but . . . Mmmm . . . Millie would be angry?"

"She'd be very angry. And Arthur already sees red."

"Arthur doesn't know."

"The hell he doesn't. He knows damn well. You made a fool of him. Sure he screws around, maybe sometimes indiscreetly. But you were even more indiscreet . . . and at our party. Arthur could fire Mark because you did your thing at our house."

"Arthur will not fire Mark. I won't permit it. Damn! I don't want to upset Millie. I should have disinvited Ken . . ."

"You? Disinvite Ken? What do you mean?"

"Well . . . you know . . ."

"I don't know."

"We've been in touch . . . by phone. That's why I suggested he accept your invitation. It was hard for us to get to know each other better on the phone. He's stuck in Malibu . . . with Tammi keeping tabs on him. I'm stuck here . . . with Arthur."

"That's why you nagged me to give a housewarming party? So you and Ken could put on a X-rated show?"

Ali laughed. "We were damn good. You should have turned on the floodlights and sold tickets."

"Right! Tammi and Arthur would have loved that. Tell me something, Ali. What if I hadn't invited Tammi and Ken?"

"Then I'd have invited them myself. And said you asked me to. I know you . . . you'd never turn them away at the door."

"Thank you for keeping me informed," Nora muttered.

"Oh, Nora! I wouldn't hurt you for the world . . . you worry too much. Relax. Everything will work out A-OK. My mother—not Amanda—she used to say that. I'll patch things up with Tammi."

Nora's impulse was to hang up. But it was tactically smarter not to. She made herself listen to Ali's stories about Ali's portrait, Ali's memoirs, Ali's tap-dancing lessons. Finally Ali had to run, but she would be in touch shortly. Mark and Nora and Arthur and she would have a candlelight dinner and gossip. Before hanging up Ali had a last aside. "You know, Nora, I admit it. I'm jealous of Tammi." Her tone was businesslike. "She has the run of the Malibu Beach Colony and Ken too." Pause. "Do you know Forbes ranked her earnings as twelfth among all entertainers. And Ken manages her money. Isn't that interesting?"

Nora heard her. She definitely heard her. Ali and money . . . till death do they part.

Ali was as good as her word. There was a short round-robin of telephone calls. Ken to Nora . . . Nora to Tammi . . . Nora to Ken . . . Tammi to Nora. All was forgiven . . . all was forgotten. The phone lines were full of "darling" and "sweetie" and "love you too." By the time Jordan returned to Hollywood, it was as though nothing had happened. A pebble had been thrown into a lake and, after a few ripples, nothing was heard of the pebble again.

The Reiners and Sterns never had dinner together. One evening while Nora and Mark were having drinks, the telephone rang. Nora answered and heard Ali . . . hysterical.

"Nora!" she cried. "Arthur's lying on the floor. He won't get up. I think he's dead." She gasped.

"We'll be right over," Nora said. "Call for an ambulance. Then call his doctor. Do you know how to give CPR?"

"What's that?"

"Never mind. Mark can do it. We'll be there as soon as we can."

When they arrived at the condo, Dorothea opened the door. Her face said all there was to say. There was nothing to be done. Arthur Reiner's heart—his spirit—had said, "Quittin' time."

The funeral service was crowded with power players . . . including mega financiers, big-time lawyers, politicos with clout. Also celebrities who did nothing except spend time being celebrities. It was almost a media event. Ali, looking stunning in black, quietly sobbed. Dorothea wore gray and sat beside her son, Roger. They were both silent and grim throughout the service. When it was over, the limo took Nora and Ali back to Ali's condo, and Nora left her to the tender mercies of the housekeeper, the cook and her masseuse, who had arrived to work on Mrs. Reiner's muscles and help her relax from the stress.

In the intervening weeks between the funeral and the reading of the will, Ali and Nora had brief conversations. Ali's voice was always on the edge of tears . . . full of exalted martyrdom.

"I miss him so much. I don't know what to do with my leftover life to live."

The theatrics deserved a rave. Nora almost applauded. Instead she listened patiently . . . poker-faced. She'd been waking up nights thinking about Ali. She had a hunch and she always trusted her hunches. Her hunch proved out. One evening as she waited to pick up Mark at Lindbergh Field—he was returning from Phoenix . . . a two-day analysis of the changes Lew Dobbs had made at Group H—she saw Ken Savage walk through the gate. An American Eagle flight from L.A. had just arrived. And there was Ali waving at him. Ken took her in his arms . . . their kiss was long and hard. Then, laughing and holding hands, they started through the airport. So much for what Ali would do with her leftover life.

Nora was so absorbed in watching Ali and Ken that Mark's breathing in her ear made her jump.

"And there go the two lovebirds . . . soaring into the sunset." His tone was mellow and rich . . . it sounded like a travelogue voice-over. Then he dropped his voice to a whisper. "Tell me, Nora, who do you think is next on Ali's A list? Ken? No. He's too entangled with Tammi's money. . . . Besides, if somehow she knocked Ken off, she would be repeating herself. That would raise suspicion. So who? Hmmm. Maybe you?" His smile wasn't nice. "Why not? You're more convenient than Hiram. And she could be such a comfort to Millie in her grief. . . ."

Nora said nothing . . . her own thoughts had been spinning down that same scabrous alley.

Chapter 15

WITH ARTHUR Reiner dead and his son, Roger, still in school, Reiner & Co. was rudderless. Mark made several attempts to reach Dorothea. Dorothea owned a huge chunk of the company. He had to talk to her about Reiner & Co.'s future. Dorothea's housekeeper told him in broken English, "Madam not *aqui*" or "Madam *ocupado*" or "Madam *no habla* with *nadie*." He left messages. Dorothea did not return his calls. Fortunately the market was acting as though it had taken an overdose of Valium. The funds did almost all the trading . . . about one hundred million shares per day. With Arthur no longer around to take the heat—just in case he blew a big one—Mark liquidated most of his customers' positions . . . especially Millie's and Dr. Abe's. One day he was sitting in his office. His feet were on his desk and he'd made a slingshot out of a rubber band. The game was to see how many paper clips he could pop into his wastepaper basket. After almost a week of practice, he'd gotten good at it. He was trying to beat his record—twenty-six in a row—when his secretary buzzed him.

"What is it, Kim?" Mark asked.

"There's a call for you. A Mr. Gus Sklar. He says he knows you. We don't know anyone named Gus Sklar . . . do we?" Kim Kelly was nosy. She was also young and pretty . . . young enough and pretty enough that Mark put up with her prying.

"I don't think so." Mark considered his options. Shoot more paper clips at the wastepaper basket or talk to this Gus Sklar. He stifled a yawn. "Put him through. Maybe I do know him." He hung up and waited for one of his lines to light up. Then . . . "This is Mark Stern. Who am I talking to?"

"I told your girl. I'm Gus Sklar."

The man's hoarse voice rang a bell. Sklar . . . Sklar . . . who the hell is Gus Sklar? Mark thought. "I'm supposed to know you?"

"Yeah. Sort of." Sklar chuckled softly. "Think back, Mr. Stern. Seventh Avenue. The Coral Tree Plaza. Can I bum a cigarette?"

Mark laughed. "You're Mrs. Dorothea Reiner's detective. What can I do for you?" Whatever the man wanted, he'd say "I'll consider it," and get rid of him. Arthur and Ali were yesterday's news.

"Well . . . Mr. Reiner's dead. I think I ought to see you. I got something you might be interested in."

"How'd you get my name?"

"I told you it would only take about an hour. I got a good friend in the department."

"Where can I reach you?"

"At 832-5650 . . . that's my office number. If my girl isn't in, I got a machine. Leave a message. But don't take too long, Mr. Stern. I got other customers for this info."

"Yeah. Sure. I'll call—" Mark was interrupted by the buzz of his intercom. "Hold for a second, Sklar." He switched lines. "What is it this time, Kim?"

"It's Mrs. Reiner. The second one. She's here. She wants to see you. When I said you were on the phone, she just whipped by me as though she owned the place. I don't know where she went."

Mark grimaced. "It's okay. I'll find her." He switched back to Gus Sklar. "Something's just come up. I'll call you back as soon as I'm free."

"You do that. Soon."

Mark and the detective hung up simultaneously. Mark then went looking for Ali. He glanced down the corridor . . . no Ali. He tried the bullpen . . . no Ali. The back office . . . no Ali. He asked himself, Where would I be if I were Ali Reiner? "Oh, shit!" he muttered. "Of course." When he opened the door to Arthur's office, there was Ali sitting in Arthur's chair behind his desk. Arthur's personal files were unlocked. Several of the drawers were half open.

"Mark! How nice!" Ali chirped in her brightest, cheeriest voice.

Mark thought about Ali's meeting Ken Savage at the airport. Ali was the merry widow. Faithful to the memory of

Arthur . . . in her fashion. She wore a navy blue corduroy pants suit and a pale blue pleated shirt set off by a triple strand of matched pearls. There was nothing to suggest that her husband had recently died.

"Sit down, Mark. I have to talk to you." She gestured to the Barcelona chairs in front of Arthur's desk.

"I'll stand," Mark said coldly. He stared at the open files and then at Ali. "What the hell are you doing . . . going through Arthur's files?"

"He was my husband. Besides, I was looking for something."

For a moment, the hard, metallic edge that lay hidden below the surface of Ali's charm was bared. It wasn't a pretty picture.

"I'll try again," Mark said. "What were you looking for?"

"Arthur's will. Mark, what do you know about Arthur's will?"

"Not a damned thing." And if I did know anything, I sure as hell wouldn't tell you, Mark added to himself.

Pensively, Ali ran her forefinger around the edge of her lips. "I was afraid of that," she said softly. "Arthur's will is to be read next week. Arthur had a copy, but I can't find it anywhere at home. So I thought of the office. Arthur kept some personal things in the office. You know . . ."

"Ali," Mark said with a show of patience, "Arthur wouldn't keep his will in the office . . . even only a copy. Sid Kramer—"

"Who is Sid Kramer?"

"Our office manager. Sid has a master key. It opens all the files. Arthur probably kept his copy of his will in his safe-deposit box." Mark didn't tell Ali that a year ago he'd swiped Sid's key and had a duplicate made. He hadn't actually stolen the key. He'd borrowed it . . . for only an hour. Two days after Arthur's death, he'd stayed late and ransacked Arthur's files. The will wasn't there. "Why don't you check Arthur's safe-deposit box?"

"I tried. A nasty man at the Bank of America wouldn't let me open Arthur's box." Ali gave a creditable imitation of a harassed bank vice president saying no to a potentially important client. " 'I can't, Mrs. Reiner. I simply can't. Not until we know you have inherited the contents of poor Mr.

Reiner's box,' the pompous little twirp squealed. I promise you, Mark, as soon as the will is read, I'm going to get that shithead fired . . . canned . . . deep-sixed.'' Suddenly Ali appeared young . . . vulnerable. "I will inherit . . . won't I?'' she asked in her little-girl voice. "Arthur promised to take care of me . . . should anything happen to him.''

"Arthur was famous for keeping his word. You'll be taken care of.''

Ali giggled. Her mood shifts came so swiftly and lasted such a short time, Mark had difficulty keeping up.

"You know what I want most of all?'' Ali said.

"No. But you will tell me.''

Ali was so trapped by her vision, she failed to hear the sarcasm in Mark's voice.

"I want Arthur's stock in Reiner & Co. I'm going to have such great fun being the managing partner. I'm a natural for the Street. Don't you agree? That I belong on Wall Street, I mean?''

Mark stared at Ali with wide-open, incredulous eyes. "You? A natural for the Street? No, Ali. You are not a natural for the Street. You're a . . .'' He caught himself.

"You're very unkind,'' Ali said. The catch in her voice was expertly done.

Mark shrugged. "The truth isn't always kind.''

Ali arched her eyebrows and grinned. "What will you do when I inherit Reiner & Co.?''

"Quit. It'll take me about an hour to collect my personal files. Jack White, Merrill Lynch, Bateman Eichler, Kidder Peabody . . . they're all lusting after my lily-white body.''

Threatening. "And you'll try to take Dr. Abe's and Millie's accounts with you. I might talk to them. . . .''

"You might not. You could get badly hurt, Ali. More hurt than me.''

A forced chuckle. "I wouldn't talk to Millie. I was teasing. You know I was teasing. Also about being a natural for Wall Street. You take everything so seriously, Mark . . . especially Wall Street.''

You're damn right I take my job seriously, Mark thought. Being poor is a shitty way to live. "I was teasing too, Ali,'' he said smoothly.

"I was counting on you to keep the employees in line.''

Again she used her little-girl voice. "You know everyone here. Stay! I'll make it worth your while."

"How?"

"Well . . . When I inherit Arthur's stock, I'll name myself managing partner. And I'll name you assistant managing partner. I'll have the title, but you'll have the authority."

Mark sat on a Barcelona chair. "Are you suggesting that I'll actually be running the firm?"

"Subject to my approval." Ali beamed at Mark.

"I'll have to think about that," Mark said.

"That's good enough for me." Ali held out her hand. "Shake, partner."

"Not yet, Ali. We'll shake after Arthur's will is read. Who knows . . . ?" He grinned. "You may not inherit the stock." He wondered what Dorothea would say about Ali's offer. "Where have the lawyers set the reading?" he asked.

Ali shook herself as though to shed Mark's doubts. "Here," she said. "I told them to have the reading of the will here."

"Don't you think you should have asked someone's permission?"

"Why? After next week I'll own Reiner & Co. Why shouldn't the will be read here?" She waved her arm around. "This will be all mine."

Mark swallowed. "What time is the reading?"

"Ten-thirty."

"I'll reserve the conference room from ten to twelve. That should give the lawyers enough time."

"Thank you, Mark. I knew I could count on you." Ali glowed as she contemplated her shining future.

"Don't count too heavily," Mark warned her. "All I said was I'd think about your proposition."

"You'll accept. I just know you will." Ali glanced at her watch. "I wish I could stay and watch you make money for me." She clapped her hands with childlike glee. "That would be fun."

"Yeah. Fun." Mark walked Ali to the door that led to the garage. He didn't want her wandering around the office. All she'd have to do is mention to a few people that she was going to inherit Arthur's stock. It could start a stampede for the exit. He walked slowly back to his office.

"Mark . . ." Kim Kelly stopped him. "Has Mrs. Reiner left?"

"Yes."

"She gives me the creeps. I don't know why Mr. Reiner married her."

Mark shrugged. "Maybe Ali was a perfect fit. She didn't need alterations."

"Alterations? What are you talking . . . Oh!" Kim blushed. "That Mr. Sklar called again. He left his number. He said he was leaving his office in a few minutes and you should call him."

"I'll call him."

Mark went into his office and shut the door. "Why the fuck is Sklar bothering me?" He looked at the pile of paper clips. Only three more baskets and he'd set a new record. Sklar could damn well wait. He fit the clip in the rubber band . . . pulled back the rubber . . . and . . . pop. Shit! He missed! Might as well get the call out of the way. He checked Sklar's number . . . 832-5650. The phone rang . . . rang a second time . . . rang a third time . . . rang a fourth time. Mark was about to hang up when the phone was answered.

"Detective Agency," a woman said.

"This is Mark Stern. Mr. Sklar asked me to call him back."

"Oh! I'm sorry, Mr. Stern. I know he was anxious to talk to you, but he had to leave." The woman's voice was slightly hoarse, almost rapsy. It told of too many long nights in too many gin joints.

"Ah. What's your name?" When Mark first started at Reiner & Co., he'd paid no attention to telephone operators and secretaries. Since then he'd learned that it cost nothing to charm the girls. Occasionally charm had its own reward . . . like inside information as to what the girl's boss really wanted.

"Frances. Frances Meeker. People call me Fanny."

"Why, Fanny?"

"Well . . . You know. Frances . . . Fanny. It's a nick-name."

Mark chuckled. "I would have thought Frances would become Fran. So why Fanny?" Mark teased her the way he teased Kim, but Fanny Meeker was a different ball of wax.

"Because I'm a woman. My fanny's my best feature."

Then, without a break, she shifted gears. "Mr. Sklar is at the Russian and Spanish Baths. That's on Market and Tenth."

"A bathhouse?"

Fanny Meeker understood where Mark was coming from. "It's not a gay boy bathhouse. It's coed. Gus goes for his health. I go whenever I can." She laughed. "Why don't you call me when you need a workout? We can sweat together." Fanny laughed. "All you have to do is pick up the phone, put your finger on the little button and push. . . ." She hung up, still laughing.

Mark looked at his pile of paper clips. He glanced at his Quotron . . . the market was flat. What the hell? He'd give the baths a try. Maybe Sklar had something worth seeing. If not, there was Fanny. If Fanny checked out, he just might put his finger on her little button. . . . His intercom buzzed.

"Yes, Kim?"

"While you were on the phone, there was a call from a Mr. Irving Buckstein of Buckstein, Kennedy and Carlson. Mr. Buckstein said he was the lawyer who drew up Mr. Reiner's will. He wants to speak to you."

"Get him for me."

"But I never make calls for you."

"Kim . . . just do it."

"Yes, sir. How high, sir? I want you to know I just saluted. I'll ring you as soon as he's on the line."

Within a minute, Mark's intercom buzzed.

"Yes?"

"Mr. Buckstein is on line one."

"Thanks." Mark pushed the lit button. "This is Mark Stern."

"Irv Buckstein here. I'm glad I caught you."

Buckstein spoke with a classic eastern seaboard, mashed potatoes accent . . . Harvard, Yale, Princeton. "I was on my way out, Mr. Buckstein. What can I do for you?"

"As I told your secretary, I drew up Mr. Reiner's will. Mrs. Reiner insisted we hold the reading of the will at Reiner & Co. That's unusual, so I thought I'd clear it with you."

"Mrs. Reiner beat you to it. You're penciled in for next Wednesday at ten o'clock. How many will there be?"

"Let's see. Myself and my secretary, the first Mrs. Reiner, her son, Roger, the present Mrs. Reiner, Betsy Feigenspan—"

"Who is Betsy Feigenspan?"

"She's in charge of the Reiner condo on Coronado. She'll represent all the retainers. Arthur Reiner was a very generous man. And you'll be there, of course."

"Me? Why me?"

"Well . . . I mean . . . Hmmm. Didn't Mr. Reiner obtain your consent?"

"To what?"

Mark could almost see the lawyer stumble and then catch his balance. "Mr. Reiner's personal accountant—William Greenberg—and I are named trustees of the estate. You've been named executor. Didn't he tell you?"

"No." Mark sounded thoughtful. "He probably meant to, but he died so suddenly."

"Yes. Very suddenly." Irving Buckstein matched Mark's thoughtful tone. "He called the day he died. He was planning to make some changes in his will. I don't know what they were or how significant."

"Now we'll never know," Mark said.

"No. Never. You will agree to serve as executor?"

"What's involved?"

"Not that much. You authorize settlement of all debts . . . pay all the bills. And make the final distribution of the net assets to the heirs. The trustees look over your shoulder to make certain you're doing what has to be done. Not that we're worried. Not in your case," Buckstein assured Mark. "You get paid only a small fee, but I hope you'll accept the responsibility. Otherwise Greenberg and I will have to appoint another trustee. Under the terms of Mr. Reiner's will, we can do that. Still . . . It would be simpler if you agree."

Mark counted to five. He wanted Buckstein to worry a little . . . to believe he was weighing his decision to accept or not to accept. He wasn't weighing a thing. Being the executor of Arthur Reiner's multi-million-dollar estate had all kinds of possibilities.

"I don't know why Arthur didn't tell me," Mark said. "But since he thought enough of me to name me as executor, I'll do my best."

"Good," Irv Buckstein said briskly. "My secretary and I will get to your office at . . . say, ten-fifteen. If that's all right with you?"

"No problem. See you at ten-fifteen."

The men said their good-byes and hung up. Mark stared

out the window. Executor of Arthur's estate. There had to be a way to make a good buck from handling the distribution of that much money. He'd think about it. Meanwhile there was Gus Sklar. If Sklar had nothing, he could use some steam and a massage.

Mark parked his car in the lot next to the Russian and Spanish Baths. The brown brick facade of the large one-story building had been recently pointed, the wood trim was a glossy white and all the windows were painted black. But what was most unusual were the signs—THE STRAIGHT PLACE—displayed prominently on all sides of the building. Mark decided the management of the Russian and Spanish Baths wasn't kidding. If he dropped a cake of soap, he wouldn't have to kneel to pick it up. He entered the building. Even in the lobby the air was stifling hot, heavy with moisture.

An old man with a completely shaved head, wearing a skullcap—a yarmulke—sat behind the counter.

"You new here," he said.

Mark nodded. "First time."

"Uhuh. You here to schvitz or kvetch . . . or both?"

Mark laughed. "Schvitz . . . like everyone else. Actually I'm looking for Gus Sklar." He wiped the sweat from his forehead. He was already dripping wet. The old man was bone-dry . . . desiccated. As though he'd long ago sweated all the fluids from his body.

"You need locker, bathing suit, towel, slippers. That costs thirty dollars . . . cash."

Mark handed the old man three ten-dollar bills.

"You follow me." He led Mark through two doors. Each chamber was hotter and more muggy. "There." He pointed to a door with a sign, MEN'S LOCKER, on it—the sign was printed in three languages . . . English, Spanish and Russian—and handed Mark a key with an elastic band that fitted around Mark's wrist. "You return key when you leave." He rocked back and forth on his heels. "You nice boy. I trust you not to keep key."

"Where is Gus Sklar?"

The old man shrugged. "You ask Robert. He give you bathing suit and towel."

Mark opened the door to the men's locker room. It smelled

like every locker room he'd ever been in . . . only more so.
Hotter, more damp, sweatier. A huge muscular man wearing
only a pair of white shorts and thonged, leather sandals came
to meet him.

"I'm Robert."

Mark nodded. He said, "I need a bathing suit and a
towel."

"Coming up."

Mark stepped into the pair of trunks Robert brought him.
"I'm looking for Gus Sklar," he told the locker attendant.

"Gus is getting the full treatment. I think the scrubber is
doing him now."

"The what?"

"The scrubber. He works you over with oak leaves. The
oak leaves open your pores. Your body gets rid of all its
impurities. Gus has a lot of impurities."

"Sklar wants to see me. Where's the scrubber?"

"No one interferes with a scrubbing. Look . . . You do
your thing. When Gus is finished, he'll find you."

"Great," Mark said dryly. "What's my thing?"

"Steam first. You schvitz. You're not used to this. Sit on
the lowest level. When it gets too hot, dump some icewater
over you."

Mark grimaced.

"Then you go for a swim. Or a whirlpool if you're a sissy.
After that, a Swedish shower. The water hits you from all
directions. And we finish you off with a massage . . . an oil
massage . . . Russian style."

"I may not survive," Mark said.

"Stop kvetching. You'll survive. We've lost a couple of
masseurs—heart attacks—but we've never lost a client."

Mark went through the entire routine . . . the schvitz, the
whirlpool, the Swedish shower, the Russian massage. It was
a hell of a workout. He then showered. As he was dressing,
someone tapped him on the shoulder.

"Glad you decided to make it. Can I bum a cigarette?"
The man chuckled.

"Gus Sklar." The detective hadn't changed much. He'd
grown a mustache, that was about it. "You said you have
something that would interest me."

"I do. Let's get out of here. There's a bar up the block

called the Dolphin. I can have a brew and a cigarette. We'll talk there.''

"Sure. Give me ten minutes," Mark said.

The detective nodded and left the locker room.

The Dolphin turned out to be a dive. It was poorly lit, the wooden bar was scarred with countless initials, and the only way to get rid of the smell of stale beer was to tear down the building. Mark slid into a booth opposite the detective. The ashtray had the stubs of three cigarettes and Sklar was on his second beer. He called to the bartender to bring Mark a Bud Light. "Jesus! The baths make me thirsty. How 'bout you?''

Mark shrugged. "When did you go on the health kick?''

"I got some aches in my chest and arms. My cardiologist says my ticker's warning me . . . get healthy or else. Cut the smoking, the drinking, eat right.''

Mark pointed to the ashtray. "That's your idea of stopping smoking?''

"Got to do it gradually. If I quit cold turkey, the shock'd kill me." He grinned. "If this detective schtick gets too tough, I'll go back to being an actor. Maybe your grandmother-in-law could get me a part. She's still got connections. . . .''

"You know Millie?''

"I knew her. . . . I was a child actor in the forties. Me and Shirley Temple, Mickey Rooney, Judy Garland. Rooney and Garland had talent. Shirley and I didn't. So Shirley became a diplomat and I became a P.I. I knew your grandmother-in-law when she was an extra named Millie Thorne. We were pretty good friends. That was before she did *Monsoon* and became a star. Now I don't know her.'' Sklar shrugged. "Times change.''

"You still working for Mrs. Reiner?" Mark asked. He made a mental note. Knew Millie.

"Nah. I was working for Mr. Reiner . . . when he died.'' Sklar's expression darkened. "Why'd you break your word about telling anyone about me?''

"I had to tell Mr. Reiner he was being followed. He was my employer. I owed it to him. It's called loyalty.''

Sklar lit another cigarette. "I figured you'd tell Reiner. . . . So I told Mrs. Reiner about you.'' He grinned. "We fucked each other. It worked out okay. That's how I got the job with Mr. Reiner.''

"What were you doing?"

"Mr. Reiner hired me to tail his wife." Sklar gave an unattractive snicker. "That's one active broad. She'd make a great working girl if she ever had to earn a living with her ass.''

"Let me get this straight. Arthur Reiner hired you to follow his wife. How'd he get your name?"

"I told you. Mrs. Dorothea Reiner gave it to him."

Arthur and Dorothea had been working together to get something on Ali . . . weird. "Why was Arthur checking on his wife?''

"So he could divorce the broad without paying through the nose. Why do you think?''

Mark tried to walk the line between being too naive and too hip. But after Ali's romp in the bushes with Ken Savage, he wasn't surprised that Arthur wanted out. "So Arthur wanted a divorce," he said.

"Yeah. But he died first. Heart attack . . . wasn't it?"

"That's what the death certificate says."

"You believe that?"

"Why not? Heart attacks run in his family."

Sklar stubbed out his cigarette and finished his beer. "The man was about to file for a divorce when he suddenly dies. I find that suspicious.''

Mark shook his head. "Convenient for Mrs. Reiner, yes. Suspicious—given Arthur's history—no. Maybe the first Mrs. Reiner'd be interested in your theory? Try her.''

"What kind of a schmuck do you think I am? I did try her . . . I thought she'd be curious. . . .''

"She wasn't."

"How'd you know?"

"You wouldn't be talking to me if she'd hired you again."

"Maybe . . . maybe not. Anyway, I held a couple of things back from Mrs. Reiner.''

"Such as?"

"A copy of all the reports I sent Mr. Reiner. Including the one I delivered the day he died.''

Mark chewed on his lower lip. "A complete report on who and where Ali screwed?''

"Plus pictures. The little lady was sometimes in a hurry to get fucked. She was sloppy about pulling the blinds."

"Pictures too," Mark said. Mentally, he ranged over the possibilities. If Ali inherited Reiner & Co. and if he stayed with the firm, Ali and he were in for some real knockdown fights. Ali was headstrong, and she knew nothing about Wall Street. Not only didn't she know anything, she didn't even know there was anything to know. The shots of Ali and her lovers would come in handy . . . if push came to shove.

"How much?" Mark asked.

Sklar looked hurt. "I told you the first time we met I wasn't into blackmail. It's bad for business. I have a bill I want paid. With Mr. Reiner dead, who's going to pay it?"

"The estate."

"No executor would touch this with a ten-foot pole."

Mark suppressed a grin. He was Arthur's executor. He could pay any bill he chose. "How much is your bill?" he asked.

"Take a look at this first." Sklar shoved an envelope across the table. Before Mark could open it, Sklar asked with a shitty grin, "You sure you're not featured?"

"If I am, someone's been very clever with the lab work. I make a point of never screwing my boss's wife." Mark opened the envelope. A single snapshot fell out. It was a grainy black-and-white shot of a woman being made love to from behind . . . doggy style. But the heads of both the man and woman were cropped.

"Not to worry. That's just a sample. The other shots are just as good, and they have faces."

"Yeah," Mark grunted.

Sklar handed him an invoice.

"Twenty-two thousand! That's pretty steep."

"I don't work cheap. That includes expenses . . . lots of expenses. That lady does not get laid in hot pillow joints."

"I'll think about it."

"You got forty-eight hours. Then I go to the present Mrs. Reiner . . . Mrs. Hot Pants herself." Sklar stood up. "Just so you shouldn't think I'm stupid, I know I could get a lot more money from the broad. Plus a jazzy weekend in Catalina."

"Why don't you?"

"I don't like her. I watched her in action. She can cut a

guy's balls off. You know how it is—once in a while a guy
can't get it up . . . happens to everyone. It happened to a
guy with her, and she took the poor schmuck apart. Made
me so pissed I almost broke in and popped her one. You
know my phone number. You got forty-eight hours.'' Sklar
slid out of the booth and left the bar.

Mark nursed his beer . . . thinking about what Gus Sklar
had offered him. The estate would pay Sklar's bill, and he'd
keep the report and photos. If Ali inherited control of Reiner
& Co., the photographs would keep her in line. And even
if—for some reason—Arthur hadn't left her his stock, the
photographs still might come in handy. At the right time, a
lot of people—especially Millie Gardiner—were going to get
a clear picture of Ali Gardiner Reiner in action. That should
knock Ali out of the race for Millie's millions.

Nora left Channel 18 early. She wanted to get home in time
to shower, dab perfume behind her ears, on her neck, under
her breasts, in her armpits. On all the places where the sex
manual said a woman should dab perfume if she wanted to
arouse a man. Recently Mark's and her sex life had gone
from bad to almost nonexistent. Mark constantly complained
of being tired. Overproblemed and undersolutioned, was his
way of putting it. And he traveled a lot . . . to Phoenix. He'd
explained how Group H was on the prowl for several more
TV stations. Since he was their investment banker, he could
make some real money. According to Mark, Lew Dobbs
wouldn't make a move without him. And when he was home
and they did make love, it was like he wasn't there. He went
through the motions . . . touched her the ways she liked to
be touched . . . kissed her where she liked to be kissed. But
the sex was joyless, mechanical. The excitement, the whoo-
pie, was gone. If she had been an inflated rubber doll—the
kind of thing the porn magazines offered for sale . . . complete with a rubber vagina—she had the feeling Mark would
be just as satisfied.

Nora didn't know what was wrong. Mark was too young
to be going through a mid-life crisis. There was no other
woman. More likely he'd gotten used to her, gotten a little
bored with her . . . sexually anyway. That's why she'd bought
a sex manual. Tonight, she'd do her best to put some sex
back in their sex life. Greeting him at the door naked, with

a martini in her hand, was a cliché. But clichés worked. So she'd do her version. . . .

Nora chose a short, brightly patterned, cotton wraparound—the kind of thing she wore over a bikini—and a pair of red thong sandals. No panties. No bra. She posed in front of the bathroom mirror. She practiced slowly allowing the wraparound to slip off her shoulders . . . off her breasts. She practiced flashing . . . whipping the wrap open. "Hey . . . look at me . . . I'm naked . . . look!" she murmured in a sexy voice. She felt silly . . . trying to seduce her own husband. Silly or not, it was the only thing she could think of. She prepared a pitcher of martinis, dry and cold the way Mark liked his martinis. And a dozen Carrs biscuits with genuine beluga caviar . . . no lump fish eggs tonight. Then she waited.

When Mark arrived home, he looked wrung out.

"Are you all right?" she asked.

"No." Mark glanced at the pitcher of martinis, the caviar and at Nora. He got it. It was let's pretend time . . . again.

"What's the matter?" Nora asked.

"Ali's the matter. She was in the office . . . looking it over . . . taking inventory. She expects to inherit the controlling interest in the firm."

"I don't believe it. Arthur wasn't a fool. He wouldn't leave her his stock."

"Don't count on it. When Ali married Arthur, she knew he was a candidate for a heart attack. Somehow she got him elected. Arthur Reiner, this month's winner of the heart-attack-of-the-month contest. Ali is a born inheritor. She could inherit the company."

"I hope not," Nora said fervently.

"So do I . . . or I may be looking for another job. Ali is a lot of things. One thing she's not is a managing partner."

Nora sat on the couch and crossed her legs. She'd put too much emotion into staging the seduction. If she didn't try now, it would be harder the next time. She smiled at Mark. "Forget Ali. Come. Sit with me. Have a drink."

Mark smiled back. Nora wanted to play games. Okay. They'd play games. "I'll wash up. I'll be right back." He hurried to their bedroom, stripped off his clothes, washed his hands and face and put on a terry cloth robe. He joined Nora on the couch. They clinked glasses, sipped their martinis, munched on the caviar and Carrs biscuits. Two martinis later, their robes were open . . . their hands caressing each other. Nora adored the touch of Mark's fingers . . . toying with her nipples . . . probing between her legs. There was only one problem . . . he wasn't hard. She tried everything she'd read in the sex manual. She used her hand, her mouth, her breasts. Nothing happened . . . he didn't get hard. Nora exhausted Mark and herself. They were bathed in sweat. Still, Mark didn't get hard.

Finally Mark pushed her away. "I'm sorry," he mumbled. "I don't know what's the matter. I'm just not with it."

Nora gave up. She closed her wrap. "Am I doing something wrong?" she said. She tried not to show how shaken she was.

Mark didn't answer. He was surprised and angry. This had never happened before. He'd always been able to get an erection. A deep part of him blamed Nora for his failure.

"It happens to everyone now and then," Nora said reassuringly. "A man can't fake it . . . a woman can."

"Have you ever faked an orgasm?" Mark sounded more angry than he realized.

"Once in a while . . . sure. I don't have to come every time I make love with you. I do come . . . almost always. But . . ."

"But not always." Mark took Nora's hand. "Look, sweetie. I'm sorry. I'm tired and I got Phoenix on my mind. When I get back, I'll make it up to you. In spades. I'll fuck your ass off. . . ."

Nora shot a quick glance at Mark. "Fuck your ass off"? Mark didn't talk like that. He was putting on an act again. For whose benefit . . . his or hers? She had to talk to someone. Ali? No way! Maybe a man? Yes! A man she trusted. A man who knew her very well, who liked her but wasn't interested in her sexually. A man who would tell her what had gone wrong. But who? She didn't know a man who fit the description. But she did know her husband. She had to solve the sex thing soon or her marriage was in trouble.

Chapter 16

NORA LISTENED to Mark's even breathing. Apparently not getting an erection didn't bother him. At least not enough to keep him up. It bothered her plenty. So much, in fact, that she wondered if maybe they ought to see a marriage counselor or a sex therapist. Or was she being silly? One failure did not mean that Mark was rejecting her. Besides, what she'd told Mark was true. She didn't always reach orgasm. Why did Mark's not getting an erection bother her so much? Was she that unsure of herself? She was reminded of the old cliché. The insecure man said, "That was great! Was it good for you?" And the equally insecure woman answered, "It was great. You're the best!" And both wondered if the other had felt anything.

Nora again ran over the names of men she might talk to. She came up with a flat zero. She had no old boyfriends in whom she could confide. She had no old boyfriends . . . period. She'd met Mark when still a teenager . . . and a virgin. During the years that they'd lived together she'd been faithful. Her sexual experience was limited to Mark.

Eventually—around three in the morning—Nora did doze. She heard Mark get up at five to go to the office. She pretended she was still asleep. When he packed an overnight bag, she remembered that he was going to Phoenix that afternoon and wouldn't be back until tomorrow evening. Still she didn't move. This was not her usual pattern. Until now—whenever Mark was going on an overnight trip—she'd helped him pack and kissed him good-bye. But after last evening's fiasco, she wasn't up to facing him. And making cheery small talk. Lying in bed with her eyes narrowed to slits, an odd question struck her. Why was Mark going to Phoenix so often? It didn't add up. Her father had taught her the basics of how the Street functioned. Investment bankers went to see

clients for a variety of reasons . . . a stock offering, an acquisition, a merger. According to Mark, Group H was looking to acquire several new TV stations. That explained the
trips . . . up to a point. But as far as she knew, Mark had
not approached any channels to see if they were for sale.
Except for Channel 18, which wasn't for sale. He had nothing
to offer Group H. So why was he flying to Phoenix so often?

Mark finished packing. Through almost completely closed
eyes, Nora saw him glance at her, frown and then hurry from
the room. She had an urge to run up the stairs after him and
make nice. She stopped herself. Maybe, by the time he returned tomorrow, she'd have sorted out a few things. Then
they'd have a loving husband/wife talk about what was happening to their marriage. She didn't believe in heart-to-heart
talks, but maybe sometimes they worked.

When Nora arrived at Channel 18, Sheri was waiting with
a message.

"Mrs. G. wants to see you," Sheri told her. "She said
you should come to her office first thing."

Nora nodded. She dropped her briefcase on her desk and
walked down the corridor to Millie's office. She was surprised to find Sara Kratz sitting at the usually vacant secretary's desk.

After the usual polite greeting, Nora asked, "What are you
doing here?"

"Mrs. G. asked me to work out of Channel 18 for the next
few months. Until the production schedule for *I Remember
Mama* is set." Miss Kratz gestured toward the CRT on her
desk. "Those numbers are the latest budget for *Mama*. I'll
have it finished in a few minutes. I'll print it so Mrs. G. and
you and Mr. Banska can go over the numbers."

"Jordan? Jordan's here?" Nora didn't realize how pleased
she sounded.

"He arrived last night. Go right in. They expect you."

Nora opened the door.

Millie and Jordan were huddled around the conference table. When they saw Nora, Millie smiled and said, "Good
morning. Come. Join us."

Jordan rose to greet her. He gave her a hug and kissed her
cheek.

The breath poured out of Nora. "When did you get back?"

she gasped. "The last I heard you were on a freighter in the middle of the Indian Ocean."

"I was. Every year I go away for a month . . . by myself. No movie scripts, no plays, no booze, no women. Just me and the silence around me. I rest and think and get healthy. This year it was a freighter in the Indian Ocean. Next year I may take the trans-Siberian railroad. Moscow to Vladivostok . . . with stops at Omsk, Tomsk, Pinsk, Minsk and all points east."

"You're teasing me," Nora said, laughing.

"A little . . . about Pinsk and Minsk anyway." He smiled. "They're west of Moscow."

Nora studied Jordan. He was wearing his usual khaki safari jacket, a khaki shirt and pants and brown loafers. His skin was still a mottled red-brown, but it seemed to her he'd gained a few pounds. The deep lines running from his cheeks past his mouth had softened and his cheeks weren't as gaunt.

"You do look well," Nora said. "The freighter agreed with you."

"Vacations agree with me. I should take more of them."

"Nora, come sit next to me," Millie said. "Jordan's been filling me in on his proposed production schedule for *Mama.*"

Nora joined Millie. "Sara said you've put together a budget."

Millie nodded. "The latest preliminary budget. I'm interested in your reaction."

"I can't give you a line-by-line reaction. I don't know enough about production costs," Nora protested.

"I realize that, dear," Millie said. "I meant your reaction to the total cost. How much of the total cost can we get back from a first showing?" Millie looked up at the sound of the door opening. "Ah! Sara! Do you have the budget?"

"Yes, Mrs. G. Here it is. I printed four copies."

Millie handed Nora and Jordan each a copy, kept a copy for herself and placed the fourth in a folder.

Nora glanced at the numbers. "Seven and a half million? Jordan, I thought we agreed on a five-million-dollar budget."

"We did." Jordan looked at her quizzically. "Did something happen while I was away?" he asked.

"What do you mean, did something happen?" Nora said.

"I mean to Tammi. When I left, she was poised at the starting gate. We couldn't get *Mama* into production soon enough. But when I got back, she was dragging her feet. Maybe *Mama* was a mistake. Maybe she shouldn't do it. Spielberg had offered her a great part. She had a baker's dozen excuses . . . none of them real. So I held her hand and offered another million and a half. The rest of the money is for . . . well . . . for just in case. Just in case Tammi needs more convincing. Or we run into production problems. Or we blow the shooting schedule. Or just in case—''

"Does Tammi often change her mind about doing a movie?'' Millie asked.

"No. Tammi's not typical Hollywood. Her word is like money in the bank. She's famous for sticking to her hand-shake deals. That's why I asked if anything happened while I was away.''

Millie looked at Nora and Nora studied the conference table . . . she felt herself blushing.

Jordan said, "Millie. Tell me about your other grand-daughter, Ali Gardiner Reiner.''

"What about her?'' Millie asked.

"The Malibu rumor is working overtime. Mrs. Ali Reiner is house hunting in Malibu. Mrs. Ali Reiner is seen around with Ken Savage. Mrs. Ali Reiner wants Ken Savage to divorce Tammi and marry Mrs. Ali Reiner—''

Nora's blush faded. It was replaced by a furious pallor. She'd like to strangle Ali. . . . She interrupted Jordan. "Grandmother—''

"Sssh, dear. You can tell me later. Jordan . . .'' Millie drew herself up. She stared at Jordan. Her stare had a chilling quality. Jordan had seen the same expression in Millie's eyes once long ago. Millie and Max were looking after him while his father was away. Milos Banska had returned to Czechoslovakia to do a film, a cinema verité on Eastern Europe after the Nazis. When the Communists took control of the Czech government, his father had fallen to his death from his hotel window . . . on the second floor. The new Communist regime insisted his father was a CIA agent and he'd committed suicide to avoid arrest. Jordan was sad about his father's death, but he wasn't devastated. His father had been away so much, he barely knew him. Not so Millie. The State Department official confirming the news was treated to the merciless stare of Mrs. Max Gardiner. It had terrified the man. Millie called the official a coward and a fool. Why would anyone try to commit suicide by jumping from a second-floor window? This was the first time since that day that Jordan had seen so much ice-cold despair encapsulated in a single glance.

"Jordan," Millie said, "there are rumors and there are truths. The two are not always the same."

Jordan sighed. "In this case, I think they are." He looked at Nora. "I talked to Tammi. She mentioned a party you gave. That's where she said it began."

"No," Nora said grimly. "That's where it climaxed. It began when Ali went to Los Angeles to contact the stars."

"That's enough, Nora," Millie said. "I take responsibility for this. I underestimated Ali's foolishness. But I'm curious, Jordan. Why did you ask if anything had happened while you were away? You knew about Ken and Ali."

"Tammi is an actress. She role-plays constantly. She has a wonderful imagination. Occasionally she confuses reality with what she imagines."

"Not this time," Nora said. "It's true about Ken and Ali."

"All right. I can handle Tammi," Jordan said. "She'll honor her commitment." He chuckled. "Ken and she have an arrangement. When they feel in the mood, they do their thing. In groups of two, four, six or eight . . . or apart. Usually Tammi goes with the flow. She understands the grass in the nearby meadow is sometimes greener. Her real bitch is hurt pride. If Ali Reiner was a great star or a great whore, Ken's sleeping with Ali wouldn't bother Tammi. But that Ken Savage, her husband, should cheat on her with a bit player . . . a small-town bimbo . . . that gets to Tammi."

Nora blinked. Was Phoenix Mark's meadow . . . with greener grass?

Millie abruptly said, "You take care of Tammi and I'll deal with my granddaughter. Nora, the budget for *Mama* is seven and a half million. Can we come out alive?"

"Not on the first showing. Even HBO—they have the most subscribers—won't go that high. Maybe for a premiere and three reruns . . ."

"What about syndication?" Jordan asked.

"That's where we pan for gold. If we hit double digits on the first showing of *Mama*, we can go after the independents and the network affiliates via the local cable systems . . ."

Nora hesitated. "It may take more than one play—maybe as many as three—to get 'Night of Stars' off the ground."

Jordan reacted to the numbers. "Millie. Nora's talking about an investment of over twenty million dollars. Are you prepared to make that big a commitment? If you're not, I have an idea."

Millie gave Jordan a small smile. "I am not offended by the suggestion that I don't know what I'm getting into. But I am offended. A little anyway. Think about me, Jordan . . . me . . . Millie Thorne. I knew how Hollywood worked in the forties. I've made it a point to know how Hollywood works in the nineties. The numbers have changed—they're bloated beyond belief—but not the business. I own a TV station. Would Millie Thorne launch a project without knowing all there is to know about cable, syndication, reruns, what have you?"

Jordan was abashed. "Sorry. No . . . It's just that . . ."

"That what?" Millie asked. "Tell us"—she draped her arm over Nora's shoulder; Jordan must include Nora in whatever he had to say—"about your idea."

"I was checking into the Grant and I ran into a man I've met. Stanley Tseng."

"Who?" Nora exclaimed.

"Stanley Tseng, big Hong Kong money. I understand he's pulling his money out of Hong Kong as fast as he can. Before the Chinese take over in 1997. He's already backed two films produced by indies . . . independent producers. Nora, are any films being shot in San Diego right now?"

"Not that I know of. Maybe your Mr. Tseng has other reasons for being in San Diego." Like Ali, Nora said to herself. She remembered Ali's gurgles about her trip to Fiji with Stanley Tseng. What a coincidence! Then there was Mark. Another coincidence. Reiner & Co.—Mark—did some trading for Tseng. Coincidences made Nora uncomfortable. Jordan's knowing Tseng was one coincidence too many. "How well do you know Tseng?" she asked.

"Not very well," Jordan said. "But since he is in San Diego, he might be interested in 'Night of Stars.' "

"He might," Millie said. "But don't talk to him. 'Night of Stars' is my baby. I've already put twenty-five million into the 'Night of Stars' bank account."

Nora wasn't surprised. As usual, Millie was several steps ahead.

Millie checked her watch and grimaced. "I'm late for an appointment. At Scripps Hospital."

Nora tensed. Scripps Hospital?

"The Scripps fund-raising committee has asked all major benefactors to meet at the hospital. They want to show us how our money is being used . . . a slide presentation. I expect it'll be a pitch for another contribution." She rose to leave.

Nora stared at her grandmother. She could see nothing in Millie's face. Still . . . She didn't believe Millie was going to view a slide presentation at Scripps Hospital. Scripps Hospital and Millie. Another coincidence.

Millie paused at the door. "Nora, Jordan's freighter jaunt wasn't all sun and sea. He's done most of the preproduction work on *Mama*. Also the casting. Bring her current, Jordan. Next time we meet, I want the professional backgrounds of the entire cast. Also the technical people. Cameramen, sets, costumes, props, lighting . . . you know what I mean. And a shooting schedule. A tight schedule, Jordan. No Hollywood bloat."

Jordan grinned. "As tight as a vir—" He coughed. "I'll be tight, Millie. Depend on it."

"I will," Millie said. "By the way, Nora, I hear Mark will be in Phoenix tonight. Would—"

"How do you know Mark is going to Phoenix?" Nora asked.

Millie held up the forefinger of her right hand. "I see all. I know all," she intoned. "Actually," she said in her normal voice, "Mark's secretary told me. I called about his buying a stock. How would you like to have dinner with me at the Farm?"

"She can't," Jordan said. "She's going to have dinner with me. I was just about to ask her first."

Millie looked first at Nora . . . then at Jordan. "I yield to your intention." She smiled. Then, with a quick hand wave, she was gone.

Nora knew San Diego, but she did not know the place they went to dinner. Jordan didn't know San Diego, but somehow he did know the Waterfront Bar and Grill . . . the oldest continually operating bar and grill in San Diego . . . way off the tourist track. Nora was taken with the smoky, low-slung ceiling, the fishnet behind the bar, and the fifty-year-old pictures of a sleepy navy town called San Diego . . . only a few miles north of the Mexican border. She didn't know a soul in the restaurant, but Jordan did know several fishermen and two beefy stevedores. He also knew the owner of the Waterfront Bar and Grill.

"Nora," he said. "This is Nancy Nichols. The Waterfront Bar and Grill is hers. Nancy, say hello to Nora Gardiner. Sorry. I mean, Nora Stern."

Nancy Nichols smiled. "Nice to meet you, Mrs. Stern." She glared at Jordan. "And phooey on you, Jordan Banska. Where's that picture? You don't show your face for years and then you're here . . ." She paused. "And without a picture, you rat." She glanced at Nora. "This Clown's been promising me a picture of himself since I've owned the joint. To hang on the wall next to the one of his father and Millie Thorne."

"You have a picture of Millie Thorne?" Nora asked.

"Right over there." She pointed to a picture next to the cash register. "Milos is on the right. That's Millie Thorne in the middle and Max Gardiner on Miss Thorne's left."

Nora had seen a few other pictures of her grandmother taken when Millie was in Hollywood. Studio publicity photos with all the life airbrushed out of the shots. This was the first picture she'd ever seen of the young Millie Thorne off the set. When she was simply having fun. "She is lovely," Nora murmured.

"Isn't she? Say . . . Jordan called you Nora Gardiner. Are you a relation of Millie and Max?"

"Nora's their granddaughter," Jordan explained.

"Well, well . . . All right, Jordan. No more excuses. The next time you show up, you better come bearing gifts . . . like a picture of you and Mrs. Stern. Or you don't get served."

"I will. I promise," Jordan said.

"You two just follow me. I have a nice dark booth in the rear. You can"—she chuckled—"have some privacy."

They ordered two steins of Carling Red Barrel. Jordan said, "Didn't Millie have a wonderful quality . . . pure passion? Sexy . . ." He whistled. "No wonder she was a star."

The word *sexy* vibrated in Nora's mind. She had an idea. Yes! She'd do it. She took a deep breath. "Jordan, I'm curious. You just said Millie was sexy. What do you mean? Most men and women agree about what makes a woman beautiful, but I don't understand sexy. What makes a woman sexy to a man?''

Jordan chuckled softly. "Sexy to a man?''

"Yes. Sexy. To you, for example.''

"That's so individual. It's an air, a . . . Nora, I don't know how to say this delicately.''

"So say it indelicately. Crudely. Jordan, I'm a big girl. A married woman. You won't shock me.''

"Would you swear it?''

"Yes!'' Nora was too emphatic.

Jordan finished his beer and ordered a second. "Let's see,'' he said musingly. "A sexy woman looks as though either she's just been well fucked or she wants to be fucked. Now! Not later in the afternoon . . . not tomorrow. Now! That's for openers.''

"What about looks? Or the woman's figure?''

"That's the package. It always helps if the product is well packaged. A pretty face, a firm pair of breasts, a nice round ass, long shapely legs get a man's juices flowing. Actually most men confuse the package with the product. Which is one reason for our high divorce rate.''

"But you don't?'' Nora said.

Jordan's grin was self-deprecating. "I've been known to make that mistake . . . twice. Two marriages, two divorces. I'm a pushover for a great ass.'' He looked hard at Nora. "Why the quiz?''

"What about me?'' Nora asked. Then she stared at the bottom of her beer glass. The moment she'd asked the question, she wished she could call back the words. Jordan was her first love. Besides Mark, her only love. Suppose he said she wasn't sexy? After last night with Mark . . . "Forget it,'' she said hurriedly. "Scratch the question.''

Jordan looked at Nora with caring eyes. He'd loved her when she was a kid, like an older brother loves a kid sister. But she wasn't a kid now. She was a married woman who attracted him more than was good for either of them. He had no compunction about climbing into bed with a married woman . . . if the woman was habitually unfaithful. But not with Nora. He knew her too well. He'd bet anything she was faithful to Mark. So why the quiz? He cared for her too much to let her off the hook without knowing what was happening.

"Nora," he said, "You're a very attractive woman . . . maybe even beautiful."

"But I'm not sexy."

"Truthfully, you are and you aren't."

Nora looked at him . . . she was close to tears. "I'm not."

"Oh boy!" Abruptly Jordan sensed he was in over his head. "Who do I fuck to get out of this conversation? You know what I mean . . . Let's drop this."

"No. Let's not drop it," Nora said with a small smile. "You fuck me. . . ."

Jordan couldn't contain his startle. "You don't mean that."

"It's like what you said about my being sexy. Truthfully, I do and I don't. It would be one way to find out if you thought I was sexy. Forget the packaging . . . test the product." She fidgeted in her chair. *What'll I do if he makes a pass?*

"That's not funny." He gulped down his beer. *If I hit on her, I'll offend her.*

"I wasn't trying to be funny. I asked if I was sexy, and you said I was and I wasn't. So which is it? Make up your mind."

"You are sexy . . . I think." *She's like a filly with great bloodlines . . . Millie Thorne and Barron Gardiner. She needs training. I could train her. . . . Knock it off, Banska.*

Nora rolled her eyes toward the ceiling. "Decisions. Decisions. Come on, Jordan." *Do something, damn you. Mark's in Phoenix. I'm here . . . alone.*

Jordan set his beer glass on the table with a thump. "Look, Nora . . . this has gone far enough. Too far. I think you're a sexy young lady—"

"Lady?" Nora interrupted.

"Would you prefer being called a sexy broad?"

"Yes!"

"No! To me you're a sexy young lady." *She sure could be . . . if . . .* "That's it. There is no more."

"Sexy young lady . . ." Nora smiled sweetly. "It will do . . . for now."

"I should hope so," Jordan said huffishly. He stared at her. *That sexy young lady had come very close to complicating their lives.*

"Let's order. We can go over the budget for *Mama* while we eat." Nora studied the menu and gave thanks for her narrow escape. *But did she want to escape? From Jordan? After all these years?*

Chapter 17

THE NEXT day Mark called Nora from Sky Harbor Airport in Phoenix. He told her he'd missed his seven o'clock flight. The next plane left at nine. But given the hour time difference, he expected to land at Lindbergh Field at nine-thirty, San Diego time. Nora spent the extra two hours catching up on her paperwork. At seven-thirty she left the station and drove into San Diego. She had a plate of linguini and clam sauce and a glass of wine at the Mona Lisa, an inexpensive Italian restaurant near the airport.

Normally Nora looked forward to meeting Mark at the airport. Just the sight of his grin as he spotted her made her feel good. Not tonight. Tonight she was playacting . . . the loving wife. She'd wait until they got home and Mark unpacked before starting their heart-to-heart talk. She didn't look forward to the intimate family drama.

"But we must talk," she murmured to herself. "Or it will only get worse."

From the Mona Lisa it was a five-minute drive to Lindbergh Field. Mark came through the gate carrying his luggage. Nora spotted him and waved. Mark waved back. They met and kissed.

"Wow!" Nora tried to smile. "After only one night. God help me if you ever go on a long business trip."

"I won't," Mark promised her. "Or if I do, you'll come with me. I don't like sleeping alone."

"Neither do I."

They linked arms and headed for the escalator that led to the ground floor of the terminal. Nora kept smiling and thinking. Mark had put too much kiss into the kiss. It reeked of greasepaint. She tried not to think why.

* * *

Nora was a better driver than Mark, but Mark always did the driving . . . whether they used his car or Nora's. Nora remembered reading somewhere, "Never criticize a man's sexual performance or his driving." It seemed that driving was a secondary male sex characteristic. Real men drove sports cars with stick shifts and one-to-one steering. Women lumbered about in station wagons with automatic shifts and soft power steering. Not this time. Unhappily aware of what she was doing, Nora slid into the driver's seat and opened the passenger door for Mark.

Mark blinked, did a double take, and tossed his suitcase into the rear seat. He sat next to Nora and studied her profile as she maneuvered her T-bird through the narrow lanes leading to the parking lot exit. Her usually mobile face was quiet . . . tight. The very lack of change warned him . . . Nora was upset. Probably his failure to perform the other night. He almost smiled. Given the right woman—like Gigi—he could perform in the sexual Olympics. Four times wasn't chopped liver. Okay. Tonight he'd give Nora a performance. To clue her, he slid his hand up the inside of her bare thigh.

"Soft. Like velvet," he murmured.

Nora suppressed an urge to open her thighs. "Not now, Mark," she said. She quickly added, "There's too much traffic."

A surprised Mark removed his hand. "How are things at the station?" he asked.

"The same as two days ago."

"Now about 'Night of Stars'? Anything new there?"

"As a matter of fact, yes. Jordan's back. With a new budget. Ali's caper with Ken Savage cost Millie a million and a half dollars. And Ali's still at it." Nora told Mark about the Malibu rumors and Tammi's reaction.

Mark snorted in disdain. "The Ali Cat strikes again." He felt relieved. Nora was bent out of shape over Ali, not him.

By the time they arrived home, Mark was convinced things were under control. He unbuckled his safety belt before leaning over to kiss her. He took her head in his hands and held it still. Then he kissed her . . . hard.

"Mmmm," Nora purred. "Nice. I'll make you a deal. You fix us two of your world-class martinis and I'll unpack your suitcase." A few drinks would soften Mark up for the heart-to-heart talk.

Mark blinked at the odd request. Normally he let no one

near his clothes. Then . . . "Sure," he said. A couple of drinks to get them in the mood. Then off to bed.

Mark carried his suitcase down the stairs to the master bedroom. "Don't forget. My brown suit goes with my other brown and beige suits."

"I know," Nora said. She was as familiar with Mark's color-coordinated closet as he was.

"And dump the shirts and other stuff in the laundry."

"I know," Nora repeated. "Now go away. You know your assignment. Scat!"

"Making a martini is not 'Mission Impossible.' " Mark grinned. Nora was always a sucker for his grin.

Nora nodded. She unzipped his suitcase. First she hung up his suit . . . color coordinated as requested. Next she slipped his shoes into the shoe caddy. Then his dirty shirts, socks and shorts went into the laundry bag. All that was left was a small zipped bag with Mark's toiletries and . . . Nora grimaced. He'd done it again. A rolled-up towel was crammed against the back of the suitcase. It didn't surprise her. Mark was a committed towel stealer. When they stayed at a hotel, he always swiped a towel . . . not a hand towel . . . a bath towel with the name of the hotel on it.

She shook out the rolled-up towel before dumping it in the laundry box. And stared. A pair of black lace panties fluttered to the floor. Automatically she picked them up. She tried not to scream. Out of her throat came a gagging, retching sound. She fingered the lace. It was the smallest pair of panties she'd ever seen . . . a tiny triangle of lace, an elastic band behind and an elastic waistband. More like a G-string than panties. The lace was still damp. Nora sat on the bed and tried to organize her thoughts. Mark had a woman in Phoenix . . . a woman who wore black lace G-string panties. She'd washed her panties and rolled them in a towel to dry. Mark had walked off with the rolled-up towel, not knowing about the panties. For a moment Nora wondered if the woman missed her panties. Maybe she came prepared with two pairs. Nora didn't think so. Any woman who wore a G-string for panties would not notice her lack of underwear. She might never miss the panties. Nora considered framing them. Or giving them to Mark to return. Despite her misery, she started to laugh. Too bad Mark didn't swipe hangers . . . you can't wrap a pair of panties in a hanger. Nora rubbed her forehead.

She silently screamed at herself. You damn fool! You think a heart-to-heart talk will save your marriage? When he's fucking a black lace G-string? You idiot! After a few minutes she stopped. Then she asked herself some questions. "Who is Miss Phoenix G-string? Is she younger than me? Prettier? Sexier? Who is she?"

"Nora," Mark called out, "what's taking so long?"

Nora took hold of herself. "Be right up," she shouted.

Nora stuffed the panties in the rear of one of her bureau drawers. She then braced herself to face Mark. Not to have a heart-to-heart talk . . . just to face him and not scream "Who is she?" Slowly she walked up the two flights of stairs. Mark and the martinis were waiting for her. He handed her a drink and reached for her with the same motion. Nora slid away. She sat on the sofa and motioned for him to sit in the chair facing her.

"Not tonight, Mark," she said. "I'm tired and I have a headache." The timeworn cliché.

Mark looked at her. He didn't like the cliché. "Jordan Banska have anything to do with your headache?"

"Jordan? No. It's a headache." Mark's Miss G-string in Phoenix didn't stop him from being jealous. It was black comedy. "What happened in Phoenix?" Nora asked. "Who did you see?"

"The usual. Lew Dobbs. Victor Ashland."

"What did you talk about?"

"You know. Group H. A new acquisition."

"You found a station for them?"

Mark shook his head. "Not yet. We talked about the possibility of acquiring more channels."

"You couldn't do that on the phone?"

"Nora, a business call is good for setting up appointments, not for cutting a deal."

"But you weren't cutting a deal."

"Why the cross-examination? You're not really interested. Let's get down to basics. . . ." He reached for her leg and caressed her calf.

Nora slapped his hand away. "I said I have a headache."

Mark heard the suppressed anger in her voice and abruptly changed his tactics. He didn't know why Nora was angry, but he did know his wife. Sooner or later she'd tell him. "Tomorrow, maybe," he said. "You'll feel better tomorrow."

"Maybe." Maybe not, she silently added. Nora swallowed the last of her martini. She held out her glass. "Another, please." Getting crocked might help her sleep. Help her forget how much more she now knew about Mark. Much much more than she wanted to know.

The next morning Mark slid out of bed. His idea was not to disturb Nora's sleep. For the first time in all the years he'd known her, she'd gotten drunk. Not falling down drunk. Nor was she a happy drunk. Hell, no! She turned into a sullen drunk. He didn't feel like facing a sullen drunk with a hangover. Not today of all days. Today was the reading of Arthur's will. For the occasion, he chose a charcoal-gray suit, a solemn suit. The reading of the will of a man who had died leaving umpteen millions was a solemn occasion. As he dressed, he practiced maintaining his solemn expression.

Once in the office, Mark inspected the conference room. Kim had followed his instructions perfectly. A new legal-size yellow pad and ballpoint pen were on the slate conference table in front of every chair. Two chairs had been placed at the head of the table . . . one for Irv Buckstein and the other for his secretary. There was a single chair at the far end of the table—well apart from the others—for him. Cards with names typed on each were lying on top of the yellow pads, telling everyone where to sit. Dorothea and Ali were on opposite sides of the table.

By the time Mark returned to his office, it was almost ten-fifteen. At ten-seventeen the intercom buzzed.

"Yes, Kim."

"Mr. Buckstein and his secretary are in the reception room. So is Mrs. Arthur Reiner," she added dryly.

"Show them into the conference room. I'll join them there."

Irv Buckstein turned out to be an average-size man with small features. Slim, except for a potbelly that stretched the buttons on the vest of his three-button suit. He had thinning brown curly hair that he parted low on the left side and combed over in a vain attempt to cover his growing baldness. Mark was surprised that Buckstein's secretary was a stout, middle-aged, black woman. Not what he had expected from an Ivy League Jewish lawyer.

"Good morning," Mark said. "Would anyone like a cup of coffee?"

"Black," Ali said.

"How about you, Irv?"

"Yes, thank you. Marion likes her coffee black. I take milk and sugar."

Mark used the conference room phone to call Kim. "Bring a pot of coffee, eight cups, and sugar and cream to the conference room."

Mark watched nervously as Ali prowled about checking the names of the people invited to the reading of the will. When she came to Dorothea and her son, Roger, she paused, pursed her lips, and looked first at Buckstein. Then at him.

At that moment Dorothea and Roger entered, followed by a strange woman.

Mark extended his hand. "I'm Mark Stern. And you're . . . ?"

"Betsy Feigenspan, sir. I've been asked to represent the household staff," the woman said. Clearly she was awed to be included in the reading of the will.

"Dorothea," Mark said. Dorothea nodded coolly. "You're Roger."

They shook hands.

Roger Reiner was a tall bean pole of a teenager with a head of long blond hair and unusually large, well-defined features. When he matured and filled out, he was going to be an attractive young man. But he didn't know that yet, and he shuffled his feet awkwardly. He glanced around the table. A look passed between him and Ali that was pure poison.

Irv Buckstein picked up the antagonism. He said in too loud a voice, "Would everyone please take the seats that have been assigned to them so we can get on with the reading of Mr. Reiner's will."

The door opened and Kim entered carrying a silver-plated tray laden with a twelve-cup pot of coffee, cups, a sugar bowl and creamer, and the appropriate flatware. Mark motioned to her to put the tray on the table and leave. He would do the honors.

After everyone had their coffee, Buckstein turned to his secretary. "Will you please give me Mr. Reiner's will, Marion." The secretary produced a document covered by a blue jacket and handed it to him. "Thank you." He touched the document lightly and began the reading. He first dealt with the gifts to the servants. Arthur was very generous, as the only partially repressed smile of Betsy Feigenspan testified. Once Buckstein completed the list of bequests to the servants, he handed Betsy a copy of the list and excused her.

Then he continued to read. "With the exception of two items of which only I am aware, I leave my entire estate to my son, Roger Reiner, and appoint his mother, Dorothea Reiner, as trustee for my son until he reaches the age of twenty-five. At that time, all control shall pass to my son."

"No!" The word burst from Ali's throat. Mark listened, fascinated. This was the Ali Cat at her screeching best. She stood up and banged the table. "I won't permit it. He can't cut me out of the will. I'm his wife. I'll fight the will. I'll beat it."

"You may try," Irv Buckstein said quietly. "But I urge you to sit down and listen to the rest of the will first."

Still fuming, Ali settled back in her chair. She glared at Roger and Dorothea. Dorothea glanced at her with distaste and looked away. Roger noisily cracked his knuckles and ignored her.

Irv Buckstein turned to his secretary. "Would you give me the envelope, please." Marion produced a large white envelope that was sealed with melted red wax. "This envelope was left in my keeping. It contains the rest of Arthur Reiner's will. You will notice that the seal is unbroken. I don't know what's in it." He produced a small penknife and attempted to slide it under the wax. About halfway through, the wax cracked and splintered. "Blast!" he exclaimed. "I'm sorry. I thought I could open it without breaking the seal."

Ali screamed, "You broke the damn seal. So what? What the hell is so important that the will had to be sealed with wax?"

"We'll soon find out," Buckstein murmured. He removed several pieces of white paper from the envelope. Buckstein scanned the contents and pursed his lips. "Rather than read this word by word—you'll all receive photocopies of the entire will—what it says is that he's set up a two-million-dollar spendthrift trust for you, Mrs. Reiner, and the will permits you to live in the condo on Coronado for the next six months. That should give you plenty of time to make other arrangements."

"What's a spendthrift trust?" Ali asked. On the surface, she seemed calmer.

"A spendthrift trust means that you do not have control over the principal." Irv Buckstein gave her the truth with no holds barred. His instinctive dislike of Ali was obvious. "Mr. Reiner didn't trust you to spend the money wisely. He considered you a spendthrift. He made sure you could never get your hands on your inheritance . . . just the income. You must select an administrator acceptable to the trustees. William Greenberg and I are the trustees. The administrator will invest the money for you as he or she thinks best. You will receive the income to do with as you wish."

"I'll fight it," Ali muttered. "If Arthur left me two million dollars, that money is mine. I won't let anyone tell me what I can do with my money. It's mine . . . Mine . . ." Gradually her words grew more incoherent until all one heard was a rumble of angry discontent.

Buckstein remained unruffled throughout Ali's fulminations. When she finally subsided, he continued. "I must tell you, Mr. Reiner specifically states that should you contest this clause—or any clause in the will—you will lose the two million dollars. You will receive nothing from his estate. Not one red cent." Buckstein slapped the table with each of his last four words.

"What about Arthur's stock in Reiner & Co.?" Dorothea asked.

Buckstein cleared his throat. "That's the second exception mentioned in this codicil."

"He left the stock to me," Ali exclaimed. "I knew he wouldn't leave me just the spendthrift trust. He did leave it to me, didn't he?"

"No, Mrs. Reiner. He did not."

For the first time, Mark spoke up. "If Roger and Ali don't get the stock, who does?"

"A number of people. You included."

"Me?" Mark made no effort to hide his surprise.

Irv Buckstein looked directly at Dorothea. "Correct me if I'm wrong, but you own twenty-six percent of the company and Mr. Reiner owned twenty-six percent. The rest of the stock is owned by the remaining partners."

"That's correct," Dorothea said.

"Mr. Reiner has chosen to leave his shares to the partners.

He's left it up to you to decide how much each partner will get."

"That was our verbal understanding," Dorothea said with relish. "When it came to business, one could always trust Arthur. Mark, I would like to meet with you later to discuss how to divide the pie. I've already decided that you'll receive an additional three percent of the stock. With what you now hold, that will make you one of the larger shareholders . . . with the exception of me, of course."

Ali had been sitting with her elbows resting on the table, her fingertips touching. Now she spoke up. "Mark, I also want to talk to you this afternoon. Mr. Buckstein, you have no objection if my monies are handled by Mr. Stern?"

Irv Buckstein said, "No objection at all. I'm sure Greenberg will agree with me that Mr. Stern is a wise choice to handle your money."

Mark glanced at Dorothea. Her face told him nothing. "I'll think about that, Ali," he said. "If I decide it isn't in the firm's best interests to manage your account, I'll find you a gaggle of good brokers who'll be happy do the job."

"I don't want another broker. I want you," Ali pouted.

"I'll have the will copied in my office and delivered to everyone at their home address by special messenger this afternoon. Does anyone object to this procedure?" Buckstein asked.

Ali started to say something and thought better of it.

"Then that concludes the reading of the will," Buckstein said. "I don't know about anyone else, but I have to get back to work."

Ali and Dorothea—with Roger hanging on Dorothea's arm—prepared to leave. On her way out, Dorothea called over her shoulder, "I'll see you at four o'clock, Mark. It would be helpful if your secretary prepared a list of the partners."

Mark nodded.

"I want to see you also," Ali said. She had regained her composure.

"I'll call you tomorrow morning, Ali," Mark said. "By then I'll know if I can handle your account."

After everyone left, Mark returned to his office. He thought about the terms of Arthur's will. Although Ali hadn't inherited control of Reiner & Co., she had inherited a couple of million. Not all bad. She had a real talent for inheriting. He wondered where the talent would lead her next.

Nora was nursing a throbbing headache. The sound of her intercom made her jump.

"Yes, Sheri?" Nora groaned.

"Mark is on line one."

Nora tensed. "Tell him I'm in a meeting. I'll try to get back to him later." She hung up the phone. She wouldn't call him back. She wasn't ready to talk to him.

That afternoon—after the market closed—Kim buzzed Mark. Mrs. Dorothea Reiner was waiting in the reception room.

"Tell her I'll be with her in a moment. Have you finished preparing the information on the partners?"

"Yes, Mark."

"Please bring it in."

Mark didn't want to keep Dorothea waiting longer than necessary, so he briefly scanned the list. He then went to the reception area and greeted Dorothea. They decided to hold their meeting in Arthur's office . . . it was larger than Mark's. They sat at the conference table.

Dorothea glanced at the list Mark had prepared for her. She then asked, "Does anyone in the firm know about Arthur's will? About the stock he left to the partners?"

"No. Not even my secretary. All she knows is I asked her to prepare a list of the partners."

"Good. Then we won't disappoint anyone when the shares are actually offered."

"Have you thought of a fair way to divide the shares?" Mark asked.

"I should think the obvious way would be best. The firm is capitalized at one hundred thousand shares. After you get your three thousand shares, the rest could be divided up on a proportionate basis. A partner who currently owns one percent of the stock can purchase one percent of the remaining twenty-three thousand shares in Arthur's estate."

"Or two hundred thirty shares. That's fine. Except for me. I get three percent. Why, Dorothea?"

"Mark, if I hadn't agreed with Arthur, we wouldn't be

sitting here. I want you to be the acting managing partner.
Until Roger is ready to take over the firm.''

Mark caught his breath. "Acting managing partner. That's
a handsome offer."

"Are you interested?"

"Of course I'm interested. Who wouldn't be?" He thought
about the three percent Dorothea was offering him. They were
talking about money . . . maybe more money than he could
raise. "How much per share do you estimate the firm is
worth?"

Dorothea consulted her notes. "Since Arthur was so generous giving out bonuses every year, the book value of the
corporation doesn't approach its actual value. Put a value on
the corporation, Mark. I'm curious what you come up with."

Mark rubbed his chin. "Last year we netted about fifteen
million dollars before bonuses. Say taxes would reduce that
to ten million. Ten times after-tax earnings is a reasonable
P/E ratio."

"So you estimate the firm is worth one hundred million."

"That's a good number."

"Which means that you'll have to pay three million dollars
for your three percent of the stock. Do you have three million?"

Mark's chuckle was both amused and sadly ironic.
"Hardly."

"What about Nora? Will she back you?"

"She would if she could. She doesn't have three million."

"She could borrow it from Millie."

"She probably could, but I'd rather go to my bank. If I
put all my stock up as collateral, I can borrow close to three
million."

"You could," Dorothea agreed. "But at a wicked rate of
interest. Banks don't like to lend money on unregistered
stock."

"I'll pay what I have to pay. I want the stock."

"I don't think you can afford that much interest," Dorothea said matter-of-factly. "I have a proposal for you."

Mark raised his eyebrows. "Yes?"

Dorothea hurried on. "I'm worried about Roger. For all
practical purposes, he's grown up without a father. Arthur
was around, but he never spent enough time with the boy.
He was too interested in the firm and his little affairs. I didn't

think it made any difference, because once Roger entered the firm, Arthur would take charge of him. Groom him to succeed. But Arthur has gone to the great unknown, and there's no one to teach Roger how Wall Street really works. To teach him the smarts. How to tough out a deal.''

Mark smothered a smile. Now he understood why he was being offered the managing partnership plus the three percent. It had little to do with him, and everything to do with Roger . . . her chickling.

Dorothea pursed her lips. ''There's no way what I have in mind can be reduced to writing, so you'll have to take my word on it. In business, Arthur's word was his bond. The same is true of me.'' She paused. ''I hope your word is also your bond. You see, I want you to train Roger. Six years from now when he comes into the firm, I want you to supervise him. See to it that he learns the ropes from the ground up. He must know the business by the time he takes over.''

''What do I get for teaching Roger to be smart and tough?'' This was no time to be coy.

''Exactly what I implied. The interim managing partnership and three million dollars . . . interest-free for ten years. With an option to extend the loan for a second ten years. If I'm satisfied with my son's progress.''

''Suppose we don't agree on Roger's progress? Because Arthur was a brilliant Wall Streeter doesn't mean Roger will be brilliant.''

''With three million dollars at stake, you'll see to it that he's brilliant.''

''Three million dollars interest-free for ten years.''

Dorothea nodded.

''You've got a deal,'' Mark said.

Dorothea gathered her papers. ''I'll leave it to you to work out the exact number of shares each partner gets. When you have the numbers, messenger them to my apartment. I'll sign off on them, and you can offer the partners their stock.''

''Most will jump at the chance.''

''I expect they will,'' Dorothea said. ''But if any can't or won't pick up their shares, that stock will be transferred to the treasury. That way you'll have stock available for any new partners you want to bring on board.''

Mark nodded.

"One more point, Mark. Ali Gardiner—I refuse to think of her as Mrs. Reiner—Ali Gardiner's account . . ."

"You want me to turn it down?"

"No! I insist you accept the account and handle it personally."

Dorothea's grin reminded Mark of a Cheshire cat poised to spring . . . to break the back of an unsuspecting mouse. "You've got something in mind?"

"Arthur said you were a very aggressive trader. Sometimes you made a lot of money for your clients."

"I do my best."

"Not this time. This time you'll do your worst."

"My what!"

"Your worst. You will lose every nickel Arthur left that tramp."

"How do I manage to do that without getting into trouble with Irv Buckstein?"

Dorothea's grin broadened to a half smile. "Somehow you'll manage it. Ali is so greedy, she'll help you." Dorothea stopped smiling. "That's part of the deal, Mark. You agree to bankrupt Ali Gardiner or there's no three percent and no managing partnership."

"How long do I have to do the job?"

"How long will it take?"

"Three years. Five is safer."

"You have two years. I will not allow that bitch to enjoy Arthur's money for more than two years."

Mark's eyes narrowed. "What's Ali done . . . besides marry Arthur?"

"None of your business."

Mark nodded. He could see a few advantages in an Ali Gardiner without money, advantages Dorothea Reiner hadn't considered.

As they walked toward the reception room, Dorothea said she would have her lawyers draw up a loan agreement. "It will probably take about a week for them to do something a second-year law student could knock out in an afternoon," she noted caustically. "There'll be no trick clauses, but you'll probably want to show the document to your own attorney."

"I'd be stupid not to. There isn't a lawyer alive who can control an impulse to work in a few goodies for a client."

When they reached the elevators, Mark waited with Dorothea until the car arrived.

"Good luck to you and Roger." She smiled.

"To Roger and me." Mark smiled back. The elevator doors closed. Mark continued smiling. If Dorothea thought he'd train her son to succeed him, she was balmy. As the acting managing partner of Reiner & Co., there were many ways to use Roger. But street smarts were something he couldn't teach. Which meant that he had a shot at becoming the permanent managing partner of Reiner & Co. Mark put aside his rosy future and hurried back to his office to call Nora. Before placing the call, he organized what he would say. He would tell Nora a lie. Like all his lies, it would be almost true. He was being given three percent of the company and the title of acting managing partner . . . all true. He was to teach Roger the business . . . also true. He was going to handle Ali's inheritance . . . again true. But he would say nothing about Dorothea lending him the money for the shares. Nora hated borrowing money . . . from her family or anyone. He'd say the stock was for free, for wiping Roger's ass . . . a lie. And he'd absolutely not tell Nora how Dorothea wanted him to handle Ali's account. Half a lie . . . a lie of omission . . . not so terrible. Mark dialed Nora's private line. No one picked up. When he called her other number, Sheri said she was still in a meeting. Mark hung up slowly. Something was wrong. What? Before he had time to think it through, the buzz of his intercom interrupted him.

"Yes, Kim?"

"Mrs. Reiner is on the line."

Puzzled that Dorothea would be calling so soon after their meeting, Mark pushed the blinking button and said, "Dorothea?"

"Not Dorothea, silly. It's Ali. I'm across the street. I waited for the Witch of Endor to leave before calling you. I do want to talk to you about my account." After her hysterical scene at the reading of the will, Ali seemed in high good humor.

"All right, Ali. Come on up. You can tell me why I should handle your account. Aside from the commissions."

"I'll be right up."

Ali actually must have been calling from a pay phone on

the lobby floor, because in almost no time Mark's intercom buzzed.

"Mrs. Reiner is here to see you."

"Send her in," Mark said.

Soon a smiling Ali rapped lightly on the frame of Mark's door.

"Come in, Ali. Sit down." Without standing up, Mark gestured toward one of two chairs facing his desk.

Ali sat in the first chair and demurely crossed her legs. "Have you thought about handling my account?" she asked.

"I haven't had time to think about it. But now that you're here, we can talk about it."

Ali smiled at Mark. The practiced smile of a good television pitch girl. "What's there to talk about? The firm will earn commissions from handling my money."

"Not that much. I'd probably invest your money in the highest-yielding AA bonds I could find. That would be it."

"Why bonds? Stocks are more fun."

"And bonds are safer."

"But I don't want safe investments, if there is such a thing. I want you to risk my money. Gamble with it the way your mother does."

"What do you know about my mother?" Mark hoped the sinking feeling in his stomach did not show.

"When I learned that Nora and you would marry, I had you checked out," Ali answered coolly. She reached into her purse and pulled out a folded piece of paper. "I photocopied one page of the report for you to read."

Mark glanced at the paper and all of his miserable childhood came flooding back. His father struggling to keep his head above water, and his mother throwing away the money on her stupid penny stocks. The nights there was only enough money in the house to have canned tomato soup for dinner. And that Ali knew everything about him was rubbing salt in his wounds. At that moment he hated Ali more than he'd ever hated anyone in his life . . . including his mother. He'd get genuine pleasure from wiping out her inheritance.

"You want me to buy penny stocks?" Mark asked.

"No. That's a losing game. I want you to buy stocks that will go up and then sell them at a profit. That way you'll make a lot of money for me . . . and bigger commissions for the firm."

"That's not what Arthur had in mind."

"We'll never know what Arthur had in mind. He's dead and he can't tell us."

Mark pretended to think aloud. "I could set up an account in the firm's name, and only a few people would have to know that the account is yours. Like our accountant . . ."

"What a wonderful idea."

"It's okay." Mark remembered the torn picture Gus Sklar had shown him. Ali the whore. When the time came, he'd enjoy treating her like one. "I'll need a letter from you insisting that I make high-risk investments. The kind of investment where you can make a bundle . . . or lose a bundle." That would cover him with Buckstein and Greenberg.

Ali's laugh was musical. "You're too good a broker to lose a bundle."

"If you say so, Ali. I'll send you a draft of a letter that I want you to type on your personal stationery. Sign it and send it back to me with my draft. When I have the signed authorization, I'll handle your account."

Ali uncrossed her legs and recrossed them. Her skirt slid halfway up her thigh. "There's one more thing, Mark. Channel 18. Millie must agree to sell it."

"Why? What difference does it make to you?"

"There's a huge commission involved."

"There is," Mark agreed. "A commission that will go to Reiner & Co."

"There's another commission," Ali said softly, "if you and I can convince Millie to sell the channel to . . ." Ali hesitated. The hesitation was not lost on Mark. "To Lew Dobbs. He'll pay me a commission."

"How do you know Lew Dobbs?" Mark asked.

"There are only thirty-six important people in the world. I know every one worth knowing."

Mark dropped the subject. When he was ready, he'd ask Lew himself. "Okay. Meeting ended. I've work to do. . . ."

Before leaving, Ali posed in the doorway. "You're a dear," she gushed. "But don't forget about Channel 18."

That evening Mark told Nora his edited version of what had taken place earlier in the day. Nora said "Yes" and "Oh my" and "That's wonderful" in all the appropriate places.

It struck her that Mark wasn't telling her the entire truth. She didn't care. Mark was having an affair. She could think of nothing else. Later, lying in bed, Mark reached for her. She brushed his hands away.

"I'm tired," she said in a voice that allowed for no change of mind.

Mark rolled away from her. His pride was bruised. And he was confused. He was Nora's husband. He had rights. Didn't Nora love him? Why was she behaving so strangely? It crossed his mind that somehow she had gotten wind of Gigi. No, he decided. Gigi and he were too professional to be caught by an amateur. Nora needed to be taught a lesson. Time alone would teach her how much she missed him.

"I have to go to New York and kick some butt," he said, staring at the ceiling. "Since Arthur's death, things back east have been drifting. I'll be there about a week." He'd go by way of Phoenix and come back by way of Phoenix.

"When will you leave?"

"Sunday morning. That way I can get an early start Monday."

Nora was glad. She needed time alone to think, to sort out her feelings about Mark. About herself. Should she tell him she knew about Miss Black Lace G-string in Phoenix? Should she insist he end the affair? Did it make any difference? It did if she wanted to hold the marriage together. But did she? Mark had betrayed her once. What assurance did she have that he wouldn't betray her a second time with a different Miss Black Lace G-string? And a third time? Could she ever trust him again? A marriage without trust was like a house divided . . . no matter what she wanted, it couldn't survive.

Chapter 18

THAT WEEK, Nora and Mark kept out of each other's way. The mornings were simple. Nora stayed in bed pretending to be asleep until Mark left for the office. During the day neither called the other. Several evenings, Mark saw clients. Other evenings, Nora worked late. When she got home, she either turned on the television set or went to bed. The few conversations they had concerned Mark's trip back east. Not only would he straighten out the New York office, while he was at it, he'd see his mother and sister. He hadn't seen either of them in several years. That piece of information generated one of their rare conversations.

"How are Shirley and Grace?" Nora asked.

"Some things never change," Mark said. "My mother's still doing it . . . still dreaming of hitting it big with one of her penny stocks." For a moment he looked baffled. Maybe it was his mother's stubborn refusal to follow his advice. "And my sister, Shirley, is up to something. She's taken a one-year leave of absence from NYU. With all the cutbacks in New York, wouldn't a sensible person try to get tenure? Not my sister. I expect the worst. The one-year leave of absence will become a permanent leave of absence."

"I hope not. For her sake," Nora added.

"For all our sakes. When whatever she's thinking of falls apart, I don't want her landing in my lap," Mark said gruffly.

Mark sounded so bitter, for a moment Nora was sorry for him. Then . . . Damn it, she thought. No one forced you to have an affair. She picked up a book, ending the conversation.

Mark went out on the deck. New York would be work . . . hard work. And much as he wanted to see his mother and sister, he dreaded it. Shirley wanted something. What? At least Phoenix would be fun. When he got back, he'd have it out with Nora. They'd have a heart-to-heart talk and work it out.

On Sunday morning, Mark made a point of showing Nora his plane ticket. A direct American Airlines flight from San Diego to JFK. He also had a ticket on a Southwest Airlines flight to Phoenix and an American Airlines flight to JFK the next day. That one he didn't show her.

He didn't have to. All Nora's instincts told her the ticket he showed her was a beard . . . a cover for his real flight plans, which included a stopover in Phoenix. The idea made her sick.

"Have a good flight," she said.

"Thanks. I'll call you as soon as I firm up my return flight. Maybe you can meet me at the airport?" Mark attempted a smile.

"I will if I can. Don't count on it."

Mark's smile faded. "I won't."

When Mark left, Nora went to her bureau and fished out the black lace G-string . . . the Phoenix G-string. She studied it, rubbed it between her fingers, rolled it up into a ball. A small ball that disappeared between her hands. By the time she returned the panties to the rear of her bureau, she was sobbing. Her marriage was a farce. When she was with Mark, she felt more alone than ever before in her life. She felt shut out. All she wanted was to be with someone. On impulse, she checked an old address book. She'd crossed his name out years ago. There it was . . . with the telephone number still readable. She sat down at her desk and dialed the number. She shrugged, waiting for the operator to cut in and say, "Sorry. This number is no longer in service." He must have moved. People in California move every couple of years. Movie people more frequently. But . . . The number rang. It must have been assigned to someone else. She started to hang up when the phone was picked up.

"Hello," Jordan said.

"Jordan?"

"That's right. Who is this?"

"N-N-Nora."

"N-N-Nora." He mocked her stutter. "Where are you?"

"Home. In Del Mar."

"Oh."

Nora imagined she heard a note of disappointment in Jordan's voice.

"I called to see . . . Are you free for lunch tomorrow? If you're not, how about Tuesday or Wednesday? Or . . ."

"Stop!" Jordan laughed. "I'm free tomorrow. Or I can be."

"That's wonderful. What restaurant?" Nora exclaimed. "I'll meet you at the restaurant."

"Don't be silly. Meet me at my house. If you're stuck on the freeway, I won't be sitting on my hands waiting for you."

"Do you live in the same house?"

"The same house in the hills."

"The house your father . . . and Millie lived in?"

"The same house," Jordan repeated. "What time can you make it?"

"I have to check with the station before I leave. Say, one o'clock?"

"One o'clock is fine. 'Bye."

Nora replaced the phone. Silently she thanked Jordan for not asking embarrassing questions. Like, Why are you driving to Los Angeles? It can't be simply to have lunch with me. That hundred-and-forty-mile drive just for lunch?

Mark took Phoenix the way Grant took Richmond. For a whole afternoon and a night, Gigi and he ate, drank and made love. The more often they made love, the better Mark felt. It wasn't just the sex. From the beginning the sex had been great. It was Gigi. With Gigi, Mark felt he could do no wrong. He was the lord and master. Did she love him? The question was meaningless. She obeyed him without question. With Nora he was never quite sure of where he stood. She loved him. He was sure of that. But did she consider him her equal? Sometimes he thought yes. Sometimes, no. But he wasn't her lord and master . . . ever. She was a Gardiner. He was a Stern. Sterns don't rule Gardiners, not in this world. But in this world, a Stern can rule a Cantrell. Gigi filled a void in Mark's life that—until he met Gigi—he was unaware of.

Mark was packing to leave for the airport when Gigi said in an offhand manner, "Did you happen to take a pair of my panties last time?"

Mark looked up. "What? No. What would I want with a pair of your panties?"

"I don't know. After you left, I couldn't find them." She shrugged. "It doesn't matter. They were too small to wear under my uniform. I drip too much. I'd stain my uniform. I only bought them to wear for you. I thought you'd get a charge out of seeing me in them."

"You mean those little lace things?"

"Uhuh. I washed out a pair and wrapped them in a towel to dry."

"You what!" Mark shouted.

"What's the matter?"

"Oh, my God!" Mark slapped his forehead with the palm of his hand. "That's what's been eating Nora."

"What do you mean?"

"I took that towel. I didn't know your panties were wrapped up inside it."

"You stole a towel from the club?"

"Swiped," Mark said automatically.

"Stole," Gigi murmured. "Stole . . . Are you saying your wife found my panties in your suitcase?"

"Yes."

"That poor woman. Is she upset?"

"Very."

Gigi sighed deeply. "I'm sorry, Mark, but we can't see each other again."

"Why not? Nora is my wife. Not yours. I'll work it out with her."

"You may, but I won't."

"You won't what?"

"Work it out with me."

"What do you have to work out? You don't know her."

"I know you. Look . . . I like you very much. But I have my rules. I live by my rules. If I didn't, I'd be a whore. No different than the girls who work the bars in Phoenix."

"What rules?" Mark asked.

"I'm not against having sex with a married man . . . a married man like you. Being married is your business. You're the one who's being unfaithful, not me. But when your wife discovers you're cheating on her . . . with me . . . then it *is* my business. I'm involved. Rule number one is, I do not break up marriages. Never!"

"But Nora already knows."

Gigi made a face. "That's what comes of stealing towels. Anyway, I'm going to give you a piece of advice. I rarely give advice, but this is a subject I really know."

"What subject?"

"What to do when the wife finds out. Listen . . . first, you tell her about me. Confess everything. Second, you promise to stop seeing me. She'll forgive you. Wives always forgive husbands who cheat. They've been doing it since forever—"

"But . . ."

"No buts, Mark. You can follow my advice or not. The choice is yours. Either way, I'm sorry, but we're history. I'll drive you to the airport. I'm still your chauffeur when you're in Phoenix."

On the way to the airport, Mark tried to talk Gigi out of her position. He failed. Only when he was about to board the plane for New York did Gigi make one concession.

"If you get a divorce and I'm not the cause of the divorce, you can come back." She grinned sheepishly. "Even if you marry another woman. As long as your new wife doesn't know about me. As I told you, I have no rule that says you can't be married."

On the flight to New York, Mark considered Gigi's advice. He decided she was right. He'd confess. Nora would forgive him. Once Nora forgave him, he'd work on a good lie to tell Gigi. One of his patented ninety-five-percent-true lies. No. Ninety-five percent wasn't good enough. In some ways, Gigi was smarter than Nora. The lie would have to be ninety-nine percent true. He'd have to come up with something good. He would. . . . He always had.

Mark spent the first two days in New York with the Reiner & Co. staff. He was given the red carpet treatment. He was the new managing partner. He expected no less. Fortunately Wall Streeters—much like the crowd in advertising and publishing—are given to changing jobs almost as often as they change their underwear. Only two customers' men remembered him as a wet-behind-the-ears trainee. They both made the mistake of greeting Mark with too much familiarity. Mark smiled and shook their hands. Later he had a word with his ex-boss, John Eckstein. Eckstein was now the partner in charge of the New York office.

"Find a reason to get rid of them," Mark said. "But don't involve me."

"They're good producers," Eckstein protested.

"Then they'll have no trouble getting jobs with other firms. I don't want them here."

"I ought to call Dorothea Reiner about this."

"You do that," Mark said. His voice was pleasantly neutral. "After you hang up the phone, you have one hour to clear out of the office. The company will buy back your stock at book value."

For a few seconds, Eckstein was speechless. When he could talk, he said, "That's less than I just paid for my new shares."

"Read the corporate bylaws, John. When you leave the firm, you're obligated to sell your stock back to the corporation. And the corporation is obligated to pay you book value. Any price above book value is at the managing partner's discretion." Mark smiled.

"Are you planning to fire the entire office?"

"No. Just every asshole who doesn't realize Arthur Reiner is dead. I'm now the managing partner."

"Okay. Suppose I don't call Mrs. Reiner . . . ?"

"Suppose this conversation never took place . . . ?"

"I see." Eckstein nervously moistened his lips. "You are the managing partner . . ."

"Good thinking, John."

"I suppose I could let them go."

"Don't suppose. Do it." Eckstein nodded. "Tomorrow morning I want to meet with the head bookkeeper . . ." Mark consulted his notes. "Lorraine Rossini. Tell her I want an itemized breakdown of all expense accounts for the last six months."

"That'll take her all night."

"If the books are in that much of a mess, she should work all night." Mark studied Eckstein's worried face and shook his head. "Not your expense account, John. You're a partner. I don't expect you to account to the other partners for your expenses."

"Aaah . . . I'll talk to Lorraine."

Mark stood up. "I'll see you tomorrow morning." In the elevator on the way down Mark debated how much longer to give Eckstein. Three months . . . maybe six at the most. He

wanted his man—a man totally loyal to him . . . not Dorothea Reiner or Roger—in charge of the New York office.

Mark left the Helmsley Palace. His mother and sister were
expecting him for dinner. On a whim he decided to take the
subway. He hadn't ridden a subway in years. It would be an
interesting experience. It wasn't. The subway was crowded.
Although the cars were clean and air-conditioned, the riders
weren't. They smelled of sweat and cheap perfume. Living
in San Diego, Mark had forgotten what it was like being that
close to that many people for such a long time. When he
exited the subway at Roosevelt Avenue—several blocks from
where his mother and sister lived—he took a deep breath of
air. And coughed. The air was heavy with the exhaust fumes
of cars and buses. People in California complained about
pollution and traffic. "They don't know from pollution and
traffic," Mark murmured. "New York has pollution and traffic."

"You okay, Mack?" a burly man asked.

"Sure." Mark tensed. This was New York . . . a violent
city.

"You're talkin' to yourself. That's the first sign a guy's
going nuts."

"I'm okay," Mark said.

"Watch yourself," the man said. "You ain't from here. If
you ain't used to it, this city can drive you nuts. And Queens
is the worst." He waved and headed for the subway entrance.

Mark walked slowly toward his mother's apartment. What
he saw wasn't what he remembered. Two-story frame houses
and rent-controlled, poorly maintained, six-story red-brick
apartment houses . . . with and without elevators. In other
parts of Queens there were elegant fifteen-story apartment
houses with doormen, elevators and terraces. People of all
income levels lived in Queens. But not in Jackson Heights.
In Jackson Heights the six-story buildings were mostly occupied by bookkeepers, taxi drivers, shipping clerks, salesmen and various working stiffs who sweated blood to keep a
roof over their heads. It was bleak. Mark felt depressed.
Either he'd changed or Jackson Heights had changed . . .
probably both. The building his mother and sister lived in
was not an eyesore, just a drab, rectangular, six-story building that gave off an air of sullenness. The kind of building you

might feel sorry for . . . if you didn't live in it and weren't already feeling sorry for yourself.

His mother's apartment was on the fifth floor. Years ago his father had said. "Never rent an apartment on the top floor. When the roof leaks—and it will—apartments on the top floor get wet." Slowly, reluctantly, the elevator rose to the fifth floor. Mark opened the door. The corridor smelled faintly of urine and antiseptic. He rang the bell to his mother's apartment. He couldn't hear the bell so he knocked on the door. He waited. No one came. He raised his fist to knock again.

The door suddenly opened, and his mother stood looking at him. Mark froze. He remembered that look. She was trying to decide whether or not she was glad to see him. For the moment the ayes had it. She made a face that on someone else would have been a smile. On Grace Stern, it looked like she might sneeze.

"Hello, Mark," she said. She glanced at his still raised fist. "Are you planning to hit me or to come in?"

Mark dropped his hand. "Hello, Mom." He stepped into the small foyer. The glow of the living room light was a pale rose that made reading difficult. For an instant Mark concentrated on his bright sunny house in California. He tried to hang on to the image like a talisman. Then he entered the world of his mother. The apartment had the overheated, stale smell that had been a familiar part of his life until he left for college. Looking around he saw the same furniture. The same tired, worn living room set . . . a green fake-leather-covered sofa and two matching chairs. The same fake Chinese lamps with shredding fake-silk shades. Against the far wall was the denim-covered hideaway couch that once had doubled for his bed. It seemed to Mark that inside the apartment time had stopped. Nothing had changed . . . nothing ever would change.

"Mark! We are indeed honored!" Shirley Stern stood in the kitchen doorway. She curtsied. "You're visiting your poor relations? Welcome. Thrice welcome." She billowed out of the kitchen holding a large bowl of spaghetti. She was followed by a large heavy-shouldered man wearing jeans and an open-throated shirt. He had a red, sunburned face and thinning sandy hair. He held a bottle of wine over his head as though he was trying to read the label through the bottom of the bottle.

Mark stared at his sister. A little too plump. In her early thirties, with frizzy, brassy hair and full breasts that were beginning to sag . . . she should wear a bra. He'd bet her curlers still littered the bathroom and strands of her hair still clogged up the sink drain. Again, nothing changed. He glanced at the table in the dining area. It was covered by a shiny polyester tablecloth, cheap stainless steel knives and forks, plastic plates and paper napkins. Set for three. Apparently he wasn't invited for dinner. That was okay. He didn't want to have dinner with his mother and sister.

"Quinn, this is my brother, Mark. I told you about him . . . about our family tycoon. Mark, this is Quinn Carroll."

"Hello," Mark said.

"Hi there." Quinn smiled.

Mark shook hands, it was like holding a callused slab of gristle.

"Are you staying for dinner? We can set another place," Grace Stern asked. She sat down heavily in an armchair next to a pile of *Wall Street Journals*.

"Don't think I can, Mom," Mark said. "I have a business dinner. But I had a few hours so I thought I'd stop by and see how you were."

"Would you like a drink?" Quinn asked in a friendly voice.

"Sure," Mark said as he sat on the other worn armchair . . . as far away from the *Wall Street Journals* as he could get. He watched Quinn move toward the cupboard where the liquor was stored. The guy knew his way around the apartment. Who was he?

"Name your poison."

"Vodka on ice," Mark said. "If you have vodka. If not . . ."

"We have vodka," Shirley said quickly.

"Good drink," Quinn enthused. "Pure vodka, made from imported potatoes."

"Absolut." Shirley smiled as she settled onto the couch. "Quinn brought a bottle. Pour me a short one, honey. Neat. No ice."

"I ought to know by now how you like your drinks," Quinn said as he made three vodkas. He handed Mark and

Shirley their drinks and joined Shirley on the couch. "Your health," he said.

They clinked glasses. Mark nodded. Shirley smiled. The room was silent as they sipped thier vodkas. Mark heard the faucet dripping in the kitchen. *Splat. Splat. Splat.* One drop every five seconds. It had been dripping exactly that way for as far back as Mark could remember.

"What are you recommending?" Grace broke into his reverie. She was a tall woman with fine features. Once she'd been considered handsome. No longer. Now she was a thin, dry, nearsighted woman with faded brown-and-white hair and a sagging jawline. "I need a killing."

"Mom . . . I . . . er . . . I don't track penny stocks."

"Not good enough for you. Penny stocks put you on Wall Street."

"Right." Mark wanted no part of an argument with his mother about stocks. The politics of his mother's penny stocks, his sister's string of affairs with married professors, his future on Wall Street had for years made up the triangular dynamics of their family. "What's with this leave of absence bit, Shirley?" he asked.

"Teaching English Lit to kids who don't want to read what I want them to is a bore. I kept flunking PC."

"What's PC?" Mark asked.

"Political Correctness. NYU is a liberal school in a liberal city. I've always considered myself a liberal. I voted for Carter . . . twice. And for Mondale and Dukakis and Clinton. But I'm not liberal enough. Not for New York and NYU." Gradually Shirley's voice had risen.

"Relax, sis," Mark said. "Why don't you try California?"

Shirley's look was half tender and half ashamed. "California. Hawaii. Sure. After all, I have a rich brother." She turned to Quinn. "Remember what I told you, baby. I practically introduced him to his heiress."

"The rich bride . . ." Quinn cocked an eyebrow.

"Rich, rich, rich. Mark doesn't bother with small potatoes. This one will inherit mucho millions."

"Oh knock it off," Mark exclaimed.

"Mark hates to give credit where credit's due." Shirley pretended to be offended.

Mark studied his sister and her current squeeze over the

top of his glass. They didn't add up. The guy was a sailor. Judging from his rolling walk and his callused hands, probably a wet-assed sailor. What was a guy like Quinn doing with a girl like Shirley? What did he want from her?

"Sounds like your sister did you a good turn," Quinn said. "I guess you owe her one."

Mark's eyes shifted around the room. The conversation had drifted into tricky channels. "My sister has a good imagination," he said.

"You mean she didn't find you a rich wife?"

"No, she didn't. Besides, Nora is not rich. Her grandmother may be rich, but Nora isn't." Mark didn't know why he felt so defensive.

"Crap!" Shirley smiled complacently and sipped her vodka. Without any warning, she asked, "You still screwing anything that moves, Mark?"

"No," Mark said firmly.

"Hey, Mark. This is me. Shirley. I know you. You're a classic bastard. Find 'em, feel 'em, fuck 'em and forget 'em. That's you. You trying to tell me that being married to what's her name . . . Cora? No. Dora?"

"I think you mean Nora," Quinn said politely.

"How'd you know my wife's name?" There was a puzzled look on Mark's face.

"You just said her name a couple of minutes ago," Quinn said politely. "Besides, Shirley talks about you constantly. She's very fond of you. Proud of you, as a matter-of-fact. You're my major competition." He chuckled.

"What did she say about Nora?"

"Well . . . you know . . . She said she introduced you," Quinn remarked in an offhand way. "Quite a matchmaker, our Shirley."

"The best . . ." Shirley applauded herself. "Stick with me, kid, and you'll wear diamonds."

It seemed to Mark that that last crack was directed at Quinn.

Grace Stern looked up from the *Wall Street Journal*. "She did find you an heiress, Mark. She did indeed."

"Now that he's married his heiress, he's too high and mighty for us poor folks." Shirley was pale.

Mark rose half out of the chair, then slumped down again. His face was egg-white, paler than his sister's.

"Mark! Loosen up." Shirley had a pained look on her face. "I did say, 'Look her up.' Which you did."

"The hell I did."

Shirley was offended. "The hell you didn't."

"You have a lousy memory."

"I have a perfect memory. You were working in a bookstore. Then you looked around. And guess what? You found her in a fast-food joint."

"Short-order cooks make more money than book salesmen. She happened to work in the same place I did."

"Lucky coincidence." Quinn grinned.

"And you didn't pull your usual stunt and dump her after the first couple of fucks," Shirley crowed. "Suddenly you were a reformed bastard. Mark, in love. Where would you be without me?" Shirley asked with sudden intensity.

Mark turned away. "You look tired, Mom," he said, trying to ignore Shirley.

"I am tired. I got a right to be tired. I've been working every day for over twenty years . . . since your father died. And up half the night reading the *Wall Street Journal.* Keeping up. Making investment decisions. You're damn right I'm tired."

"I send you a check every month."

"A small check," Shirley interjected.

"I use the checks to buy some interesting stocks."

Mark made a face. "Penny stocks. You should forget your penny stocks, Mom. Let me do some professional investing for you."

"We like different things."

"I'd do better for you than you do for yourself. Those penny stocks are losers."

"Xerox was a penny stock."

"Which you sold," Mark said.

"I made a profit."

"A small profit."

"That's our Mark," Shirley boasted to Quinn. "Now that he's married that heiress I found for him, he'll stick to her like glue. He knows you don't find real heiresses growing on trees."

"Shut up, Shirley! For Christ's sake! Drop it!"

"Mark . . ." Quinn leaned back on the couch. "Come on. There's nothing wrong with a man marrying a rich woman. Women marry rich men all the time. If it wasn't for Shirley . . .''

"All right," Mark said. He could have kicked himself for not getting where Shirley was coming from sooner. "You want something from me. What do you want?"

"Well . . ." Shirley hesitated and then said with a combination of embarrassment and fake good humor, "In case you got amnesia about how much I did for you, I took out an insurance policy."

Mark said without emotion, "You don't have to blackmail me to get money."

"Who said anything about blackmail?" Shirley protested.

"You did. Why? You know I send Mom money all the time. My own money. If I had more, I'd send more."

Grace Stern again glanced up from the paper. "Mark, I saw a tombstone a while ago. It had a thick, black border. It said a Mr. Arthur Reiner of Reiner & Co. had died. He was your employer, wasn't he?"

"That's right, Mom."

"Who's the new managing partner?"

Mark searched frantically for an answer. Not a true answer. An answer that would stand up in case Shirley got it in her head to check. There was none. He'd have to break a rule . . . tell a lie that was not ninety five percent true.

"Dorothea Reiner is now the majority shareholder. She'll pick the new managing partner. . . . Whoever she picks will run the firm until Arthur's son, Roger, takes over."

"Hold it right there, brother," Shirley said. "As I remember it, Dorothea Reiner is the ex Mrs. Reiner. What about the current Mrs. Reiner . . . Mrs. Ali Reiner?" She smiled at Mark's startled look.

"What do you want, Shirley?" Mark sputtered.

"Money. Lots of money."

"How much is lots of money?"

"Half a million," Quinn said softly. "That's the minimum."

"What! I don't have that kind of money. Nora and I just bought a house. We . . . Never mind. Why do you need a half million dollars? That is a lot of money."

"That's nothing compared to what we'll make when I find the ship," Quinn said.

"What ship?" Mark asked.

"A seventeenth-century Spanish galleon. It went down off the Florida Keys loaded with gold and jewels. I have a damn good notion exactly where the galleon foundered."

"You want me to gamble a half million dollars—which I don't have—on a crazy treasure hunt? You're kidding!"

"We're not crazy and we're not kidding," Shirley said. "You know, Mark, I was thinking that someday soon . . . well . . . Someday soon we might double-date. You and your rich bride. Quinn and me. You could bring her here for supper. Don't you want her to meet your family?" There was a look of such misery in Mark's face that Shirley ended weakly. "Sorry. Bad joke. Forget it. Your heiress was born to ritzier ways. She uses a better class of toilet paper."

"You were invited to the wedding party."

"I had a stock that needed watching," Grace Stern explained. "I couldn't go."

"And I'd just found Quinn. I couldn't take a chance on losing him."

Lose him! You dumb broad. Once you told him about Nora and me, you couldn't have held him off with an AK-47. "I don't have a spare half million. Not this week anyway," Mark said, trying to turn the request into a joke.

"Next week will do," Quinn said. "Or even next month."

"I don't have the money, and if I did, I wouldn't back a crap shoot treasure hunt. That's worse than Mom's penny stocks." Mark stood up. Seeing his family had been a mistake, but like so many mistakes, it was a mistake he'd had to make. "I'll be in touch," he said.

"Sure you will," Shirley said. "Send money, Mark. Or we'll be in touch."

"Shirley, stop it," Grace Stern said. "He doesn't have the money."

"I don't.' Bye, Mom." He kissed his mother on the cheek and left without saying good-bye to Shirley or Quinn.

After leaving the building, Mark looked for a cab. A side street in Jackson Heights wasn't on the cruising cabs' main route. He started for the subway entrance . . . then stopped. He turned and looked up at the fifth floor. There was Shirley, sitting on the windowsill as she always used to. She waved and blew him a kiss. Mark waved back. Despite the clumsy blackmail attempt, Shirley was his sister. He would always wave back.

PART 8

Nora
1993

Chapter 19

NORA EXITED the San Diego Freeway at Santa Monica Boulevard and headed east. Jordan still lived in the unfashionable part of Los Angeles . . . the Hollywood Hills. Not in fashionable Beverly Hills, Bel Air, Malibu or any of the canyons . . . Coldwater Canyon, Laurel Canyon. That he chose to live where he did was typical of the man. He also didn't go to power breakfasts, power lunches or power dinners. When he ate, he ate. He didn't work the room trying to cut a deal while he ate. And he didn't care if the maître d' showed him to the Good Table or to a table with a good view of the Good Table or to a table in the part of the restaurant known as Siberia . . . with a potted palm between his table and the Good Table. He didn't drive a Rolls-Royce, a Bentley, a Mercedes or an Excalibur. To the best of Nora's recollection, he drove a Land Rover . . . a huge four-wheel-drive vehicle that could ford a three-foot-deep river and climb a nearly perpendicular cliff. He was Jordan Banska . . . second-generation producer/director . . . a Hollywood aristocrat. If he wanted to live in the Hollywood Hills . . . well . . . No one questioned an aristocrat, a brilliant filmmaker whose movies won awards and made money. He could live anywhere . . . geniuses were famous for their eccentricities.

Between the usual delays at Costa Mesa and the construction at LAX, Nora was late. The heavy Santa Monica Boulevard traffic made it worse. She hit every red light. At Wilshire Boulevard it took two light changes before she made it through the jammed intersection. As 1:15 became 1:30, she grew apprehensive. Suppose Jordan had grown bored at having to wait for her and left? He was famous for his short fuse. She considered pulling over and phoning him. Dumb! By the time she found a public phone, she could be at the house. At 1:40 Nora turned left on Doheny. Soon she was winding her way up the steep, narrow streets that curved around the Hollywood Hills. Although it had been ten years, Nora remembered each turn in the road. Except for a few new houses here and there that—through brute strength—clung to the sides of the hills, nothing had changed. Unlike the rest of L.A., the Hollywood Hills were trapped somewhere in the 1920s and 1930s. Many of the old houses had a story to tell. Of wild parties where famous stars let their hair down and danced naked in the sun. Of writers—drunk on the easy Hollywood money, cheap gin and the benign climate—trying to complete one last money-making script before they went back east to write the great American novel. Of the talkies and the decline of careers that ended in booze, drugs and suicide. Men with the talent and the drive to make their kind of movies—movies the major studios in the thirties wouldn't touch—once lived in the Hollywood Hills. Milos Banska had felt at home in the Hollywood Hills. That was why he'd bought the house from Millie after she married Max. The hills were like no place else in L.A. And Jordan Banska—like his father—belonged in the Hills.

Nora rounded a bend in the road and turned into a narrow driveway. On both sides of the driveway were high concrete walls dripping with bright red bougainvillea. It seemed to her the driveway went straight up to the sky. She prayed her T-bird could make the grade. It did. The driveway led to a small parking area . . . enough room for three cars at most. The old Land Rover—the same car Jordan drove ten years ago—stood in one corner. Nora parked next to the Land Rover, got out of her car and paused for a moment to reorient herself. The white, two-story, faintly Spanish-style house had one thing in common with many of the houses in the Hills. Whichever side of the house faced Beverly Hills, West L.A. and the rest of the valley . . . that side was the rear of the house. The terrace, the swimming pool and Jacuzzi, the built-in barbecue were on that side of the house. The front of the houses usually looked out on nothing . . . a wall, a steep bank or an equally steep hill. Nora wondered if she should go directly to the terrace or ring the front doorbell. Her father had used the house as a second home . . . a bolt hole. Whenever things got too tough—he'd gotten clobbered in the market . . . a woman resented being kissed off . . . Hiram was appointed to a still more prestigious office—he escaped from

Millie and her. And headed straight for the safety of Jordan's house. Ring the bell, Nora decided. It's been so long. You're a stranger in this house.

A concrete path led from the parking area to the front of the house. Nora pushed the bell. She heard the *bing-bong, bing-bong* sound. No one came to the door. She rang again. *Bing-bong. Bing-bong.* There was no sign of life inside the house. "Damn!" she muttered. "He didn't wait." Disappointed, disgusted—close to tears—she turned away.

"Nora?" a voice called out. "Is that you?"

"Yes. Where are you?"

"Here."

Jordan appeared around the corner of the house. His lightly tanned skin was glistening with lotion, and he was wearing a bathing suit. At least what might pass for a bathing suit in the fleshier fleshpots on the Mediterranean. A pouch in front that barely covered his pubic hair was held up by a string around his waist . . . it looked like a male model's posing pouch. Automatically she compared Jordan's body to Mark's. They were about the same height. Although Mark had bigger bones, he rarely exercised. He wasn't fat . . . not yet. But there was a roundness, a sleekness—almost like a seal—about him. Jordan was lean. The muscles of his arms and legs were long, hard ropes. And his stomach was a washboard . . . not an ounce of excess flesh anywhere. In spite of herself, Nora felt the heat rising in her body. Her bra felt too tight . . . her nipples hardened and pressed against the fabric.

"What are you staring at?" Jordan said, laughing.

"You know very well what I'm staring at. I thought we were going to have lunch. Or is that thing you've got on Hollywood's latest idea of an informal dining costume?"

"It is if you're having lunch next to your pool."

"Is that what we're doing?" A thin film of perspiration oozed through the pores of her skin.

"We are. Come." Jordan escorted her around the corner of the house.

Nora glanced around the terrace. Almost nothing had changed. Not the green grass rug covering the concrete or the pool or the two-person Jacuzzi or the lounge chairs or the Saltarini iron-and-glass table that was set for two. Nothing had changed except for the bushes. They'd gotten larger and thicker and higher. Jordan once claimed that even a man with

two black thumbs—like him—could grow roses in Southern
California. The patio was totally protected from prying
neighbors, if there were prying neighbors in the Hollywood
Hills.

"I thought it would be more pleasant to eat here rather
than in a restaurant. Here, no one at the next table will try
to listen to our conversation. No waiter to hover over us. We
can kick off our shoes and relax."

"You've kicked off a lot more than your shoes."

"Do you mind? I think you told me you were experienced
. . . a married woman . . . unshockable. Should I put on a
pair of shorts?"

"No. I mean . . ." Anything she said would be a mistake.
She smiled. She was aware Jordan knew exactly what he was
doing. The bathing suit was his way of breaking down her
defenses. The dinner at the Waterfront Bar had cued him. She'd
talked too much. Much too much. Now she didn't want to talk.
She only wanted the comfort of being with someone . . . No!
She wanted to talk about Mark. No! She didn't want to talk
about Mark. What did she want? She didn't know.

"You look a little warm," Jordan observed. "Why don't
you slip into something more comfortable?"

Nora giggled. "I didn't bring anything more comfortable."

"How about a bathing suit?"

"I didn't bring one."

"I have plenty of suits. In the pool house. Over there."
Jordan gestured in the direction of a small, one-story pool
house at the far end of the pool.

"Like the one you're wearing? I think not."

Jordan grinned. "Not exactly like mine. There's a collection of bottoms and bras in there . . . all sizes and colors."

Nora studied her nails. The idea of wearing some other
woman's bathing suit didn't appeal to her. "I'll pass," she
said.

Jordan shrugged. "I've made a chef's salad . . . ham, turkey, cheese, bacon . . . the works. And I have several bottles
of a nice wine on ice. Relax in one of the lounges while I
bring out the food." Without waiting for Nora's response, he
turned and walked toward the house.

Automatically, Nora's eyes followed him. The rear of the
suit consisted of a narrow strip of cloth barely wide enough

to cover the crack between his buttocks. She gasped and quickly looked away. The thin film of perspiration on her forehead beaded and ran into her eyes. It stung. She wiped the sweat away with the back of her hand.

It took Jordan a few minutes to carry the salad and wine from the house to the poolside table. He then announced, "Lunch is served. Come and get it."

Nora's next feat was a tricky bit of navigation. She walked in one direction—toward Jordan—while looking in another . . . away from Jordan. And she did so without tripping over anything. Her effort was wasted. There was no way to avoid seeing him. The table was glass. Every time she looked down at her plate, she saw more of Jordan than she wanted to. Jordan served the salad and filled her glass—a red-wine glass—from a one-and-a-half-liter bottle of a white zinfandel. The salad was crisp and cold. The wine dry and slightly fruity. The perfect wine to drink on a hot day by a pool. Nora pecked at her salad but she finished her glass of wine . . . taking large swallows.

As Jordan refilled her glass, he said, "Take it easy on the wine, Nora. And eat your salad. It's not a good idea to drink on an empty stomach."

Like an obedient child, Nora hurriedly stuffed her mouth full of salad. "It's very good," she said. Since her mouth was half full, her words were muffled.

"Swallow your food before speaking," Jordan teased her.

"Yes, Daddy. Thank you, Daddy."

During the lunch, Nora thought a lot and said little. She looked anywhere but at Jordan. What had made her think she could talk to him about Mark . . . about their sex life? Was she crazy? Almost silently, they ate and they drank. Actually Nora drank and Jordan ate. The first two glasses of cold wine refreshed her. The next two glasses of cold wine made her feel hot and uncomfortable. She blotted the perspiration from her forehead, wishing she had brought her own bathing suit. Maybe it was just as well she hadn't. She owned a number of sensible one-piece bathing suits. Not a string bikini like the suits hanging in the pool house. She visualized a typical girlfriend of Jordan's. She remembered her father's succinct description of one of Jordan's women. "All tits and ass." When she excused herself to go to the bathroom, the back of her white linen dress was soaked. Her dress was meant for

an air-conditioned restaurant on Rodeo Drive . . . not a table
next to Jordan's pool under the hot sun.

While Nora was in the john, Jordan thought about sex . . .
and the Byzantine-like fuckups that can happen in a marriage. On that subject he was an authority . . . a two-time
loser. In his experience, anything that could go wrong between married people would go wrong. And what went wrong
first was usually sex. He understood why Nora wanted to
have lunch with him . . . to talk about her marriage. Her
husband. Her sex life. To get his advice. He doubted she
would talk freely at a restaurant. With him in a pair of slacks
and a safari jacket and Nora in that dress. Which was why
he'd set up the lunch by the pool and worn his nothing of a
bathing suit. He knew from experience that when one person
is fully clothed and the other almost naked, the fully clothed
person is usually uncomfortable . . . embarrassed. The idea
was to embarrass Nora into changing to a bathing suit . . .
the more naked a woman was, the more relaxed she became.
Ideally, they should both be stark naked. But for this talk that
was out of the question. So he'd compromised. If Nora could
be persuaded to change to a bathing suit, she'd let down her
guard and spill out her worries about her sexiness. . . . Such
nonsense. Then he would offer sage, mature advice. Ease her
fears. And she would go back to San Diego a happy, contented woman. Their lunch would have served its purpose.

Nora rejoined him. The first thing she did was pour another glass of wine. "Look," she said, placing the bottle
upside down in the ice bucket. "A dead soldier. Do you have
another soldier . . . a living soldier?" Her voice was slurred.

"Don't you think you've had enough to drink?" Jordan
asked.

"I'm fine. I'm sweating so much you can taste the wine
on my skin. I mean I can taste the wine . . ."

Jordan regretfully put aside the wine-tasting idea. Instead
he said, "I'll make you a deal. I'll open up another bottle if
you get out of that dress and put on a bathing suit."

"But I . . ."

"I know. You're wearing a girdle and you feel naked without it."

Nora flared. "I've never worn a girdle in my entire life."

"Few women need girdles," Jordan observed. "They wear
them anyway."

"I don't!"

"I believe you. Change to a bathing suit and I'll get the wine."

Screw it, Nora thought. I'll look like what I look like. She stood up, marched around the pool and entered the pool house. The sun baking on the roof had turned the small room into a cauldron. Nora couldn't get out of her clothes fast enough. She stood naked, staring at the wisps of brightly colored cloth hanging on the many pegs. She reached for a green suit. She held the bottom against her and blinked. "Oh sweet Jesus." A tiny triangle in the front . . . another triangle in the rear. Or was the front the rear? No. The label told her the front was the front. "What the hell!" she muttered. "Jordan's seen enough women. We're all pretty much alike." Still, when she pulled on the bottom of the suit and looked in the full-length mirror, she blushed. Her tan lines were wrong . . . there was white skin on the tops of her thighs and hips. And the suit didn't cover her pubic hair. She always shaved so the hair didn't show when she wore one of her normal bathing suits. This wasn't a normal suit. She tried to stretch the fabric. No go. Like most tall, lean women, she had smallish breasts. The tiny bra almost fit. She looked again in the mirror and shrugged. What you sees is what you gets.

"Ready or not, here I come," she sang out as she opened the door. The patio appeared to be empty. Where the hell was he? She walked to the edge of the pool. Suddenly Jordan popped to the surface of the water. He was looking straight up at her. She had the sensation he could see through the cloth . . . see her crotch. Her hands dropped to cover herself . . . she felt silly. Jordan hoisted himself out of the pool. In doing so, he splashed water on her. Nora took a step back, lost her balance and fell into the pool.

Jordan dove in after her. "Isn't this better?" he said.

"I guess so," Nora sputtered.

"Do you want to swim some laps?"

"I want some more wine."

"The wine is over there." Jordan pointed to a white Styrofoam block floating at the far end of the pool. The block had been molded to hold a bottle of wine and two glasses.

"What a lovely idea!" Nora swam to the shallow end of the pool. When she stood up, her breasts popped free of the bra. Quickly she turned her back to Jordan and tucked them into the bra. "Sorry about that," she said over her shoulder.

"Why be sorry? You have the breasts of an eighteen-year-old. Lovely breasts."

Nora didn't hear him.

It was just as well. Jordan's penis was beginning to harden. Damn! He hadn't considered that possibility. But what could he do about it? Beside the obvious?

Nora poured herself a glass of wine. "Come." She gestured to Jordan. "I don't want to drink alone."

Jordan joined her. Several glasses later, the bottle was empty.

"You know what I'd like?" Nora asked.

"What?" Now Jordan was feeling the effect of the wine.

"More wine. Do you still keep your wine in the old wine closet?"

"Yes."

"I know where that is. I'll get it," Nora said.

"I'll go with you," Jordan said. He stopped.

The sight of Nora rising from the water made him catch his breath. Her buttocks were larger and more muscular than he'd expected. His penis was hard as a rock. Double damn! If Nora saw his erection, she'd never trust him. Crossing the terrace, he picked up a towel and hurriedly wrapped it around his waist. He handed a second towel to Nora. "Dry yourself," he said.

In the house, Nora selected another bottle. They sprawled in the comfortable chairs—towels wrapped around their waists—as they shared the third bottle.

When Nora finished her second glass, she waved the empty glass in the air, chanting, "Nobody loves poor Nora. Mark doesn't want her. Jordan doesn't want her. Nobody wants her." Then she stretched out her legs and giggled. "I'm drunk." She sang in a tuneless voice, "Drunk last night. Drunk the night before. Gonna get drunk tonight like I've never been drunk before. . . ." She stood up. The towel dropped to her feet. She faced Jordan and swayed back and forth in front of him. "Don't want to get drunk alone, Jordy. Not fair to let me get drunk alone. Come on. Get drunk with me."

Jordan gazed at her yearningly. That asshole she'd married didn't appreciate her. He wanted to hold her in his arms . . .

comfort her . . . tell her she was the most exciting woman
. . . Nooo. Can't say that. . . . Can't even move. He was
trapped in the chair with a full erection. If he held her, she'd
feel it.

"You're drunk enough for both of us," he said.

"I'm not drunk enough for me. Dance with me, Jordy."
She reached for Jordan's arm . . . missed his arm and stopped
herself from falling by catching hold of his towel-covered
thigh. When she straightened up, she pulled the towel with
her. Her eyes got big and round. "Look at that." She
grinned.

Jordan grabbed the towel and covered himself.

Nora tried to pull the towel off again. In the struggle, she
fell against him.

"Kiss me, Jordy," she whispered. "You've never kissed
me like a grown-up woman."

Jordan Banska was not steel. That Nora was married didn't
matter. That she was Barron Gardiner's daughter didn't matter. What mattered was that she was a beautiful woman wanting to be kissed. And he wanted to kiss her. He kissed her
. . . gently at first and then deeper. His tongue played with
the tip of her tongue . . . with the roof of her mouth. Tick-
ling. Caressing. She raised her arms so he could remove her
bra. He kissed her nipples. His fingers slid lightly down her
spine . . . lingering here and there. His nails traced patterns
on her back. His hands slipped under her suit and cupped her
buttocks . . . pressing her against him. He broke the strap
holding the bottom of her suit together and tossed it to one
side. He fondled her wetness. She opened to his touch.

Nora moaned in her need . . . her happiness. Jordy wanted
her. The room teetered wildly. She felt dazed with joy. Then,
abruptly, she slid into darkness. . . .

Jordan caught her as she fell away, lifted her naked body
and carried her to his bedroom. Only when he placed her on
the bed did he realize she'd passed out.

"Shit!" he softly hissed. He covered Nora with a light
blanket and headed for the bathroom. What he needed was a
cold shower.

Jordan sat for a long time on the patio thinking about what
had happened. And what hadn't happened. He ached for
Nora. But part of him was relieved they hadn't made love.

Mentally, he listed again and again the reasons for not making love to Nora. She was too young. He was too old. Too jaded. She was married. A faithful wife. She was Barron Gardiner's daughter, Millie Gardiner's granddaughter. He was Milos Banska's son. The Gardiners and Banskas were already too tangled up with each other. He'd known Nora since she was a child. He had no right to take advantage of her. What he refused to consider was the possibility that he loved Nora. That in a way he'd always been in love with her. Years ago, innocently . . . as an older brother might love a very young sister. Now, passionately . . . as a man loves a woman.

"Hello there."

Jordan looked around.

Nora had put on his bathrobe. She was standing in the doorway looking miserable.

Jordan hurried to her.

"I really made a mess out of that," Nora said in a low voice. "What I remember, at least."

"What do you remember?" Jordan asked.

"Almost everything. Up to the point where you . . ." A deep blush suffused her cheeks. "We didn't make love," she finally said.

"No. We didn't."

"Why? Was I so unattractive?" She looked like she might cry at any minute.

"You were very attractive. You were lovely. But you were smashed. And there are rules about things like that."

"What rules? Who made the rules?"

Jordan grinned. "I did."

Nora touched his arm. "Thank you . . . I guess." She rubbed her head. "I don't feel so good."

"I wonder why?" Jordan's grin broadened. "I have just the thing for you. Vitamin C. Lots of vitamin C. Best thing in the world for hangovers. Sit and contemplate your sins. I'll be back in a moment." He disappeared into the house and quickly returned with what looked like a large glass of orange juice.

"Orange juice?"

"It was orange juice. It's now orange juice plus. I have done weird and wonderful things to it. Just drink it."

"Yes, master." Nora gulped down the juice, offering a silent prayer that it stay down. There was a moment of nausea. Then her stomach settled. She attempted a smile. "I guess I made a fool of myself."

"We both did."

"What's wrong with me, Jordy?"

"Nothing, as far as I can tell."

"How would you know? My father once told me a man doesn't know anything about a woman until he makes love to her. Then he knows everything about her worth knowing. You didn't make love to me. You don't know anything about me."

"Barron was wrong. Sometimes making love gets in the way of knowing a woman. I know you very well."

"But you don't know if I'm good in bed. If I'm a good f—"

"Nora, listen to me. I think I know what's going on, but I want you to tell me about it in plain and simple language. What's wrong? Why the questions about your sexuality? How good you are in bed? Or not good? Sex isn't a contest. There are no winners and losers."

Nora turned away. "This is very hard," she said.

"Tell me something that isn't hard."

Nora wanted to say, Being with you isn't hard. She didn't dare. The moment for them had passed. "It's Mark," she whispered. Then she was silent. Nora was a private person . . . talking about her sex life to anyone, especially to Jordan, was difficult. Eventually she quietly described her marital problems . . . and the impasse she was at. When she finished, she looked helplessly at Jordan.

Jordan wanted to take her in his arms, hold her, make love to her. He couldn't. She was too open, too vulnerable. "Okay," he finally said. "I don't know Mark. But I do know something about men. I don't think there's a man over the age of twenty-five who—once in a while—doesn't have trouble making it. Even with a woman he loves. It has nothing to do with you."

"It's happened to you?"

"Of course it's happened to me." Not often, thank God.

"What do the women do?"

"Get angry and go home. Or go to sleep. And we do it the next morning. The smart ones play a game. It's called Fantasy. They work out a fantasy that would amuse and arouse me."

Nora was in way over her head. Sometimes she fantasized

when making love, but her fantasies were about Mark. "What kind of fantasy?"

Jordan shook his head. "Not important. Everyone has different fantasies. You're going to have to figure out Mark's."

"Oh!"

"And as for the woman in Phoenix? Listen, Nora. There are three kinds of husbands. One." He held up the forefinger of his right hand. "A man who occasionally runs across a woman. The timing is perfect. They go to bed. Afterward they go their own way. They may never see each other again. Or they might bump into each other and wonder why on earth they went to bed the first time."

"But Mark is seeing this woman steadily."

"I said there were three kinds of husbands. Two." His middle finger shot up. "A man who regards any woman as fair game. Single, married, pretty, not so pretty. It makes no difference. All he asks is that she's female."

Nora thought of Arthur Reiner. That was a pretty good description of Arthur. But not Mark.

"Three." His ring finger joined the other two. "A man who is bored at home and meets a woman he finds exciting. They go to bed. The sex is great. If the woman is willing to break up the man's marriage, she sometimes has a husband."

"Mark?"

"Maybe. How did you find out about the girl? Was it an accident or did he set it up so you had to find out?"

Nora thought about that. She finally said, "I don't know." She told Jordan about the panties rolled up in a towel.

"An accident? Maybe." Jordan leaned forward. "Does Mark realize that you know everything?"

"No."

"Okay. Tell him you know he's having an affair. Don't confront him. Just tell him. Listen to what he says. If he asks you to forgive him, forgive him. I'm not suggesting you forgive and forget. Just forgive him. He'll promise never to cheat again. He probably will. Maybe next time you'll be lucky."

"Lucky?"

"If you're lucky, you won't find out. If you do, either he's careless . . ."

"Mark isn't careless. Not about anything."

"Then he wants you to know he's cheating. Maybe he's angry at you and wants to rub your nose in it. Or it's a power

play. Or . . ." Jordan hesitated. "This is getting complicated. First things first. Talk it out with Mark. He'll probably
beg you to forgive him. Which you will do. That's it for
now." Jordan stood up and brought his hands together, making a loud clapping sound. "Are you planning to stay over
in L.A.?"

"No. I have to be at the station tomorrow morning. I played
hooky today."

"It's almost five-thirty. I suggest we have an early dinner
. . . in a restaurant. By the time we finish, the going-home
traffic will have cleared off the freeway. You should have a
straight run to San Diego."

"I'd like to have dinner with you," Nora said with a smile.
"And thank you for everything."

"Fa niente." Jordan made a mental note. He'd do his own
checking on Mark Stern. He was certain the Phoenix romp
wasn't the first time Mark had strayed. The more he knew
about the guy, the better prepared he'd be the next time it
happened. And it would happen again. And Nora would again
find out. Some men never learned. He stared at Nora. Was
he one of them?

On the way home, Nora thought about Jordan. His advice
was good advice. Reasonable. Logical. Sane. She did love
Mark, and she wanted him to love her . . . to make love to
her the way he used to. But now there was a new complica-
tion . . . Jordan. Was she also in love with Jordan? She didn't
know. She wanted him badly. She'd wanted him since she
was a teenager. If she hadn't passed out, they'd have made
love. Then what? Nora rubbed her eyes. She made herself a
promise. Next time—if there was a next time—she'd stay cold
sober. She hoped he didn't have a rule about making love to
her . . . stone-cold sober.

Chapter 20

THE STRETCH Cadillac limousine wound through Manhattan on its tortuous way from the Helmsley Palace to JFK. Mark slumped in the rear seat of the car. He could have turned on the television set or poured himself a drink to help pass the time . . . as usual the traffic jam leaving Manhattan was horrendous. He did neither. His eyes were closed as he considered the flight back to San Diego. He still had two return tickets . . . one with a twenty-four-hour stopover in Phoenix and the other a direct flight from Kennedy to Lindbergh Field. He took both tickets from his breast coat pocket and studied them regretfully. Given a choice he'd take the American flight to Phoenix. He shook his head. He didn't have a choice. Reluctantly, he opened his attaché case and slipped the ticket with the Phoenix stopover under a pile of papers. He closed the attaché case and spun the tumblers that locked it. Not even Nora knew the combination. He would cash in the ticket in San Diego. And keep the money. That was his arrangement with the travel agent for Reiner & Co. . . . one of the perks that went with being managing partner. Like the suite at the Helmsley Palace . . . at five hundred dollars a day. Like the limousine that—except for the one subway ride to see his mother and sister—had chauffeured him around the city . . . at three hundred dollars a day. Like the first-class seat on the plane . . . fifteen hundred dollars round-trip. The one week in New York cost Reiner & Co. close to ten thousand dollars. A lot of perks. Still, Mark felt no qualms about spending the money. First, it wasn't his money. And second, he'd saved the firm more than one hundred times the cost of the trip by cleaning house in the New York office.

The expense account chiseling that he'd uncovered ran into tens of thousands of dollars. And that was for openers. There was more . . . the expensive antique furniture and fine oil paintings the partners had ordered for their offices . . . at least that's what the invoices stated. But when he dug a little deeper, he discovered that most of the antiques and paintings ended up in the partners' homes. He'd considered asking for a ten percent cut, but decided it was too risky. One of the clowns might get it into his head to call Dorothea. Dorothea would have a fit. Besides, the money he'd get was small change compared to what he expected to make as managing partner. Smarter and safer to be a Boy Scout. The New York partners squealed like stuck pigs, but they agreed with his suggestion as to how they could repay the company for the art and antiques that furnished their homes. The money was to be deducted from their salaries and commissions. For this quarter at least, the New York office would show an unusually handsome profit.

Given what else he'd discovered, it wasn't surprising that Eckstein allowed the partners to steal from the company. He was following the example set by their late managing partner, Arthur Reiner . . . actually, by the wife of their late managing partner. Ali had charged the antique furniture and expensive art with which she'd furnished the condo to the New York office of Reiner & Co. The checks had been signed by Les Nelson, the New York controller, and countersigned by Arthur. Mark had photocopied a half dozen checks . . . in order to check Arthur's signature on the checks against documents he knew from firsthand experience Arthur had signed. He found it hard to understand why Arthur would steal from himself. To save taxes? Mark didn't think so. Arthur was too smart to risk an income tax evasion charge. He'd learned his lesson from the Helmsleys. Since they were caught with their fingers in the company cookie jar, charging the business for personal expenses had dropped to the bottom of a long list of executive officer rip-offs. But it was the kind of stunt Ali might pull. He'd bet the ranch that somehow she had convinced the controller to go along with the scheme. Somehow? That's a laugh. Ali only had one asset to trade for Nelson's cooperation . . . her ass. Once Nelson agreed, Ali went to work on Eckstein. Fucking two men or two dozen men to get what she wanted was Ali's style. She used her ass as though it was a renewable natural resource. With Nelson and Eckstein on board, everything got charged to the New York office

overhead. It occurred to Mark that Arthur's will made no
mention of the furniture and art in the condo . . . only that
Ali had to get out in six months. He wondered if Arthur knew
how valuable the furnishings were. Because a man was a
smart businessman did not mean he knew anything about the
high cost of art and antiques. If Nora hadn't told him what
Ali had bought and how much everything had cost, he would
have had no idea that the furnishings in the condo were so
valuable. That brought up another question. Who actually
owned the antiques . . . Ali, Arthur or Reiner & Co.? Reiner
& Co. paid for everything. Logically, Reiner & Co. owned
everything. And he was the managing partner of Reiner &
Co. He could . . . No, he couldn't. Nora wouldn't sit still
for his having the most valuable pieces moved from Ali's
condo to their house. But . . . Mark grinned. He could arrange for Christie's to pick up everything in the condo and
put the contents up for auction. Ali could spend the six
months in the condo without any furniture. She'd love that.
Then he had second thoughts. It wasn't right to put a natural
resource out of business. He'd leave Ali her bed . . . her base
of operations. Nora wouldn't be able to say a word. No matter how much Ali bitched to her.

Nora? Mark closed his eyes again and sank deeper into the
soft leather seat. He'd had a very successful New York trip.
Now he had to figure out how best to handle his wife. Compared to Nora, everything he'd accomplished in New York
was like winning a minor league game. Nora was the majors
. . . the show. If he lost Nora, he'd lose both Abe's and Millie's accounts. And if Millie asked her to, Dorothea might
fire him. In San Diego, Dorothea and Millie were heavy-
weights. If they put out the word, no San Diego brokerage
firm would hire him. He'd have to begin again in another
town . . . and as of now he didn't have enough money to
begin again. When he did . . . Mark grinned. Anything could
happen. Meanwhile, he had to pour oil on troubled waters.
Several times during the week, he'd considered calling Nora
to apologize and beg forgiveness. And each time he decided
against making the call. His plea for a second chance was
best done in person . . . not on the telephone.

The limo pulled up in front of the American Airlines terminal. Mark checked his watch. Three o'clock. He had a
solid hour and a half before the plane was scheduled to de-

part. That was the way he liked it. Arriving an hour ahead of departure time was cutting it close. He watched as the driver removed his luggage from the trunk and handed it to the uniformed black man who handled curbside check-in. Even in blasé New York, anyone arriving in a maroon stretch Cadillac limousine got attention. The limo said "Look at me. I'm rich. I'm important." And when Mark gave the attendant his first-class ticket, the attendant almost saluted.

"It's good to have you flying with us, sir." Mark nodded. And when the attendant stapled the baggage receipts to Mark's ticket, he said, "Thank you for choosing American. Your plane leaves from gate forty-two. Have a good flight."

"Thank you." Mark handed the man a ten-dollar bill. He had arrived in a limousine and he had a first-class ticket. Ten dollars was a nice touch, a way of living up to his new image.

"Will you need me any longer, Mr. Stern?" the chauffeur asked.

"Not on this trip, Mike," Mark said. He gave the chauffeur a fifty-dollar bill . . . a splendid touch . . . more living up to his new image.

"Thanks, Mr. Stern. Will you be coming back soon?"

"If those jokers in my New York office don't get their act together, damn soon." Mark's crack was not a casual gripe. Skyways Limo was hired by the New York office traffic manager, who reported to Les Nelson. He was confident whatever he said to Mike would get back to Nelson and from Nelson to Jack Eckstein. Which was exactly what he wanted to happen.

Mark sauntered toward gate 42. There was a short wait at the metal detection gate . . . the alarm kept going off. Then he figured out that his belt—a wide leather belt with silver studs and a heavy silver buckle that Gigi bought for him in Phoenix—was triggering the alarm. The belt safely went through on the conveyor and he passed the metal alarm. Since he already had his seat assignment, he settled himself in one of the many empty seats close to gate 42. He had about a half hour before any American Airlines employee would start checking in passengers. He had a sudden hunch. Call Nora now. Tell her your flight and when you're landing. Ask her to meet you at the airport. Her answer will clue you as to which way the wind is blowing. He always followed his hunches. He'd make the call . . . but not on Nora's private line.

Nora was about to break for lunch when the intercom buzzed.

"Yes, Sheri?"

"Mr. Stern is calling from New York?" Sheri's voice rose at the end. She was asking a question. Do you want to talk to him?

"Put him through," Nora said. She heard the connections click as Sheri transferred the call from her line to Nora's.

"Hello, Mark," Nora said cautiously. "How are you?"

"Okay."

"How was the week?"

"Exhausting. I'll tell you about it when I see you."

"Uhuh. Why the call?"

"Well . . ." Mark spoke rapidly in broken, staccato sentences. "I'm at JFK. . . . My plane leaves at four-thirty . . . one-thirty your time. We're supposed to land at Lindbergh at ten-fifteen . . . seven-fifteen your time. . . ."

"I can figure the three-hour difference." Nora grimaced. She sounded more sarcastic than she'd meant to.

"Will you meet me at the airport?" Mark blurted out. "Please?"

"What airline are you flying?"

"I showed you the ticket before I left. American Airlines. Flight seventy-nine."

"Is it a direct flight?" Nora asked. "No stopovers?"

Automatically, Mark started to ask what she was talking about. He stopped himself. Nora knew about Gigi. No . . . not about Gigi. She knew about some girl he was screwing in Phoenix. "It's a direct flight," he said.

Nora mentally kicked herself for asking. A five-and-three-quarter-hour coast-to-coast flight had to be a direct flight. She said, "I'm really backed up here. I'll try to break away in time. If I'm there, I'm there. If not . . ."

"I'll take a taxi home."

"Okay, Mark. Good-bye."

" 'Bye."

Nora hung up without wishing Mark a safe flight. She tilted her chair back. She'd meet him at the airport all right. The sooner they talked the better. But she didn't want Mark to feel too sure about her. For almost six hours—while he ate lousy airline food and watched a movie he'd probably already seen—he could damn well worry if she'd be waiting for him.

At Lindbergh Field, Nora took her time deciding where to sit. She chose the far side of the gate from which Mark would exit. She wanted to see Mark before he saw her. Flight 79 arrived on time. That Mark was the first passenger off the plane made Nora smile. And when she saw him nervously glance this way and that, her smile grew broader. She composed her face—put on her "life is real, life is earnest" expression—before standing up. Mark spotted her, waved and hurried toward her. He reached her. When she didn't respond, his arms slowly dropped to his sides.

"Did you have a good flight?" Nora asked. Using the same tone of voice she could have asked, Did you have a good tennis game?

Mark shrugged. "The plane left on time. The plane landed on time. These days, that's the definition of a good flight."

"Yes. One takeoff, one landing. That is a direct flight." Nora smiled. She knew she was being snide.

Mark started to say something and stopped himself. "I checked my bags. We'll pick them up in baggage claim." He wanted to make nice . . . but not too nice. To walk the delicate line between a husband returning to his loving wife after a short business trip and a husband returning to a troubled marriage because his wife knew all about him. He said, "I gather you had less work to do in the office than you thought?"

"I have more work. I packed a briefcase. I'll work at home."

Mark waved his attaché case. "I have work to do at home."

They walked toward the escalator . . . without touching each other. They talked . . . without saying what either wanted to say or the other wanted to hear.

"You survived New York," Nora said. She was thinking of all the times her father went to New York and came home beaten down, on his shield.

"Surviving New York is like riding a bicycle. Once you learn how, you never forget."

Barron never learned. "How is the New York office of Reiner & Co.?"

"A mess. I had to fire the bigger fuckoffs. The guys I used to work with."

"That must have been hard on you."

Mark heard the first note of sympathy in Nora's tone. He played up to it. "It was," he said. "But I'm the managing partner. Like Eisenhower said, 'If you can't stand the heat, get out of the kitchen.' "

"Truman," Nora automatically corrected him.

"What?"

"Truman. Harry Truman said that."

"Eisenhower."

"Truman."

Miss Know-it-all knows all, Mark thought. Won't hurt to agree . . . even if she is wrong. He smiled. "Okay. Truman. If Eisenhower didn't say it, he should have."

"He didn't."

Their attempts at talking grew more and more strained. By the time they'd collected Mark's bags, neither had said a word in five minutes.

Mark carried his bags to the gate leading from baggage claim. His stubs were checked against the luggage tags before Nora and he were allowed to leave. After stowing the luggage in the trunk of the car, Mark asked, "Do you want to drive?"

Nora blinked. There was a perceptible pause before she said, "Yes." She added, "In my car, I drive." She didn't like the way that sounded and wished she could take the words back.

Mark stiffened. "Right," he said. He waited for Nora to get behind the wheel of the car and unlock the passenger door. Cool it, he told himself.

On the way home, Mark struggled to make conversation. He mentioned how he thought Ali had ripped off the company.

"I don't understand," Nora said. "Why did Arthur permit it?"

"Arthur didn't know. Nelson and Eckstein covered for Ali."

"Why would they risk their jobs?"

Mark chuckled. "I guess Ali made them an offer they couldn't refuse."

"What could Ali offer them?"

"You figure it out."

Nora took her eyes off the road for a moment to glance at Mark. "I think you men are crazy. What's so special about sleeping with Ali?"

"I don't know," Mark said. "I may be the only old friend who hasn't slept with her." He was all innocence.

"How did you miss her?" Bite your tongue.

"I managed." He sounded virtuous.

Nora frowned. She'd never considered the possibility of Mark and Ali. He disliked her so much. But now she wasn't sure. Either way, it was a rock she didn't want to turn over.

Mark rested his head against the back of the seat. "I'm beat. Long flights knock me out."

"If God wanted man to fly . . . you know . . . man would have wings and tail feathers and so forth. Flying is psychologically exhausting."

So is talking to you, Mark said to himself. He closed his eyes and pretended to doze. I've got to make a lot of money, he thought. Not just a nest egg. A lot . . . millions. During the rest of the drive home, Mark considered ways—legal ways and not-so-legal ways—to make millions. He dismissed most of the schemes as either too small or too crooked or—and this was the biggest hurdle—taking too long to bear fruit. He was more aware of his strengths and weaknesses than most men. He loved Nora, but he loved her in his own way. And his way did not include being faithful. Shirley had once called him cunt happy. It was true. Next to making money—a lot of money—nothing was as exciting as getting laid. Not just getting laid. Getting laid by a girl he'd never had before. He wouldn't be faithful to any woman . . . not to Nora . . . not to Gigi. Even if Nora forgave him this time, it would happen again. He was in a race. A race to make a pile of dough before Nora found out about his next woman. Or the woman after the next one. Because sooner or later she would find out.

Nora pressed the clicker that opened the garage door and guided her T-bird into the vacant space. Last night in bed alone, she'd had time to think. Jordan said she should forgive Mark. And that Mark would probably cheat again. Should she keep on forgiving him? Jordan hadn't gone into that. And what about her? If she hadn't gotten drunk, Jordan and she would have made love. She'd have been as unfaithful to Mark as he'd been to her. She'd wanted Jordan to make love to her

. . . she still wanted him. How much difference was there between mental infidelity and physical infidelity? She didn't know.

Mark and Nora sat on deck chairs. The fog rolled in, isolating the terrace from the rest of the world. Both wore jeans and heavy sweaters to keep warm in the cool dampness. Mark warmed a snifter of brandy by rubbing it between the palms of his hands. Nora sipped a dry sherry. The silence grew oppressive as each waited for the other to speak first. In this contest, Nora had an advantage. She knew Mark was unfaithful. But Mark didn't know if she knew. Not for sure. Not for absolutely, one hundred percent, sure.

Eventually Mark managed a small smile. He said, "I've given up snitching towels from hotels."

"Oh? What brought on that decision?"

"People use towels for all sorts of things. . . ."

"Like drying a . . . a sweater?"

"Right. Like drying a sweater."

"When I'm staying in a hotel and I wash my bras and panties, I wrap them in a towel," Nora said. "A lot of women do."

"Must be a secondary sex characteristic. Men don't dry their underwear in a towel."

Nora shrugged.

"Er . . . Nora?"

"Yes?"

"About Phoenix."

"What about Phoenix?"

"Damn it!" Mark muttered. "You're making this hard."

"Do you think discovering my husband is screwing some broad in Phoenix is easy?"

"Why call her a broad?"

"Because she is a broad. Who else would wear panties like those?" Nora hated the way she sounded . . . like a jealous wife. There wasn't that much difference between the G-string he'd brought home and the G-string she'd worn for Jordan.

Mark almost told Nora that the panties had been bought to please him. What a lousy idea.

"I don't care what she is," Nora said. "I do care that you've been sleeping with her." Nora put her drink down

and swung her feet off the lounge. She sat up facing Mark.
"Why, Mark?"

Mark finished his brandy in one swallow. He shifted his
position to face Nora. Their knees were almost touching. "I
don't know," he said softly. "It just happened." He had a
thought . . . he'd tell Nora a lie. Not one of his patented,
ninety-five-percent-true lies. He didn't have time to invent
one of those. But since Nora and Gigi would never meet, it
made no difference. "I broke it off on my last trip to Phoenix," he said ruefully. "She knew I swiped towels. I think
she put the panties in the towel in the hope that you'd find
them. Her idea was you'd walk out on me, and I'd go back
to her."

"Would you?"

"No." Mark took Nora's hands in his. They were ice-cold.
"I love you," he said. "I love you very much. I know how
badly I've hurt you. I'm so sorry." There was a tiny catch—
the merest trace of a sob—in Mark's voice.

Although Nora didn't move a muscle, inwardly she cringed.
She'd seen this act before. The whole thing was a performance for her benefit. What she didn't know was how far it
went. He said he was sorry that he hurt her. Was he sorry
that he hurt her or was he sorry she'd found him out? He said
he loved her. She had to believe that was true. Otherwise
their eight years together was a farce . . . a black comedy.
Nora was tougher minded than most people, but she refused
to face that possibility.

"Can you forgive me?" Mark begged.

"What?"

"Can you forgive me? Please?" Mark had waited until this
moment to plead. Now he pulled out all the stops. "Please!"
he whimpered.

Nora thought again how close she'd come to making love
to Jordan . . . how much she still wanted to. She pulled her
hands away, stood up and walked to the railing. She stared
at the fog for a while. Then, slowly, she turned to face Mark.

"Listen to me, Mark. I don't want a divorce any more
than you do. I love you, and I'll try to make this marriage
work." Her voice dropped an octave . . . became almost
menacing. "But I warn you. Everyone is entitled to one mistake. You've made yours. No more affairs or I walk." She
added silently, That goes for me too. Jordan is off-limits.

Mark stood up. He joined her at the railing. Hesitatingly—half expecting Nora to pull away—he put his arms around her. She remained in his arms. He kissed her. Lightly at first. Then—when she kissed him back—deeper. ''I love you,'' he murmured in her ear.

''I love you,'' Nora said.

After kissing each other for a long while, they finally left the deck and started down the stairs to their bedroom. Nora remembered what Mark had told her the night he couldn't make it. Make love to me, Mark, she prayed. Don't try to fuck my ass off.

Chapter 21

NORA LOOKED at herself in the bathroom mirror and didn't like what she saw. She was thin. She'd always been slim, but now she was thin. Not slim. Classy women were nicknamed Slim. Like Lady Slim Keith. Gary Cooper's wife . . . Slim. And Lauren Bacall was called Slim. The nickname was a compliment. But nobody was nicknamed, Thin. Nora made a face. Slim was elegant. Thin was too close to skinny. If she lost any more weight, she'd be skinny.

Nora turned and looked over her shoulder at the way her white jeans fit her rear. They didn't fit, they bagged. She'd lost ten pounds . . . in the wrong places. It had happened over the month since Mark and she had patched things up. Instead of being happy that she still had a marriage, now she worried when the next shoe would drop. Who would be the next Miss Phoenix? Her uneasiness had affected her appetite. She wasn't eating right, and it showed. It also affected the way she treated people. She snapped at her co-workers at Channel 18 so often that Pat Yokum had stopped calling her, Norakins. Now she was Lady Macbeth. It even affected her natural curiosity about meeting new people, going to new places. Like tonight. She didn't want to go to a party on Lew Dobbs's yacht.

"Mark," she called out.

"What is it?"

"Why are we going to this dumb party?"

"It's not a dumb party. And we're going because Lew Dobbs invited us." Mark stuck his head into the bathroom. "And we're late. The party was called for seven-thirty. So we could see the sunset from Lew's yacht in the middle of San Diego Bay."

"I can see the sunset from our deck," Nora complained.

"You're being unreasonable. That's not like you."

"It's like the new me," Nora murmured.

"What? Never mind." Mark glanced at his watch. "We were supposed to leave a half hour ago." He wanted to say, If you're not ready in five minutes, I'm leaving without you . . . he didn't have the nerve. The invitation included both of them. Lew had written "Bring your wife" along the bottom of the invitation. It was more than an invitation . . . it was a command performance.

"All right. I'm coming." Walking up the stairs, Nora groused, "I don't know why he didn't rent a private room in a pricey restaurant for this shindig. I can see it now. His lousy little boat will bounce us around like corks. Half the party will get seasick. Instead of watching the sunset, they'll be leaning over the railing throwing up. Polluting the bay even more."

"Are you finished?" When Nora didn't answer, he said, "It's not a lousy little boat. It's a ninety-foot motor sailer."

"How would you know? Unless Dobbs moors the boat in Phoenix?" Nora heard herself and winced. She was being bitchy.

Mark gritted his teeth. When Nora was in one of her moods, the best thing he could do was shut up. These days her moods were like spring showers. They came suddenly, without warning, thundered down on anyone around, and blew over quickly.

"We'll take my car," Mark said as they entered the garage.

"Are you asking me or telling me?" Nora snapped. She wished she could stop. She couldn't. Lew Dobbs reminded her of Group H . . . of Miss G-string in Phoenix. She didn't want to meet Dobbs. She didn't want to think about Phoenix.

"I'm asking you." Mark was determined to be reasonable.

"I'm sorry, Mark," Nora said. "We can take your car. I know how much you like to drive." Although she meant to be agreeable, there was a cutting edge to her voice. It said, You like to drive, but you're a lousy driver.

As Mark backed the Aston Martin out of the garage, Nora said, "I told you months ago I didn't like Lew Dobbs."

"Nora, please be nice to Dobbs. He owns Group H. I'm his investment banker. One of these days, I'll find him another TV station." Mark headed toward Pacific Coast Highway. He'd take PCH to La Jolla before picking up the freeway. Nora liked that stretch of PCH. It ran right along the ocean.

"Then you'll have a legitimate reason for going to Phoenix. Won't you?"

"I always had a legitimate reason. I still have a legitimate reason. It's called cultivating a client."

Nora stopped herself from making a crack about what else he'd cultivated.

When they reached the San Diego Yacht Club, Mark parked in the visitors' parking area. He checked the invitation. Dobbs's yacht was moored in slip 32. There was a small map of the marina attached to the invitation. Slip 32 wasn't actually a boat slip. It was a mooring at the far end of the marina where only the largest yachts tied up. Mark guided Nora in the direction of the mooring.

Even before they found slip 32, Mark spotted the huge white motor sailer. Two tall masts . . . one fore and one aft. A teak cabin in the middle of the boat. It had a fly bridge and a second tiller directly under the fly bridge in the fore cabin. The hull was broken by a long line of portholes. Nora's first thought was that Barron would have loved to own the motor sailer. She immediately changed her mind. Barron loved to sail. The owner didn't sail this yacht . . . this boat needed a professional crew and a full-time captain. The deck was so high above the pier that, instead of a gangplank, one climbed a staircase to board the boat. The first ten steps were parallel to the yacht and led to a landing. Owners of huge motor sailers tended to be older men . . . they needed to rest for a moment after climbing a flight of stairs. The second ten steps were at a right angle and ended at a gate that, when shut, was part of the railing. The stairs had rubber on all the treads, railings on both sides to keep a guest from falling into the bay and a banister to hang on to . . . just in case. When they reached the steps, Lew Dobbs waved and walked partway down to meet them on the landing. He was wearing a white captain's hat, an open-throated white shirt, a double-breasted blue blazer—the buttons looked like twenty-five-dollar gold pieces—white jeans and white leather boots. His massive frame filled the landing.

"Glad you're here," Dobbs boomed out. "I was worried you guys wouldn't make it." Without any change in inflection, he said, "So this is your filly, Mark. Don't blame you for keeping her hidden."

"I'm not a filly, Mr. Dobbs—"

"Lew, little lady. You call me Lew." He looked over his shoulder. "Bosun. Pipe the Sterns on board."

For the first time, Nora noticed a very pretty woman standing in the shadows. She was wearing a traditional sailor's uniform . . . so tight she could have been poured into it. She held a bosun's whistle in her right hand. When she blew it, it made a shrill, whistling sound.

Mark tripped. He went to his knees. If it hadn't been for the railing, he would have fallen into the bay.

"Are you all right?" Nora asked. It wasn't like Mark to stumble.

"I'm okay." Mark pointed to one of the rubber-covered treads. "It's loose."

"Gigi." Dobbs motioned to the girl in the shadows. "What are you doing back there? Hiding?"

The girl stepped into the light and stood next to Dobbs. When Dobbs draped his arm over her shoulder, Nora felt, more than actually saw, her shiver. Making nice with Lew Dobbs was not joy galore.

"Gigi, you know Mr. Stern." Dobbs grinned at Nora. "Gigi works for Group H. The beautiful lady with Mr. Stern is his wife."

Gigi acknowledged the introduction with a nod. "I'm Group H's chauffeur, Mrs. Stern."

Nora's eyes narrowed. "You meet the planes," she said.

Both women knew what Nora meant.

"When I choose to," Gigi said unabashedly.

"Come on, Sterns," Dobbs said. "The party's going on in the main cabin. I invited three couples besides yourselves. You already know some of them. Gigi, tell the captain everyone's on board who's coming on board. He can cast off. Then you join us. Maybe help with the drinks." He slipped his arms under Nora's and Mark's and hustled them toward the rear of the boat. As they walked, he carried on a monologue. "You're a lucky man, old buddy. I'm not as lucky as you. Never found the right filly." He nudged Nora in the ribs with his elbow. Nora hoped he hadn't cracked one of her ribs. "That's you, Nora . . . the right filly. I'm not married, so my good friend Gigi agreed to fill in as my hostess."

"Your good friend," Nora murmured. Was Lew's good friend also Mark's good friend in Phoenix? She glanced at Mark. He was looking this way and that . . . quick, darting glances. Appraising the boat, Nora guessed, and she forgot about Gigi.

The motor sailer slowly slid away from the dock. Whoever was at the tiller knew what he was doing.

"Here's the main cabin," Dobbs said.

Unlike most boats, one walked up several steps to enter the cabin on this one. Nora glanced around. The floor was carpeted. One corner was taken up by a permanent wet bar. Comfortable easy chairs, lamps and tables were scattered about the large cabin. Very impressive. She was surprised to see Pat Yokum chatting with a nice-looking man. She wondered if the man knew he was wasting his time. A second look made her wonder if the man really was wasting his time . . . they were standing that close. Her surprise at seeing Pat was nothing compared to her shock at seeing Ali. Ali was in the far corner. Her back was to the door. She was concentrating on a stocky man of average height. The man's expression was bland . . . almost to the point of looking bored. Only his eyes—the dark, light-absorbing eyes of an Oriental— were alive.

"Everyone," Dobbs called out, "front and center. We got here the Sterns. Mark Stern and Nora Stern. You can figure out for yourselves which is which." Ali laughed and waggled her fingers at Nora and went back to charming her date. "That there filly is Pat Yokum. You already know her. And that stallion pawing the ground next to her is Cousin Leonard Gerard." The way Dobbs introduced Gerard made it sound as if the man's full name was Cousin Leonard Gerard. Dobbs then introduced Victor Ashland and Bobbi Weeks.

"Nice to meet you, Nora," Ashland said. "Mark talks about you all the time."

"Does he?"

"Says you're the real brains at Channel 18."

Nora shot a quick glance in the direction of Pat Yokum. Pat was fuming. "Mark exaggerates," Nora said. "Besides, I'm not in programming. That's Pat's department. I'm in sales."

"That's not the way Mark tells it," Ashland insisted.

Bobbi Weeks stepped between Ashland and Nora. "Mrs.

Stern, I'm Mr. Ashland's private secretary. Can I get you a drink?''

Nora studied the woman. With different makeup, a more flattering hairstyle and a less frozen expression, she'd be quite attractive. She was wearing a simple black dress-for-success dress, stockings and low-heeled pumps. Perfect for the office, wrong for a yachting party. And she was afraid. What was she afraid of? Meeting her? Mark's wife? Was she Mark's Phoenix fling? An uptight secretary in public . . . a sexual athlete in private?''

"I'll get Nora a drink," Mark said.

Bobbi Weeks stepped back. "If you need anything, Mrs. Stern, just ask."

Nora joined Ali and her Oriental friend. She hadn't seen Ali since Arthur's funeral. That is, not officially. And unofficially only once in the airport with Ken Savage. She'd been avoiding Ali, but the continued silence at Ali's end of the phone was very un-Ali-like.

"Hello, Nora." Ali grinned at Nora.

Nora swallowed hard. The grin and the words reminded her of the long-ago Friday night dinner when Millie first introduced them. "How have you been?" Nora asked.

"Surviving," Ali caroled. "I'm a survivor. I'll explain later. Anyway, two months of mourning for Arthur was more than he deserved. So I'm out of mourning."

"Yes, you are." Nora took in Ali's tight-fitting white sequinned jumpsuit.

"Nora, this is Stanley Tseng. Stanley's a dear. He's the reason I rejoined the human race."

"Mr. Tseng." Nora held out her hand.

"Mrs. Stern." Tseng took Nora's hand and expertly brushed it with his lips.

"You're a famous man, Mr. Tseng. Between Arthur Reiner, my husband and Ali, I think I know all about you."

"I hope not everything, Mrs. Stern. I'm an international banker. If you knew everything about me, I would have to leave the country."

Nora smiled at the good-humored warning that she mind her own business.

"Here's your martini, Nora," Mark said, joining them. "How are you, Stanley? And you, Ali?"

"We're very well, Mark," Stanley Tseng said. "How are you, and why are you serving the drinks? Where's Gigi?"

"I don't know," Mark said. "Why should I know? I'm not her keeper. Ask Lew. She works for him. Not for me."

Nora glanced at Mark over the top of her glass. Why so defensive?

"No matter," Tseng said smoothly. "I have to see you tomorrow, Mark. I want to transfer assets from . . ." He glanced at Nora and smiled. "Your wife tells me she knows all about me. I am aware that husbands in America sometimes confide their business dealings to their wives. The practice is barbaric. Why burden a woman with dull business talk?"

Another warning. Nora looked at Mark. No reaction. Whatever was making Mark tense had nothing to do with Stanley Tseng.

"I talk to Nora about business when the business concerns her." Mark's smile was a carbon copy of Tseng's.

"Ah. There's Gigi," Tseng said.

Mark's smile faded.

Tseng motioned for the girl to come over. "A whiskey and soda, Gigi. No ice."

"I know, sir. Would you like a freshener, Mr. Stern?"

"N-no. I'm fine." Although the temperature in the luxurious cabin was comfortable—even a little on the cool side—he was sweating.

Nora's eyes darted from Mark to Gigi and back to Mark and back again to Gigi. Then she got it. Miss Priss in her uptight dress might be Victor Ashland's lady friend, but she wasn't Mark's. Gigi, the girl who met the planes, was.

"How about you, Mrs. Stern? Would you like another martini?" Gigi's smile was easy, natural.

"No thank you, Gigi. I'm fine."

Nora took note of the girl who met the planes. Mark was as nervous as a cat in a strange room. If he could, he'd slide along the wall. But Gigi had it all together. She was so smooth that Nora questioned her own judgment. She looked again at Mark. His mouth was tight. His eyes were fixed on the ceiling. Nora felt a tinge of disappointment. Poor Mark. If he had behaved naturally, she'd never have guessed. She glanced at Gigi. Oddly, she admired the woman. Could she do as well if their roles were reversed? Could she keep her cool if she met her lover's wife? She didn't know.

"Bring me a white wine," Ali snapped.

Nora winced at Ali's tone. The charm she ladled over Stanley Tseng was missing. To Ali, Gigi was a servant. Charm was never wasted on a servant.

"Okay, you stallions and fillies," Lew Dobbs called out. "Everyone out to the cabin. It's sunset-watching time."

While the rest of the party watched the red sun sink into the Pacific, Nora wandered around the deck of the motor sailer. She could see all the sunsets she wanted from the deck of her house. But the boat was a floating mystery. From the teak decks to the teak window trim to the shiny bright work, everything about the boat said money. This boat was a huge hole in the water into which tons of money had been poured. Nora glanced into the galley. Two cooks were preparing dinner. She turned away and stopped dead in her tracks. Gigi was leaning against the rail, watching her. At that moment, she wished with all her heart to have back the ten lost pounds.

Nora lifted her chin and squared her shoulders. "Why aren't you looking at the sunset?" she asked.

"The sun has set. And the sunsets in Arizona are more spectacular."

Nora had no small talk.

"Would you like me to show you around the boat?" Gigi asked.

"I've taken a turn around the deck."

"Have you seen the cabins? The owner has done them up real nice."

"The owner? What owner? Isn't Mr. Dobbs the owner?"

Gigi laughed. "Lew Dobbs own a boat?" She shook her head. "Lew owns TV stations, not boats."

"But this . . . ?"

"Rented. By the week."

"You could have fooled me," Nora said.

"Lew isn't trying to fool anyone. At least not about owning a boat. Come on. I'll show you the cabins."

"Sure," Nora said.

The cabins were reached from a hatch in the rear of the boat. There were four identical cabins on each side of the mahogany-paneled corridor. Each had built-in twin beds, a night table between the beds and two built-in bureaus. Cabins one and two shared a bathroom, as did cabins three and four, five and six, and seven and eight. The bathrooms were so luxurious, it would be wrong to call them heads. Whoever had designed the interior of the motor sailer knew about the ocean . . . that even a ninety-foot boat bounced around in a high sea. There was nothing loose to fly about. Even the prints of famous racing sloops—they were all named *Ranger* and a number—were screwed into the walls. What struck Nora as strange was that only one of the eight cabins was occupied.

"Mr. Ashland?" Nora asked.

"And Bobbi. She had to come."

Nora nodded. "Where does the crew sleep?" she asked.

"There are four bunks up front and a small cabin for the captain."

"Ah. What about you? Sorry about that. None of my business."

Gigi shrugged. "It's all right." She pointed to a set of double doors at the end of the corridor. "The owner's cabin. Right now it's the renter's cabin. Complete with king-size bed and all the comforts of a five-star hotel. Including maid service. Me," she dryly added. "I'll show you." She started for the door.

"Thank you, but I've had enough of the tour." Nora felt panicky.

"It's just a bedroom."

"I'm getting claustrophobic. Is there anywhere on this floating palace where we can just sit and talk?"

"There's a small deck in the bow of the boat. It's real private. I don't think Lew knows about it. When I want to get some sun—like all over—I go there."

Nora grinned. "The sun's set, but let's give it a try." She followed Gigi past the main cabin. Through the portholes, she could see that the party had divided into two groups. Victor Ashland and Bobbi Weeks were chatting with Mark and Pat and Cousin Leonard. Lew Dobbs and Stanley Tseng surrounded Ali. Ali's face and body language were teasing, seductive, animated as she played one man off against the other. Past the crew's quarters, the deck grew narrow.

"Be careful," Gigi warned. "Don't want you falling in the drink. The bay smells real bad."

"The bay stinks."

At the bow of the boat was a small deck . . . about six feet square. Half the space was taken up by an inflated rubber mat.

"My hideaway," Gigi said. "Lew's a big load. Once in a while, I got to put it down." With a single fluid motion, she dropped to the mat, her legs tucked beneath her. She patted the space next to her. "Set yourself," she said. "It's nice here."

Nora joined her. Her movements were equally supple.

The women sat quietly for minutes . . . each waiting for the other to say something.

Nora finally acknowledged she was in a losing position . . . she was more curious about Gigi than Gigi was about her. She took a deep breath. "Sorry about the stupid crack I made earlier."

"What crack?"

"About your meeting the planes."

Gigi shrugged. "It wasn't stupid. It's what I do."

"You don't work?"

"Sure I work. If you think meeting the planes isn't work, you're wrong." She smiled. "I'm very good at what I do."

"I'm sure you are," Nora said. "You've got a great figure. When I was a teenager, I always wanted to have a figure like yours. I still do."

"And I wanted to be tall and slim like you. Kind o' aristocratic looking."

"Why? Men prefer your figure to mine."

"I guess most men do," Gigi admitted. "They go for the sizzle . . . the package."

Nora was startled. "You sound like a friend of mine. He told me men confuse the package with the product."

"You got a smart friend. Did he also tell you once the package is opened, it's thrown away?"

Nora shook her head.

"It is. Believe me. I know."

Nora said nothing.

"Mickey and I didn't last long."

"Mickey?"

"My ex. I got married at sixteen. Didn't know shit about sex. I just spread my legs and he banged away. It only took him two months to get bored."

"Couldn't he have . . . "

"Taught me how to make love?" Gigi shook her head. "Maybe he could have, but he wasn't interested. Or maybe he didn't know how himself. Mickey was a chaser. He chased women. I think he enjoyed chasing them as much as catching them. When I caught on, we had a fight. He beat me up real bad. Put me in the hospital. Then he hightailed it out of Phoenix. Fast. At least once a week I go look at the tire marks he left running away."

"You mean the skid marks on the road?"

"That's what I mean. Black, burned-rubber marks. They're still there. Those black lines help me keep my priorities straight. I know I can get left. But now it isn't because the product isn't as good as the package. I'm very good at what I do."

"You mean driving?" Nora was off balance.

Gigi glanced at Nora. Nora looked back. Their eyes met in a mute exchange of sympathy and understanding.

"You know what I mean, Mrs. Stern. I mean fucking."

Nora swallowed.

"Now when a man leaves me it's not because I don't know my business."

"Why is it then?" Nora held her breath.

"Because sometimes they love their wives . . ."

"Ah . . ."

"And sometimes I send them back."

"You what!"

Nora listened as Gigi explained the rules by which she lived. When she finished, Nora knew why Mark had taken a direct flight from Kennedy to San Diego. Again she knew more than she wanted to know. "The men who love their wives? Why do they . . ."

"Climb into bed with me?"

Nora nodded.

"Look, Mrs. Stern . . ."

"Nora. My name is Nora."

"Okay. You see, Nora. For me there are two kinds of men." Gigi chose her words carefully. "Most men—and women, for that matter—can meet someone. Like me, for instance. If the timing is right they fall into bed. The next morning, they go their own ways. No harm done, and a good time was had by all. But then there are the chasers. A chaser is always looking for women. Sometimes, when the man is attracted to the package, he sticks around for a while. But soon he's off to the races . . . on the next chase. He never quits.''

"What about the product?" Nora asked. "Suppose he really likes the product?"

"A chaser can't tell the difference. If he could, he wouldn't be a chaser."

Nora thought of her father. Barron was a chaser. While caressing a woman, he would glance over her shoulder. Who else was around? Was Mark a chaser? She wanted to ask Gigi. She couldn't. Mark was off-limits.

Gigi stretched and rose to her feet. "I got to be getting back. Lew'll be wondering what happened to me. And I don't want him to come looking for me. You can stay. You probably want to think about what I said."

Nora rose. "I'll go back with you. I'll tell Lew we had a girl-to-girl chat."

"Lew'll like that."

Nora and Gigi looked at each other and both began to giggle. They could read each other's mind. Lew Dobbs might like their having a heart-to-heart chat. Mark would have a hemorrhage.

Dinner consisted of a variety of dishes from the sea. Shrimp, scallops, Maine lobster. And a choice of vegetables. Bottles of red and white wine and Mexican beer were passed around the table. Ali entertained with stories about movie people. Stories she could only have picked up from Ken Savage. Who was sleeping with whom. Who was pregnant and had an abortion. Who was pregnant and didn't have an abortion . . . even though her husband was not the father. Who had paid off his male lover to save his macho image. Everyone except for Mark and Stanley Tseng laughed in the right places. Nora had never seen Mark look so uncomfortable. Stanley Tseng simply wasn't interested. Then, as Ali took a breath, Nora saw Stanley Tseng motion for her to quit. Ali stopped playing hostess. Lew Dobbs took over. He told how he'd acquired several TV channels . . . a combination of money, persistence and intimidation. Nora watched Tseng smile . . . he approved of intimidation. Victor Ashland also smiled. But Bobbi Weeks played with a sharp fruit knife. She looked as though she might climb over the table and go for Lew.

Nora was finishing her second cup of coffee when Ali tapped her on the shoulder.

"Let's take a turn around the deck. I have a dreadful story to tell you. About what Mark did to me."

Nora glanced at Mark. He seemed in a trance . . . his eyes were burning holes in the bottom of his coffee cup. She rose and left with Ali. What else had he done? Wasn't Gigi enough?

As they walked around the deck, Ali told Nora how she'd spent a week at the Golden Door. When she returned, her beautiful condo was stripped bare.

"It was naked," Ali said with one of her practiced half sobs. "Everything was gone . . . except for my bed. The furniture, the rugs, the paintings. Everything."

Nora was all sympathy. "That's terrible. What did the police say?"

"I didn't call the police. I was going to. Then I found a note on my bed . . ."

"A note?"

"From Mark. It was a very strange note. He said he'd left the bed because my bed is my office, where I work. If I worked hard, I might make enough money to buy my own furniture. What did he mean by that?"

Nora couldn't help laughing. "You know what he meant."

"It was a disgusting suggestion." Ali couldn't suppress a giggle. "I'm a gifted amateur, not a professional. Mark had no right to steal my things."

Nora stopped walking. She leaned against the railing and looked hard at Ali. "They aren't your things, Ali. They never were."

"I selected every piece in that condo. I poured myself into the tables and paintings and—"

"You didn't pay for them."

"Well . . . no . . . Of course not. Arthur paid for the furnishings. He was my husband. That's what a husband is supposed to do . . . furnish the house."

"Stop it, Ali. The way I understand it, Arthur didn't pay for the things you bought."

"Of course he did."

"Of course he didn't. Mark told me Reiner & Co. paid for everything."

"It's the same thing. Arthur Reiner and Reiner & Co."

"It's not the same thing, and you know it. Reiner & Co. paid for the furnishings. Reiner & Co. owns the furnishings."

"And I suppose Mark didn't have the best pieces shipped to your house?"

Nora grew indignant. "He didn't, and he'd better not. He arranged for Christie's to auction them off."

"Everything?" Ali sniffed. She was back in her poor pitiful Pearl role.

"Everything."

Ali made a disgusted face. Then, in one of her typically abrupt mood shifts, she smiled. "When I married Arthur, I did one smart thing. I kept my beautiful condo in Hillcrest. And I completely furnished it."

"Did Reiner & Co. also pay for those furnishings?"

"None of your business. You'd tell Mark," Ali pouted.

"No . . ."

"Ah. There you are. I wondered what happened to you." Stanley Tseng crossed the deck. He glanced at the downtown San Diego skyline. "Are you admiring the view? It's not Hong Kong, but it is . . . shall we say interesting?"

Nora resented his patronizing tone. "You're right," she shot back. "San Diego is not Hong Kong. But it will still be part of the United States in 1998."

"Touché." Tseng smiled. "Sad but true. By 1998, the sun will have set on still another part of the British empire."

"You should move your money from Hong Kong to America," Ali chirped.

Tseng placed his fingers on Ali's lips. "Ssssh, Little Dove. You must not talk about money. Your talents lie in other areas."

Nora waited for the explosion . . . there was none.

"Speaking of money, tell me, Nora . . ." He stared hard at her. "Why won't your grandmother sell her station to my good friend Lew Dobbs?"

"Speaking of money, why should she sell it?" Nora asked.

"For a good deal of money. The best reason to sell anything."

"Grandmother doesn't need more money."

"Ah. A strange attitude. In the real world, everyone needs more money. And everything has a certain value. If one is offered more than the value of a possession, logically one should sell."

"Money is only one way to measure value," Nora said.

"Nora, don't be stubborn. It's the best way," Ali insisted. "If you'd like me to, I'll help you persuade Millie. Together we can't miss. We'll change her mind, and—"

"Stay out of this, Ali," Nora flared. "I don't want to change Millie's mind."

"You are against the sale?" Tseng asked.

"Flat-out against it. So don't waste your breath on me."

"How sad. I suggest, Nora, that you learn to change your mind. The winds of change are blowing. If one doesn't bend to them, one can be broken."

In the dim light, Nora could not see Tseng's face. But his tone was chilling. "Mr. Tseng, are you threatening me?"

The voice was soft. Caressing. "No, Nora. I never threaten. I am advising you. . . ."

Nora brought the tips of her fingers together. "Mr. Tseng, now I'm curious. Why do you care if my grandmother sells Channel 18 to Dobbs?"

"Lew is an old friend. I enjoy doing favors for my friends."

"Like making the winds of change blow?"

Tseng smiled and shrugged. "If you believe it to be so . . . then it is so."

Nora stepped closer to Tseng. Her temper was rising. "Listen to me, sir. I will not advise my grandmother to sell Channel 18. Not to Lew Dobbs. Or anyone else. And as for your winds of change, call them off. Or the Gardiner family will change your life. And not for the better."

"Nora!" Ali exclaimed.

"Don't Nora me, Ali. I don't know why you want Millie to sell, and I don't care. But as long as I have anything to say, she won't sell. Have I made myself clear?"

As Nora stalked toward the main cabin, she heard Stanley Tseng's voice. "Very clear, Mrs. Stern. Very clear indeed."

Mark didn't talk as they drove home.

"I like Lew's girlfriend," Nora said. "What's her name?"

"Gigi. I think."

"That's right. Gigi. We had a short talk. She's smart and nice. How long will Dobbs be in San Diego?"

"I don't know. Why?"

"We could invite Dobbs and Gigi to dinner. It would be an interesting evening."

Mark glanced at Nora. Her face was guileless. He didn't know what to think.

Nora tried two dates for her proposed dinner. Mark vetoed both. He had reasons. His reasons had reasons why neither date worked. Nora enjoyed watching him squirm . . . and admired his inventiveness. After the third vetoed date, the game lost its fun. It was too sad and too serious. She stopped ticking off dates and lapsed into an anxious silence. She remembered Stanley Tseng's words. He was right. The winds of change were blowing. Over all their lives. Nothing was the same today as it had been even six months ago. Not Mark . . . or her feelings for him . . . or even her idea of herself. Then there was Ali. In an odd, frightening way, Ali was the biggest change of all. Mark was simply a standard-issue unfaithful husband. Ali was stranger. For no reason she could give, Nora felt a twinge of alarm. Was it her imagination? Probably. Except that Ali was connected to Fu Manchu Tseng. Thinking that over, Nora felt real fear.

PART 9

Millie and Nora
1993

Chapter 22

MILLIE PICKED up her cards and arranged them. She was an experienced bridge player . . . it was impossible to tell by watching her sort her hand how many cards she had in each suit.

Mindy Wolff opened the bidding. "One spade," she said.

"Pass. I haven't had a single decent hand all night," Ali complained.

The Wolffs looked pained. Ali had committed a bridge no-no. If the Wolffs won the bidding, whichever one of them played the hand would play Millie for the missing high cards . . . finesse through Millie, end-play Millie, squeeze Millie. And if Millie happened to have a strong hand, Ali's comment warned Millie not to expect much support from her partner.

"Two spades," Eugene Wolff said. He had only five points and a three-card spade suit . . . barely enough to make the bid. If Ali had kept her mouth shut, he might have passed. As it was, his major reason for the two-spade bid was to make it more difficult for Millie to enter the bidding.

"Two no-trump," Millie said. She was asking Ali to bid her strongest suit, no matter how poor a hand she had.

Mindy was a fine bridge player. She said, "Three spades." That would shut Ali out of the bidding. Whatever Millie did, she'd have to do it without any information from her partner.

Ali grimaced. "Pass."

"I pass," Eugene said.

Millie rubbed her chin with the knuckles of her hand. "Five diamonds," she said.

"Double." Millie and Ali were vulnerable. With the ace and king of spades, the ace and king of clubs and a protected queen of diamonds, she envisioned a nice five-hundred-point penalty . . . at the least.

Ali shook her head. "I'm sorry, Millie. I have to pass."

Millie put her cards facedown on the table. "Ali . . ."
Her voice showed her irritation. "I know you can't do anything about the cards you're dealt, but you *can* keep your
mouth shut."

Ali looked properly contrite. She'd been so delighted when
Millie invited her to make a fourth at her weekly bridge game.
She looked forward to showing Millie how well she played.
But all night she'd had such terrible hands, she never had a
chance to show off for Millie. It didn't occur to her that the
thing about bridge is that one can play well even with poor
cards. Defending against a difficult contract takes as much
ability as making the difficult contract.

"Pass," Eugene Wolff said. He hoped Mindy could use
his two queens and a jack.

"Redouble," Millie said.

Mindy blinked and passed.

Ali studied her hand again. She opened her mouth . . .
and closed it. One warning from Millie was enough. But
Millie would forgive her. Her distribution was a perfect fit
for Millie's hand.

Ali passed. So did Eugene. Mindy led the king of spades.
When Ali put down her hand, the Wolffs knew they were in
trouble. Ali had five diamonds, five spades and three hearts.
Although Ali had no points, she was void in clubs and had a
long spade suit. Obviously, Millie was void in spades. The
Wolffs were going to be cross-ruffed to death. And they were.
In the end, they made one trick . . . Mindy's protected queen
of diamonds.

"Five diamonds, doubled and redoubled, plus an overtrick," Millie crowed. "Let's see. That's four hundred points
for the game, eighty points for the overtrick and seven hundred points for the rubber." She totaled the score and added
it to the running total for the evening. "Not bad," she said.
"We've played ten rubbers and the damage is just under five
thousand points. At a penny a point, we each owe Mindy
and Eugene fifty dollars, Ali." Now that the game had ended,
her irritation at Ali appeared to have evaporated. She stood
up. "Would anyone like a nightcap?"

"No, thank you," Mindy said. "Eugene has to drive.
Carlsbad isn't that far, but still . . ."

"You don't want to risk it. Of course," Millie said. She
looked at Ali.

Ali's musical laugh had the ping of crystal. "I'll risk it," she said. "We can have a little gossip."

"That would be pleasant. Wait here. I'll show Mindy and Eugene out."

"You don't have to do that," Eugene protested.

"I want to," Millie said. She slipped her arms under Mindy's and Eugene's and guided them from the enclosed porch. When she returned, she asked Ali, "What can I get you?"

"Cognac—Remy Martin—and soda."

Millie nodded. "That sounds good to me." She went to the portable bar Oscar had set up in the enclosed porch and made the two drinks. After handing one to Ali, she suggested they take a turn around the pool. "It's a warm night. I can use a breath of air."

"So can I," Ali said. She smiled, and as always her face lit up. "I have several juicy stories you may not have already heard." Her tone hinted at the salacious. She was playing on Millie's well-known love of any kind of gossip.

The women stepped onto the terrace and down the few steps that led to the wading pool. As they strolled around the pool, they sipped their drinks. Ali was in no hurry. Juicy gossip does not become overripe and spoil if it is not told immediately. It ages like a good steak and becomes all the more titillating when finally whispered. She waited until they'd taken a complete turn around the pool.

"Millie, I went to a party on a yacht last week," she said.

"Did you?" Millie said. "I'm sure the party was very interesting, but it can wait."

Ali picked up a note in Millie's voice. It suddenly occurred to her that she hadn't been invited to make a fourth at bridge because of how well she played bridge. She waited for Millie to continue.

"Some time ago Jordan Banska told me something I found hard to believe. So I looked into it. Unfortunately he turned out to be correct."

Ali continued to sip her drink.

"The story Jordan told me had to do with you. . . ."

"Me!" Ali finished her cognac and soda . . . she could have used another.

"You and Ken Savage."

"Oh, that!" Ali scoffed.

"Oh, that!" Millie expertly mimicked Ali's tone. "Your

little adventure with Ken Savage cost me one and a half million dollars.''

"One and a half million . . . How?''

"Tammi found out.''

"Tammi always knew about us,'' Ali protested.

"Not exactly. The way I understand it, Tammi knew about you and Savage at Nora's party. . . .''

"Nora told you.''

"Only after Jordan spilled the beans.''

As they continued to walk, Millie glanced at Ali. Her trained ear had picked up a hint of deep-rooted jealousy— even hatred—in Ali's voice. To be filed for future examination. So many of her hopes rested on Nora and Ali remaining close . . . as close as sisters.

"Nora had no right—''

Millie interrupted her. "Listen to me, Ali. Nora had every right to tell me the facts. She was not being judgmental. Neither am I. I don't care if you sleep with half the marines in Camp Pendleton. But I do care that your romp with Savage cost me a lot of money. And more important, it threatened 'Night of Stars.' It still does. You and Savage are meeting in Malibu, and Tammi is furious. I want you to stop the nonsense and stop it now.''

"My goodness, Millie. I never realized you took such an interest in my love affairs.''

"Only when your love affairs get in my way.''

"I wouldn't deliberately hurt you for the world.'' Ali oozed sympathy and understanding. "But actually Nora has it all wrong. So wrong it's really quite amusing.''

"What is? You and Ken?''

"Yes. Ken and I. And Nora. I would love to promise that I'll stop seeing Ken. But I can't.''

"You can't? Or you won't?''

"I can't. It's a matter of tenses. How can I promise to stop doing something in the future when I've already stopped doing it?''

"You and Savage are no longer . . . ?''

"More than a month ago.'' Ali waved the ring finger of her right hand in front of Millie's nose. "Look,'' she gloated.

"I noticed the emerald when we were playing bridge. It's a nice stone.''

"Nice! It's beautiful! A gift from an admirer.''

"Other than Ken Savage?"

"Oh, Millie." Ali laughed. "Ken Savage does not give expensive presents to women. If he was sure Tammi wouldn't find out, he'd have the women pay him . . . for services rendered. He really is very good."

Millie nodded. "It's a talent. Now I am curious. Who's your latest conquest?"

"That's part of what I wanted to tell you. Stanley Tseng gave me the ring. I think he'll ask me to marry him." There was more wishful thinking than confidence in Ali's words.

"Don't get your hopes too high," Millie said. "From what I understand, Tseng is a Hong Kong businessman. In his case, *businessman* is a polite word for *barracuda*. He uses people . . . men and women. I don't think he's marriageable. He may even be already married."

"No, Millie. I'm sure he's not married. And he is kind. He often goes out of his way to help his friends."

"So there's another side to him. The Good Samaritan. How does he help his friends?"

"Well, take Lew Dobbs, for example."

Millie made a face. "I'd rather not."

In her eagerness to say what she'd been told to say, Ali ran roughshod over Millie's reaction. "Stanley knows all about Lew's offer for Channel 18."

"Lord! Why didn't Dobbs take out an ad in the *Wall Street Journal*? Is there anyone who doesn't know about his offer?"

"Stanley thinks the offer is more than fair . . . it's generous."

"It may be generous," Millie admitted.

"Then why is Nora so set against your selling the channel?"

Millie knew exactly why, but her curiosity was aroused. What was Ali's interpretation? "Suppose you tell me."

"Nora doesn't care what's best for you," Ali stated firmly. "She has a cushy job, and she wants to hang on to it."

Millie heard again Ali's deep resentment of Nora . . . this time more overtly expressed. She smothered her dismay. "I don't believe that, Ali. Nora is very good at what she does. She could easily get as good a job with another channel."

"Then she's a very poor businesswoman."

"How would you know? Are you such a good businesswoman?"

"Me!" Ali chuckled. "Lord no! I wouldn't know a good business deal if it hit me between the eyes. Unless it was a piece of jewelry or an antique table. But I trust Mark's judgment. He's a good businessman. If a little . . ." Ali grinned knowingly and wiggled her hand. "Shall we say, tricky?"

Millie raised an eyebrow, but she didn't pick up on the word. Instead she said, "Mark thinks I should sell the station?"

"Oh, yes."

Millie's smile was sarcastic. She remembered how hard Arthur Reiner had pressed her to sell. Why wouldn't he? Reiner & Co. would earn well over a half million dollars if she sold out. "Do you think Mark has an impartial opinion?"

Ali was unreceptive to nuances . . . except her own. "Mark knows what's best for you. That's why he's in favor of your selling."

"You don't think the fee he'd earn would influence his judgment?"

"Not where you're concerned. And Mark is so bright. I've always admired his business sense. Even if he cuts corners."

"That's the second time tonight you've said Mark isn't quite straight. How do you know he cuts corners?"

"I was married to Arthur Reiner. Arthur said Mark was good but he must be watched." Ali giggled and licked her lips. She'd come to the second half of her instructions. "I find men fascinating. Arthur and Mark were so much alike. They were both committed to making money and to sleeping with as many women as possible. Mark has picked up where Arthur left off."

"Are you saying that Mark sleeps around?"

"Oh, Millie . . . Remember, I mentioned the party on the yacht? There was a girl there named Gigi Something or other. Now she's Lew Dobbs's girl. Before Lew she was Mark's girl."

"How do you know that?"

"I got it straight from the horse's mouth . . . from Lew himself."

"Gigi Something or other gets around," Millie said dryly.

"Mark's had other women before Gigi."

Millie almost asked if Ali was one of the other women. She didn't. She didn't want to know.

"That's why Mark is so fascinating. He's smart. He's borderline dishonest. And compulsively unfaithful. You never know what he'll do.''

"Do you think Nora would agree with your description of Mark? Or find it interesting?"

Ali pouted. "No. Nora is blind. She has to be. She takes little flaws in people too seriously. She's so uptight. If she really understood Mark, she'd be miserable."

"You wouldn't mind having a husband who is compulsively unfaithful? You wouldn't get uptight about a little flaw like that?" Millie asked.

Ali thought about Arthur and made a quick shift. She smiled. "I don't think so. I modeled myself after you. You're not uptight about anything."

Millie couldn't help smiling. It was so easy to underestimate Ali. Just when you think she's painted herself into a corner, she comes up with a sly way of flattering you. "I am uptight about a few things, Ali." Millie looked at her watch. "It's almost midnight. I must be at the stables tomorrow morning at seven."

Ali looked properly abashed. "I've kept you up too late. I'm sorry. But please do me a favor. Think about Lew Dobbs's offer. I know it's a generous one."

"I'll think about it, Ali."

After she showed Ali out, Millie returned to her bathroom and turned on the indoor Jacuzzi. Ali's description of Mark had disturbed her far more than Ali had guessed. Compulsively unfaithful was bad enough. She remembered Max and their marriage all too well. Neither Max nor she believed in monogamy. But borderline dishonest was far worse. As she undressed, she thought about Mark and Nora. Did Nora love Mark because he was so like Barron? She hoped not. She stepped into the Jacuzzi and relaxed as the water and air jets gently massaged her body. As she slipped into a half-awake, dreamlike state, Barron's face drifted into her mind's eye. Handsome as a movie star, energetic, brilliant, daring . . . on the brink of a brilliant Wall Street career. With one flaw . . . a flaw that had turned out to be fatal.

Millie would never forget that disastrous morning. She was having a late breakfast when she heard the phone ring. She continued eating her bacon and eggs . . . either Oscar or Rosa would pick it up.

Rosa bustled into the breakfast nook carrying a telephone. "Madam, it's Mr. Barron. He says he must speak to you." She plugged the phone into a jack next to Millie's chair. "On line two."

"Thank you, Rosa." Millie picked up the receiver. "What is it, Barron? Why aren't you on the floor of the exchange?"

"I think I've done myself in," Barron said. His usual self-mocking tone was strained.

"How?"

"I'd rather tell you in person. If you're not busy, I could be there in about thirty minutes."

"I'll expect you." Millie had an appointment for a dress fitting that she would cancel immediately.

"Thank you," Barron said.

Millie hung up the phone. What on earth had he done that was so disastrous?

When Barron arrived, he didn't bother to say hello. He plunged into his story. He talked and talked. Feverishly. Millie, who was seasoned on the workings of Wall Street, got the gist of what had happened immediately. Barron had arranged for the private sale of a large amount of unregistered stock. Both the buyer's and seller's companies were important customers . . . there was a juicy commission in it for Barron's firm. If he hadn't played the fool. The Gardiner Company—his company—had neglected to register the stock with the SEC. Nor did it file a 146 Private Placement with the SEC. It did nothing. It simply sold the unregistered stock. A criminal offense.

"How could you be so careless about a business transaction?" Millie asked.

"Well . . ." Barron fidgeted. "The seller, Ralph Bedwell, has a beautiful wife. Sally Bedwell. We snuck away for ten days to Puerto Rico."

"Ralph Bedwell didn't object?"

"The Bedwells have an arrangement. While we were at Dorado Beach, the sale of the stock was completed."

"You never saw the stock certificates . . . the typed-in legend?"

Barron shook his head. "No. I was having too much fun. It never occurred to me that anything might be out of order. I told my assistant to finalize the sale of the stock. And I left . . ."

"Tell me the truth, Barron." Millie's voice was stern. "Did Bedwell tell you the stock was unregistered?"

"He never said a word. If he had, I wouldn't have arranged for the sale. I know selling unregistered stock is a criminal offense."

"He wanted to sell the stock fast?" Millie's face was stony.

"Very fast. His company was tight for cash. That's why he hadn't registered the stock. It takes over a year for the SEC to approve a registration. Even a one-forty-six takes at least six months."

Millie was scrambling for answers. "Barron, think. If you can prove he didn't tell you the stock was unregistered, he goes to jail. Not you."

"How can I prove a negative? He says he told me. I say he didn't." Barron looked whipped.

"So it comes down to whose word the SEC believes?"

Barron had the grace to look embarrassed. "Not quite. Sally says she heard Ralph tell me the stock was unregistered."

"Sally? The woman you took to Dorado Beach?"

Barron nodded.

"The woman who has an arrangement with her husband?"

Barron looked grim.

"That's some arrangement. They took you, Barron. You've been had."

"I know."

"The question you must ask yourself is, Was the fucking you got worth the fucking you're going to get?" There was no humor in Millie's smile.

The trial was quick. A securities fraud had been committed . . . someone had to take the fall. Not Bedwell. Not the buyer. Barron was the obvious choice. He was found guilty of selling unregistered stock. Punishable by a fine of two hundred fifty thousand dollars and/or a prison term of one and a half to three years. After listening to the verdict, Millie decided it was time to call in a marker.

On the morning of Barron's sentencing, Oscar drove her to 100 Center Street . . . the criminal courts building. A clerk ushered her through a side door into Judge Aaron Sonnenberg's chambers.

The judge was a man in his sixties, portly, with thick white hair. He was in his shirtsleeves . . . his judicial robe was hanging on a coat tree next to the door that led to his court. He stood up to greet Millie.

"It's been too long, Mrs. Stein," he murmured.

Millie gently corrected him. "Mrs. Gardiner. I now use my first husband's name."

"Mrs. Gardiner."

"Yes, it has been too long. But New York is such a busy city. It's difficult to keep up with all one's friends."

The judge flushed slightly at being referred to as a friend by Millie Thorne Gardiner Stein. "Please sit down," he said. "You know, if you weren't you, I would never have agreed to see you. Not this morning anyway."

"But I am me and that makes it all right." She smiled at the judge. "Leo often said if I ever needed a favor, I should ask Aaron Sonnenberg."

"Leo . . ." The judge stroked his jaw thoughtfully. "Leo Stein. A very impressive man."

"You know, Aaron, Leo was very meticulous. He kept meticulous records—canceled checks and the like—long after the IRS requires."

Judge Sonnenberg sighed. "Of course, you have those checks."

"Of course."

"Mrs. Gardiner. Leo has been dead many years. What is it you want of me?"

Millie smiled appealingly. The sweet, foolish widow. "My son, Barron, did a stupid thing. He allowed his hobby to interfere with his business."

"I don't follow you."

"Barron's hobby is women. His business is Wall Street. Instead of minding the store, he was indulging his hobby."

"Ah. The beautiful Mrs. Bedwell. The jury didn't believe your son's story. Why should I?"

"The jury had nothing to gain by believing Barron. You do."

Judge Aaron Sonnenberg looked hard at Millie.

"Judge, do you remember when you were an assistant district attorney?"

"I remember, Mrs. Gardiner. Very clearly. Are we going to talk about the parking meters?"

"Yes. Some five thousand parking meters that Leo sold to the city."

"Mrs. Gardiner. I agreed with your late husband, with Leo Stein, that there was nothing to the rumor that the traffic commissioner had been . . . er . . . shall we say, handsomely taken care of to accept the bid of a firm Leo controlled. I investigated the matter," the judge said huffily, "and I dropped the case. Those parking meters were the finest that could be bought. They're still in use."

Millie raised her hand. "Please, Judge Sonnenberg. We both know Leo had his own way of getting things done, but no one—not even his worst enemies—ever claimed that he provided the city with less than the best."

"A great man."

Millie bowed her head for a moment, in silent memory of the late, great Leo Stein. "Still," she said, "you could have embarrassed him."

"I chose not to."

"That's right. And in return Leo set up two bank accounts. Fifty thousand dollars was deposited in each account. The money paid for the college educations of both your sons. I understand your older son is now an assistant district attorney . . . he's following in his father's footsteps. And your younger son is in the State Department. It would be awkward for both boys if . . ."

"I can't overrule the jury and find your son innocent." There was a frantic, pleading note in Judge Sonnenberg's voice. He had no idea what Millie would ask.

"Judge." Millie sounded bereaved. "You surprise me. Would I ask for something impossible?" Millie was now the judge. "No. You can't find him innocent. He isn't innocent. But you can fine Barron the maximum . . . two hundred fifty thousand dollars. And you can sentence him to one and a half to three years." Her sense of the theatrical made her pause for a moment. "Then you can suspend the sentence."

"Suspend the sentence?"

Millie nodded. "You can suspend the sentence."

There was a heavy silence. Finally the judge said, "If I do this, you will hand deliver Leo's checks to me."

"That's part of our arrangement." She would, as a matter of good business practice, make photocopies.

After a few seconds' deliberation—was there any way out? . . . there wasn't—Judge Sonnenberg agreed.

Millie concentrated on Barron as he stood to be sentenced. He stood ramrod straight, his eyes fastened on the judge. Considering that he didn't know the fix was in, he was behaving admirably.

Barron listened as the judge set the fine . . . and nodded. He kept listening as the judge sentenced him to prison. He again nodded. Only when the judge suspended the prison sentence did he show any emotion. He looked straight at Millie . . . his eyes were moist. Millie risked a small smile. Barron looked away . . . across the courtroom at something that wasn't there. He knew she'd gotten him off. He didn't know how she'd gotten to the judge, but he knew she had. That was why the judge had suspended his sentence. And he hated her for it.

Millie was suddenly aware of what she'd done. Catching the desolate look on Barron's face, she saw with startling clarity her monumental blunder. With the best of intentions, with care and compassion, she'd injured her own son. Barron had wanted to go to jail . . . to pay for his self-indulgence. Jail would have been a kind of purification. But her meddling had hobbled his pride, destroyed his sense of himself as a man who could accept responsibility for his mistakes. She'd only wanted to minimize the damage. Instead she'd made it worse. Millie gasped at the damage she'd done with her act of unwanted mercy. Would she ever forgive herself? Would Barron ever forgive her?

Barron had one last price to pay. The New York Stock Exchange barred him from trading securities . . . other than for his own account. But his brilliant career was over. He would never be a power on Wall Street. Worse. His pride— his sense of self—was shattered.

With an effort, Millie roused herself . . . returning to the present. She'd been in the hot water so long her fingers were wrinkled. As she dried herself, she continued to think about Barron. The disaster had broken his nerve, his confidence in his ability to handle the rough-and-tumble of the Street. Even his personal investments did poorly. He retreated to the only safe haven he knew . . . women. His hobby, women, became his career. And what had been his career, Wall Street, be-came his hobby. But all that was long ago. Now the shadow moves, Millie thought. And there is Mark. Who might or might not be as bad as Ali claimed. Either way, Millie knew she must stay out of Nora's life . . . not interfere. She'd say nothing to Nora. Nothing to Mark. Nothing to anyone. She'd watch and wait. She didn't mean to make the same mistake twice.

Chapter 23

IN THE beginning, Millie seldom used the cottage at Spa Pacifica. But in the last few years, she felt more and more often the need for the peace and tranquillity of the cottage. Her headaches were becoming increasingly severe and they exhausted her. Recently a new and ominous symptom had appeared. Along with the headaches, she would suddenly get very cold and weak, her teeth would chatter, her hands and arms would tremble violently. Even her stomach shook. The fits never lasted long. But when they gripped her, no matter how hard she tried, she was unable to control the shaking. It was as though she was in the advanced stages of Parkinson's disease. She wasn't, but the symptoms were strikingly similar. Every morning she offered a prayer: "Do not let this happen to me in public." So far the Lord had granted her wish . . . she hoped he would continue to be merciful.

On this visit, Millie had been at the spa for ten days . . . resting, doing mild exercises, husbanding her strength. The night before she planned to leave, she went on a Moon Walk. The gravel paths that wound among the hills surrounding Spa Pacifica were plentiful. Rarely did one encounter another Moon Walker. The theory was that the magic of moonlight worked best on those who walked alone. Rounding a bend in the path, Millie was surprised to see a figure standing a short distance off. Not recognizing the woman, she was prepared to walk silently around her. But as she passed, she realized it was Dorothea Reiner. She couldn't ignore Dorothea . . . not even on a Moon Walk.

Millie stopped and asked softly, "Are you enjoying the moon?"

"What!" Dorothea shook herself out of her reverie. "Oh! Millie. It's you."

Millie started to smile, then her smile closed on itself.

391

Dorothea did not look well. She had always been a large, robust woman . . . energetic almost to a fault. Now she looked gaunt and exhausted. Millie got the impression that every movement Dorothea made, every gesture, was accomplished only by a great exercise of will.

Tentatively, Dorothea took hold of Millie's arm. It was as though she was afraid Millie was a creature of her imagination and—if she released Millie's arm—Millie would silently melt into the darkness. Dorothea pointed to a stone bench a short distance along the path. "Sit with me, please," she entreated. She was actually pleading.

Millie had never heard Dorothea plead for anything. "Of course," she said in a gentle voice.

As the women walked the few feet to the bench, Dorothea continued to cling to Millie's arm. And when they sat silently on the bench, Dorothea still did not release her arm. Millie was prepared to wait as long as necessary. She would play by Dorothea's rules.

After a few minutes, Dorothea said, "Thank you for staying with me."

Millie shrugged. "I was happy to find a reason for resting. Moon Walks can be tiring."

There was another short silence. Then Dorothea said, "I know this is a rude question, but how old are you, Millie? You seem ageless, but no one is ageless."

Millie smiled. "Let's say I'm too old to play Juliet and not old enough to challenge Methuselah."

It wasn't an answer, but it seemed to satisfy Dorothea. "I'm fifty-three going on one hundred. When your son, Barron, died in that terrible accident, how did you survive?"

"Mothers have survived the deaths of their children for as long as they've been giving birth."

"I know. But what did you do?"

"I mourned. And every day I reminded myself that I had another son and granddaughters."

"Granddaughters?"

"Nora. And Ali too." Millie quickly added, "Ali isn't my granddaughter by blood. But sometimes it's easier to think of her that way."

"I'm glad she's not really your granddaughter," Dorothea whispered. "I have Roger. He hasn't helped."

"What hasn't he helped?"

"He hasn't helped me get over Arthur's death. It's so strange. For years—when Arthur and I were married—I didn't care what he did. We lived our own lives. We were more like friendly strangers than husband and wife. And when he met Ali, I didn't try to break it up. Actually I was pleased. I even encouraged Arthur to marry her. I thought, At last I'm free of Arthur. What a fool I was."

"A lot of women have discovered freedom can be lonely," Millie said. "It's cold out there."

"I'm not lonely. I've had too much money for too long to be lonely. A rich woman who complains of being lonely usually complains because she thinks that men want her for her money. Often they do. But what she doesn't realize is that she and her money are one. They're joined at the hip. There's no difference between a man wanting a woman for her pretty face, large bosom and long legs and a man wanting a woman for her money. Except a pretty face ages, a large bosom sags, long legs get varicose veins. But money . . . money lasts forever. Much longer than a face-lift or a body-lift."

"I seem to be missing something," Millie said.

"Ali. You're missing Ali."

"Ali?"

"I'm sorry, Millie, but she's a dreadful woman. I'm sorry she's related to you . . . even by marriage. I was right to divorce Arthur. But I'm terribly sorry I let him marry Ali. It was the worst mistake I ever made."

"Why?"

"Because she murdered Arthur."

"What!"

"I blame myself for what happened. I can't sleep. I can't eat. I've cut myself off from all my friends. My lovers. I know Roger is worried about me, but I can't help myself. Guilt is a terrible thing."

"Dorothea," Millie said firmly, "Ali did not murder Arthur. Arthur died of a heart attack."

"Yes and no. Yes, technically he died of a heart attack. But, no. He didn't have to die of that heart attack."

"You'd better tell me what you're talking about."

"I want to. There's no one I want to tell about it more than you. I have to warn you."

Millie made a face. "Please, Dorothea. Just the facts . . . no melodrama."

"You want the facts. Fine. Here are the facts. I was talking on the telephone to Arthur when he had his attack."

Millie listened, her face a mask.

"He told me he'd hired the detective I'd suggested, and he had all the evidence he needed to divorce Ali. I heard Ali scream, 'I'll never divorce you. Never.' They had a terrible fight. Violent."

"A violent fight? What do you mean?"

"Arthur shouted, 'Stop hitting me. Damn it! Stop it! You know what the doctor said.' I heard Ali laugh. Arthur must have held the phone close to his body. I could actually hear the sound of her punching him. I think on his chest. I was terrified."

Millie nodded. Beneath her mask was a grim fear.

"Then I heard Arthur choke. 'I can't breathe,' he said. 'The pressure. It's crushing me.' Arthur asked Ali to hurry and bring him his pills. 'Which pills, darling?' Ali said. 'You have so many.' Arthur said she knew which pills. I heard poor Arthur gasping for breath. Then he fell to the floor. Ali picked up the phone and said, 'Good-bye, Dorothea.' She hung up."

"What did you do?" Millie asked.

"I hurried to their condo. Betsy Feigenspan, the house-keeper I hired for Arthur, was waiting for me. She told me she found Ali sitting on the floor beside Arthur's body. Ali was laughing her fool head off. I checked in the bathroom. Arthur's pills—the pills that might have saved his life—were in plain view. Ali didn't give Arthur the pills. She wanted him to die."

"That's a very serious accusation."

"I know it is. I saw several lawyers. They said I have no proof. And they're right. I have no proof, but I know it's true. Ali murdered Arthur as sure as if she'd fired a bullet into his heart."

"It sounds more like an accident," Millie said.

Dorothea's hand tightened on Millie's arm. Although the grip was painful, Millie made no attempt to free herself.

"Listen to me, Millie." The intensity in Dorothea's voice was undeniable. "I believe Ali has killed once. I believe she can kill again. And since you are her grandmother . . ."

Millie made no effort to correct her.

Dorothea rushed on. "I'll put it another way. You said it

sounded like an accident. Maybe Arthur's death really was an accident. Maybe. Still, you should watch out. Ali is accident-prone . . . for other people. She's a fatal accident waiting to happen . . . to someone else.''

''A fatal accident waiting to happen,'' Millie said to herself.

Dorothea sighed and stood up. ''I can't tell you how much better talking to you has made me feel. It must be the way Catholics feel after confessing and being granted absolution by a priest.''

''I have no power to grant absolution,'' Millie said. ''But I'm glad you feel better.'' They smiled at each other. Then they separated and silently continued their Moon Walks . . . each lost in her own thoughts.

If Dorothea felt better, Millie felt worse. The burden of Ali had shifted from Dorothea to her. Even though Dorothea believed Ali to be a murderess, Millie didn't. At least she tried not to. Arthur's death had been a terrible accident . . . nothing more. Still, Dorothea's story reminded her of another terrible accident. For that reminder, she would never forgive Dorothea.

It had been a warm June night. Millie was awaiting the arrival of Sir Charles Neville in a haze of anticipation. They were to have dinner à deux in her apartment. When Sir Charles entered the drawing room, Millie rose to greet him. She was wearing a vintage Saint Laurent dinner gown. Anyone who saw her slender straight body, her lithe energetic movements would find it hard to believe she was somewhere in her early sixties.

''I thought about you, Charles. While in my bath,'' she said. ''Or to be more accurate, I thought about Phillip. He'd set his heart on your being a success. A pity he never lived to see it. I think he would have been more than satisfied.''

''I doubt it,'' Sir Charles said. ''He was never satisfied. Not with himself or me. But maybe this time . . . I don't know.'' He leaned forward, kissing Millie on the cheek.

''He would have been pleased,'' Millie insisted. ''He wanted so much for you.''

''Possibly. He didn't do much with his own opportunities.''

''And now you're making up for his failures.'' She smiled

with pleasure as she seated herself. "I'm proud of you. I've always been proud of you."

"I know that." Sir Charles gazed at Millie with affection. In his eyes, she was as she always had been. A slim, white-haired woman with fresh skin and facial bones that aged but didn't grow old. Still a great beauty.

Oscar appeared at the door and gazed at them questioningly.

"I'll have a Tanqueray martini, straight up," Sir Charles said.

"So will I," Millie said. She was actually in one of her periodic wine phases when all she drank was white wine. But for Sir Charles, she would make an exception. She leaned back and studied her guest as he lounged on the couch facing her. His face was cleanly drawn, fastidious . . . a face that spoke of Eton, Oxford and generations of English landowning gentry. There was a slight resemblance to herself. Which was odd, since he wasn't family . . . rather, an old family friend. He came by this status via his father. Many years ago, Millie and his father, Sir Phillip Neville, had planned to elope. But their timing was off. Phillip was divorced, but Millie was still married to Leo Stein. At the last minute, she refused to leave Leo. It would have broken the poor man's heart. Then Leo left her by dying. But Phillip had remarried by the time Millie was widowed. He couldn't leave the new Lady Jessica. It would have broken the poor woman's heart. As a consolation prize, Millie and Phillip had brief, discreet, tempestuous flings through the years, which never disturbed the sanctity of his marriage. Millie inherited many millions from Leo . . . which she didn't need. And when Lady Jessica was thrown from a horse and killed, Phillip also inherited millions . . . which he *did* need. Their attraction was intense, but so was their business sense. So they had the best of both worlds . . . romantic memories and financially secure futures.

"At least I didn't settle for the clergy or the army," Charles said. "So many younger sons do."

"I never thought either God or the military were right for you."

"They weren't. I like politics, but I have no taste for speeches on village greens. In churches. Opening bazaars.

Attending political party dinners. Putting on more weight than I need.''

Millie inclined her head. "You could do so many things."

"Up until now I've avoided doing anything with singular success."

"Tell me exactly what this new post is." Her eyes were bright and full of genuine interest.

"Assistant to England's ambassador to the United Nations." Charles gave her a judicious and contented smile. "It gives me ambassadorial rank."

"Wonderful! A real chance to use your talents." Her judgment brooked no opposition.

"I hope so. That's why I accepted the post. To prevent my life from being a complete waste . . . spent playing polo and skiing and smashing little white golf balls."

Millie chuckled. "You also accepted the post to stop the scoundrels from wasting any more of my money. I've given millions to charities to aid third-world nations . . . money thrown away. Instead of providing food and medical services for starving, sick people, the money has built huge palaces with swimming pools and tennis courts for scoundrels. And that doesn't include the money they've hidden in numbered Swiss bank accounts. I depend on you to stop all that."

"I'll do my best. But I have a full plate. . . ." He gave her a rapid rundown of his responsibilities. As he spoke, his gestures were lively, active, even theatrical.

"Full plate or not, you will do the right thing," Millie stated affectionately. "I believe in you, Charles."

"You always did. When I was a child, I used to wish you were my mother." Sir Charles Neville gazed at Millie with admiration. Long ago she had come to terms with herself and followed her own nature. She was a woman he judged to be happy. Although not always what people of her day called a "good woman." She'd had two marriages . . . hardly tranquil marriages because Millie wasn't tranquil. But full of the rich, glittering life she wanted. As far as he knew, she had never been bored. She had enjoyed her life . . . she still enjoyed it. "I've always thought Hiram and Barron lucky devils to be your sons . . . especially Hiram. I've been jealous of Hiram all my life. You must know that."

Millie laughed. "Stop it, Charles. Your mother loved you very much."

"My mother, the Lady Jessica, was a stout heart. But she lacked imagination."

"But if I'd been your mother, you wouldn't be the Charles you are now. There's the gene pool to consider. That sort of thing."

"I'd take my chances on your genes working to my benefit. I'd be an improved model of Charles Neville." For a man in his mid thirties, his smile was surprisingly spontaneous and boyish. "I'm curious, Millie. Did you refuse to marry my father because he was Church of England? Not Jewish?"

"Don't be silly." Millie inclined her head. "Charles, I wasn't born Jewish. I was born a Presbyterian. Leo was Jewish."

"Oh. I see. So you converted."

"Twice. When I married Leo, I converted to Judaism. And when Leo died, I became an Episcopalian."

"That's exactly what I mean. You're imaginative. Open-minded. Unprejudiced. You can live with the idea of one world and many religions. I wish people were more civilized . . . like you. Instead of religious zealots. Zealotry in any form is a very dangerous disease."

Millie sighed. "Sometimes I dread the future. I worry about my grandchildren . . . my great-grandchildren. One Hitler and one Stalin in a century is more than enough."

"I think we've about seen the last of that type. Even when the Israelis blew up the Iraqi nuclear power plant, Saddam did not get good reviews on the telly. And the telly is everywhere." Charles smiled hopefully. "Enough serious talk. I just want to look at you and forget that most of the Third World is in chaos." He literally shook himself, shedding his concerns much as a dog shakes himself to shed water. His smile broadened. "You do look wonderful. You're ageless."

Millie smiled back. "My secret is happiness. I've probably been happier than most. It keeps one young. It's not been all moonlight and roses. . . . But all in all, I'm quite happy," she reflected.

Oscar returned with their drinks and silently bowed himself out.

"It shows. More ageless than Dietrich . . ." Charles cheerfully sipped his martini. "How is my rival, Hiram, anyway? I don't think we've spoken three times in the last eight years. Not since he married that beauty. Amanda . . . isn't that her name? The news traveled transatlantic. I hear she's a stunner. I was jealous of that too." He was mildly embarrassed. "In fact, I mean to uphold a family tradition. I'll court Amanda the way my father courted you. Father lost out to Leo. Maybe I'll win . . . even up the score."

Millie's face was suddenly somber.

Charles looked surprised. "I can't have offended you . . ."

"No. You haven't. . . . It's just that . . . Amanda is not possible."

"My dear. It's too late for you to become a prude."

"I'm not a prude, Charles. I have no opinion about the pros and cons of adultery. For your father and me, it worked very well. For others . . . I don't know. Actually, people's sex lives don't interest me . . . unless I'm involved." Millie paused. "Frankly, I wish it were possible."

"You mean she already has a—uhmm—a friend?"

"No . . ."

"Then who's my rival . . . besides Hiram?" Charles looked puzzled. "Or is she hideously faithful? I can't believe it. Amanda is reputed to be a beauty. Beauties are seldom faithful . . . although they can be dreadfully dull."

Millie hesitated. "Amanda was a beauty."

"Amanda was . . . Oh!"

"Hiram is still in mourning." Millie's misery was as immediate as a child's.

"What a pity! How long ago did it happen?"

"Almost six months."

"What was it? A sudden illness?" He wanted to comfort her.

"No. An accident. Skiing. She was killed." Millie's explanation was blunt . . . to the point. She wanted to change the subject.

"Really. Oh dear . . ." Charles shook his head. His expression was both shocked and subdued. But he had something more to say. "How strange. The world is full of depressing coincidences. You know I'm an avid skier. Been skiing since childhood. This winter I saw a dreadful skiing accident . . . an Alpine horror story."

"That is depressing," Millie said dully.

"In Davos. A woman. Really a beauty. She had a daughter. A difficult, headstrong girl."

"Davos?" Millie lifted her head.

"The woman was an absolute stunner. She and her daughter were staying at the same lodge as I. The stunner and I hit it off immediately. You know how it is. Never made it to bed, though. Pity. I'm sure we would have . . . if we'd had a little more time. The night before she died, we did have a long talk."

"What was the woman's name?" Millie asked.

Charles grinned. "She wouldn't tell me. She said, 'Call me Madam X.' I think she wanted me to know that if we did go to bed, it would only be a one-night thing. Which was splendid with me. So I told her my name was Phil Battenberg. Little Philly Battenberg."

"Philly Battenberg? Oh! You mean Phillip Mountbatten? Prince Phillip? Queen Elizabeth's husband?"

"The one and only. I don't think Madam X got the joke."

Millie nodded. "Probably not."

"We had a few drinks, and the lady started to talk. She told me that she wanted her daughter out of her life. That she was afraid of her."

"Afraid of her own daughter?"

"She believed her daughter capable of anything . . . even murder."

"Of murdering her own mother?" Millie was paying total attention.

"I'm not sure of this, but I got the impression the daughter wasn't really her daughter. She was her stepdaughter. There was an inheritance of some sort involved. Madam X planned to give the girl her inheritance just as soon as the ski season ended. Then it would be good riddance to her."

"What happened?" Millie asked. Her question appeared to be no more than natural curiosity.

"We arranged to meet at the Octagon at the top of the mountain for breakfast. But I was late . . . my bindings needed to be adjusted. By the time I got off the lift, Madam X and her stepdaughter were standing at the head of the slope. I heard the girl say, 'You're afraid. You're too old to ski anyway.' And Madam X said, 'I'll show you who's afraid.' Before I could stop her, she pushed off. The stepdaughter followed. I skied over to the slope and stopped. I wanted to bed the woman, but I'm not crazy."

"I don't understand."

"There were avalanche warning signs posted at the top of

the slope. No one was supposed to be skiing on that slope. It was such a glorious day, an avalanche was the last thing you'd worry about. But the stepdaughter should have known better.''

"Why?"

"I watched them. The stepdaughter was a fine skier. Almost world-class. Skis locked together. Tight parallel turns. At best, Madam X was a poor intermediate. She could barely traverse the slope."

"Then what?"

"Then disaster. Avalanche Control fired a cannon shot into the slope to bring down the avalanche. That's how they control the danger. They create an avalanche when no one is on the slope.''

"But Madam X and her stepdaughter were on the slope."

"Avalanche Control had posted warning signs. They didn't know the foolish women had ignored the signs. The stepdaughter was able to ski away from the avalanche. Madam X tried . . . she didn't make it. I saw her fall. In seconds she was buried under tons of snow."

They were silent for a moment. Then Millie said, "A horror story indeed. But there's more."

"You always were intuitive. There is more. What happened then is very strange. When the avalanche ended, I skied down the slope to help the rescue team find Madam X. On the way down I saw the stepdaughter, who, as I told you, had managed to ski away from the slide. She was herringboning up the slope to help in the search for Madam X." Charles fidgeted and crossed his legs . . . and uncrossed them. "She had the oddest look on her face. It wasn't fear. It gave me a queer sensation. . . ." He hesitated.

Millie prodded him. "Go on," she said.

"To be frank, it was an uncanny feeling. Like watching a lioness nose around its kill. I swear it. I actually felt she was praying they wouldn't find her stepmother." He coughed into his fist. "They didn't. Not the rescue team. Not the Red Cross. Not anyone. There wasn't a chance. Poor Madam X was buried somewhere on the slope under sixty feet of snow. . . ."

The conversation stuttered to a halt. Finally Millie asked, "And the stepdaughter?"

"I don't know. I left that afternoon for Australia. The surfing in Australia is wonderful.'' He hesitated. ''Never found out Madam X's name. Didn't want to know. Still don't. I know her death was an accident. But . . .''

''Is that all?''

''Isn't that enough? Anyway, that's my Alpine horror story.''

Millie's eye were steady. ''I have a favor to ask, Charles.''

''Ask away.'' He looked at her curiously.

''I would like you never to repeat this story to Hiram. Hearing it will reopen the wound, remind him of Amanda's accident. I want my son to heal.''

''Of course. . . . Never . . . I won't say a word.''

''Thank you, Charles.'' Millie closed the subject. ''I'll ring for Oscar. He'll give you a refill before dinner.''

''I can use one.'' Charles half regretted having told the story at all. He tried to rid himself of the odd feeling that this woman, whom he'd known and loved all his life, had become, for the moment, a stranger . . . utterly mysterious.

Millie sat quietly in her cottage thinking about Dorothea and Amanda and Arthur and Ali . . . at the mercy of her terrifying imagination. She felt empty. Drained. The safe, sunny future she'd imagined for Nora and Ali was threatened, and only she knew the source of the threat. She asked herself a question. Had Ali known that Avalanche Control was going to fire the cannon that morning? She couldn't believe it. Not her Ali. For a moment, Ali's catlike face flashed before her mind's eye. Millie could see the intelligence, the genuine charm. How could this have happened? she wondered. She'd taken such care. Millie took a deep breath. She would handle the dreadful possibility in her own way . . . as she'd handled all the other dark, disordered events of her life. She'd call Dorothea in the morning. By then she'd think of a good reason for asking Dorothea for the name of the detective she'd mentioned. Until she knew more, Ali had to be watched constantly . . . kept under twenty-four-hour surveillance.

Chapter 24

PAT YOCUM looked at the toilet paper. Her relief was palpable. Her rear end was sore as a boil—she wouldn't be able to sit comfortably for a week—but thank God she wasn't bleeding. Unless boys were built differently than girls back there, she didn't know how gay boys did it that way night after night. Lenny had wanted to do it to her the first night. She'd said, "No way, Jose." It had taken them a month of haggling—who would do what to whom—but eventually they'd reached an accommodation. Once a week they did it his way . . . usually she gave him head. According to Lenny, she was no Christal. But he admitted that for a girl she wasn't half bad. And once a week they did it her way . . . mostly he went down on her. He was no Juno, but Juno didn't have a cousin named Lew Dobbs. And once a week they did it the way a boy and a girl are supposed to have sex. Considering that neither of them were turned on by mom-and-pop sex, they did okay. But once every other week it was what Lenny called "Dealers Choice." Tonight was Lenny's turn to be the dealer. He chose what he always chose. Okay, she thought. Next week was her turn. She'd borrow Juno's leathers, her thongs and her silky whip. They'd play a game called Mistress and Slave. She hummed. "Just you wait, Lenny Gerard. Just you wait. You'll be crying 'Help!' and it'll be too late. Just you wait." She pulled several pieces of toilet paper from the roll and touched herself again. "Whew! No blood."

When Pat returned to the bedroom, Lenny was contentedly lying on top of the covers smoking a cigarette. He looked at her and smiled. "That was great, kid," he said.

Pat dropped on the bed next to him. "As good as with Christal?" she asked.

"Don't be bitchy," Lenny murmured. "Christal is . . . well . . . different. But for a girl, you're okay."

"Thanks," Pat said dryly.

They held hands as though they were bona fide lovers. Not two people with a private agenda that required they have sex with each other. Lenny's agenda had to do with his rich cousin, Lew Dobbs. He wanted to work for Dobbs and get rich too. If Lew knew Lenny was gay, he'd never hire him. Pat was Lenny's beard. Pat's agenda was to be on the inside when Lew Dobbs took over Channel 18. She was hopeful that she could convince Dobbs to offer her Nora's job. Next to sleeping with Dobbs himself, sleeping with Cousin Lenny was the best she could do. It should give her a very inside track.

Lenny finished his cigarette and turned off the light. He started to talk. One of his peculiarities was his addiction to aftersex pillow talk. In the beginning, Pat had tried to hold up her end of the conversation. But she soon discovered that he didn't expect her to talk to him. He wanted her to listen to his ramblings. Her occasional "Yes" or "Really" or even "Hmmm" contented him.

"You know, sweetie," Lenny mused, "I don't understand my cousin."

"Oh?"

"Lew's strange."

"How strange?"

"Well. He's real rich. At least I think he's rich."

"Hmmm."

"He owns a bunch of TV stations. At least I think he owns the stations."

"What!"

"Lew's name is on the door, but there's this guy . . ."

"Stanley Tseng? Isn't it? From the yacht party?"

"Yep—him. Stanley Tseng. Chinese, I think."

"Asian anyway."

"Yep—Whenever Tseng shows up, Lew jumps. I think Comrade Tseng has put a lot of money into Lew's TV business."

"Hmmm."

"He may be the money behind Lew. The Dobbs branch of the family was the poor branch. The Gerards never mixed with the Dobbses."

"Snob."

"Until Cousin Lew came along, they were dirt-poor farmers. . . ."

Pat broke a rule. She asked a question. "Didn't Cousin Lew strike it rich in oil?"

"Don't think he did. I kind o' remember he went somewhere . . . maybe Hong Kong. And came back with a big bank account. That's when he bought his first TV station."

"Hmmm."

"Maybe he hit it big at the crap table in Macao."

"Maybe."

"Maybe Stanley Tseng is the money behind Lew. Maybe I ought to pay more attention to the wily Oriental."

Maybe I should too, Pat thought. She kissed Lenny lightly. "Enough, Lenny baby. I got to get my beauty sleep. Big day at the office tomorrow."

Lenny yawned. "I got a big day too. Satellite wagering at Del Mar. I wish Lew would give me a real job."

Me too, Pat thought. " 'Night, Lenny."

" 'Night, Patty baby."

They pulled up the covers. Lenny was asleep in seconds. Pat couldn't sleep. If Lew Dobbs wasn't the boss, she was wasting time with Lenny. She felt a sudden sharp pain in her rear end. She slid out of the bed and padded across the room to the bathroom . . . just to make absolutely sure she wasn't bleeding. She wasn't. It was a gas attack brought on by nerves.

Pat arrived at Channel 18 early. She wanted to have a talk with Tim Rourke. Tim wasn't her favorite person, but he was the smartest of her co-workers. If anyone had a line on what was going on, her money was on Tim. She knocked on the door to Tim's office.

"Door's open. Come in."

Pat stuck her head in the office. "Got a minute, Tim?"

"For you, Patti Cake. Always."

Pat sat in the chair facing Tim's desk. She scrunched up her face. "I wish you'd stop calling me Patti Cake."

"I wish you'd stop calling Nora Norakins. Or Lady Macbeth. What's on your mind, Pat?"

"Channel 18. Is Nora's grandmother . . . I said Nora. Is Mrs. G. selling the station?"

Tim chuckled. "I hear you, Pat . . . I said Pat. Get in line. That's the sixty-four-dollar question."

"So what do you think, Tim?" Pat leaned forward. "Will she sell?"

"There's a theory that anything is for sale. If the price is right. And the timing is right. And the person making the offer is right."

"I hear Lew Dobbs has made Mrs. G. a very high offer."

"I think Dobbs hired a PR firm to publicize the offer. Any day now I expect to see the billboards along the freeway announcing, 'Lew Dobbs has made a very high offer for Channel 18.' Or maybe he'll go for skywriting. Or a plane with a trailing sign flying over downtown San Diego. Or ten-second IDs—"

Pat raised her hand. "Enough! Will Mrs. G. accept Dobbs's offer?"

"I told you I don't know. She says she won't. But that may be a negotiating position. Or maybe she means it."

"Why wouldn't she sell . . . if the price is right?"

Tim scratched his head. "Maybe she doesn't like Lew Dobbs. From what I hear, he's an easy man not to like."

"You saying she might sell to another buyer?"

"She might."

"So if Lew isn't the real buyer . . ."

"What do you have in mind?" Tim sat up straighter. He had a sudden feeling this session with Pat wasn't more Channel 18 "will she or won't she sell?" bullshit.

Pat veered off in another direction. "If Lew Dobbs does buy the channel, will he fire Nora? I repeat . . . Nora. What do you think, Tim? Will he?"

Tim grimaced. "He won't have to fire Nora. She'll quit. Haven't you heard she doesn't like Dobbs?"

"I heard. I just don't believe it." Pat closed her eyes for a moment. When she opened them, she asked, "But what if someone else—not Dobbs—takes over?"

"What someone else? There is no someone else."

"Maybe there is," Pat said slowly.

"You know something, Pat. Tell your old friend Timmy all about it."

"Last night, Lenny . . ."

"Lenny? Lenny who?"

"Gerard. My latest. Lenny told me that maybe Lew Dobbs isn't playing with his own deck of cards."

"That's not funny."

"It wasn't meant to be funny."

"How would Lenny Gerard know whose deck of cards Dobbs plays with?"

"He's Dobbs's cousin."

Tim softly applauded. "Aaah. Patti Cake—I mean, Pat—I have to hand it to you. I wondered why you dumped Juno. If Dobbs takes over . . . Nora goes bye-bye and Lenny and you . . . Cute. Not nice, but cute." Tim stopped clapping. "If Dobbs doesn't own the deck, who does?"

"Did you ever hear of Stanley Sung? Something like that anyway."

"Tseng," Tim said automatically. "You mean Stanley Tseng."

"That's the guy."

"Stanley Tseng . . ." Tim tugged thoughtfully on his lower lip. "You think Tseng is backing Dobbs?"

"I don't think anything. I met Stanley Tseng once. Lenny thinks Tseng is backing his cousin. What I want to know is, would Nora quit if Stanley Tseng took over?"

"I don't know."

"Would Tseng fire Nora?"

"Again. I don't know."

"Damn! Damn! Damn!" Pat literally stamped her feet in frustration.

"That's what you get for betraying your true love for money."

"I could learn to hate you, Tim Rourke."

"Don't hate me, Patti Cake . . . I mean, Pat. I want to check out a few things. But if I'm right, I could do us both a big favor."

"What favor?"

Tim raised his right hand. His thumb and pinky were folded together. "Trust me, Patricia. I was an Honor Scout."

"Doesn't say much for the Boy Scouts of America." She smiled seductively. "You do right by me, and I might do right by you."

"I'll count on it."

After Pat left the office, Tim thought for a while. Stanley Tseng . . . Big money . . . Very big Hong Kong money. Korean money. Malaysian money. Indonesian money. He shook his head. Dobbs would be a fool to risk getting involved with Tseng. Still . . . In the last few years a bunch of smartass business types had turned out to be dumb crooks. Why? He answered his own question. Because they were caught . . . that's why. He wondered how many more crooks were still regarded as big business brains because they hadn't been caught. Maybe Lew Dobbs was one of them? Tim made a phone call . . . to make sure he knew the law. After that he talked to Nora.

Nora swung her desk chair around to face Tim. "Give that to me slowly," she said.

"I heard a rumor. Lew Dobbs is backed by Stanley Tseng's money."

Nora remembered Tseng. His pressing her to get Millie to sell the station to Dobbs. His thinly veiled threat. Now the connection between Dobbs and Tseng was clear. "I guess it's possible," she said. "So?"

"So plenty. If it's true, that Tseng character—and Dobbs—have a nasty problem. Unless Tseng has become an American citizen."

"I'm missing something. What?"

"A little quirk in the law. While a foreigner can own a movie studio, a newspaper or a magazine, the electronic media are off-limits. The theory is that the airways belong to the American public. Only an American citizen can own more than twenty percent of a radio or TV station. If Tseng's money is behind Dobbs and Tseng isn't an American citizen, the FCC and the attorney general will pay them a visit."

Nora considered Stanley Tseng. It was not likely he was an American citizen. He operated in the shadow world of international hot money. Few rules. Fewer regulations. No enforcement. Playing with banks like BCCI was his game . . . not the Bank of America. Unlike so much of the world, where governments were for sale to the highest bidder, in America money might buy a committedly corrupt senator, or a greedy judge, but not an entire country.

"With a Summons and Complaint?" she asked.

"Worse. Dobbs and Tseng will be forced to sell everything. That's for openers. There are also criminal charges. In fact, anyone involved with those boys' acquiring TV stations is hanging out in the breeze . . . bareassed.''

Nora took this in. "Isn't that interesting?"

"Interesting?" Tim frowned. Nora's lukewarm reaction wasn't what he'd expected. "It's a gift from heaven. Why interesting?" Tim asked. "I figured you'd be ecstatic. If it's true, Dobbs can't force Mrs. G. to sell the station in any way, shape or form."

"You don't get it. My grandmother has told you the station isn't for sale. Dobbs can't force her to do anything. She's an army tank when she wants to be. Nodody budges her. Period. End of discussion."

"If Tseng is behind Dobbs, I'm sure Tseng has other means of persuasion besides money."

Nora thought about that. "He'll threaten Millie." She shook her head. "Grandmother won't like being threatened. He'll be sorry he ever heard of San Diego."

"Maybe. Everyone has holes in their kimonos. Tanks, in Mrs. G.'s case."

Nora studied Tim's body language. He was pushing her. "Tim. Why do I get the feeling you're after something?"

Tim leaned back and gave her a funny grin. "Because I am. And you're the only one around here who's smart enough to help me."

"You want Luddy's job," Nora said.

"Everyone wants someone else's job. Yeah. I want to be station manager. And I figure if I help Mrs. G. keep the channel, she'll owe me one. Luddy, Sim, Pat—the whole bunch of them—are sure she'll sell out. Eventually. Because they want her to. I don't think she will, and I don't want her to. If I'm on the winning side, I hope to be rewarded. . . ."

"What do you want me to do?"

"Tell Mrs. G. about Tseng. She has contacts in Washington. She can find out if Tseng is a citizen."

"Even if he isn't, we still don't know if he's the money behind Lew Dobbs."

Tim sucked in his cheeks and chewed on them. "I think you'll come up with something . . . if you put your mind to it." He stood up. "That's it for today. Luddy has called another damned meeting for nine-fifteen. If I make station manager, the first thing I'll do is shitcan nine-fifteen meetings. But until that glorious day dawns, the ball, my dear Nora, is in your court. My advice is, wack it!'' He waved as he left Nora's office.

Nora had had no difficulty following Tim's thinking. Her head hurt. It led straight to Mark! Tim knew Mark was the investment banker when Dobbs bought Group H. He knew Mark was pushing Millie to sell. He figured Mark would know where Dobbs got his money. Nora winced. Tim was wrong. Mark couldn't know anything. If he did, he wouldn't have handled the deal. Would he? Nora reached for the phone. She jabbed at the numbers. Her call was picked up immediately.

''Mr. Stern's office.''

''Kim, this is Mrs. Stern. I want to speak to Mr. Stern.''

''I'm sorry, Mrs. Stern. Mr. Stern is on a conference call between Phoenix and our New York office.'' She hesitated for a moment and then whispered, ''It's a huge order, and he's working on getting the best price for a client.'' She giggled. ''Our Mr. Tseng is in a buying mood today.''

Nora looked out of the window for help. ''Mr. Tseng is in Phoenix?''

''Yes.''

''Figures. Tell Mr. Stern I want to see him. It's important. I'll be there in about thirty minutes.'' She hung up before Kim had a chance to ask her any questions she didn't want to answer.

''So Dobbs and Tseng know each other. They may even do business together. What are you driving at, Nora?''

''Does Tseng own into Dobbs's TV operation?''

''How do I know?'' Mark's nose was bent out of joint at Nora's butting into his business. ''I'm his investment banker, not his accountant.''

''Ask him.''

''Are you nuts? You want me to piss off one of Reiner & Co.'s biggest corporate clients? But that won't satisfy you . . . not Nora Gardiner. . . .''

Nora noted that recently, whenever Mark was irritated at her, he called her Nora Gardiner. Did he resent it that much? That she was a Gardiner?

''What you also want is for me to stick a burr up the ass of a very big trading account. Any other clever suggestions on how I can commit business suicide?'' Mark's tone was venomous.

"I'm not trying to harm you, Mark. I'm trying to save you!''

"Save me? Save me from what? Making too much money?''

"That's not fair.'' Nora was hurting so badly, she was beyond anger. "What you're doing is dangerous.''

"Why dangerous? Lew Dobbs bought Group H. His signature is on the agreement. Dobbs is an American. You don't have any proof that he used Stanley Tseng's money.''

"But suppose he did?'' Nora persisted.

Mark stood up and went to the window. He looked out at San Diego. The high-and-mighty Gardiners thought they owned the city. Owned him. They didn't. All the resentments that had been percolating for months now finally crystallized. A new Mark emerged. When he was rich enough, he'd dump Nora. Little Miss Rich Bitch. She'd find out how little of him she really owned. As for San Diego . . . screw it. They could take their town and stick it where the sun never shines. He spun about.

"If Lew did cut a deal with Tseng, I don't know anything about it. And I don't want to know.''

"Mark, you're too exposed. Don't you see it?'' Nora was desperate.

"No, I don't see it. All I see are big fees flying out the window. My fees.'' Mark returned to his desk. Still standing, he placed his palms on the desk and leaned forward. "You come barging in here. You louse up my entire day with your crazy ideas about Lew Dobbs. Now get this straight. I can't make Millie sell Channel 18. I would if I could, but I can't. You could, but you won't. Okay. That's your decision. How I run my business life is my decision. I will not dump Lew Dobbs. That's final.''

Nora stood up. She glared at Mark. "I can't deal with that much dumb greed. You do what you have to do. So will I.''

"Like run to Millie with your shitty story.''

"Maybe.''

Nora slammed out of Mark's office. Driving down the winding ramp, she tried to think rationally about her feelings for Mark. Was this Mark Stern the real Mark Stern . . . the man she loved and had married? She didn't know. Did she still love this man? She didn't know. Did she want to divorce him? She didn't know. So what was she doing? Mark would never agree to give up Dobbs's business . . . he loved money too much. Was she using Dobbs and Tseng as an excuse for getting a divorce? If she was divorced, Jordan might . . . Nora shook her head. At that moment, she didn't like herself very much.

Mark stared at the closed door . . . literally trembling with fury. Tseng and Dobbs. Dobbs and Tseng. His thoughts jumped from one to the other, then back again. Minutes passed before he was able to think clearly. He remembered the phone call Lew had made before agreeing to the terms of Ashland's employment contract. Now the call made sense. His mouth twisted into an imitation of a smile. He pressed the intercom button. "Kim, get me Lew Dobbs."

"This is quite a spread you have here, Mrs. Gardiner."

"Thank you, Mr. Sklar. I like it."

They were sitting in comfortable rattan chairs. The colonnade protected them from the hot sun. Just a few yards away the wading pool reflected the pale blue of the sky.

"I thought I'd seen some beautiful layouts, but I never seen nothing like this."

Millie's smile acknowledged the compliment. Normally she would have gone directly to the reason she'd asked to see the detective, but there was something about the man's attitude—something she couldn't put her finger on—that said to her, "Let him do his thing." She only hoped he'd be quick about it.

"The fancier the spread, the more the owners need my services. I wonder why that is?"

Millie had no comment. She took a cigarette from an alabaster box and inserted it into her favorite jade holder.

"Can I bum one of those?" the detective said.

"Certainly. If I'd known you smoked, I'd have offered you a cigarette. These days so many don't smoke."

"I'm trying to kick the habit . . . gradually," Gus Sklar explained. "That's why I don't carry a pack."

"Cigarettes are an addiction . . . like alcohol or drugs. I don't believe a nicotine addict can gradually cut down on cigarettes any more than an alcoholic can gradually stop drinking."

"I know. I should do it cold turkey, but . . ."

Millie shrugged and offered him a cigarette and a book of matches . . . she never judged another person's vices. "Mrs. Dorothea Reiner thinks highly of your work," she said.

"I'm good," Sklar said. "The best in San Diego." He'd long ago found modesty in his line of work was a waste.

"Your fee is five hundred dollars a day . . ."

"Plus expenses."

Millie nodded. "When can you start?"

"Maybe first, Mrs. Gardiner, you'd better tell me what you want me to do." He smiled as he said, "Five hundred dollars a day buys my time . . . it doesn't buy my taking anyone down."

Millie returned his smile to show her appreciation of the detective's bad joke. Then she stopped smiling. "If I wanted someone taken down, I wouldn't use local talent. What I have in mind is a round-the-clock surveillance job. Twenty-four hours a day."

"Ah. Who am I supposed to watch?"

"One of my granddaughters. Mrs. Ali Gardiner Reiner."

Sklar's eyebrows rose. "Mrs. Reiner is your granddaughter?"

"Not exactly. She's my stepgranddaughter. But *stepgranddaughter* is such a clumsy word. . . ." Millie stared at the detective. Was he laughing at her? "Did I say something funny?" she asked.

"No. There's nothing funny about having a stepgranddaughter. You know I've tailed Mrs. Reiner before?" Sklar said.

"I know. The first Mrs. Reiner, Mrs. Dorothea Reiner, told me. It should be easier the second time around."

"It will be. What am I looking for?"

"Anything and everything. I want a weekly written report. But if she does anything unusual, an immediate phone call."

"Unusual? Very little that lady does is usual. She gets around."

"So I've heard," Millie said dryly. "I have no interest in her sex life. Unless there's something about the man that you think I should know."

Sklar stubbed out his cigarette. "When do I start?"

"As soon as you leave here. You'll want a retainer."

"A week in advance."

Millie pulled a small checkbook from the pocket of her Levis. "Thirty-five hundred dollars. I set up a special account for this purpose. The checks don't have my name on them. . . ."

Sklar laughed. "You're good for the money. You always kept your . . ." He bit down on his lip.

"Mr. Sklar, what am I missing? Ever since you arrived, I've had a strange feeling you know something I don't."

A queer, shy look crept over the detective's face. "You don't remember me. Do you?"

"Should I?"

"Nah. Why should you? I've changed. But you might remember Baby Gustave."

Millie took a quick puff on her cigarette, then crushed it out. She stared at the detective. "Baby Gustave? Gus Sklar? You?"

"Me."

"You've changed." It was all Millie could think to say.

"You haven't. Not much anyway."

Millie's lower lip trembled. She took hold of Sklar's hands. "I was too young, too frightened . . . Without your mother's help, I don't know what I'd have done."

"She knew how you felt. But my money was on you. You're a survivor. One way or another, you'd have figured something out."

Millie gave him a strained smile. "Maybe. I don't know. Where is your mother now? Does she still live in Hollywood?"

"She died a long time ago."

"I wish I'd known. I could have helped."

"Nah. She was too fat and I had no talent. Besides, you were out of the game by then . . . married to Max Gardiner."

For a few moments neither could think of anything to say. Then Millie blurted out, "Do you still want to work for me?"

"More than ever."

Millie's grip on Sklar's hands tightened. "You know who she is?" she whispered.

"Yeah. I figured it out when I saw you. There's something about the way you hold your head. The way you move. Your mouth when you smile . . ."

"Is it that obvious?"

"Nah. It's not obvious at all. To anyone except me. Because no one else knows what I know."

Millie sighed and let go of Gus Sklar's hands. "Shall I make the check out to you?"

"The Gus Sklar Agency, Inc."

As Millie walked the detective to the door, she said, "I want Ali Reiner watched very closely. No slipups. Please!"

"No slipups." He hesitated before saying, "Look, Millie . . . to me you'll always be Millie Thorne and seventeen years old."

"Thank you." Millie tried to smile.

"You didn't ask me, Millie. For that I thank you. But I want you to rest easy. What I know, I know. No one else knows, and no one else is going to know. You can bet the farm on that."

Millie looked grave. "I already have bet the Farm. So thank you again, Baby Gustave. I'm depending on you. . . . Help me win my bet."

Chapter 25

NORA TRIED to concentrate on Channel 18's advertising schedule. It was tricky. Her mind would shy away from the time slots . . . veering over to Mark. His temper. Her temper. He was her husband. How could she make him see what he was doing? The danger? She didn't know, so she was seeing Millie around five-thirty . . . to ask for advice. She'd tell Millie everything she suspected. Between them, they must convince Mark the risk wasn't worth the reward. The buzz of her intercom startled her. She pushed down the lit button. "What is it, Sheri?"

"Your friendly Ford dealer is on the phone. Someone named Ted wants to talk to you."

"Thanks." Nora shifted lines. "This is Nora Stern."

"Mrs. Stern. We've gone over your car with a fine-tooth comb. We can't find nothing wrong. It runs beautiful."

"It runs lousy," Nora insisted. "If I step on the gas and then quickly take my foot off the pedal, the engine stalls. And the only way I can keep it from stalling in reverse is to work the brake and the gas at the same time. That car is still under warranty."

"Only the power train, Mrs. Stern."

"Only the power train. Right. Ted . . ." Nora took a deep breath. "Let's take this from the top. What is the power train supposed to do?"

"Well." Ted Menotti figured he'd better keep it simple or the silly broad would get confused. "The power train makes the car go."

"Very good, Ted. And when the engine stalls, can the car go?"

"Nooo." Ted held on to the word. He saw where the broad was heading, and he didn't like it.

"You're getting the picture, Ted. So if the car stalls, there's something wrong with the power train. Right, Ted?"

"I dunno, Mrs. Stern."

"You don't know. What's your title, Ted?"

"Manager of the service department."

Nora heard the pride in Menotti's voice. "You have a very important job, Ted, but I didn't buy my car from you. I bought my lemon from Mr. Rush. Now you be a good guy and switch me over to Mr. Rush."

"I dunno."

"Do it, Ted. Or I promise you, a bolt of lightning will strike you right in the middle of your left ear." It'll pass through and out your right ear without hitting anything, she added silently, glaring at the phone.

"Well . . ."

"Ted, were you ever in the military?"

"Sure. I learned to be a mechanic in the army."

How the hell did we ever beat Iraq? "Ted, when you were in the army, did anyone ever tell you to duck when the brass walk by?"

"Sure. You don't duck . . . you don't survive."

"Now's a good time to duck, Ted. Pass me on to Dave Rush and get out of the way. Do it, Ted."

"Okay. You fight it out with the boss."

The phone clicked. Nora waited. She was rewarded by a dial tone. "Shit!" she muttered. She had to check the number of Rush Ford before dialing.

"Rush Ford. The best price and the best service is our motto. Can I help you?"

"No. But Dave Rush can."

"Who shall I say is calling?"

"Nora Stern."

"One moment, Nora."

Nora! Only in California would a switchboard operator call someone she didn't know by her first name.

"This is Dave Rush. You want to talk to me?"

"Yes, I do. This is Nora Stern."

"What can I do for you?"

Nora explained what was wrong with her car and the problem she was having with his service department.

"I'm at a loss. If Ted can't find anything wrong . . ."

"Mr. Rush, if you're really at a loss, I suggest you look

hard for yourself . . . very hard." She rarely name-dropped, but she wasn't getting anywhere. "I bought that car from you three years ago. When I bought the car, I wasn't married. My name was Nora Gardiner. I worked for Channel 18. I still work for Channel 18. My grandmother, Millie Gardiner, owns the channel. Our local news department would be interested in the difficulty a customer can have—"

"Ahem." Rush cleared his throat. "Would you be kind enough to hold the wire for just a moment, Mrs. Gardiner-Stern?"

"I'll hold. But please don't disconnect me. My temper is getting frayed."

"I won't disconnect you. I'll be right back." Nora waited. In less than a minute, Dave Rush was back. "A team of mechanics is going to give your car a complete going over. I'm confident we will find out what's wrong."

"I believe you will, Mr. Rush. How long will this take?"

"We'll have the car ready for you tomorrow morning by—"

"No! I told your service department when I brought the car in this morning that I needed it by five o'clock. I was promised the car would be ready by five."

"But we can't complete the . . ." Dave Rush cleared his throat for a second time. "I'm going to put you on hold again."

If he disconnects me . . .

Rush didn't. "Mrs. Gardiner-Stern, I believe I have a solution that will please you. Can you drive a stick shift?"

"Yes. I learned to drive on a Jaguar with a stick shift."

"Good. Last week I took in a Porsche 944 in a trade. It's not a new car, but I've had it completely gone over. It's a cream puff. Would you accept the loan of the Porsche—at no charge—until your car is running to everyone's satisfaction?"

"Mr. Rush, I would accept a pickup truck that ran well, but the Porsche will do." Nora checked her watch. "My secretary will drop me off at your dealership at five sharp."

"The Porsche will be gassed up and waiting. And thank you for your patience, Mrs. Gardiner-Stern."

"Thank you, Mr. Rush." Nora hung up the phone shaking her head. No wonder the American automobile companies were in trouble. It wasn't the cars . . . it was the damn service departments that were screwing up buyer loyalty. She made a note for the news department. "Run story on automobile service departments."

Mark leaned back in his chair, placed his feet on his desk and closed his eyes. The trading day had ended hours ago. Although it was only a little after four o'clock, the entire office had left . . . except for Kim. Kim was waiting at the receptionist's desk. She'd buzz him when they arrived. The meeting was crucial. It would help him get out from under the Gardiners. . . . Where the hell did Nora come off storming in yesterday and howling at him like she owned him? Demanding . . . Not asking . . . Demanding he stop doing business with Dobbs. "Who the hell does she think she is?" He answered his own question. "Nora Gardiner, that's who. San Diego's version of Princess Di . . . a 'royal.' " Last night she'd given him the silent treatment. Fixed herself a sandwich and shut herself up in the office. She'd actually locked the door . . . as if he couldn't kick it in any time he wanted to. He hadn't. He'd broiled a steak and thrown together a salad. Cracked open an expensive bottle of wine . . . a Nuit St. George, a present from Queen Millie herself. He'd priced the wine . . . one hundred twenty dollars a pop. That he couldn't taste the difference between the Nuit St. George and a decent jug wine like Gallo Hearty Burgundy was beside the point. Nora was sure to find the empty bottle. She'd be pissed that he'd polished off Queen Millie's present without offering the princess a sip. Which was exactly why he did it . . . to piss Nora off . . . keep pissing her off. His intercom buzzed.

"Yes, Kim?"

"Mr. Dobbs and Mr. Tseng are here."

Mark took a deep breath. He couldn't remember being this calm before an important meeting. Why shouldn't I be calm? he asked himself. I've got all the cards. He stared at the phone. He'd heard a strange edge—almost like the buzz of an electric motor—in Kim's voice. Another time he might have asked what was bugging her. Not tonight.

"Show them to my office, and then you can leave."

"But . . . I can't leave."

"Go away, Kim. I'll give you a full report tomorrow morning."

"Y-yes, sir."

Mark waited. There was a knock on the door.

"Come," Mark called out.

The door opened and Stanley Tseng entered . . . followed by the giant figure of Lew Dobbs. To Mark's surprise, they hadn't come alone. Another man—an Oriental—clumped through the doorway. He took his post to the left of the door.

Mark didn't say a word. He just glared at the man. He'd been raised on the streets of New York. His street smarts were bred into his bones. This man was an Oriental . . . he could also have been Italian or Hispanic or black or Irish or even Jewish. A "soldier" was a "soldier" was a "soldier."

Stanley Tseng sat in one of the chairs facing Mark's desk. Lew Dobbs settled himself in the other. "You asked us to meet with you," Tseng said in a conversational tone. "We are here. Now tell us why are we here?" He smiled at Mark.

The game being played out in Mark's office took on a sur-realistic quality. The threat of violence drifted through the air, but Tseng smiled benignly at Mark.

Mark was too angry to feel fear. "You're here because . . . because . . . I . . . want . . . in." There was a perceptible pause between each word.

"In what?" Tseng asked.

"Group H, for openers. I want a piece of the action."

"Old buddy, you're getting too big for your britches," Lew Dobbs roared.

Tseng waved his forefinger at Dobbs, telling Lew to shut up. He'd handle Mark. "You are not satisfied with the hand-some fees Reiner & Co. receives each time Lew acquires a new channel? Arthur was content with the arrangement."

"I'm not Arthur Reiner." Mark started to add, I'm not as rich as Arthur was. Instead he added, "Besides, Arthur did not know what I know."

"Exactly what do you think you know?"

Mark gave Tseng a smug smile.

"I'll ask again. Why should Lew agree to do this?" Tseng asked.

"Lew doesn't have to agree to anything." Mark saw no point in beating around the bush. "You do. Since Lew bought Group H with your money."

"You've gone loco, son."

"Lew. Please." Tseng studied Mark. "Why do you be-lieve this to be the case?"

"I don't believe it. I know it."

"You know it." Despite his slight accent, Tseng managed a credible imitation of Mark . . . a mocking imitation.

"I have my sources."

"And you think you can prove this in a court of law?"

"If necessary." Mark snickered. "But it won't be necessary for me to prove anything in court. The FCC, the SEC, the IRS and the attorney general will do that for me. If they look for proof, they'll find all the proof they need. I imagine a close look at the corporate books—"

"Damn you, boy . . ."

"What do you want for your . . . shall we say, cooperation?"

"Twenty percent of Group H. Plus twenty percent of any new stations you buy."

Dobbs was half out of his chair before Tseng motioned for him to sit back.

"That's too much," Tseng said, still smiling.

"I don't think it is," Mark snapped. "You'll still have eighty percent of something. That's better than one hundred percent of nothing."

Tseng thought about that. "My problem is a simple one, Mark. If I agree to blackmail now, what is there to prevent you from using the same blackmail next month? Or next year? Or at any time in the future when your greed gets the better of your judgment?"

Mark looked Tseng directly in the eye. "I want twenty percent. No more. No less. You have my word on that."

"Of course. We have your word."

"You can take your word and stick it. . . ." Dobbs was trembling with rage.

"Be reasonable, Lew." Although Tseng didn't raise his voice, something in his tone stopped the three-hundred-pound Lew Dobbs dead in his tracks. "The man has information. Information has a certain value. The question is, how much value?"

"Twenty percent," Mark said.

"Who else knows of our alleged arrangement?"

"My lawyer," Mark lied. He hadn't thought to protect himself. He would, first thing in the morning.

"Your insurance policy. A wise precaution. Blackmail is a dangerous game. No one else knows?"

Mark didn't answer.

"No one else?" Tseng mused. "All right, Mark. We will give you the twenty percent. But you must be taught a lesson. So you will never again try to blackmail me." Without turning around, he made a beckoning motion with his right hand.

Another man—also an Oriental—entered the office. He was holding Kim. He'd twisted Kim's arm behind her back . . . her face was scrunched up in pain.

"Let Kim go," Mark shouted. "She knows nothing about this. She's my secretary."

"I know that," Tseng said. "First we will play Let Us Pretend. Let us pretend that your charming secretary is your equally charming wife." He nodded to the man holding Kim.

Kim screamed as the "soldier" ripped her blouse off. She wasn't wearing a bra. With her free arm she tried to cover her breasts. The "soldier" slapped her across the side of her head . . . hard. Her eyes glazed. The "soldier" then tore apart her wraparound skirt. Kim slumped to her knees . . . all she had on were a pair of bikini panties and her shoes. The "soldier" reached down . . . his face was impassive . . . he was doing his job. He grabbed hold of her panties. If he was told to rape the girl, he would . . . But there would be nothing personal in the act.

"Damn it!" Mark shouted. "Tell your muscle boy to knock it off. I told you she knows nothing."

"And I said, Quite so. The girl knows nothing. We are playing Let Us Pretend. . . ."

Mark stood up. "Right," he snarled. "Let's pretend. Let's pretend Kim is Nora Stern. Nora Gardiner. That's the operative word. Gardiner. Your boy can do a number on Kim, but you won't let him go near Nora Gardiner. Millie Gardiner would nail your hides to the wall. So what are you proving?"

Stanley Tseng remembered his conversation with Nora Stern on Dobbs's yacht. He'd made a threat . . . the threat had been a mistake. One mistake was unfortunate. To repeat the same mistake was inexcusable. He made a motion. The "soldier" let go of Kim's panties and stood up.

Kim remained on her knees. She was shaking and sobbing.

"You're both right and wrong, Mark. I would dare . . . but I admit it would be a blunder. However, you are not a Gardiner. I do not believe Mrs. Millie Gardiner would . . . How did you put it? Nail my hide to the wall? If I touched you. Because you can't explain to her what happened to you and why. Mark, I insist on knowing who informed you of my arrangement with Lew." He motioned to the "soldiers." "Li. Chou. Hurt him. Don't kill him. Hurt him."

Mark tried to defend himself, but he had no chance. The "soldiers" were professionals. The first held him while the second beat him about his chest, his ribs and his stomach. He thought his bones were cracking and his muscles were being torn to shreds.

Mark was not a physical coward, but soon he'd had enough. Why should he protect Nora Gardiner? The Gardiners could damn well protect themselves. "Nora told me," he gasped.

"I thought so," Tseng murmured.

The punishment continued nevertheless. Soon Mark was choking and gasping for air. It ended just before he lost consciousness. The "soldiers" dropped a dazed Mark alongside Kim.

Stanley Tseng knelt. "Now you will remember how dangerous it is to blackmail me. You own twenty percent of Group H, Mark. You're a greedy man. Consider yourself fortunate. I've had men killed for less." He placed his hand on the trembling Kim Kelly. "I apologize for causing you fear, young lady. It was stupid of me, but Mr. Stern made me very angry. Still, that is no excuse." He took a money clip from his pocket. "Here," he said as he placed the money on the floor in front of Kim. "There is only about a thousand dollars there, but it is all the cash I am carrying. Tomorrow a messenger will deliver to you a proper recompense." He glanced up at Lew Dobbs. "Lew, give me your jacket, please."

Lew Dobbs quickly shrugged off his jacket.

Tseng covered Kim with Lew's jacket . . . it was long enough on her to be a coat. "Also, I place you under my protection. No matter what happens in the future, you will not be troubled. Do you understand?"

Kim nodded.

Stanley Tseng stood up. "Come to Phoenix tomorrow, Mark. We will complete our business at Group H headquarters." He glanced at Lew Dobbs. "Nora Gardiner Stern? We must think long and hard what to do about Nora Gardiner Stern."

"You're damn right," Lew Dobbs said.

With a "soldier" leading and a "soldier" bringing up the rear, the four men marched, single file, from Mark's office.

After driving a few miles up and down PCH to get the feel of the car, Nora decided Rush was right. The Porsche ran smooth as silk. She turned east on Encinitas Boulevard and headed toward Rancho Santa Fe. There were a half dozen traffic lights on Encinitas Boulevard. Several times when she looked in the mirror, she noticed a black pickup truck with huge, oversized wheels behind her. The pickup rode so high off the ground she couldn't see much more than the tires and the shiny, stainless steel bumper. Nora thought nothing of the pickup . . . it would probably turn off at Camino Real. It didn't. She continued east on Encinitas Boulevard. When she hit another red light at Manchester, the pickup was still close behind. A little too close. Nora didn't like being tailgated. The light turned green. She shifted into low gear and sped across the intersection. Encinitas Boulevard became Rancho Santa Fe Road. The pickup truck followed her. When she shifted into second gear and took the very sharp left onto El Mirlo at too high a speed, she hoped she'd lose the pickup. She didn't. The pickup couldn't corner like a Porsche, but once the road straightened out, there it was. Nora was disconcerted when she saw the pickup closing in on her. Okay, she thought. You win. She slowed down and waved the pickup by.

Many of the roads in Rancho Santa Fe were cut into the side of a hill. On one side of the road was a steep bank, on the other an equally steep drop-off . . . like a gully or a ravine. As chance would have it, the ravine was to Nora's right. The pickup truck drew level with her. The wheels were almost as high was Nora's car. She slowed down still further to make it easier for the truck to pass. But instead of passing her, the driver of the truck turned the wheels so the truck bumped against her car . . . hard. The truck weighed more than twice the Porsche. Nora fought for control.

"What do you think you're doing, you idiot?" she screamed.

The wheels of the pickup banged into her car again.

The Porsche was forced to the right. The car was half on the paved road and half on the packed dirt alongside the road. Nora tried to edge back onto the asphalt.

The truck hit her again . . . the Porsche was knocked sideways. The car's right wheels were dangerously close to the drop-off.

"He's trying to kill me," Nora said in a shocked whisper. The need to survive sharpened her thinking.

As the pickup edged closer to bump the Porsche for a fourth time, Nora downshifted and stood on the brakes. The pickup hurtled past her front fender. Before the driver could regain control, the truck was half off the road. Nora shifted from first to third gear, turned to the left and floored the gas pedal. The Porsche responded with a burst of speed. It flew by the left side of the floundering pickup. It was impossible for Nora to spot who was behind the wheel. She threw the car into fourth gear. She hit eighty miles per hour. Downshift and brake to make the left turn onto Via de Fortuna. Back into fourth gear. Sixty. Seventy. Downshift and brake to turn right on El Montevideo. Back into fourth gear. Sixty. When Nora glanced in the rearview mirror, the pickup truck was nowhere in sight. She'd lost it. "Thank you, Lord," she murmured.

Nora's adrenaline was still flowing when she arrived at the Farm. She was driving much too fast, and she skidded to a stop in front of the gate. Her tires left black marks on the road.

Juan Carillo looked out the window. When he didn't recognize the car, his hand crept closer to his pistol. Then he saw Nora and relaxed.

"Señora drive *a toda velocidad."*

"You betcha," Nora said.

"E peligroso," Juan said.

"Muy peligroso," Nora agreed. It's a hell of a lot safer than being forced off the road, she reminded herself. I could have been killed. *"La puerta,* Juan. Open the gate."

"Sí, señora."

The gate slid sideways. As Nora drove up the driveway, she glanced over her shoulder at the road. The black pickup was slowly cruising by the gate. She glimpsed a man behind the wheel. The sight made her hands shake so violently she had to stop the car. Suddenly she realized the driver of the pickup wasn't some drugged-out kid playing a stupid, dangerous game. What had happened was an attempt to murder her. But whoever wanted her dead wanted it to look like an accident. The would-be murderer knew who she was. He had

been waiting for her. He knew where she was going. Which
road she would take. The only thing that had saved her life
was that she happened to be driving a Porsche . . . not her
T-bird. Her T-bird was an okay car, but it couldn't brake,
steer or accelerate like a Porsche. She'd never have been able
to maneuver her T-bird around the pickup. Nora put the
Porsche in low gear and continued up the driveway.

When she pulled up in front of the hacienda, Carlos met
her. He looked at the Porsche's badly dented fender. *"La
señora* have accident?'' he asked.

"La señora almost had a bad accident,'' Nora said as she
slid out of the Porsche. She walked around the car. *"La
señora es muy fortunado.''* She shook her head as she
thought, Dave Rush! He is going to have a hemorrhage. No
he won't. I'll make it up to him.

The news that Nora had been in an accident reached Millie
before Nora did. It was routed from Juan to Carlos to Miguel
to Oscar. And then to Millie.

Until Millie reassured herself that Nora was all right, her
concern was tangible . . . one could almost reach out and
touch it.

"I was very frightened,'' Nora admitted. ''I still am. I'm
not used to being a target of choice. I wish I'd seen the driver
clearly or had the sense to note the truck's license plate. I
didn't. I was too scared. But now I'm furious. What happened was attempted murder. I could have ended up just
another accidental death statistic.''

Millie caught her breath. "What did you say?''

"That someone tried to kill me. But the police would have
called it an accidental death. That's what it would look like.
There are no paint marks on the Porsche. Just the crinkled
fender that could have been caused when the car went into
the ravine. I'm the only one who knows the damn truck tried
to push me off the road. And I'd be dead, so I couldn't argue
with the sheriff.''

"You'd be another accidental death.'' Millie's voice was
harsh and uneven. After a few moments, choosing her words
with care, she said, "But you didn't die. You're here now
and safe. Thank God for that.'' She shook her head. "None
of this makes any sense.'' What she didn't say was that she
was starting to fear it might make too much sense. To escape

her thoughts, she touched Nora's hair. "It used to be long and silky."

"But it's still black."

"Like Barron's."

"Not like Mark's." Nora swallowed and then found her voice. "Mark is the reason I wanted to see you today."

"Mark? What about Mark?"

Nora said, "He's done something dumb. And illegal. Which is worse."

Their eyes met in pure misery. It all sounded so familiar to both of them . . . so like Barron. "What dumb, illegal thing did Mark do?" Millie asked.

Nora told her. She told her about Mark and Lew Dobbs . . . about Lew Dobbs and Stanley Tseng. And how Mark refused to listen to reason . . . to obey the law. Because he was greedy.

Millie considered what Nora had said. "Thank you for telling me about Dobbs and Tseng," she said.

"Why thank me? You know I would tell you. You're you. I'm me. Even if I'd wanted you to sell the channel to Dobbs— which I don't—I would tell you."

"And I would tell you if I meant to sell the station. I don't. So don't worry, please." Millie took a deep breath and exhaled slowly. "But what can I do about Mark?"

"Talk to him. Tell him what you think."

"You believe I can change his mind?"

"Yes. I do."

"I don't," Millie said humbly.

"He values your goodwill."

After a little while, Millie said, "Mark won't thank you for talking to me."

Nora's face fell. "I guess he won't. But he's refused to listen to me."

"What will you do?"

"He's so dishonest, I don't know what to do." Without meeting Millie's eyes, Nora stood up. "I guess there's nothing more to say."

"Wouldn't you like a drink? I'll ring for Oscar."

"No. I have to get home. I suppose I should be worried about driving . . . the pickup truck might be waiting for me. But if I'm too scared to drive a car, I might as well spend the rest of my life in bed. With the covers pulled over my

Davidyne Mayleas

head." She faced Millie. "I'm sorry I dumped all my troubles on you."

"I'm sorry you're having troubles."

Nora leaned over and kissed Millie lightly on the cheek. "Somehow they don't seem so bad after talking to you. I don't know what I would ever do without you." She turned on her heel and was gone.

Millie made an enormous effort not to go after her . . . to offer some meaningless but comforting words. She knew she mustn't . . . or how would Nora ever learn what to do without her?

After Nora left, Millie went to the library to make a phone call. The attempt on Nora's life concerned her far more than Mark's dishonesty. She hoped Nora was wrong . . . that the near accident had been just that . . . a near accident. That it had nothing to do with Ali. She dialed a number.

"Detective agency."

"This is Mrs. Millie Gardiner. I would like to speak to Mr. Sklar."

"One moment, please."

"Millie?"

"Yes. I know this is soon. You've only been on the job one day. But I want a report on Ali Gardiner's last twenty-four hours."

"What's happened?"

"I'm not sure that anything's happened."

"I have three good men—ex deputy sheriffs—on her tail. I'll collect their reports tomorrow and messenger the reports over to you."

"All right. Watch her closely."

"Will do, Millie."

"And can you keep an eye on Mark Stern . . . my grandson-in-law?"

"For money I can do anything."

"Do it, Gus."

He laughed. "Formerly Baby Gustave."

"Formerly." She laughed too.

Millie hung up the phone. She sat for some minutes incapable of doing anything. She thought of tears, but she was beyond tears. There was nothing to do but live . . . if she could do that.

A blast of Arctic cold forced aside the mild San Diego air. Millie's teeth began to chatter, her arms and legs trembled. She tried to make her way to her bedroom when a crushing blow to the top of her head brought her to her knees. She refused to surrender. Her vision narrowed to a single purpose. She must reach the safety of her bed. Foot by foot, she crawled through the deserted hall. When she finally arrived at her bedroom, she was bathed in sweat. She was freezing and sweating at the same time. It seemed to take forever to get from the bedroom door to her bed. And an eternity before she was able to haul her shaking body onto the bed. She rolled the bedspread around her. All she could do was wait and hope the seizure would pass. First she felt a strange, unnatural relief . . . it lasted about five seconds. Then the trembling and pain returned. The next time the relief lasted ten seconds. Then fifteen seconds. Finally the unnatural cold disappeared. The pounding in her head and the uncontrollable shaking ended as suddenly as they had struck. She had survived another attack.

Chapter 26

WHERE WAS Mark? Why wasn't he home? Nora could hardly sit still . . . she had so much to tell him. Maybe her lucky escape would teach him something . . . bring him to his senses? But the moment he entered the house, she saw something was wrong. He moved slowly, cautiously . . . like a fragile old man who was terrified he might fall and break his hip. Walking down the stairs to their bedroom, he hung onto the banister. Nora silently followed him. Mark half closed the bedroom door. Nora didn't follow him. She stood in the hall and peeked through the opening. Mark carefully removed his jacket. He winced as he worked his arms free of the sleeves. He had more difficulty pulling off his tie. Nora was afraid he didn't have the strength to unknot the tie. When he unbuttoned his shirt, Nora gasped. His chest and stomach were covered with ugly black, red and purple bruises.

Mark heard her. He faced the door. "Stop spying on me," he said. "Come on in. Get a close-up look at what happened when I followed your brilliant advice."

Nora entered the bedroom. "What are you talking about?"

"You told me about Tseng and Dobbs, and you wanted me to dump them. I thought about it and decided you were right."

"You did?"

"Yeah. I did. More fool me. So I had a meeting with Dobbs and Tseng. I told them I thought I knew what was going on. If I was right, I wanted out."

Nora wanted to believe him.

"They offered me a piece of the action—twenty percent— if I'd keep my mouth shut. I told them to fuck off."

Nora stared. The world was full of the unexpected.

"That's when they did a number on me."

"Dobbs and Tseng beat you up?"

"Not Dobbs and Tseng themselves. They brought two musclemen with them. The goons beat the shit out of me. It was a warning to shut up."

"Did you tell them I was the one who told you?"

"Sure I told them. So what? You're a Gardiner. They won't touch you. Millie would have the entire San Diego police department—plus the marines and the navy—after them."

Nora chewed on her lower lip. Too many coincidences. "You tell Dobbs and Tseng about me. Then I almost get killed. Is there any connection?"

"You almost got killed? How?"

Nora explained what had happened and how lucky she was to be driving a Porsche.

Mark listened. Then he asked, "What time did all this happen?"

"About five." Nora followed his thinking. "What time did you give them my name?"

"Four thirty. . . . There wasn't enough time . . ."

Nora nodded. "No. They didn't have enough time to set me up."

Mark said with some impatience, "That's a pretty lousy story. But I gotta soak myself in hot water before I break into little pieces. Then I need eight hours' sleep. We'll talk it over in detail tomorrow night . . . when I get back from Phoenix."

"Phoenix! I thought you dumped Dobbs and Tseng."

"I have. But I haven't dumped Victor Ashland. Remember, Ashland used to own Group H. He sold out to Dobbs for big bucks. Now he's asked to see me. I think he wants me to find him a station."

Nora gave in. "At least Ashland's legitimate. I'm going to fix myself a drink. Do you want one?"

"Later." Mark watched her go. He started to laugh and stopped. It hurt too much. He was a mess, but he was proud of himself. He told some of his best lies under pressure. This lie was proof positive. When he signed the papers, he'd have his twenty percent. And Ashland might actually want to buy a TV station. That part of the lie might turn out to be true. As Mark soaked his aching body in the tub, he thought about the future. He'd siphoned almost one hundred thousand dollars from Arthur's estate. Kickbacks from some legitimate creditors in return for fast action on their bills and a few judicious payments to dummy companies he'd set up. With one thing and another—if he kept his eye on the ball—he'd soon have enough money to kiss the Gardiners good-bye.

"I read your report." The telephone receiver nestled between Millie's ear and shoulder. "Let's say it's provocative."

"What my boys see is what you get," Gus Sklar stated. "No more. No less."

"She went with Mr. Tseng to Los Angeles two nights ago. To have dinner with Mr. Savage."

"Yeah. Then, as you see, the three of them drove to Savage's house in the Malibu Colony. Naturally, my guy didn't try to follow them into the Colony. He'd never have gotten by the gate at the entrance."

"Naturally."

"He waited for them to leave. Finally they did. They left the Colony at ten o'clock the next morning . . . that was yesterday."

"I read it all." Millie's tone was somber. "I believe Ali Reiner made breakfast for both men."

"You believe right. And she probably straightened up the bed. I told you, Millie. Your grand— Sorry. Your stepgranddaughter gets around."

"She does indeed. Keep up the good work, Baby Gustave. I'm depending on you."

"I will, Millie. I won't let you down. I've been watching Stern. There's nothing going on there . . . not so far as my guys can tell."

Millie's laugh was cynical. "Maybe we'll get lucky and you won't have anything to report."

"Maybe. But don't count on it."

"I won't." Millie's face was as grim as her tone. "Just keep me posted. 'Bye." She hung up. She thought for a while before making another call. When her call was picked up by an answering machine, her instinct was to hang up. Then she said, "Jordan, this is Millie Gardiner. Call me as soon as you—"

"Millie. Hang on for a second. I'll turn off the infernal machine." There were a few clicks, and the answering machine went off. "Sorry about that. The machine is my first line of defense. I get so damn many calls."

"Why don't you use a message service?"

"Two reasons. One, I'm paranoid. I wouldn't want the service to know who's called me. Second, the girls can be so impressionable. If a star, a director, a celebrity type happens to call, the girl on the board gets starry-eyed and tongue-tied."

"Some things never change . . . especially in Hollywood. Speaking of Hollywood, where is Tammi Meredith this week?"

"In Canada. She has about three more weeks' shooting. When she finishes the movie, she'll take a short vacation. Then we start rehearsals for *I Remember Mama.*"

"Where's Ken Savage?"

"Where Tammi is, Ken is not far away."

"My sources tell me Mr. Savage was seen in L.A. the other day."

"He does fly back to L.A. regularly. Tammi has business interests . . ."

And Mr. Savage has other interests. . . ."

"Ali Reiner?"

"Ali Reiner." Millie sighed.

"Damn her! That woman will blow the whole—"

"Not if we play our cards right. Jordan, I need your help with another problem. I think I can kill two birds with one stone."

"As long as one of the birds is Ali Reiner . . ."

"It is. I don't want to go into this on the phone. Can you come to Bienvenida?"

"When?"

"The sooner the better."

Jordan thought for a moment. "I still owe Columbia the final cut of my new film. It'll take another week."

"That's all right. Come next Wednesday. Plan to stay a few days."

"You sound serious."

"I am."

"Does Nora know?"

"No. I don't want her to know."

"I understand." He didn't understand at all, but he relied on Millie's judgment. "I'll be there," he said.

"Thank you, Jordan."

Lenny Gerard lounged in a chair watching Lew Dobbs

throw his clothes into a suitcase. Lew was furious. Lenny could guess why. Lew had slammed only a few minutes ago. Tseng socked it to him. Lenny had been in the next room listening . . . listening hard. They had a knockdown fight about giving some clown twenty percent of something. Lew didn't want to do the deal. Tseng did. He finally told Lew, "We'll do it my way. Is that clear?" Lew gave in.

Lenny studied his hulking cousin. He'd been minding his business for months . . . waiting for Lew to offer him a job. Now it occurred to him that Lew couldn't offer him anything. Maybe he ought to pay attention to Tseng? Without thinking, Lenny asked, "Lew, what kind of a stunt are you and that Oriental pulling?"

Lew howled, "What the hell are you talking about?"

Lenny got the picture. He'd made a mistake. "Nothing." He smiled. "I don't mean nothing."

Lew sat on the bed. "Jesus! Let's have it, Lenny. I've had a rough day. I'm in no mood to play games."

Lenny didn't like being talked down to. "Well . . . you see . . . I figure you and Tseng . . . you're in some kind of deal together." As he spoke his confidence grew. He remembered what his mother always said: "The Dobbs branch of the family are poor trash." "I get the impression Tseng put up the money for your TV stations. Which makes him your boss."

Dobbs shook his head slowly. "You get the impression . . . Jesus! Who the fuck gave you the right to get impressions? You tell this impression to anyone?"

"No. Yes." He saw Lew's piggy eyes become as large and as round as the silver dollars he used as buttons. The expression on his face was murderous. "No!"

"Which is it, Lenny? Yes or no?"

"No!"

"You're lying. Damn it! I hate a liar." Lew picked up the phone and dialed a number. "Stanley. You'd better get your ass over here. I think I found a swamp rat."

Lenny started to get up. When he was halfway out of the chair, Lew said, "Sit, cousin."

Lenny froze, half in and half out of the chair. His hands were on the arms of the chair, and he balanced himself by resting his weight on his hands.

"I said sit." Lew made a threatening gesture with one ham-size fist. Lenny collapsed into the chair.

They were silent for a few minutes. Then Lenny complained, "I have to go to the bathroom."

"You sit there. I don't care if you piss in your pants."

"I care," Lenny said. For a second time, he started to rise.

Lew took a step toward him.

A knock on the door stopped Lew. He opened the door.

"Come in, Stanley. Cousin Lenny has a story to tell you."

"I gotta go to the bathroom."

"I said—"

"Lew," Stanley Tseng said, "we want Cousin Lenny's cooperation. He'll be more cooperative after he obeys nature's call. Won't you, Cousin Lenny?"

"Yes. Thank you." Lenny hurried to the bathroom. He barely made it to the john. The feeling of relief was unbelievable. As he zipped up his fly, he tried to understand why he was so frightened of Cousin Lew. Why was it such a big deal if Cousin Lew did business with Stanley Tseng? He washed his hands and returned to face Lew Dobbs and Stanley Tseng.

"Lew says you think he and I are in business," Tseng said.

"You are. You put up the money to buy the TV stations."

"How do you know that?" Tseng asked.

"I don't know it. I just guessed it. From watching the two of you together."

"He told that piece of shit to someone," Lew roared.

"Did you tell anyone?" Tseng asked.

"I may have," Lenny admitted.

"Who?" Tseng was a model of patience.

"A girl . . . A girl I've been balling. She's a doll."

"I'm sure she is. Why did you talk about your cousin and me?"

"I don't know. We'd just finished fucking, and . . . well . . . I felt like talking. It didn't mean anything."

"Of course it didn't," Tseng murmured. The truth was he hated pillow talk. Once, when he was a young man, he'd talked too much to a girl. And he'd lost an important arms sale. A competitor had used his own virginal sixteen-year-old daughter as bait. Afterward, the girl—no longer a virgin—told her father everything Tseng had told her. The father underbid him and got the order. Years later—when he met the girl . . . now an ambassador's wife—she smiled at him. And he smiled back. What else could he do?

"Her name is Pat Yocum. Pat works for Channel 18. She's the program director," Lenny explained.

Stanley Tseng rubbed his forehead. "I remember her. The party. She knows Nora Stern," he said softly.

Lenny shrugged. "Sure. She knows her."

"For the want of a nail a shoe was lost."

"What's that mean?" Lew Dobbs asked.

"Nothing."

"That's Shakespeare," Lenny said. "I think it's from *Richard III.*"

"It is. Shakespeare gave a simple explanation of how a war is lost." It could apply to this war, Tseng told himself. "Cousin Lenny, go home. And do not talk to anyone else about your cousin and me. Do you understand that?"

Lenny nodded.

"Go." Tseng pointed toward the door. He waited for Lenny to close the door behind him before saying, "So now we know something more."

"We know everything. My asshole cousin told his broad. The broad told Nora Gardiner Stern. Nora Gardiner Stern told her husband . . . and we're twenty points lighter."

"Probably."

"I'll arrange to take care of the broad."

Tseng shook his head. "My people will pick her up. She might have told someone else, who, in turn, told Mrs. Stern." His lips were compressed in a thin smile. "Or that someone else told still another person who told Mrs. Stern. Until we know the facts, you do nothing."

"And after we know the facts?"

"Everyone must be taken care of."

"You're talkin' about another fuckin' Valentine's Day massacre."

Stanley Tseng studied his perfectly manicured nails. He'd been careless in his dealings with Lew. He'd not given sufficient weight to the fact that Lew was an American . . . not an Asiatic or even a European. Asiatics and Europeans were used to following orders without question. Obedience was bred into them, Americans were different. Often, he'd had to convince Dobbs to do what he told him to do. Cousin Lenny had overheard their arguments. Everything that had gone wrong followed from that. He considered his boast . . . to take care of those who knew too much. An idle boast. There were too many messy links in the chain, including the Gardiners. Stanley Tseng was not a man who fought the odds. His survival had often depended on an acute sense of the tides of war . . . when to cut his losses. It was time to cut his losses and move on. Tomorrow morning he would start transferring funds from banks in Dallas and New York to accounts in Switzerland, Luxembourg and Lichtenstein. In forty-eight hours he'd be clean. Of course, if by some miracle things held together, he must dispose of Lew. He needed an American who would follow orders without question. It occurred to him Cousin Lenny might be that American. Besides, there was a nice irony in the change from big dumb cousin to little dumb cousin.

"Madam. There's a Miss Stern on the telephone. She wishes to speak to you?"

"Nora?" Millie gave Oscar a puzzled look.

"No. Miss Stern. Miss Shirley Stern."

"Shirley Stern? Who in the world . . . ?" Millie made a grimace of disgust. "I am getting old. Mr. Stern's sister?"

"I believe so, madam."

"I'll take the call." Millie straightened out her papers and picked up the phone. "Hello. This is Millie Gardiner."

"Oh! I appreciate your coming to the phone. You must be very busy." Shirley spoke rapidly . . . her voice squeaked.

"Not too busy to talk to Mark's sister. What a clear connection. You sound as if you're in San Diego."

"I am. I'm calling from a pay phone in Lindbergh Field. We just arrived in San Diego. A TWA flight."

"We? Is your mother with you?"

Shirley laughed a little hysterically. "No way. Grace will never move an inch out of Queens. One of her penny stocks might move an eighth of a point. I'm here with a friend."

"Are you going to be in San Diego long?"

A few seconds passed before Shirley said, "I don't know. It depends. . . ."

"Ah. Where are you staying?"

"I made a reservation at the Holiday Inn at Hotel Circle."

"I won't hear of it. I insist you and your friend stay with

me. I have a large house. You'll have far more privacy and comfort than in any hotel."

"That's very kind of you," Shirley said uneasily. "But I don't . . ."

"I do. I'm going to put you on hold for a moment." Millie pushed the hold button and rang for Oscar. "Oscar, where is Mario?"

"Right here, madam."

"Good. Don't let him leave." She switched back to Shirley. "Are you still there?" she said.

"I'm still here, Mrs. Gardiner. Barely. I'm running out of change."

"All right. Collect your luggage and have a cup of coffee. In about forty-five minutes go outside the terminal . . . in front of the TWA sign. My limousine should be waiting for you. It's a white stretch Cadillac. The license plate is FARM 1. The driver's name is Mario. He'll bring you here."

"You're very kind," Shirley repeated.

"Nonsense, Shirley. You're family. I wouldn't have it any other way." After Millie hung up, she smiled. The invitation had nothing to do with kindness or family feelings. She'd insisted Shirley Stern stay with her because she was very curious. Why had Shirley called her? Not Mark? And what were Shirley and her friend doing in San Diego? She hadn't asked because she was confident Shirley would tell her at the earliest opportunity.

Millie was waiting at the front door to greet Shirley and her friend. She didn't know what to expect. But when Shirley stepped from the car, she was satisfied. Shirley's bone structure and features gave evidence that the same gene pool had shaped both Mark and her. But it was as though Shirley's maker had not sifted her through a fine enough screen when she was formed. He'd permitted impurities to coarsen what could have been a lovely face. And what Shirley did to herself didn't help. Her frizzed copper-colored hair might have been cute on a dolllike whore. On Shirley the hair wasn't cute. And maybe an anorectic sixteen-year-old model could have worn the very short stretch-wool black dress Shirley had chosen . . . with a black patent leather belt and thigh-high black boots. Shirley couldn't. Her large breasts, full hips and thighs made a joke of her outfit. Just looking at Shirley made Millie uncomfortable. Millie glanced at the large man who was with Shirley. His skin was rough, and he wore well-washed jeans, a blue sports shirt and sandals. There was something about him that reminded her of tall-masted sailing ships. She'd seen many men like him, men who belonged to the sea . . . who remained on the land only because they lacked the means of returning to the sea. They made an odd couple, more original and quirky than Millie had expected from Mark's family.

Millie walked the half dozen paces to the car. She held out her hand. "I'm Millie Gardiner. And you're Shirley."

"Yes. I'm Shirley." But Shirley didn't shake hands. She just stood and stared at the house. Millie had long ago become accustomed to the look on many faces the first time they saw Bienvenida. Still, Shirley Stern's reaction was interesting. The house seemed to paralyze her . . . she couldn't move.

"That's some house," she said at last.

"It looks big. It is big. But it's also my home. And it's comfortable. You'll see . . ." She reached for Shirley's hand and grasped it. The women shook hands. "Come. I feel I already know you. Mark's talked so much about you."

"Mark's talked about me?"

Millie heard an edge in Shirley's voice. She turned to the seaman. "Hello," she said. "I'm Millie Gardiner."

"Hi. I'm Quinn Carroll." His voice was deep and rolling.

"Carlos, tell Oscar that I would like Miss Stern and Mr. Carroll placed in the blue suite." She smiled at Shirley. "The blue suite has a private terrace. You can see the ocean from the terrace."

"How far are we from the ocean?" Quinn Carroll asked.

"About two miles . . . as the crow flies. A lot longer by road."

"Only two miles . . ."

Millie linked arms with Shirley and Quinn and guided them into the house. "Come with me," she said. "I'll give you the nickel tour."

As they went from room to room Shirley's eyes grew round. "This is some place," she said. "There's something about it that reminds me, spiritually anyway, a little of Casa de las Cuentas. You know. D. H. Lawrence's *The Plumed Serpent*. I think Lawrence might have found happiness here."

"You've read Lawrence?" Millie tried to smother her surprise.

"Didn't Mark tell you I'm an assistant professor of literature at NYU? He must have. He spoke so much about me." Shirley enjoyed her own sarcasm.

"I'm sorry. Of course he did. I don't know what I was thinking of."

"You weren't thinking."

"Drop it, Shirley." Quinn Carroll didn't raise his voice, but Shirley heeled.

"I'm sorry, Mrs. Gardiner. . . ."

"Millie. Please. We are related."

"By marriage. Courtesy of my brother."

Millie glanced at Shirley. Under that outrageous outfit was an angry, frightened woman. That Shirley had called her and not Mark made no sense.

When Millie walked her guests around the wading pool, Quinn took more interest. "Do you swim in that?" he asked.

"No. It's more decorative than utilitarian. Just looking at the water is refreshing."

Quinn smiled and nodded.

"There's a fifty-meter lap pool and pool house behind the garage."

"Two pools. You get it, Quinn? That costs money."

Millie shrugged . . . she hadn't thought about the cost in many years. "Are you hungry?" she asked. "Airline food . . . even first-class airline food is still airline food."

"We flew tourist," Shirley said proudly. "But they fed us."

Millie floundered. Shirley was like an electric eel.

"Would you like to see your suite? You can bathe and change if you like."

"I'd like that, ma'am," Quinn said.

"Please. Ma'am makes me feel old. My friends—"

"Of whom you have so many." Shirley couldn't shut up for the life of her.

"Quit it!" Quinn said.

"My friends call me Millie."

"Millie. Is that short for Mildred?" Quinn asked.

Millie nodded. "I think so. But I never saw my birth certificate. I was born in a small town in Kansas. If the records didn't get buried in a dust storm or didn't burn up in a fire,

the rats probably ate my birth certificate decades ago. I've
always been called Millie.''

"Your parents weren't rich?'' Shirley asked.

"No! We were dirt-poor. Dust bowl poor. My father and
I migrated to California in the thirties. They called us Okies.''

"You've read John Steinbeck?'' Shirley asked.

Millie smiled. "I've not only read *The Grapes of Wrath,*
I've lived *The Grapes of Wrath.''*

"That wasn't the best of times,'' Shirley said.

"It wasn't the worst of times either.'' Millie quickly added,
"Sorry about that. I couldn't resist.''

Shirley sounded almost good-humored. "If I'd thought of
it, I'd have said it myself.''

Millie heard the change of tone. Shirley's anger was ebb-
ing.

"I'll go for that bath,'' Quinn said. "Then maybe you,
me and Shirley here can have us a nice talk.''

Millie motioned for one of the servants to join them. One
was always on duty . . . ready to respond to her commands.
"Rosa,'' Millie said, "please show our guests to the blue
suite.''

"Sí, madam.''

"You go ahead. I'll either be here or in the library. When
you're ready, they'll find me. And then, Quinn, we'll have
that nice talk.''

While Shirley and Quinn were in their suite, Millie called
Nora at the station. "Did Mark tell you that his sister and
her boyfriend were about to descend on us?''

"No. He didn't say a word. He's in Phoenix.'' Nora
thought for a moment. "I don't think he knew they were
coming. What's Shirley like?''

"Well . . . she's different.'' Millie described Shirley's outfit and her spleen.

"Do you want me to come over? Pay you a surprise visit?
I'm very curious to meet my sister-in-law.''

"I don't think so. Not today anyway. We'll see about tomorrow.''

"Millie the Mysterious strikes again.''

"I'm not being mysterious. They're here for a reason. I
think they'll talk more freely if we're alone.''

Nora reluctantly agreed. "But call me as soon as you know

anything. If I'm not here, I'll be home . . . waiting by the telephone.''

"I'll call," Millie promised. She hung up and rang for Oscar. "Roll one of the bars onto the colonnade. Next to my chair. And set two more chairs and a table there. I'm going outside. I'll have a glass of Chenin blanc while I wait.''

"Yes, madam. Is there anything special I should include in the choice of beverages?''

"Beer. A half dozen bottles . . . light and dark beer.''

"Thank you, madam.''

The glass of wine was waiting for Millie beside her favorite chair. She sipped the wine, placed the glass on the table, closed her eyes and allowed the tranquillity of Bienvenida to wash over her. She wasn't aware that she'd dozed off until she opened her eyes and saw Shirley and Quinn watching her.

"Welcome back," Shirley said. "I hope we didn't disturb you.''

"No, no. If I nap too long in the afternoon, I won't sleep well at night. No one has fixed you a drink. Oscar is slipping.''

"He tried, but we waved him away. You were asleep, and . . .''

"Thank you, Shirley.'' Millie pondered the change in the woman. Even her clothes were different. She wore white pants and a simple white cotton blouse. "I'm awake now. What would you like?''

"Vodka. Absolut. Straight up . . . if you have it," Shirley said.

"I'm sure we have a bottle of Absolut somewhere in the house. And you, Quinn?''

"The same, ma'am.''

Millie raised her hand. As if by magic, Oscar appeared. "Our guests would like Absolut vodka. Is there a bottle of Absolut in the bar?''

"Yes, madam. As always.''

Millie watched as Oscar made the drinks. Then, as magically as he had appeared, he disappeared. It was a talent she valued highly. While they sipped their drinks, Millie noticed that Shirley held her glass in her left hand . . . her hand farthest away from Quinn. And Quinn held his drink in his right hand . . . his hand farthest away from Shirley. Since the table blocked her view of their free hands, she guessed they

were holding hands. How nice, she thought. She was surprised when Shirley and Quinn placed an attaché case on the
table. They hadn't been holding hands. They'd been holding
the attaché case.

"Millie . . ." Shirley sounded tentative. She took a deep
breath. "Could I have another drink?"

"Of course." Millie started to summon Oscar.

"No!" Shirley exclaimed. "I'll do it myself."

"As you like."

"You can freshen me up," Quinn said.

Shirley went to the bar and filled the two martini-size
glasses to the brim.

That's a lot of vodka, Millie thought.

"Show Millie what you have, honey," Shirley said.

"Now?"

To Millie, Quinn looked worried.

"Now!"

Quinn opened the attaché case. He brought out an old book
and a folded map. "Would you look at this, ma'am?" Quinn
asked.

"Call her Millie. Damn it! She told you to call her Millie." Again Shirley sounded hysterical.

"It's all right, Quinn," Millie said soothingly. "If you're
more comfortable with ma'am, I'll answer to ma'am."

"Thank you, ma'am. Here." He opened the book to a
specific page and passed it to Millie. "Read this, please."

Millie wished she had her reading glasses. She had to squint
to make out the words. "In the year of our Lord, 1608, in
the month of October, on the day of the twenty-third, the
great galleon, *Puerto de Veracruz*, foundered in a hurricane
off the coast of Florida . . ." Millie looked at Quinn. He was
mesmerized. To him, this wasn't a book. This was the Holy
Grail.

"I don't understand," she said. "Why am I reading this?"

"This is why, ma'am." Quinn unfolded a maritime chart
of the waters surrounding the Florida Keys.

Somewhere to the south and east of Key West—Millie's
ability to read the chart was limited—there was a hand-drawn
circle with an *X* in the middle. "Let me guess," she said.
"That Spanish galleon. It sunk here." She jabbed at the *X*.

"That's right, ma'am. The galleon was loaded with gold
and silver—"

"They always are," Millie said.

"—bound for King Phillip II of Spain."

"Who else?"

"Look here, ma'am." Quinn produced several ancient-looking metal plates from the attaché case. The plates were pitted and encrusted with the residue of centuries of immersion in salt water.

Millie examined the plates. "From the galleon?" she asked.

"That's right, ma'am." Quinn explained how he and a friend of his had been looking for this galleon for over twenty years and how they'd finally pinpointed—within a ten-square-mile area—where the galleon had gone down. "We had a small boat—a thirty-foot sloop—and using scuba equipment, we found these. Now we need a much bigger boat, the right equipment and the resources to search the ten square miles of ocean bottom . . . foot by foot."

Millie maintained a carefully neutral expression. The man wasn't a fool. He couldn't expect her to fund the expedition.

"We need your help," Shirley said.

"I don't think I—"

"Not your money," Shirley quickly interjected. "I said, your help."

"How can I be of help?"

"You can talk to Mark."

"Mark? I don't understand."

"Mark owes me money. A lot of money. Enough money to pay for our share in the treasure hunt." Although Shirley was doing her very best to remain calm, her voice became strident. She told Millie how, when Mark was in New York, she'd asked him for the money. And how he'd claimed he didn't have it. "He lied to me," Shirley exclaimed. "He didn't tell me he'd been made managing partner of Reiner & Co. He has plenty of money. He just won't pay me what he owes me."

"How much money did you lend Mark?" Millie asked.

"I didn't lend him any money. Mark is the first Stern to have any real money. I did him a favor . . . a big favor. And he promised me, if things worked out, I could count on his help whenever I needed it. I need his help now, and he won't do anything." Shirley was close to tears.

"What kind of a favor did you do for Mark?"

"I introduced him to your granddaughter."

"You what!" Millie's stomach started to churn. Here, in the peace and beauty of Bienvenida—her safe place—she was about to see it again . . . the ugly face of life. "How could you have introduced them? Mark and Nora met at college. You didn't know Nora at Ohio State?"

"I didn't know your granddaughter personally. I still don't. But I did know about her."

"You're straining my patience, Shirley. What exactly are you trying to say?"

"Here." Shirley took a scrapbook from the attaché case.

Millie gingerly opened the scrapbook. She did not want to know what was in the book, but she found it impossible not to look. There were only two items. A newspaper clipping stating that Nora Gardiner, heir to the Gardiner fortune, had decided not to attend Radcliffe. She was going to work her way through Ohio State as a waitress. The second was the invitation to Mark's and Nora's wedding.

"I'm sorry. I still don't understand," Millie said.

"Mark was at Ohio State. I sent him a photocopy of the clipping."

"Ah." Millie rose. She went to the bar and poured herself another glass of wine. She turned and leaned against the bar. "So, thanks to you, Mark knew who Nora was and where to find her."

Shirley nodded. "It clicked. I thought it would. Girls have always liked Mark. And as they say, the rest is history."

"That's the favor you did Mark."

"That's it. He owes me."

"I see. How much does he owe you?"

"Five hundred thousand dollars. That's all. A lousy five hundred thousand."

"There's nothing lousy about half a million dollars. You didn't pick that number out of the air, did you?"

"No, ma'am," Quinn said. "That's what I need to cover my share of the cost of finding the *Veracruz*."

Millie was tempted to ask if Quinn had known about Shirley's great expectation before he attached himself to her. She didn't ask. She suspected the answer—if truthful—would have devastated Shirley. Instead she asked, "What do you want from me?"

"I want you to make Mark pay his debt."

"Or else, Shirley? There's always an 'or else,' " Millie said.

"Or else I'll show the clipping to your granddaughter."

"She won't thank you."

"I don't want to be thanked. I want to be paid what Mark owes me."

Millie returned to her chair. She thought about Shirley Stern. In her thirties . . . her looks fading . . . frightened . . . desperate. Shirley saw Quinn Carroll and the treasure hunt as her way out, possibly her only way out. Millie remembered a time when she was frightened and desperate. She'd done what she had to do, taken the only possible way out. But Shirley had made a bad miscalculation. Mark was the managing partner of Reiner & Co., but he didn't have a half million dollars. And if Nora found out the truth . . . ? Millie began to perspire. She knew her granddaughter. Nora was proud, and because she was proud, she was vulnerable. That Mark might have married her for her money would be a terrible blow to her pride. To her marriage. Millie respected that pride. And she knew how fragile pride could be. Once she'd failed to consider Barron's pride. She mustn't make the same mistake again. She considered her options. Yes, she could write Shirley a check for the clipping. But that meant paying blackmail. When Quinn didn't find the treasure—and he probably wouldn't—there was nothing to stop Shirley from coming back for more money. Unless . . . Millie had an idea. Maybe there was a better way.

"Shirley," she said, "am I right in thinking you don't want to hurt your brother and my granddaughter?"

"I just want my money."

"Mark doesn't have it."

"He does. He's the managing partner."

"That's right. And in two or three years—if he's successful—he will be worth a lot more than a half million. But right now—today—he doesn't have it."

"Damn!" Quinn muttered. "I knew this was a lousy idea."

"He really doesn't have the money?" Shirley asked.

"Believe me. He really doesn't." Millie looked again at the maritime chart and then at Quinn Carroll. "Quinn, tell me more about yourself . . . about how you got interested in the sunken galleon." She listened as Quinn—slowly at first and then with growing enthusiasm—spun out the story of his lifelong love affair with the sea. And how he and his friend had stumbled across the story of the sunken treasure. He'd spent half his life looking for the treasure.

"And now that I've finally got a fix on it, no one except for Shirley, here, will believe me. And she has no money. I'm a sailor. If a boat has a mast, I can raise the sails and take it anywhere in the world. But I don't know anything about raising money," he concluded bitterly.

"Maybe you know more than you think," Millie said cautiously.

Quinn and Shirley just looked at her.

"I'm a gambler. I own a breeding farm. There's no bigger gamble than breeding horses."

Quinn and Shirley were afraid to say anything. When one is witness to a possible miracle, one must be careful not to interrupt the magic.

"Would you be interested in selling me a piece of the action . . . for, say, half a million dollars?"

Shirley swallowed. "How big a piece?" she asked.

"Fifty percent of your share in the venture."

"What about that?" Shirley pointed to the newspaper clipping.

"I'd like to have it for my own family scrapbook, but it's not a deal breaker."

Shirley tossed down her drink. "It's yours. It was supposed to be my insurance policy. Now . . . Who needs it?"

Millie closed the scrapbook. "Tonight, the three of us will have dinner here. And tomorrow we'll see my lawyer and then my banker. Once you get your check, you'll be on your way."

"Yes, ma'am," Quinn said. "We'll catch the first plane back to New York."

Millie lowered her eyes. Barron, she said silently. I didn't understand until it was too late. But I did learn something. I did better with your daughter. Now will you forgive me?

Millie had no belief in the existence of life after death. Still, she half believed she heard the sound of faint laughter and a familiar mocking voice saying, "I will . . . if you will. . . ."

Chapter 27

MARK FINISHED going over his analyst's report on the state of the TV industry. He wanted to throw up over the report. The networks were in the shithouse. Except for a few independents, the specialized superstations—ESPN, CNN, A&E—and the cable operations, no one was making money. What was he missing? For the life of him, he couldn't see why Ashland wanted back into the business. But he did. More important, Ashland had given Reiner & Co. a handsome retainer and a year's exclusive to find him a property. His intercom buzzed.

"Yes, Kim," he said.

"They're here again," Kim whispered.

"Who's here again?"

"Those men."

Mark stiffened. "The men who . . . ?"

"No. Not them. Mr. Tseng and Mr. Dobbs. They're alone."

"No musclemen?"

"I don't think so. Mr. Tseng brought me a lovely bracelet. The diamonds almost look real."

"Don't kid yourself. They are real."

"You mean it? I could kiss him."

"Tseng doesn't expect to be kissed. Just show them in and disappear for a while."

"Okay."

Mark stared at the door. What the hell was Tseng up to? When they'd met at Group H, he'd made it plain he didn't want to see either of them in San Diego. Jesus, he thought. If Nora gets wind of this, my ass is grass. I'm not ready to cut out. There was a knock on his door.

"Come in," Mark called out.

Kim opened the door and then scuttled for safety.

Tseng entered the office with Dobbs close behind. Dobbs shut the door, and the men seated themselves in the chairs facing Mark's desk . . . as if they owned the place.

"We agreed you wouldn't come here," Mark said. He made no attempt to conceal his anger.

"We did. Times change," Tseng said.

"Old buddy, you're going to be real happy we're here."

Mark frowned. Lew was so full of himself, he looked as if he was about to burst.

"That twenty percent you cut out of our hides." Lew shot a quick glance at Tseng. "Out of my hide. I reckon you earned it."

Mark said nothing. Until he knew what Dobbs was talking about, there was nothing he could say.

Tseng appeared to find Dobbs's enthusiasm and Mark's silence amusing. "You don't know what's happened . . . do you?"

Mark sipped what was left of his morning cup of coffee. The coffee tasted cold and bitter . . . that didn't matter. What mattered was it gave him a few seconds to think. One reason he was a successful trader was the speed with which his mind worked under pressure . . . assembling the available information, letting the information tell him whether to buy a stock or sell it. His brain worked so quickly, his decisions seemed instinctive. Now he understood why Dobbs and Tseng were in his office, why they had broken their promise. He didn't know how he knew but he did.

"Wrong, Stanley," he said. "I expected it to happen. I just didn't know when. I've been working on Millie . . . all the time. She's finally decided to sell Channel 18 to you."

"So it would seem. She wants much too much for the channel, but we'll negotiate. She'll give a little. We'll give a little. . . ." Tseng shrugged. "She asked us to meet at her office to cut a deal."

"How much is Millie asking?"

"One hundred twenty million."

Mark's eyes opened wide. "Reiner & Co. is your investment banker." It was a statement, not a question.

"I think if you work it right, Reiner & Co. might handle both sides of the transaction. The way you did when Lew here bought Group H."

"Well, son. How do you feel now about our coming to see you?"

Mark grinned. "I know about killing a messenger who brings bad news. But I never heard of anyone killing a messenger who brings good news."

"A wise philosophy," Tseng said as he rose to leave. "One final point. Your charming secretary? She is aware the diamond bracelet is genuine?"

"I told her it was."

Tseng nodded. "You will tell her I consider my debt paid."

"I'll tell her," Mark said.

"We'll call you after the meeting, old buddy. Once you know the final terms, you can start drawing up the papers." Dobbs swaggered out of the office. Tseng followed. It occurred to Mark that if he were Lew Dobbs, he would not let Stanley Tseng get behind him. He'd want Tseng where he could see him at all times.

After the men left, Mark did a mental double take on Millie. Why was she selling Channel 18 to Dobbs and Tseng? Nora had to have told her about the Tseng/Dobbs connection. And that the arrangement was illegal. So why? Mark smiled. The deal confirmed his philosophy. Everything and everyone was for sale . . . if the price was right and the timing was right. Mark whistled. One hundred twenty million for an independent station in the San Diego market. The price was right. He frowned. But the timing. Why had Millie decided to sell now? His eyes fell on his analyst's TV report. His frown faded. Millie was some smart broad. Now was the right time to sell. The longer she waited, the less Channel 18 would bring on the open market.

Millie led Dobbs and Tseng to the conference table. Jordan was waiting for them.

"Gentlemen," she said. "This is Jordan Banska. Jordan, I understand you already know Mr. Tseng. This is Mr. Lew Dobbs."

Dobbs and Jordan shook hands.

"I've been an admirer of your work for a long time," Tseng said. "And of your father's work."

"Thank you," Jordan said. "One can never have enough admirers."

"And of your films, Mrs. Gardiner." Tseng was at his charming best. "Or should I say Miss Thorne?"

"You're too kind. I haven't been Miss Thorne for almost half a century."

"Any time you elect to be Miss Thorne again, I would be honored if you allowed me to finance the film."

"A tempting offer, Mr. Tseng."

"When you lovebirds are done sniffing each other, maybe we can get down to business," Dobbs said.

"Business." Millie's fingers drummed on a manila folder in front of her. "Yes. I suppose we should get down to business."

"A hundred twenty million is too much for this joint," Dobbs said.

"It probably is," Millie said.

"How does sixty million sound? I think that's a damned generous offer. If I were you, I'd take it seriously." Dobbs's negotiating technique was simple. Pound at the person on the other side of the table until he'd beaten him into the ground.

"I do take it seriously," Millie said. "And I urge you to take my offer just as seriously."

Stanley Tseng tensed. From the moment he'd entered Millie Gardiner's office, his survival instincts had gone into overdrive. Jordan Banska's presence only added to his concern. "What offer, Mrs. Gardiner?" His manner didn't change. He was still his charming self.

"This offer, Mr. Tseng." Millie opened the file and slid two pieces of paper across the table . . . one went to Stanley Tseng and the other to Lew Dobbs.

Tseng scanned the offer and smiled. He congratulated himself on getting his money out of the country.

Dobbs exploded. He rose to his feet with such violence that his chair toppled over backward. "You crazy, stupid, old broad! Sell out for one dollar?"

"Are you asking me if I'm crazy or are you telling me?" Millie said. She was amused by Dobbs's theatrics.

"I ain't asking you nothin'. I'm telling you to back off." Dobbs slammed his fist down on the conference table.

Jordan stood up. His hand whipped down and across the table. Much like a tennis player hits a backhand, the callused side of his hand sliced into Dobbs's arm just above the elbow. The chop paralyzed Dobbs's arm.

"Sit down," Jordan said. He didn't raise his voice.

"Jesus! What did you do to my arm?"

"I'll tell you what I didn't do. I didn't break your elbow. But if you don't sit down, I will."

"Sit down, Lew," Tseng said. "The man knows karate . . . probably a black belt. He can easily break your elbow. What is called for is talk . . . not bluster."

Lew used his left hand to pick up his chair.

"This seems quite simple," Tseng said. "For one dollar and other valuable considerations . . ."

"What valuable considerations?" Dobbs exclaimed.

Tseng glanced at Dobbs with contempt. "Mrs. Gardiner means she will not inform the authorities of our arrangement." He smiled.

"She has no proof," Dobbs muttered.

"She doesn't need proof. Remember BCCI. Once the government begins an investigation, they'll find proof. Lew, I do not wish to testify, under oath, before a committee of United States senators. And neither do you."

"A wise decision, Mr. Tseng."

I have no interest in my government's version of alphabet soup . . . the attorney general, the IRS, the FCC, the SEC. Providing you agree to all my terms." Millie matched his smile.

"For one dollar and other valuable considerations, we will sell Mrs. Gardiner Group H and our other television holdings."

"I ain't selling for any one dollar," Dobbs stormed.

"There's more, Mr. Tseng," Millie said.

"True, Mrs. Gardiner. We will agree never to buy another TV or radio station in the United States." Stanley Tseng continued to smile.

"Goddamn it! No!" Dobbs roared.

"Yes, Lew. I will lose a great deal of money, but . . ."

"There's always Europe, Africa, Asia . . . the entire world," Millie pointed out.

"That's okay for him, but what about me?" Dobbs was as furious with Tseng as he was with Millie. "I'm an American. I'm not a fuckin' Oriental. If I lose my American operation, I lose everything."

"Quite right, Mr. Dobbs," Millie said. "You are an American. Even more than Mr. Tseng, you owe your country obedience to your country's laws. You broke the law. So you will lose everything.''

Dobbs moved his arm as feeling began to return. ''You got another problem, lady. Doesn't she, Tseng?''

''I don't know, Lew. It all depends . . .''

''What problem?'' Millie asked.

''Well, maybe you can put the arm on Tseng and me, but how you going to handle your son-in-law?''

''Mark?'' Millie braced herself. ''What has Mark got to do with this?''

''Mrs. Gardiner,'' Tseng said, ''your son-in-law found out about the arrangement . . .''

''I know that,'' Millie said.

''You may not know that in return for his silence, we gave him twenty percent of Group H.'' Tseng's smile was maddening.

It came back to her with a rush . . . Ali's description of Mark. Ali had been wrong. Mark was more than a little dishonest. How would Nora take it? She'd buried Shirley's scrapbook, but she couldn't bury this. This time she couldn't shield Nora.

''Mark will sell on the same terms as you,'' Millie said.

''You're lying,'' Dobbs snarled. ''If he doesn't, you going to report him to the alphabet soup? The hell you are.''

Jordan intervened. ''The hell she isn't.'' he said pleasantly. ''If for any reason, Millie finds it difficult to turn in Nora's husband, I'll do the job for her. I don't like the bastard.''

''Ah.'' Tseng looked at Jordan. ''I understand. Speaking of Mrs. Stern, will you indulge my curiosity. Am I correct in thinking Mrs. Stern told you about Lew and me?''

''No,'' Jordan lied. They'd come to the reason Millie had wanted him at the meeting. ''Nora knows nothing about the game you two are playing.''

Millie's face was open and guileless. ''If she did, she would have told me.''

''It's not important,'' Tseng said. ''But if Mrs. Stern did not inform you, might I ask who did?''

Jordan laughed. ''You trusted the wrong woman, Tseng. Ali Reiner talks too much . . . after sex.''

''Pillow talk?''

"You can call it that. Ali has diarrhea of the mouth. Some women do."

"And some women don't." Tseng remembered his sixteen-year-old virgin. She didn't talk. He did.

Jordan pressed his point. "Ali Reiner is generous. She pillow talks to everyone."

For the first time in the meeting, Stanley Tseng was angry. At himself for his lack of judgment in trusting Ali. But he was even more angry at Ali . . . for betraying him with Jordan Banska. The sexual betrayal was meaningless. The night he'd spent with Ali and Ken Savage . . . they'd each had their turn between her legs and then they'd enjoyed her together. It wasn't sexual betrayal . . . it was far more dangerous. She'd betrayed a business confidence to Banska. In the shadow world of international hot money, confidentiality is crucial. It was fortunate he'd trusted her only with the television matter . . . and that only because he thought she might be useful. Still, for that betrayal she must be punished.

"May I make a call?" he asked. "I believe you'll find it interesting."

Jordan glanced at Millie . . . she nodded. "Go ahead," he said.

"I would like you to listen to the call, Mrs. Gardiner."

Millie went to her desk. She waited until Tseng had completed dialing before picking up her extension. The phone rang several times before the call was answered.

"Hello."

Millie winced. Even though she'd expected that voice, the hurt went deep.

"Ali. This is Tseng."

"Where the hell have you been?"

"Here and there. Why?"

"Ken Savage is waiting for a call. He's agreed to listen to your offer."

"My offer?"

"You know. That you'll make it worth Ken's while if Tammi quits *I Remember Mama.*"

"I did say that, but I've changed my mind. I am no longer interested in buying Channel 18 or in Miss Meredith."

"Stanley! You promised! You can't change your mind," Ali wailed.

"What did I promise you, Ali?"

"You'd take care of me when Millie sold you the channel. I'm to get a nice commission." There was just the suggestion of a sob in Ali's voice.

"That's true. But, as I said, I'm not buying Channel 18. By the way, Li Yung told me you paid him to run Mrs. Stern's car off the road."

"He didn't do it. He's a lousy driver."

"I know he didn't succeed."

"You should fire him."

"I have. For acting without my permission, Li has . . . lost his driver's license. Permanently!"

"Good!"

"Ali . . . do you dislike Mrs. Stern that much?"

"Dislike her? For heaven's sake, of course not. She's my oldest friend . . . my only friend. I like her. Maybe I love her." Without any emphasis, Ali added, "But she was in my way."

"For that she had to die. That's what I thought." Tseng sighed. "But you failed to ask my permission to hire Li Yung."

"Stanley . . . It was such a little thing. I didn't want to bother you."

"Murder is not a little thing. You are never to go near any of my men again. And you are never to try to contact me. If you disobey me in this, I will be forced to confiscate *your* driver's license. Also permanently!" He put the receiver down slowly and faced Millie. "Mrs. Gardiner, this twist of fate has permitted you a more intimate glimpse of another side of Mrs. Ali Reiner. I hope it will prove useful to you. More useful than knowing Mrs. Reiner has proven for me. I suggest you take this experience as a warning." In an abrupt shift, his tone changed, and he said, "You have papers for Dobbs to sign."

"Yes," Millie said.

"I'm not signing nothing," Lew Dobbs insisted.

"Lew, you must learn not to be a bigger fool than necessary. You will sign the papers. Li Yung's departure has left an opening on my staff. You are big. You are strong. You will fill that opening."

"I'm no muscleman."

"Do not argue. When you learn to follow orders whether

or not you agree with me, we will consider other duties. May
I have the agreement, Mrs. Gardiner?''

Millie returned to the conference table. She opened her
folder and produced three copies of the agreement. Tseng
scanned the document.

"It is as you have said.''

In short order, the agreements were signed by Lew Dobbs
and Millie and witnessed by Tseng and Jordan. Then, quixotically, Millie produced an Eisenhower silver dollar from
her pocket.

"I'm a fair woman, Mr. Tseng. You've made me a fine
deal . . . and given me valuable information. Under the circum-
stances, I owe you one. I don't want you to walk away empty-
handed. Since you're a gambler, let's gamble. Call it.'' Millie
spun the silver dollar. Tseng watched the flashing coin.

"Heads,'' he called out.

"Tails,'' Millie said.

The coin began to wobble. The spin grew more flat. Finally the coin settled on the table. Eisenhower's face was up.

"Well, well,'' Tseng said. "Eventually one's luck does
change.'' He pocketed the coin. As he stood up, he studied
Millie. "I lost a great deal of money today, but you lost more
than money. I will recover my losses. Will you?'' He stared
at Millie in the light of his merciless appraisal. Then he
turned. "Come, Lew.'' With Lew Dobbs two steps behind,
he walked quickly from the office.

Millie watched them go. When the door closed, she buried
her face in her hands. Her shoulders heaved violently with
dry sobs.

For the moment, Jordan didn't know what to do. He had
always thought of Millie as beautiful . . . as strong. But
somehow Tseng had touched a supersensitive nerve.

"What am I going to do?'' Millie asked, struggling to
regain her composure.

"Well . . .'' What could he say in the presence of so much
raw pain?

"I have to warn Nora.''

"About Mark? About his lies?''

"About Mark. And about Ali. . . .''

Millie was grim. Jordan had never before seen her look so
grim.

"Nora can take it. Don't worry. She's very strong.''

"Is she?"

"Stronger than you know," Jordan said clumsily.

"Barron wasn't strong." She gave him a pale, exquisite glare.

"I know how Barron was," Jordan said in a humble, hand-to-mouth way. He hoped somehow to ease Millie's pain. "And I know how hard you tried to protect him. That was a mistake. But afterward—after the mistake was made—you had nothing to do with the way he chose to ruin his life. He could have built a career in Hollywood. I talked to him about it. He was a California Gardiner. Millie Thorne's son. Every door was open to him. Barron wouldn't walk through the open doors."

Millie smiled through a mist. "Thank you for saying that, Jordan. And thank you again for your help today."

Jordan stood up. He recognized that she wanted him to go. "You're welcome for everything. I'm always available. You know that."

There was an odd, friendly, but slightly awkward silence . . . as if something was still unsaid. Millie broke the silence. "Would you be of service to me once more? I have a last favor to ask."

"Ask anything."

"Take care of Nora."

At that moment there glowed for Jordan a sharpness of irony. "I will if she'll let me." His tone was wistful.

"She'll let you. She'll need someone. Someone she can trust. Lean on. I don't want her to feel alone. . . ."

Millie's tone struck Jordan as full of despair. There was something he didn't understand. "I'll be there. But why?"

"Why? Why what?"

"Why would she need me that badly? She won't be alone. She has you."

"Ah, yes. Me." She looked at him. Again Jordan sensed he was missing something. "She does have me. But later. Remember I asked this favor."

"I'll remember," he said. He turned away in confusion . . . taking her words as a dismissal.

After Jordan left, Millie sat quietly. Life was always unpredictable . . . the turns of chance, the luck of the draw, the cheats of hope. Well, she still might manage something. It occurred to her how rich she truly was . . . that since marrying Max she'd been able to buy whatever she wanted. Might there now be a new use for her wealth? A use that would counter fate? Thinking this, she picked up the phone.

"Sara. Get me Nora, please."

Mark waited all day for the call from Tseng. When it didn't come, he tried to reach Tseng at Channel 18. Sara Kratz told him that Mr. Tseng and Mr. Dobbs had come and gone. And Mrs. Gardiner wasn't taking any calls. Mark then called Group H. Bobbi Weeks took the call.

"They're not here, Mr. Stern. I don't know what's going on. A moving van and four men showed up a couple of hours ago. They cleaned out Mr. Dobbs's office. There's nothing left. It's like Mr. Dobbs decided to jump off the face of the earth. Isn't it marvelous!"

"No. It isn't marvelous. Where's Victor?"

"He's on a long-distance call. Talking to Mrs. Millie Gardiner."

"Cut in," Mark demanded. "I want to talk to Victor."

"I can't do that."

"Can't or won't?"

"Take your choice, Mr. Stern."

As Mark slammed down the receiver, his intercom buzzed. "Yes, Kim?"

"It's Mrs. Stern. She would like to talk to you."

Nora wandered around the living room. She'd done the unthinkable. She'd called Mark and demanded he come home. She'd told him she wanted a divorce . . . and why. She remembered Millie's words.

"This is a decision you have to make. No one can make it for you. Not if you love him. What I have given you are the facts, not opinions. Love is beyond opinions. . . . "

Love, Nora thought. The word itself had tricked her. Love lied. How could she live with Mark knowing how he lied? Knowing he would always lie. How could she live with herself? This was not the first time she had thought about life without Mark. But this was the first time she meant it. Before telephoning him, she had mentally listed the pros and cons of their marriage. Once sex would have been one of the great pros. Now it was pure con. She conned Mark. Mark conned her. Their chemistry for each other had changed.

There were still a few pros. Mark was smart. Good-looking. Funny. A money-maker. He could be charming. But she didn't like him anymore.

Driving home, Mark no longer felt the panic and hysteria that had made him drop everything and rush home. Now his indignation was rising. What the hell was the matter with the princess? She said she was having new locks put on the doors. She was throwing him out. She was getting a divorce. His indignation changed to fury. The princess had betrayed him. How dare she try to dump him? Before he was ready to dump her? Despite his rage, his mind was a supercharged engine running on all cylinders. His arguments against a divorce were lined up like a crack drill team. His sales pitch for marriage was fine-tuned. His lies were eager to be told.

When Mark entered the living room, Nora stood waiting . . . her back was to the door. "What's the matter with you?" were the first words Mark said.

Nora turned and looked at him. "Nothing is the matter with me. I said I want a divorce."

"You can't be serious."

"I'm dead serious. You're an inveterate liar. Also a thief. I want a divorce and I want you out of this house tonight. Pack a suitcase now. You can send for the rest of your clothes tomorrow."

"Just like that." He snapped his fingers. "You want to get rid of me. Throw away all the years we've been together."

"Not just like that." She snapped her fingers. "If you think this is easy, you're crazy. But I've made up my mind. It's over."

"I don't believe it."

"Believe it. I want a divorce. I told you why."

Mark poured himself a shot of gin. "So I told you a dumb business lie. I suppose I shouldn't have lied . . ." He swallowed the gin.

"Right. You shouldn't have lied. But you did. And you will again."

After a momentary pause, Mark said, "You're mad because I was unfaithful once. Just once! Some men are unfaithful all the time. You're mad for no good reason."

"I'm not mad, Mark. I'm sad. But enough is enough."

"You really want this stupid divorce?"

"I really do. As soon as I find a divorce lawyer, he'll call you."

Indignation wasn't working. Mark changed tactics. He would make a play for sympathy. "Look. I've done some damn fool things. A lot of husbands do. They grow older . . . get smarter. That's how a marriage grows. Give me a second chance."

"No. I know you too well."

"How about a separation . . . for a while? You'll miss me."

"I may. But I still want a divorce."

Mark could no longer contain his fury. "You are a bitch!"

"And you, lover boy, are a lying bastard. Always looking out for number one."

"Listen to me, Miss Tight Ass. I looked out for you. I busted my balls to look good for your precious Millie. Now you shit all over me. Thanks a bunch."

"If that's how you see it, you're welcome a bunch." She watched him grope for control.

"It's your old lover, Jordan. Isn't it? You've been shacking up with him. You're dumping me for him."

"I haven't been shacking up with Jordan. Or anyone else."

"Come off it, Nora. Now who's lying?" His voice shook. "You're about as faithful as your grandmother was . . . as your father was. The talent runs in the family. You want a divorce? Okay. I'll give you a divorce. It'll be the divorce of the decade. The tabloids will have a field day. Spreads on the Gardiners. Milos and Max and Millie. A cozy ménage à trois. And you and me and Jordan. Plus God knows who else. Then there's your crook of a father, Barron Gardiner. The *Enquirer* and the *Star* will eat you up alive."

"Get out of here, Mark. Before I call the police."

"Temper, temper, Princess Nora. Watch your language. I may quote you." He slammed out the door.

Nora started to shake. There was no school for divorce. No courses. But somehow she'd gotten her degree.

Chapter 28

MILLIE OPENED her eyes. She was puzzled to discover that she was looking up through the blurred branches of a tree at a gray sky. Several moments passed before she realized she was lying on the riding trial. How had she got there? The last thing she remembered was urging her hunter jumper, Gray Dawn, into a slow canter. No. She remembered a bolt of pain that seemed to split her skull . . . much the way a lightning bolt splits a branch from a tree. She must have passed out and fallen off her horse. Gingerly, she flexed her arms and legs . . . no broken bones. But her body was sodden wet with sweat, and she was cold. She thanked God that she wasn't shaking herself to pieces. That phase of the attack must have passed while she was unconscious. She raised her body . . . resting herself on her elbows. Gray Dawn—two Gray Dawns . . . the real horse and a second image—was standing on the side of the trail. She was seeing double. His two necks were bowed as he nibbled on the grass. Millie sat up. Every bone in her body ached. Some fall, she thought. Oddly, her head didn't ache. She took off her hard hat and touched her head with the tips of her fingers. The result was both strange and frightening. She could feel her head through her numbed fingertips, but her head felt nothing. It was as though the fall or the attack had severed the nerves that connected her scalp to her brain.

Millie put on her hard hat and struggled first to her knees and then to her feet. Staggering a little, she approached Gray Dawn. The horse heard her footsteps. He raised his head and waited for her. Millie reached for the reins. She blinked, trying to rid herself of the double image. Her effort was useless. Wherever she looked, she saw two of everything . . . one real image and a second image to the left of the first. Millie closed her left eye. "Ah. That's better," she sighed.

Keeping her left eye closed, she gathered Gray Dawn's reins. She wondered if she should walk her horse back to the Farm or try to ride him. It was about a five-mile walk . . . Millie doubted she had the strength to walk her horse for five miles. She set her left foot in the stirrup and tried to swing onto the saddle. She was only able to sprawl across the saddle on her stomach. Laboriously, she worked her right leg over Gray Dawn's back. She was then able to sit up and fit her feet into the stirrups.

She risked opening her left eye. She still saw double . . . two trees, two fence posts, two stones by the side of the trail. The double image assaulted her brain. She cringed under the attack and immediately closed her eye again.

"Home, boy," Millie whispered to her horse.

Gray Dawn nodded his head at hearing the command . . . he knew his way back to the stable.

With Millie precariously perched in the saddle—at any moment she expected another attack—the horse picked his way through the maze of trails. By the time they'd arrived at the stable, the double image had come together. Millie was able to dismount and hand the reins to a groom. As she walked up the slope to the house, she thought about the attack. This was the worst yet. Her month-to-month lease on her life was running out, and there were still many things that must be done before God foreclosed.

Millie drew a hot bath. She stripped off her sweaty clothes and soaked herself in the tub . . . her catching a cold and then possibly pneumonia was asking for God to act before she was prepared. She picked up the phone by the tub and called Nora.

"Mrs. Stern's office."

"Sheri, this is Mrs. Gardiner. Is Nora there?"

"Yes, Mrs. G. I'll put you right through."

There were the usual clicks as the circuits opened and closed. Then, "Grandmother? How are you?"

"I'm fine, Nora," Millie lied. "About tonight. My usual Friday night dinner. Could you come about an hour earlier? Before the others arrive? I have a number of things to go over with you."

"Of course. I'll bring you up to speed on Mark's latest stunt. He's asked the court to place a lien on the house . . . so I can't sell it."

"Do you want to sell the house?"

"Yes. The house has too many memories . . . both good and bad."

"We'll talk about that tonight."

"One thing, Grandmother. Jordan wants to start rehearsals for *Mama* in about a month. Tim and Pat and I have gone over the possible number of commercial time slots. Do you want me to bring the schedule with me?"

"Not tonight, dear. We already have a full plate."

"Oh!" Nora hesitated. "All right. I'll be there around five-thirty."

After hanging up, Millie made three additional phone calls. When she hung up after the final call, she was satisfied. The set, the actors, the lights, the props were all in position. She wasn't acting in this production . . . she was the director. She would call out, "Lights. Camera. Action. Roll 'em." And roll 'em she would.

"Good evening, madam," Oscar said. "Your grandmother is waiting for you outside . . . under the colonnade."

"Thank you, Oscar." Nora's eyebrows rose. Why was everyone so formal tonight?

"If you will follow me, madam . . ."

What was happening? First Juan, then Carlos, then Miguel and now Oscar. They've known me since I was a kid. Tonight they treat me as if I were some kind of rare, delicate flower. Why?

"I know the way, Oscar. I've known the way as long as you have."

"I'm sorry, madam. I'm only following Mrs. Gardiner's orders."

Nora rolled her eyes toward the ceiling. Millie . . . what are you doing? she silently asked.

Millie was seated in her favorite wicker chair, waiting. Nora stared at her grandmother. Instead of one of her Friday night costumes, she was wearing white jeans and a white sports shirt. A bottle of Dom Perignon champagne—mist still escaping from the bottle—and two glasses stood on a table next to her. A second wicker chair had been placed by the table.

"What's up?" Nora said breezily as she sat down in the empty chair. "We celebrating something?"

Millie smiled at Nora. "In a way, yes. I like your jumpsuit. Velvet suits you . . . it's your material."

"Thanks. But what's with the jeans? We doing a beach party tonight?"

"No. I'll explain later. First, let's have a drink." Millie filled the twin tulip-shaped glasses three-quarters full.

Nora noticed something disturbing. Millie wasn't exactly sure where the glasses were . . . she almost missed one.

"A toast, Nora. To the future."

"To the future."

They clinked glasses and sipped their champagne.

Millie refilled their glasses. Again Millie almost missed Nora's glass.

Millie took a big swallow of champagne. She began to speak. She looked and sounded relaxed, almost casual. She had the practiced ease of a professional who had played the same role thousands of times. "I have a story to tell you, Nora," she said.

Nora smelled the greasepaint. Heard the roar of the crowd. What was happening?

"This is not easy for me, so please try not to interrupt any more than necessary."

Solemn-faced, Nora nodded, placing her glass on the table.

"As you know, your great-grandfather, my father, Andy Thorne . . . well . . . My father lost the family farm in Kansas during the Great Depression. First came the Depression and then the dust storms blew the land away." Briefly, Millie recounted the family story Nora had heard again and again. How Millie and her father had made their way across the country to California and how they'd ended up on Jude Castelli's farm. But for the first time Millie told Nora how her father had been killed and how she came to live with Jude Castelli. There was no melodrama in the telling, only dry facts. But the bare bones still echoed with the stark reality of that harsh, terrifying time. Nora shivered. "You know I ran away from Castelli when I was a young girl. What you don't know—what only one living person knows—is that when I ran away I was pregnant with his child."

"You were pregnant!" The shock burst from Nora. "Millie, I . . ." Millie's stony expression stopped her. "Sorry. I'll try not to interrupt again."

"Thank you," Millie said, picking up the thread of her story. She did not spare herself in the telling . . . not the pain of remembering how she gave the baby up for adoption. "I was too young. I had little money and no job. I was desperate. I knew if I kept my baby, neither of us would survive. But if I agreed to the adoption, we both had a chance." She'd been speaking very quickly. Now she paused to gather herself . . . then she went on. "You know what happened to me. Now I'll tell you what happened to my daughter."

"The baby was a girl?"

"Yes. A girl."

"You kept track of her?"

"Of course. She was mine. I loved her. Once I had the money and freedom to do something . . . I did something."

Nora put a few dates to Millie's story. Her daughter was older than Barron . . . older than Hiram.

"I considered contacting the Sloans . . . the family that adopted my Jenny. That was their name . . . Jim and Harriet Sloan. But I'd given up that right when I agreed to the adoption. And the Sloans loved Jenny. They took care of her as if she were their own flesh and blood. She thought she was. So I felt it wiser to leave well enough alone." Millie sipped some champagne and then continued. "Jenny grew up far away from me. In Sandusky, Ohio. She became a book-keeper." Millie laughed uncertainly. "I suppose she inherited my head for numbers. She did the bookkeeping for a number of local businesses. One of them was an undertaker. . . ."

Nora stared at Millie. While she tried to keep a calm face, she couldn't believe what she was hearing.

"Eventually she married Henry Kjytekka, the undertaker's assistant."

There was an uncomfortable pause while Millie cleared her throat and Nora repeated the name to herself. How could it be a coincidence?"

"A few years later Jenny and Henry had a baby. . . ."

Nora was again working the time frames in her head. That baby was either a little older than she . . . or a few years younger. A year or two either way at the most.

"Now I had a daughter and a granddaughter to take care of. So I arranged for Henry Kjytekka to start an insurance company. I used a front—a 'dummy'—to provide him with start-up money. And I privately guaranteed his loans at a bank where the chairman was a personal friend. Henry was smart and a hard worker.''

Nora couldn't bear it any longer. She burst out, "He founded Ohio Casualty, didn't he?''

Millie gave her a look that brought Nora up short. It told her she was to have no more sudden insights. Millie would tell her story in her own way.

"Yes. He founded Ohio Casualty. It's odd,'' she mused. "I can control many things, but not life and death. My mother died very young. Breast cancer. So did my Jenny. Also breast cancer.'' She eyed Nora. "You do go for regular gynecological checkups?''

"Annually. Pap smear. Base line mammogram. The works.''

"Good. Anyway, after a period of mourning, Henry remarried. He chose a very beautiful young woman, Amanda Wiesnewska. After Henry married Amanda, I made it my business to get to know them. The chairman of the bank introduced us.'' Millie smiled. "Also Henry remembered Millie Thorne . . . that didn't hurt. Then Henry suddenly died . . . he had a massive coronary. He left Amanda a rich widow with a stepchild . . . whom you know. My other granddaughter . . .''

"Ali,'' Nora said softly. She tried not to appear resentful at not being told the truth sooner.

"Ali. Like you, my granddaughter. I wanted somehow to bring Ali into my world.''

"How did you manage it?'' Nora whispered. "I mean get Uncle Hiram to marry Amanda?''

"I didn't manage it. Hiram managed it himself. Amanda met him at some cocktail party in Washington. A beautiful woman with too much money is like a vacuum. She attracts all sorts of men. She attracted Hiram.''

A happy ending followed. Uncle Hiram married Amanda.'' Nora gave Millie a wry smile. "You said Hiram managed it himself but I sense your presence. You had nothing to do with Uncle Hiram's and Amanda's being at the same cocktail party?''

"Well . . .''

"You remind me of the spiderwoman spinning her web.''
Millie chuckled. "I suppose I did stage-manage it a bit. I

was enthusiastic about Hiram's marrying Amanda. Maybe I am a spiderwoman. But, Nora, a spiderwoman isn't born. Things happen. Not all good. Like any woman, I have my share of spilt milk. So what would you want me to do? Sit down and weep? Or try to clean up the mess? I try to clean it up. I suppose sometimes I do behave like a spiderwoman.''

"So that's how Ali came into our lives.''

"That's how. But with Ali I got a lot of things I didn't bargain for. More spilt milk. Ali is what Ali is. I loved her very much. . . .''

Nora looked down. She wasn't going to compete for Millie's affection with Ali or anyone else.

"I still love her. I had great hopes for the two of you. I wanted you to be like sisters. Not now.''

"You've given up on us?'' Nora raised her eyes.

"Not on you. On Ali. . . .''

"Why?''

Millie's mind seemed to have wandered. Her gaze wandered around the patio, the statues, the massed bright flowers, the wading pool. And finally, Nora. She closed her eyes for a moment. "I've loved living here.''

"You sound as if you're thinking of living somewhere else . . . of moving.''

"Not of moving. I'm thinking of dying.''

Nora didn't want to think of Millie dying. She laughed. A pleasant, human-sounding laugh . . . with no depth or darkness. "We all die sooner or later.''

"I'm dying sooner.''

"Don't tease me, Millie. I'm a quick scare.''

"I'm not teasing, dear. I'm dying.''

Nora stared at her.

"It's something of a medical miracle that I'm still alive. That I've lived this long.''

Nora took in the full force of Millie's words . . . it was like a punch in the stomach. "That's why you were at Scripps?'' she gasped.

"You know that? It doesn't matter. Yes. I've been going to Scripps regularly.''

"Regularly?''

"For years. On and off. For checkups that do no good.''

Nora fought to remain calm. "What is it? What's wrong?''

"A tiny air bubble. An embolus somewhere in my brain.

Apparently I've had it from birth. It can't be reached . . . it can't be operated on. Now, after years of lying quiet, the bubble is getting larger. One of these days it will burst an artery . . .''

For an instant Nora couldn't speak. Then she asked, "There's nothing you can do?"

"What I can do, I am doing. One can't do more than live."

Nora closed her eyes to keep the tears back. Awkwardly, like a child, she wiped them away with the back of her hand.

"It's the hankie gap again," Millie tried to smile. "I was afraid this would be a tearjerker." She rose. "I'll get you—"

"No! Don't get me anything." Nora opened her wet eyes, grabbing for Millie's arm with one hand and wiping her eyes with the other. "Please sit down."

Millie nodded and resumed her seat. Nora stared at her, seeing her grandmother now as she had never seen her before . . . as threatened, as haunted and as gallant. She tried to match Millie's courage.

"What can I do?" Nora asked.

"Help me make up for my mistakes . . . mop up my spilt milk?"

"Which mistakes?"

"For one thing, bringing Ali into the family."

"I understand that now. She's your granddaughter too. You love her."

"Yes, she is. But she's other things." Without dramatizing or embellishing the bare facts, Millie told Nora the full story of Ali.

Nora was filled with horror. "Good Lord!" she said when Millie finished. "She sounds like a monster."

"I don't know what she is. But she's mine . . . my granddaughter."

"Amanda's death was an accident. So was Arthur's. I was almost an accident." Nora winced. "But she's family."

"She is family." Millie raised a cautionary finger. "Nora, she doesn't know that. I have no intention of telling her the truth, and I don't want you to. Ever!"

"I see," Nora said. "Yes. It's better she never find out."

"She'll be here any minute."

"Here! You invited her here?"

"Not to dinner. To talk. I have an idea I want to explore with her."

"Tell me what you're thinking."

"Not yet . . . later. Now you must take my place at the table."

Nora looked bewildered. "Your place?"

"Yes." Millie sounded amused. "I admit you're a little young to be cast in the part. It carries with it a great deal of responsibility. But I learned something in Hollywood. If one wants to work, one takes what is offered. You are being offered the role of Matriarch. Play it as a young matriarch. Will you accept the role?"

A discreet knock made them both look up. Oscar was standing in the doorway.

"Mr. Stern and Mrs. Reiner have arrived."

"Mark is here too!" Nora exclaimed.

"To talk. Like Ali." She turned to Oscar. "Escort them to the library. They are not here for dinner. Wait with them until I join you. I'll be along in a minute. . . ."

"Yes, madam."

"And, Oscar. I will not be at the table this evening. Mrs. Nora Gardiner Stern will greet the guests and sit where I usually sit."

"Yes, madam." Oscar didn't blink. He turned to Nora. "Should you need any assistance, madam, you can depend on me." He bowed slightly and backed into the house. His English upbringing told him all he needed to know. He had witnessed the end of a reign. A queen had abdicated. Long live the queen.

Millie looked at her watch. "Will you accept the role?"

"You mean the role of Matriarch? Where will you be?"

"With Ali and Mark. We have things to discuss. I'll tell you about it after dinner. I'll be here. Waiting for you."

Nora started to say something, but Millie gave her a strange look that brought her up short. It told her there was nothing to say. To protest . . . to object . . . to show any dismay about Millie's condition would comfort only her, not Millie.

"I accept," Nora said

"Good. Your guests will be arriving any minute. I've also invited Jordan."

Nora couldn't help laughing. "Jordan! You never quit. Now I'm in the spiderwoman's web."

Millie smiled. "I do what I can. He's anxious to talk to you. I asked him to wait until tonight." She stood up, holding her glass of champagne. "Let's finish our champagne and get on with our lives." She raised the glass. "A toast to your future," Millie said.

"And to yours," Nora said, avoiding Millie's eyes.

They toasted each other's future.

Millie paused in the library doorway, observing the scene. Mark was seated at one end of the couch, Ali at the other end . . . as far away from each other as they could get. Off in the corner was Oscar, a discreet policeman.

"Thank you, Oscar," Millie said. "You may go now."

"Yes, madam." Oscar left the room and closed the door behind him.

Millie went to the chair behind her desk. She glanced at the two of them. "Thank you for coming on such short notice," she said.

"I'm always glad to see you, Millie," Mark said. "Is Nora here?"

"Nora's here. It's Friday night. Where else would she be?"

"You look tired, Millie," Ali observed.

"I am tired. The two of you make me quite weary."

"That's not fair, Millie. I've called you every day. You never take my calls," Ali complained. She glanced at Mark. "Nora's divorcing him. She's not divorcing me. Why are you angry at me?"

"Nora isn't divorcing you, Ali. I am."

"Millie!" Ali was all injured dignity. "What a thing to say!"

"I mean it."

"Why? What have I done?"

"Do you remember Stanley Tseng's call? His last call to you? He made that call from my office. I listened on an extension."

Ali cast about frantically for an explanation. "Oh, that!" she exclaimed with a smile. "Didn't you know I was leading him on? I've been trying to get information on him. To give to you, Millie."

"Ali! This is what tires me. Your lies."

"I don't lie," Ali protested. "I never lie."

"You constantly lie. Remember how you grieved for Amanda?"

"Yes. I loved her."

"You didn't love her. You didn't even like her. Amanda's death was one of the more profitable accidents in your life. You owe her a great deal for dying so conveniently."

Mark looked smug. "I knew it. I always knew it."

"You shut up, Mark Stern." Ali's voice was strained. "What are you talking about, Millie?"

"Amanda's accidental death wasn't an accident at all. Somehow you arranged it. When Amanda died, you inherited a great deal of money. Neither was Arthur's death completely accidental. Or unprofitable for you. And if Nora had been killed in that car accident, you expected to replace her in my will."

"Stanley is disgusting." Ali's voice was shrill. "I wondered why he talked the way he did. He tried to implicate me in what happened to Nora. What you didn't hear because he hung up too fast was that I was only doing what he insisted I do."

"Ali, be quiet!" Millie spoke in a low, cold voice. "Your lies don't serve you well. What you're saying is you obeyed Tseng's instructions to have Nora murdered."

Ali paled and tried to curl up into a tight ball.

Millie's tone became official. "Listen carefully, Mark. If you and Ali do not want to go to jail, you will both do exactly as I say."

"Jail!" Mark's chest tightened. Breathing became difficult.

"Jail, Mark. You will sign over your twenty percent ownership of Group H to Nora. And you will agree to a quiet, civilized divorce. When the divorce is final, you will marry Ali."

"What!" Ali exclaimed.

Millie arched an eyebrow. "Yes, Ali. Mark will be your next husband."

"Mark and I have nothing in common. He's common! Illiterate! Uncultivated!"

"All true. But, like you, he believes in marrying for money. That gives you a basis on which to build a lasting relationship."

"Be reasonable, Millie," Ali pleaded. "If Mark marries

me, Dorothea will fire him on the spot. I can't marry an ordinary customers' man. He'll have no money. No! I will not marry Mark."

"Mark will remain the managing partner of Reiner & Co. Dorothea has already agreed. That should enable him to make enough money . . . even for you, Ali."

Mark had been silently listening to Millie spell out the terms of his survival. The word *jail* had frightened him out of his wits. Now he got up and walked around the desk. He bent over Millie. "Why, Millie?" he asked. "You've got me cold. Why let me off the hook?"

"I have other plans for you. Besides, I understand that— except for some money you stole from Arthur's estate . . . money you will return—you're doing a good job as managing partner. So it's in both Dorothea's interest and mine to keep you there."

Mark didn't know what to say. He retreated to the safety of the couch.

"I've alerted Dorothea to the danger . . . you won't get the chance to steal any more money."

"I wouldn't steal from Dorothea," Mark protested. "I'd never bite the hand that feeds me."

"You already have," Millie said with resignation. "You bit my hand. So my account and Dr. Abe's will be moved to another brokerage house. Give Dorothea any reason you can think of . . . after you clear it with Nora." She smiled expansively at Mark.

"There's one flaw in your plan," Mark said. He had to find some way to avoid marrying Ali. "If Ali and I marry, she gets me. But what do I get? Bubkus! An old Jewish expression. Ali is broke. She's lost most of the two million she inherited from Arthur."

"According to Dorothea, you lost her money," Millie said. "But she'll be rich again. When Hiram dies, Ali will inherit Amanda's millions, which are still in trust for her."

"Hiram won't die for decades," Ali protested.

"That's right. Especially since Nora will warn him about you. You will not be able to orchestrate another accident."

Mark heard Millie's words loud and clear. "My God, Millie. That's great for Hiram, but what about me? The more money I make, the quicker I could die. Ali has a patent on accidents."

"You will have to be careful, Mark. But you can manage it."

Mark tried another tactic. "She'll be unfaithful. Ali can't keep her legs crossed."

"And you'll be faithful? Please, Mark. What about Gigi? You've been seeing her again."

"You've been sleeping with that whore?" Ali stamped her foot. Incredibly, she sounded like a betrayed wife.

"She's not a whore!" Mark started to say something, then stopped himself. "She's none of your business. You and me . . . we're not married yet." He looked at Millie. "This could be a deal breaker. You give me a choice between jail and being murdered. That's some choice."

Ali knew when to quit. She gave Mark a coy smile. "Let's not fuss, Mark. You've wanted to go to bed with me for years. I told you a long time ago it was a pity Nora met you first . . . that we'd make beautiful music. Now we will. I'll bet you're great in bed."

"I'm okay," Mark mumbled.

"He is," Millie agreed. "Ali, as a wedding present, I give you proof." She slid a packet of snapshots in Ali's direction.

Ali stared at the pictures. She licked her lips and grinned. "You are good. Better than I expected." She handed the snapshots to Mark.

Mark glanced at them and turned to Millie. "Where did you get these?"

"Gus Sklar. He did some work for me."

"My detective," Mark exclaimed.

"No. My detective." Ali snorted. "When we marry, I'll hire him. I'll need a good detective."

"He won't work for you. He also took pictures of you in bed with half the men in San Diego."

Ali rose. As she sashayed toward the door, she said, "Sklar was in the remaining half. All the more reason he'd rather work for me."

"Damn you!" Mark exclaimed as he hurried after her.

Millie watched them leave with some relief. The pain was beginning again. Oscar entered and waited silently in front of the desk.

Millie picked up a letter that had been on her desk through-out the meeting. She said to Oscar, "When the dinner is over, give this to Mrs. Stern."

"You don't want to give it to her yourself?" Oscar looked puzzled.

Millie took her amusement where she could. "If I'm awake, Oscar, I will hand it to her. If not, you do it."

"Yes, madam."

"Thank you, old friend," Millie said almost to herself.

For the first time in their long relationship, Oscar smiled. "Thank you, madam, for being who you are. For taking a green stripling from the streets of London. You've made my life very pleasant." Then, embarrassed at his own words, he turned and left the library.

Millie picked up the letter and reread it. The meeting had gone as she'd described it in the letter . . . with a few minor variations. As she had written, the affair had a kind of symmetry. Yes, she could see to it that they went to jail, but this way was better. Their punishment fit their crimes. Two greedy, dangerous people would be locked together in a marriage made in hell. They'd never have a moment's peace . . . they'd never be able to turn their backs on each other. Millie added a short footnote. If either showed signs of not keeping to the deal, Nora must bring charges. There is no statute of limitations on a criminal act. Satisfied, she inserted the letter in an envelope and sealed it.

Millie leaned back in her chair. The pain grew more demanding. She waited for the trembling to begin. Instead, slowly, magically, the room began to change . . . dissolve. She was no longer sitting in her chair. She was walking in a field of tall corn under a bright blue sky. She had a sense of awe . . . of joy and expectation. She could see her father standing on the porch. He was so young and strong and proud. He was waving to her as though she were still a child. Couldn't he see how old she was . . . that she'd lived to be older than he? Then she saw someone else she hadn't ever expected to see again.

"Milos!" she called out. "Milos. Here! I'm over here. . . ."

Coda

WHEN JORDAN and Nora entered the Waterfront Bar and Grill, Nancy Nichols was waiting for them. She stood with her hands on her hips as though daring them to pass.

"You know what I said the last time? No picture, no dinner."

Jordan handed Nancy a flat package wrapped in plain brown paper.

Nancy ran her fingers around the package.

"Open it up," Nora suggested.

Nancy unwrapped the package and held it up to the light. "You did it!" She laughed. Then she walked to the place on the wall where the picture of Millie and Milos and Max hung. She held the new photograph next to the old one. The frames were identical. So were the poses . . . except the new photograph was of Jordan and Nora. "That's perfect," Nancy said. "Two generations of Banskas and Gardiners. What took you so long?"

"Nora and I got married," Jordan explained, smiling. "We've been on our honeymoon."

"You married this drunken, womanizing clown?" Nancy shook her head. "You're out of your mind."

"I've reformed, Nancy," Jordan said.

"I'll believe that when I see it."

"Believe it," Nora said. "I keep a razor-sharp knife by my bed. One mistake and he'll be talking soprano."

Nancy roared with laughter and clapped her hands. "I could learn to love you, Nora Gardiner Banska. Go stuff your faces. Tonight's on the house."

Jordan held Nora's hand for luck. This was the first complete reading of the play. "All right, everybody," he called out. "I want the cast on stage. Sit in the chairs behind the

475

long table. And the rest of you, sit anywhere out of camera range.'' He waited as Tammi Meredith and the cast of *I Remember Mama* settled themselves in the wooden chairs. When they were ready, he looked around. The station executives— Luddy Poole, Sim Crumb, Tim Rourke and Pat Yocum— were huddled in a far corner. He took a deep breath. If they were lucky, it would be there now. That magical chemistry . . . the theatrical quicksilver that could rivet an audience. He raised his hand and pointed at Tammi.

''For as long as I can remember the house on Steiner Street has been home . . .'' Tammi concluded her speech with ''. . . but most of all I remember Mama.''

Jordan squeezed Nora's hand.

Nora's eyes were misting. ''I remember Millie,'' she whispered.